SWEET PRINCE

CHRISTER KIHLMAN

SWEET PRINCE

A NOVEL

TRANSLATED BY JOAN TATE

PETER OWEN · LONDON AND BOSTON

ISBN 0 7206 0606 3

Translated from the Swedish *Dyre Prins*

UNESCO COLLECTION OF REPRESENTATIVE WORKS
European Series

This book has been accepted in the European Series
of the Translations Collection of the United Nations
Educational, Scientific and Cultural Organization (UNESCO).

PETER OWEN PUBLISHERS
73 Kenway Road London SW5 0RE
and
99 Main Street Salem New Hampshire 03079

First published in Great Britain 1983
© Christer Kihlman 1975
English translation © Joan Tate 1983

Photoset and printed in Great Britain by
Villiers Publications Ltd, Ingestre Road, London NW5 1UL

There was once a man of forty-eight who was satisfied with his life. His name was Donald Blaadh and he considered he had been successful in everything he had done. When he was young, he had had great dreams for the future, and all his dreams had been fulfilled. He had everything he had wished for, money, women, influence. Less honour had come his way, but that did not worry him. He had never aspired to honour. He was healthy, content and sober.

Donald Blaadh was a rich man. He had started with empty hands, as empty as two hands could be, and now, thirty years later, he was rich. He owned, and until quite recently had been Managing Director of, a flourishing import firm. Nowadays he was Chairman of the Board and, in addition, a director on the board of a large construction company in which he held a considerable number of shares. Other deals to conceal. It was not exactly yesterday he had worried over how his money was to suffice.

Donald Blaadh did not ask himself whether he was happy, in the certain knowledge that he had no need to, because he surely was. He lacked for nothing. Wasn't that sufficient evidence of happiness? He had had five wives, three in legal matrimony, and a great many other women as well. Certainly. Altogether, he had six children, but he was not particularly close to any one of them. He had found time to beget them, but not to love them. Sometimes, awareness of this caused him an irritating sense of imperfection.

He had gone a long way. His childhood home had been poor, grey and joyless. Nowadays, he had no need to deny himself anything. But the years and experience had taught him it was wise to deny himself a great deal. Donald Blaadh had no intention of dying of a coronary. His habits, except when it came to women, were more spartan than dissolute. There had been a time when he could hardly imagine himself eating anything else but pheasant à la something or other, or venison this or that, with a whole bottle of vintage wine (at the

5

appropriate temperature – how many times had he not sent a bottle back because the wine was either too cold or too warm). But that was quite a long time ago. Nowadays, he preferred cabbage rolls and cranberry sauce, or black-pudding and a glass of non-fat milk.

His father, whose name was Brynolf, had been the caretaker of a large stone apartment house in Helsinki owned by the well-known Lehtisuon-Lehtinen family. In those days, Donald had been called the caretaker's nasty little brat. Today he was on first-name terms with prime ministers, foreign ministers, provincial governors and eminent industrialists. More significant relationships to conceal.

There was once a man who was satisfied with his life. His name was Donald Blaadh. He was forty-eight and considered he had succeeded in all he had undertaken and that even the wildest dreams of his youth had been fulfilled. He had had everything he could wish for, money, women, power. Honour only so-so, but he didn't mind that. He had never aspired to honour. He was healthy, content and sober.

During various periods of his life, Donald Blaadh had lived with five women, three in legal matrimony. Together, they had borne him six children. He did not particularly like children, but he liked begetting them. His eldest son, Miles, was already twenty-seven, a successful business man, a lawyer and economist in record time, recently appointed financial director of a large firm. Donald's pride, the apple of the family eye. Miles' sister, Rosa, was dead. She had died of an overdose of amphetamine in London two years earlier, and that was the first time Donald Blaadh had brushed with the thought that in some respects he had been perhaps inadequate.

The youngest child, Hans, or Hannu, was only three. Hannu's mother was much younger than Donald, so young in fact, she could have been Donald's daughter. They had lived together for a few years, conceived a son, then parted company with no drama whatsoever. Hannu's mother, Elina, was going to get properly married to a contemporary sociologist who lived on a research grant, and Donald himself had become acquainted with Vanessa.

The three middle children were all born of the same marriage, which had lasted for over ten years and had seemed very happy. Gunnel was very beautiful and had never really managed to overcome her bitterness over the divorce. Donald left her for Elina;

6

she was given custody of the children, and for many years did her best to ensure that Donald saw as little as possible of his children. They were two girls and a boy, Anna, Torbjörn and Carola. Torbjörn was now almost adult. He was going to be an artist and drank too much. He had left Gunnel and moved in with Donald. A child of sorrow.

Donald Blaadh was rich. He owned an import firm he had taken over twenty years earlier from his elder brother Emil, who had emigrated to America. He was also part-owner and on the board of a construction firm responsible for some of the capital's least attractive suburbs. Mm. Mm.

Over the years, Donald Blaadh had been accused by his enemies of a great many ugly things. He had been called an unscrupulous boor, a criminal, a bounder, an upstart and an opportunist, as well as other insults jealous people are apt to throw at their more successful fellow men. At first it had hurt, but one gets used to it. Donald Blaadh had quickly got used to it. He had good contacts in all the most important political parties. He had always avoided being politically active in any particular definite direction, apart from when he was young, immediately after the war, when for a while he had been a member of the Communist Party. Business first, he used to say.

It would be wrong to say my life has been *very* successful, although I've done good work from time to time. On the other hand, no one can deny that I've managed to manoeuvre myself into a position which makes me exceptionally influential.

The most closed doors in this country willingly open when I knock on them. And I quite often do knock on them. Nowadays. That's part of my duties.

What duties?

They listen to my advice. I am offered assignments which never become public.

Besides, it's a long time since I found myself in a situation in which I had to take orders from anyone. I am my own boss. I have striven towards that all my life, deliberately. As early as when as a young student and a communist, I cheated my brothers of their share in the smallholding we inherited from my paternal grandfather.

In this world, honesty does not last longest.

Life has taught me three things.

7

Straightforwardness does not get one very far, unless one knows how to use it as a function of cunning. Straightforwardness is a virtue only to the innocent, and the innocent are never happy, for they are always the ones who are deceived and get the kicks. But on the other hand, what a wonderful weapon straightforwardness is, when subordinate to the first principles of cunning in a world that pretends to value straightforwardness so highly, while in reality it simultaneously acts and rolls on according to different and far from such exalted rules and guiding principles.

One does not go far with honesty. Cheating and betrayal are far more certain routes to security and freedom-from-cares than assiduous labour and abiding by the law. For this world has been created in such a way by the cunning, the greedy, the untrustworthy, that to be law-abiding is the greatest foolishness and assiduous labour futile endeavour. Obey the laws in small circles and no one will notice you transgressing them in greater ones. And industrious-as-an-ant will always be an ant in the circles of the big boys. But he who is more cunning than the cunning and more untrustworthy than the untrustworthy finally takes home the largest kitty. Because he has the sense to wear that expression which induces confidence.

Never fear people. Fear death, thunder and the serpent's sting if you cannot help it, but don't be afraid of people; because the most terrible person is frightened somewhere within him, weak in his loneliness, and can be disarmed with ease. With an intimate expression, a gesture of indifference, a flick of the finger. It comes down to the art of acting. The most overbearing bigwig loses his nerve when faced with someone even more overbearing. He who bellows collapses when confronted with a superior bellower. And the well-mannered leader with his firm, calm authority does not escape ulcers and depressions when he finally finds himself fundamentally seen through. Bluff, my dear Watson.

As Machiavelli says, one should be sufficiently cunning that on appropriate occasions one acquires enemies in order to gain yet greater respect by striking them down. What a wise maxim when transferred to our modern everyday level. How well Machiavelli knew the human character and the movements of the human flock. Sheep.

Perhaps I appear disillusioned and cynical. But aren't illusions simply a consequence of ignorance and inexperience, a sign of a poor conception of reality? Illusions are not the same as expectations, and I have a great many expectations. Many hells-on-earth have existed, possibly many paradises – and still exist at this very moment. But although I believe in neither hell nor paradise as future prospects for me and my fellow men, I have never ceased to hope for a better world.

Cynicism is again a term applied to oneself by others. No wise person calls himself cynical. But a person who distinguishes himself as having greater perspicacity than average is often labelled cynical out of sheer envy. His life appears to be so much easier, characterized by such audacious freedom. In the mind of the extreme puritan, one is cynical simply by refusing to allow oneself to be weighed down by meaningless guilt. Sometimes cynicism is nothing but freedom from superstition.

There was a time when I could experience a euphoric sense of lust and arrogant joy when, having gone through the excitement, I finally saw that I had succeeded in what I had intended. And by God, I allowed myself to enjoy that wonderful joy to the hilt. Nowadays I am more accomplished and have become more blasé over the years; I no longer embark on enterprises in which I cannot be certain to succeed.

I am a man in my prime, conscious of death, cancer, thrombosis, road accidents, as a constant incalculable factor, but otherwise unreservedly prepared to enjoy the multitude of highly spiced possibilities of the prime of life. Free from temporal worries, free from all banal kinds of human dependence, but strong and secure in the knowledge that what I am and what I have achieved in life are the durable fruits of hard work, my own efforts and purposefully completed calculations. I will be forty-nine next year. Humanly speaking, I have more than a half a lifetime behind me. But my will to act is as firm as ever it was in my youth, and the world of my imagination is as crammed with the future as it ever was then.

I have always felt a certain alienation among what are known as intellectuals; not a sense of inferiority, but a difference in character. Compared to them, I have seen myself clearly as a man of practical dealings, of immediate action, of quick decisions. Arguing without deciding, weighing up without acting – no, I'm no intellectual in the pretentious, planless or irresponsible sense. On the other hand I have never had any reason to doubt or question my intelligence. I have always been perfectly aware that I am an exceptionally intelligent person.

I have never claimed to be one of God's best children, those who gain on the celestial swings what they lose on the earthly roundabouts. On the contrary, I have tried to obey the rules of the game as thoroughly as possible, as they are inscribed in the secret book of the powerful of this world. As a consequence, I have lied and betrayed whenever I have thought it to my advantage, and given and accepted bribes with the same warm hand. Don't think that I mention this with any kind of confessional contrition in mind. In my own eyes I appear to be a far from unsympathetic person. On the contrary, my own altruism has sometimes been remarkable, my sense of justice, my social conscience. It is simply that the question of morality and immorality is so tremendously uninteresting, of secondary importance. Or, to put it bluntly, wool pulled over the eyes of the credulous, whose main task in life is to be kept on course and to obey the coachman's arrogant jerk at the reins.

But I shall cease philosophizing.

I have had five wives, more or less legalized: Sinikka, Gunnel, Elina, Laura and Vanessa. I have begotten six children: Miles, Rosa, Anna, Torbjörn, Carola and Hannu.

I have two brothers: Emil and Oskar.

My father's name was Brynolf, the poor wretch, and he was commissionaire at the National Theatre.

My mother was religious and what would her name be if not Saimi.

I myself am called Donald, which shows in an almost macabre way that my wretched parents must have had a few confused ambitions left in life at that late stage, just before my birth.

It is a long time since the very thought of my parents gave rise to contempt and bitterness, but on the other hand it would be untrue to maintain that I remember them with love, or even affection. My greatest ambition in life has always been not to be like them.

And by God, I have succeeded.

Now I really must begin at last.

This is incomprehensible. For forty-eight, or anyhow twenty-eight years, since I came back from the war and went into business after a brief communist intermezzo, I have lived with the idea that I am able to do what I want to do, and that I do not want to do what I am unable to do. And now suddenly this. Or should it be called 'this business'? It is laughable, foolish and, as I say, incomprehensible.

10

I have defied ministers and chief editors, I have brought municipal leaders to their knees, feeling nothing but decisiveness, annoyance and perhaps occasional contempt. And now I am here on my own, quite alone in front of (at?) a typewriter, and for the first time in my life I am feeling personal uncertainty, or straight fear of the task, if I am to be quite honest. I fumble my way ahead in a quagmire, and that quagmire is nothing but myself, expressed or made concrete in language I should know as well as the back of my hand and which is consequently precisely the same as that with whose aid I have most often defied those aforementioned ministers, municipal leaders, etc. I don't even know how to begin.

I have now been here for three months with the most peculiar feeling of childish incompetence and impotence, telling myself that if I can't begin in some other way, then I should begin quite simply with the simplest of all sentences, in other words: 'Now I really must begin.'

But the very moment I set about writing that down, the objection arises: 'Wouldn't it be better to say: . . . Now I really must get started?' And so I sit there hesitating again. And yet all the time I know that fundamentally it is a matter of total (complete?) indifference which words I use. As long as the content is (remains?) the same.

Am I afraid of language, afraid to express myself in writing? Because in some way it is not my field? But I've composed hundreds of memos, reports, even one or two more serious articles in recent years, without feeling the slightest inhibition when confronted with the task. Afraid of myself?

Could I really be afraid of myself?

Because it is myself in question. My life. What it has been like.

The starting point was a kind of pride; essentially nothing but a need to share with myself some of the satisfaction I felt over what I had achieved with my life. Now I know perfectly well that it is not really considered distinguished to be proud of oneself. But as I am not particularly distinguished in any respect whatsoever, I think I may grant myself the luxury of being honest on this point.

On the other hand, I cannot deny there is a certain amount of envy involved alongside the pride, an envy concerning my relatives, my so-called 'family'. They are indeed distinguished. But I am not. They have called me bastard and upstart and opportunist and God knows what else, while sitting there like a gathering of seedy bores, being as distinguished as distinguished. Actually, it is wrong to talk about envy, because I don't envy them their dismal empty existence and all that makes their life bitter and false and hopeless.

But when I compare what they have done with what I myself have done, and the social prestige they so self-evidently enjoy with the social prestige I have had to fight to acquire for so many hard years, then a crystal-clear sense of injustice keeps besetting and angering me, and which I now once and for all wish to correct. All those Blads and von Bladhs and Lehtisuon-Lehtinens, those alcoholic doctors and mediocre professors and roaming (German?) doctors of philosophy sitting on their high horses and living off daddy's and granddaddy's money. Those dismissed directors and pensioned-off industrialists. And last but not least, little Jacob von Bladh, the painter.

I called myself Blaadh, to mark the distance, but at the same time to show that I was no worse than they. Father, who was a caretaker and had Brynolf as his first name – his surname was just Blad. A fig-leaf. The social fig-leaf. The social fig-leaf people. The lower orders. The proletariat. He hadn't even the sense to become a communist.

This then was the situation. About six months ago, I felt an irresistible urge to write my memoirs. Not that I in any way felt I had lived my life, that I was kaput, finished, or anything like that, far from it; I'm not even fifty yet. But quite simply because I wanted to say what it is like to begin at the beginning, from the bottom, empty-handed, in fact as empty as two hands can be, and twenty-five or twenty-eight years later be rich, so rich that one need not deny oneself most things. I shall dedicate my book to His Grace the little painter, Jacob von Bladh.

External circumstances appeared to be so favourable, in fact in some way challenging. I suddenly had more time than before. After almost twenty years of laborious but successful management of the firm, I had a kind of attack of indolence or lightheartedness, and perhaps rather rashly, I handed over the day-to-day administration and immediate responsibilities to younger hands. Younger men, although not inexperienced for that reason. At the same time, I had – as it's usually called – promoted myself to Chairman of the Board. That meant the sudden end of the regularity of my life, which had become habitual over the decades. A great many duties remained, but the (partly self-inflicted) duty of being in place at eight-thirty precisely every morning was no longer there. I found myself roaming round my large, silent apartment without knowing what to do.

Slightly like being retired in some way. I had imagined it all as desirable, at last having time to do nothing. It didn't suit me. It was unpleasant. I suddenly had time to think. I thought. Perhaps that was why.

Naturally I kept in daily contact with Reino L., my successor as managing director. I had meetings and appointments and private consultations. But it was not quite the same as before. It was not really my concern as before. In a peculiar way I started feeling left out. I thought I'd done my bit and done it damned well, and it felt good, for sure, in some ways a great relief. And yet.

Filling the emptiness of life with work. Deciding the character of the work so that it became dynamic and meaningful. I had done that, hadn't I? I must do it again. The emptiness of life! That, too. To be able to afford the emptiness of life!

When I say I started thinking, I really mean I started evaluating. I started looking at myself, my life and my activities, the people around me, with new eyes, an evaluating look. I noticed that, before, I had somehow regarded all of life from the point of view of work. What was good for the firm was good on the whole, and all the better the more profit it produced. On the whole. A simple and accessible philosophy of life. But now I realize, as if a decisive change had taken place in my attitude to life, in my judgement, my whole consciousness, that there were other equally important bases of evaluation. Reluctantly, I was forced to admit I actually had understood that far back in my youth, at the time when I joined the Communist Party. But I forgot it in the course of time, losing that insight into the storms of life.

What were the people I had done business with like, apart from being good or bad business men? Like me? Ordinary simple people with family responsibilities and sexual appetites? Deep down, was I really that humdrum and one-track-minded? Was it really so uninteresting and empty to be ordinary and simple? I couldn't believe it. They lived as if in a dream in which sensations were moulded in advance and expectations served up ready-made. A lasting marriage as a base, often a wholly childish dependence. Children who turned out all right or didn't, and were consequently to be boasted about or not mentioned. And then, as a change, the happy little incidents, a girl to sleep with, a new motor launch, a larger apartment to show off. As if that actually were their whole happiness and their whole life, the sum total of realized desires. Their existence was to produce goods and distribute them on the market. That was

13

what we talked about. Goods were the primary concept of life. Hatreds, aggressions, provoked by wage demands, tax increases, social democracy, cultural activities, art. They never hesitated over what was good or bad in politics. The right was good, the left a catastrophe. In world politics, they were Nixon's men, but Kennedy had been best of all, as he had been both on the right capitalist lines and able to soothe more sensitive consciences with his liberal rhetoric. Was there not an anguish, a fear, at the root of their life experience, their imagined reality? A fear constantly threatening to break out, which had to be controlled and suppressed through boldness and arrogance; a shabby limited world of experience, rigidly held and crudely adapted opinions? What did they risk beyond what was prescribed by their bourgeois way of life? For to a great extent it must have been simply a matter of daring. They did not even dare read a left-wing paper in public, and maintained, apparently quite seriously, that socialism meant losing one's summer place, a purely individual loss of freedom, that is. So neurotic. Did I possess their anguish? Was I afraid in the same way as they were?.

Suddenly I had created a distance between myself and my colleagues and business friends, and I didn't really understand why or how it had happened. It was distasteful, to some extent a betrayal, and just because of that, so much stronger that I had to gain something constructive out of it, a clarification, a kind of captain's protest. And so the thought of writing down the whole thing was near at hand.

Now I must at once have it said that in contrast to my so-called cousin, the incomparable portrait painter, Jacob von B., I see nothing negative or slightly contemptible in being 'plain and ordinary'. On the contrary. To a great extent I have always regarded myself as a plain ordinary man, i.e. without neuroses or profundity and fortunately lacking in complicated or unusual ambitions. But both because of my nature and because of circumstances I have been able to influence, my life has perhaps been several degrees stormier than average. It is possible I have done a trifle more than others, I have risked a trifle more, I've taken chances where others would not have done, and I've placed myself in positions other people would not have placed themselves in. My weak point has always been my emotions, the difficulty always being how to keep them in check.

About ten years ago, I acted for a while as the Minister of Defence in the interim government. First and foremost, it was my

14

emotions that in the final count jiggered my activities even then. It would be untrue to say it is a painful memory just because I caused a scandal. Because I did cause a scandal. I have sufficient sense of humour to be able to laugh at it all now, as well as at the time. But a scandal is a scandal, inevitably containing an element of humiliation which one would have preferred to have avoided. My emotions played tricks on me. I shall return to that. This was at the time when I was still a plain ordinary man and happily married for the second time. To Gunnel.

It was the women who changed me, of that I am convinced. Each woman has not only been another woman, but she has opened a whole new and wonderful world for me to live in. How deeply and unconditionally I have loved them all.

Nothing is more nourishing than a woman's love, and in that respect I have been fortunate. I have loved and been loved, and that has changed me, in actual fact so profoundly that the man I am today barely resembles the desperate and disillusioned youth returning from the war in the late autumn of 1944.

My life is about women, how they intervened and turned me upside-down and influenced me and persuaded me to change my attitudes and way of life. My life is about what I learnt from women, about how they continuously and each in her own way formed the basis of my existence and world of experience. And yet those women are not included in what I consider important and significant in my life. I mean what I have achieved and attained, my position in society, my wealth, influence and connections.

Now what do I mean by that? That cannot correspond with reality, can it? When my first marriage was dissolved, that was expressly because Sinikka refused to approve – let us say – certain aspects of my financial activities. She saw my withdrawal from the Communist Party as shameless opportunism, i.e. that I had in some way sacrificed my political convictions on the altar of my financial ambitions. Which I suppose I had. It could equally well be maintained that, during my long marriage to Gunnel, I would never have been successful in business or in my social ambitions had I not had her constant, unalterable support, encouragement and loyalty, her understanding of the thousands of unwritten laws, or, to put it succinctly, her social background.

What am I trying to say? That to be alone is strong? Am I trying to devalue women and sentimentalize love? Or have I unconsciously

15

given expression to a doubt, a secret uncertainty, lying behind what I am finding so extremely difficult to express and explain at this moment, namely how impossible it is to give a truthful picture of one's own life, to write one's own autobiography?

One should begin at the beginning and end at the end. It's no more difficult than that. But my beginning was such that for a large part of my adult life I have denied or suppressed it, so that by now the picture has been partly wiped out, or anyhow certainly become distorted, perhaps unrecognizably. While the end . . ., well, naturally I don't know what that is. But the end that I do know and can take in, in other words what exists today – to be perfectly honest, I don't acknowledge that, either.

(All the time I am writing this, struggling with these horribly intractable, questionable, perhaps quite meaningless words, a name aches within me, my heart calling a name in silent despair . . . Miles! Miles! Why?)

But this was not to be about Miles; it was to be about myself and why it cannot at this moment even be about myself. I know I am expressing myself badly and I sense that I am becoming more and more obscure all the time. Isn't life obscure? Miles is my eldest son. Was.

Now I must confess something. I have already written three chapters of this opus, one on my childhood, one on my youth and one on my adult life, from the years of success. I started with my youth, what things were like when I came back from the war, from the front, possessing nothing, literally not even owning the clothes on my body, my army uniform, I mean, and without the slightest idea what my future would entail. Then I tried writing about the present. By recounting a true episode, a conversation 'at an exalted level', I wanted to indicate how that future has taken shape in reality. In actual fact, perhaps I simply needed to boast about my present influence and connections in high places? But it was when I tackled my childhood that the difficulties seriously started to accumulate. I could not write about my childhood. Was I ashamed of it? Or had I forgotten it?

No, to be truthful, I did not appear to have forgotten. On the contrary, I sat there feeling myself remembering everything very clearly, horribly clearly. But in the wrong way, quite the wrong way. I noticed as soon as I had a written a few pages. My parents cannot have been as I remember them. Or as I thought I remembered them.

16

So impersonal, so colourless, so repugnant, so featureless in their terrible limitations. My whole childhood, the memory of my childhood, I mean, was irremediably stamped, soiled, by the hatred, the shame, the humiliation I have associated with them all my life. What was the point of producing distorted pictures of the first years of one's life, if from the very start one knew perfectly well they were nothing but distorted pictures? What is the truth about Mother and Father, about our timid mouse-like life in the cramped, draughty, damp and unhealthy caretaker's quarters in the wooden building across the yard? What was it really like? Truly? I didn't know. For the memory of my eternal discontent, my indefatigable defiance, naturally cannot have brought to the surface more than a small fraction of what had really happened, the way things really were.

Father died of tuberculosis in 1943, the year when food shortages were at their worst. I left school and went to the front shortly afterwards, as a volunteer, as I was not yet conscription age. Mother was left alone at home with Oskar and her sewing-machine, stove, broom and Oskar's heart complaint. Those are the facts. But facts of that kind are not worth writing about, are they? They are true of everyone in some form or other. Each and every one of us has his own sad wretchedness. Life is like that, we all know that. Being a child and becoming adult is actually the most mutual of all human experiences. And the most banal. Facts need a context, an overall view, a kind of framework of knowledge of life, to be interesting and worth recounting and writing down. Is that not true? But I lacked that context, that framework of knowledge. The hatred and shame had distanced me or shut me out from context, knowledge, a general view.

(Miles! Rosa! Was that why? If it was . . . no, don't forgive me!)

I said at the beginning that my starting-point, or so I thought, was a kind of pride. It was also a kind of arrogance, a kind of contempt. Why shouldn't I be able to if others were? Write my memoirs, I mean. Or rather, why shouldn't I be able to do much better what others had done so damned badly? I thought of that diffuse bunch of mediocre politicians, officials and academics who 'after a lifetime's work', as they say, or 'when they had left the arena', felt called or even chosen to put down the memoirs of their lives. How astonishingly poverty-stricken those memories had then turned out to be. Deplorable, unimaginative or lying accounts of human lives and human deeds 'in the service of the public' as it was called, stamped with a kind of advanced dullness beneath exaggerated responsibility and peppered with platitudinous or cheap political reasoning and flat, foolish, or ingenuous comments 'on life'.

I knew I could do better. I knew that. Even if my ambition to 'be at the service of the public' could never measure up to my ambition to make money and live a good life in general. I was not famous in their pompous and pretentious sense. I had never needed to risk being afflicted with self-importance as an occupational disease or a status symbol. Not even as Minister of Defence was I self-important; everyone who had dealings with me at the time would testify to that – apart, of course, from certain staff officers whose self-importance was the actual meaning of life, and consequently that was the only way in which one could make oneself understood to them. But I've gone around in damned great black cars, all right. Chauffeur-driven and all. And not just as Minister of Defence.

But why write about it just because I am proud of it? Isn't that pretentious, a painfully conspicuous overrating of oneself? Is it because I am one of those people who have to compete in all fields, and win in all, fighting on all fronts and being victorious? Decathlete through thick and thin? General Custer off on a new adventure? Everywhere and always? Strong is best and most beautiful? How silly and meaningless! When I seem to know the picture will be crooked, anyhow, the experiences untrue, the statements false? I know so little about my own experiences. How could I know anything at all about other people's?

Is that not an understanding and a starting point?

Yes and no.

If only I could kill my doubts. Or at least in a convincing way show that they are justified. For I have begun to doubt myself.

That is my real starting-point.

Vanessa is absent, gone away. Jacob persecutes me. Torbjörn drinks and smells unpleasant. I have never in all my life been so lonely as I am now. And Miles . . . is there a single fragment left of that assured, tremendous self-satisfacton, that utter self-confidence, which to such an extent characterized me only a few months ago, when I was still working as before, when it happened, this business with Jacob? One cannot write about one's childhood, one's past, when the whole of one's present world is falling round one's ears. One cannot write about the past while the world burns.

So write about the present.

CHAPTER ONE *(Youth)*

'Blad.'

'von Bladh.'

That was how it began and the year was 1944. I was twenty and had just come back from a war that had wiped out my childhood faith. If I had ever had any.

I was with a friend from the front called Seppo. He had been promoted to sub-lieutenant a few weeks before the Armistice, for bravery in the field and exceptional services in the noble art of killing. Or in reality as a consequence of the insanely quick turnover of sub-lieutenants. I was a corporal for some reason, and had been elevated to university student a few months earlier during a confused leave which almost ended in a court martial. I was like that even then, obstinate and reluctant to obey orders. We had liquor in our packs and we sang and bawled, our joy desperate at having survived it all with our lives intact and more like a kind of rage during which one was prepared to murder both children and the old.

Weary of book learning, whining teachers and childish duties, I had joined the army as a volunteer straight from school just over two years earlier. My father had died shortly before, broken by undernourishment and galloping consumption. Only my mother, Saimi, and my brother Oskar remained at home, and I was not on very good terms with either of them. They kept on bringing up what a weighty financial sacrifice my schooling entailed. 'I'm off to the front then,' I said. I was seventeen, trained in the hard school of the back yard and not exactly an innocent. Yet the corresponding army life was far from what I had imagined. I was inflamed by war propaganda. In my youthful receptivity for all that was lofty, I had absorbed the fatherland like a drug. I had dreamt of a hero's halo, soon to be transformed by life at the front into the least attractive and most loathsome thing of all.

I learnt to kill and avoid death. I learnt to fear and protect myself against my own fear by encapsulating it into a hard cocoon of hatred. That was not much on which to build a future when peace came and life was to start again and be lived in a right-minded and edifying manner with assiduity, love and obedience to the law. I returned as an anonymous number in the savage multitude.

Arriving in Helsinki, we were tired and drunk. I had not considered playing the rôle of returning warrior and rushing back home into the arms of Saimi and Oskar. Seppo's childhood home, a large apartment in Arkadia Street, was empty, so we went there. His father was a doctor still serving at an army hospital in Villmanstrand, I think. The rest of the family were still evacuated to the family farm in Österbotten. Seppo had no keys. We had to ring the caretaker's bell and ask him to open up for us. Seppo addressed him with the same condescending amiability the gentlemen had shown when speaking to Father where I had grown up. I found this disturbing and suddenly realized I was in a situation which in some respects was abnormal and which did not correspond to anything else I had been involved in.

So now I had to play the rôle of – equal – guest in a gentleman's home. And although our friendship at the time was unwavering, in an unpleasant, uncomfortable way I was shy, taken unawares by the tension between inherited humble timidity and an almost raging desire to go wild and smash the furniture and all those refined knick-knacks. I escaped into deathly fatigue and fell asleep in full uniform in Seppo's mother's bed, while Seppo went off to buy some food and alcohol. For several days we wandered round this apartment, eating, drinking, bawling, spewing, bathing, sometimes almost unconscious from drink and exhaustion, incapable of deciding anything about the future or doing anything constructive. There was money in the bank, an inexhaustible source, and a bank-book rapidly commandeered from Österbotten. I smashed a handsome standard lamp of shiny brass and some kind of antique vase, but that didn't worry Seppo, who was going round in a kind of drooling drunken daze. The autumn days outside were clear and flaring, but that had nothing to do with us. We were not concerned with the outside world. We'd had enough of that.

Awakening occurred slowly and reluctantly, as if from a very deep sleep full of confused and tormented dreams. Neither of us had anywhere to go where we could have taken up our lives again. Seppo was already home, and I had no intention of returning home. Both of us lacked a fixed point in the world with people and tasks that would have tempted and challenged us into fresh endeavours. All we had was our childhood homes, but now we had reached the age when the security of home had for us been hopelessly forfeited. It was precisely from its grasp we had to free ourselves to be able to lead our own lives.

An ugly vacuum arose in our existence, which slowly, very slowly, began to be filled with the surrounding reality.

For the time being we had the apartment at our disposal, but it was clear it would not be long before one of the parents would appear, demanding an explanation for the ruined furniture, the vanished ornaments, the filthy bedclothes, the spewed-on carpets and so on. Seppo considered he had nothing to reproach himself with. He had single-handedly killed eight people, been promoted to lieutenant and awarded a medal, and if his mother and father had any comment to make, they could go to hell. Anyhow, he did what he felt like. But for me the situation was different. I was not only a guest in the house, but also a guest in their social class. Whatever happened I would sooner or later have to go and find another place to live. The thought of the arrival of the doctor and his wife, or until further notice the colonel and his lady, and my own departure, began to become more and more disturbing.

Seppo had bought most of the food and alcohol we consumed during those days on the black market, to which he appeared to have unlimited recourse. I had no money at all and was living on my friend's generosity and the still very strong sense of comradeship life at the front had created. That, too, would vanish one day; I realized that. Worst of all was that I had not had a woman for a very long time and my prick was beginning to rebel violently. There was a lot I ought to have done during those days, but only one single thing I simply had to.

So I said to Seppo that I was going out to find myself a cunt and presumed he had nothing against coming with me.

'You can't do that in those clothes. You stink,' he said.

It was true, of course. I had not changed my underclothes for several weeks and the uniform I was still wearing was stiff with dirt. In other words I had a valid reason for going home and kissing my mother on the cheek. I had to find a complete set of clean civilian clothes. I was not reckoning on remaining long in that nest of sorrow and sighs. We decided to meet a few hours later outside the Luxor on Great Robert Street, where they were showing a film with Betty Grable and Carmen Miranda.

As long as I could remember we had lived in the same wretched hovel, two small draughty rooms, dripping with damp, in a ramshackle wooden building in the back yard of 76, Skarpskytte

21

Street. They were the caretaker's quarters, with no conveniences. In the 'twenties, there weren't even water or drains, and the privy was in an unheated storeroom alongside. Mother carried water from the wash-house on the opposite side of the yard. Suddenly I can remember the gnawing of rats in the larder and woodbox at nights. Family bliss was cramped then, five people sharing the few square metres. Mother and Father and I and brother Emil and brother Oskar. I slept in the same bed as Oskar for some years. In 1932, Emil went to America and we had a little more elbow-room. I did not go into that melancholy yard, so full of bitter memories, with the joy of reacquaintance.

Mother opened the door when I knocked. She seemed far from pleased to see me.

'So you're back, are you?' she said, in her plaintive, squeaky voice. 'I thought you were rotting away in the Russian forests when you didn't let us know and when the peace came and all.'

'Well, here I am now, anyhow,' I said.

She had aged a great deal since I had last seen her, was more shrunken and wrinkled and greyer. She was as thin and brittle as a dragonfly. Her short, brushed-back hair also seemed thinner, not even grey, but quite colourless. Her fingers, deformed by rheumatism and endless work, were fumbling nervously with the buttons of her worn green cardigan. Then she quickly pressed her hand against my uniform coat and I put my hand over hers, almost without knowing what I was doing, holding it there for a moment against my heart. A lump came up in my throat, however that happened, and I was just about to put my arms round her when she said something that at once removed any desire to be friendly.

'Ugh, how you smell,' she said. 'I'd say you've been drinking. Oskar says the soldiers drink something terrible. I wouldn't have believed it, but then that's how things've gone with this war. . . .'

'Where are my clothes?' I broke in.

She was on her way into the kitchen now.

'Do you want some coffee?' she said, without turning round.

'Where are my clothes?' I repeated.

She did not reply.

I went over to the cupboard where I used to keep my personal belongings. They were all gone. Oskar had clearly been there, bag and baggage. At first I didn't realize what it meant. Then suddenly it hurt terribly. They had eliminated me. They had stopped counting on me as son and brother. They had done what the war had not succeeded in doing, killed me. Then as usual I quite unexpectedly became terribly angry.

'What the hell does this mean?' I yelled.

She still said nothing.

I went across, took her by the shoulders and turned her round. Her eyes flickered. It was like holding the corpse of a bird between my hands. She was afraid, her eyes suddenly blinded with tears. She stammered. Incoherently, she explained she'd been sure I'd been killed, that Oskar had said so, that he'd read in the paper that my whole unit had been wiped out.

They really had killed me.

'For Christ's bloody sake!' I shouted as loudly as I could.

It was all a great muddle of sorrow and despair and wounded self-esteem and guilty conscience and raging fury. I had despised my mother, ignored her and treated her badly, but in my youthful self-absorption, despite everything, I was making all the ordinary maternal demands on her. I could not see that this tragic misunderstanding could partly be seen as a logical consequence of my own actions.

I was very upset and felt a need to see blood. I left her without another word and started walking almost blindly, first along Högberg Street past the burnt-out, smoke-blackened ruins of Jägar Street and the dreary rows of boarded-up shattered windows. I was seething with hatred. I turned up Bergman Street in the direction of Skeppar Street, my hands clenching and unclenching automatically. It was almost evening, the street empty of people and vehicles. Then a wretched lieutenant steps out from a porchway a little farther on and comes walking towards me. I look him straight in the eye as he passes, but do not salute. I have done the same thing with a colonel once before with devastating results, but they were not to be repeated this time.

'Hey, corporal!' he calls after me.

I stop and turn round.

'Why the hell didn't you salute?' he says, almost friendly in his reproach. Peace had recently been declared and it wasn't so important any longer, at least not for a certain type of reserve sub-lieutenants and lieutenants.

'Go kiss your arse,' I say (just like the last time), taking a few steps towards him.

23

He stares at me, incapable of speech. He seems to be one of the soft sort.

'Are you drunk?' he says.

'No, are you?'

Not until then does he become angry and shout something I don't catch (as I'm already thinking about other things).

I hit him with my right exactly between the eyes and feel the bone in his nose giving way with a small crunch. The skin on my knuckles splits and starts bleeding. He staggers back a few steps, blood spurting out of his nose and his eyes blind from watering. Then his right hand starts fumbling for his holster. I lock his arm back and drag him into a porchway. I hate him totally without reservation. I hit him as hard as I can in the midriff and he doubles up, gasping. He gets a kick in the face and falls, then lies on his side as he semi-consciously tries to protect his face with his hands. I kick him as hard as I can in the head and the kidneys, time and time again, then walk quickly away. I feel a bit better. I have worked off the worst, but the throbbing desire to strike out still has not left me.

When I ring the bell at Seppo's, no one comes to the door. I sit waiting on the stairs for a moment, about to give up and almost crying when suddenly he appears, very smart in civvies, and colossally drunk. He has been out to buy some more alcohol. He has been to his uncle's and drunk brandy and been given ten thousand marks as a reward for bravery in the field. The uncle was drunk for the second consecutive week, utterly crushed by the terrible fate which had befallen his fatherland.

I'm allowed to borrow some of Seppo's clothes. I drink practically nothing, but Seppo keeps drinking all the time, simply getting drunker and drunker.

'No woman'll want to fuck with you in that state. Take it easy, for Christ's sake,' I say.

He takes no notice of my well-meaning advice. I leave him and the last thing I see is him sitting on the floor and, with a dangerously unsteady hand, filling a tumbler with neat aquavit. 'Here's to eight dead Russians,' he mumbles, apparently now at the sentimental stage.

I get hold of a couple of girls in Kajsaniemi Park and offer them cigarettes. I tell them about life in the trenches. When we've finished smoking, I get rid of the plainer one and screw the other up against a tree. She's a bit reluctant at first and I have to take a stranglehold on

24

her with one hand while I rip her pants with the other and force two fingers between her thighs. I've hardly got it in before it comes for me. Anyhow, then she soon catches on, and we go over to the goods station and continue in an empty goods wagon. After coming eight times, I'm ready and wondering how to get rid of her. She seems exhausted. I feel in a tremendously good mood. I tell her I must go and have a pee, and then I slowly creep away.

It's the middle of the night and rather cold. I shiver. My hands are cold, my buttocks strangely chilly. But it feels good all the same, in every way; for the first time since God knows when, I'm almost exhilarated, almost so that I can begin to think there is peace in the land and what will happen now and that I ought to start on something useful and all that and Mannerheim and Paasikivi and Herta Kuusinen. That's how edifying a good screw is after long abstinence.

I just walk and walk, my hands thrust deep down in my pockets. On the north side of Töl Island Bay, a gang is sitting round drinking and solving the problems of the world.

'Which bloody side are you on?' they say threateningly.

'Come on over and I'll bash you one!'

'Go to hell, bloody class-traitor.'

'I've just bashed in the head of a fucking officer an hour or so ago, and I'll do the same to any bugger who asks for it,' I say, stretching my hands out towards the warmth of the fire.

They make room for me and hand round a bottle. It tastes like shit but warms me nicely. They talk grandly about hanging Mannerheim and his gangsters from the nearest lamp-post, getting lost in macabre details and laughing loudly for a long time. They plan to crush the exploiting bourgeoisie and set up a dictatorship of the proletariat. It is liberating to hear them setting it all out. In a superficial and inarticulate way, I become class-conscious that night and lose my political virginity.

Towards morning, I return to Arkadia Street. Seppo is gloomy and has a hangover. He seems unusually reserved, almost unfriendly, and I sense that a divide has opened between us, which can no longer be bridged, but on the contrary, will become deeper and deeper as we slowly grow into our respective rôles in the reality of peacetime.

But for the time being things are all right. I sponge money, houseroom and black market connections off Seppo, the difference from the early days being that now it is conscious and premeditated. Seppo is dependent on me, clinging to what is ingrained, as he finds it terribly difficult to free himself from the effects of war and adapt himself to the bourgeois peacetime reality of student life he is predestined for. Letters full of advice and orders from his mother and father keep coming at shorter and shorter intervals, but Seppo just drinks and one day confides in me that he has almost begun to long to be back to the front and the trenches and dug-outs and the sound of exploding grenades.

We go into town these days. We've got used to the ruins, the shattered boarded-up windows, the stacks of wood, the parks turned into primitive air-raid shelters. The shops are empty, there are queues for food every day, people are thin and badly dressed and everywhere there are traces of a long, devastating war, and Soviet troops patrolling the streets with their stone faces and short necks.

We dance in the joyful peace of Järnvag Square with the communists and weep over the cruel armistice with the bourgeoisie in bourgeois homes, now gloomy nests of defeat. Everything is transformed, the wrong way round, and I don't know which camp I belong in. Seppo is timid and uncertain in the Square and insolent and aggressive among his bourgeois equals. It is more complicated for me, all the same. I have never before sung the Internationale, but now it feels good and right from my vocal cords. On the other hand, the decorative, patrician homes of Seppo's world are what I have always longed for, aspired to belong to. It's hard to know. The only thing I know with any certainty is that I don't want to be like Father and Mother, that never, ever, will I be as bloody wretched and poor as they were.

During Father's time as commissionaire at the National Theatre, I had got to know an actress who became my first mistress. I was fifteen years old then, she almost twenty years older. She called me her 'lovely boy' and for a long time her bed was a second home to me. I had not seen her since I'd joined the army and become a 'brave boy', but now I renewed the contact and introduced her to Seppo. Naturally she had aged, like everyone else. So had I. But my affection for her remained, and a small shred of desire. She had been married and divorced a couple of times and was now very lonely. She lived in Fänrik Stål Street in a two-roomed apartment almost grotesquely overcrowded with lace and velvet draperies and mats and old porcelain and small glass ornaments. She was not happy and her gratitude for our simple attendance on her was sometimes painfully

26

exaggerated and sentimental. But for a brief while she served as a kind of fixed point in our uneasy, planless existence. Her name was Helga. Helga Norin.

The three of us went round the city's inns together, she and Seppo taking it in turns to be financiers. My rôle as sponger was not humiliating. I paid for myself in my own way. It could be said that I gave Helga my youth and Seppo my wisdom. I was financially dependent on them, but their dependence on me was at a deeper level and concerned their loneliness and anguish. For Helga, I was sexual pleasure, human proximity. For Seppo, I was the the only human support on offer in his unhappy post-pubertal post-war attempts to adapt to a cramped and joyless bourgeois reality.

One evening we were at a restaurant in Great Robert Street. We had been playing Alan Ladd and Peter Lorre with the notice 'Weapons should be left in the hall' on the wall by the entrance to the dining-room, arousing the porter's ire with the noise. We were still at an age when we became excited and boisterous very easily and our smooth youthful faces did not arouse spontaneous respect in the head-waiter. Neither was Helga a well-known actress. In other words, from the very start we incurred disapproval. We were smoking some Lucky Strikes Helga's brother in the merchant navy had given her, and the packet was left on the table to show that we weren't just anybody. That was rather childish, of course, and naturally American cigarettes did not have any apparent effect on the head-waiter. We were eating some kind of tough, indefinable mincemeat, dog-meat according to Helga, with beetroot and last year's rather sour potatoes. It all tasted foul. Seppo suggested it was crow-meat, while I overstepped the mark as usual and suggested Jew.

The head-waiter was disapproving of our arrogant questions, and the waitress became more and more tight-lipped, which made us even more exhilarated and expansive, and we jabbered on like a couple of silly kids. Then they sudenly stopped serving us and instead of the round of cheap brandy we had ordered, we were presented with the bill. Seppo was furious. He was not exactly blind drunk, but certainly far from sober. He called for the head-waiter, but extraordinarily the head-waiter was absent. Seppo started shouting obscenities as loudly as he could about Finnish inns in general and this one in particular; then the head-waiter was suddenly there, inviting us with considerable emphasis to leave immediately or else. . . .

Seppo called him all kinds of things such as bounder, idiot, imbecile, fag, insinuator and Sjdanov's private little arse-licker. All conversation at the tables round us ceased and everyone sat waiting intently for what was going to happen next. The head-waiter tried to pluck up courage as best he could, but he was noticeably frightened, having clearly grasped where we had been for the last few years and knowing from bitter experience what to expect from enraged front-line soldiers of our age. Helga made feeble attempts to mediate and smooth things down.

'I've killed eight Russians single-handed, and now I'm going to fucking well make mincemeat out of you, you bloody sod!' shouted Seppo.

'You are drunk, sir, and it'd be best if you went home to bed,' said the head-waiter.

'You're a fucking insinuating drunken fag yourself. Bring those drinks or I'll tear out your guts, by Christ and . . . hang you up on that lamp over there by your own intestines,' bellowed Seppo.

I saw the porter appear in the doorway and stand there watchfully.

'Please leave at once, or I'll call the police.'

'Bugger the police. D'you know what I'll do with the police if you call them? I'll piss on the police. . . .'

He was so angry now, words failed him.

'Seppo, dear, let's go now before anything awful happens,' whispered Helga, tugging cautiously at his sleeve.

He jerked his arm violently away, sending Helga reeling. Then he suddenly grasped the table with both hands and lifted it with glasses, ashtrays, half-empty soda-water bottles, tipping the whole lot at the head-waiter, who fell backwards against the neighbouring table in an indescribable mess of salads and half-consumed meat. The porter rushed across, ready for action, and guests here and there at the nearby tables rose and approached threateningly. I saw that Seppo was just about to leap on to the head-waiter and go for him, so I grabbed his wrist and started dragging him over towards the exit. Helga had gone on ahead. The porter stopped us.

'You don't get away with it that easy,' he hissed. 'You've bloody got to pay for this.'

I hurled Seppo into Helga's arms and called to her to get him out as quickly as possible. Then I hit out, first with the right, then the left, and the astonished porter squinted, put his hands to his face and

28

slowly collapsed. Then I ran. Helga and Seppo were already out on the street.

'Come on, run!' I shouted.

We ran.

We rounded corner after corner, Helga between us in a firm grasp, as she found it hard to keep up with her thirty-eight years, her smoker's lungs and tight skirt. We ran tight-lipped and purposefully at first. I was expecting a police-car to appear at any moment and stop us. But nothing happened. We were gasping from exhaustion. Then the tension gradually receded, the further away from the inn we got. I giggled. Suddenly I felt an irresistible desire to laugh. I stopped and howled with laughter. Helga and Seppo were infected and also started laughing. We stood there breathlessly and just laughed and laughed.

'Head-waiter crushed between two tables . . .'

'Fried head-waiter with potatoes and beetroot, only four marks fifty . . .'

'Head-waiter hanging by his own guts . . .'

We laughed and laughed.

We were down in Albert Street near the park, and it was Seppo's idea that we should pay a call on a crazy relative of his, an artist who lived nearby. We had nothing to drink at home, neither in Arkadia Street not at Helga's, and we were merry and as thirsty as hell. It was hardly ten o'clock. This artist relative had his studio in the attic of a house with a view out over the opera house and Gräsvik harbour, the shipyard and the sea beyond. He was at home when we rang the bell and said von Bladh and I said Blad as we shook hands, and that was how everything started, as I said before.

I had never met anyone like Jacob von Bladh before. We disliked each other on sight. He was distinguished and I was brutish. Or rather, he was in fact not at all distinguished, as he was dirty and untidy, and I was far too intelligent to be a brute. We didn't conform to each other's patterns, the prescribed social patterns of prejudice.

Jacob von Bladh was quite a large man with a heavy, squat body. His face was red, his hair thin and straggly and reddish, not trimmed, and he had red freckles everywhere, right down his neck and on his hands, his chin and cheeks covered with several days' stubble. His eyes were small, pale blue and watery, his nose fleshy and covered with small holes from blackheads, his lips thick and rather loose. His voice was light, almost feminine, and did not at all match the heavy body. He was exceptionally ugly, but in some inexplicable way not directly repellent. He had a charming, rather clumsy but courteous manner, testifying to a good upbringing and solid social background, which presumably made an impression on a certain kind of woman, regardless of his ugliness. He had a kind of warmth which also testified to his humanity. He could say peculiar, bizarre things, the meaning of which I could not grasp. For instance, about himself: 'Ignorant of the warrior's noble art but a warrior of art'. What the hell did he mean by that?

Seppo indicated not very sensitively, nor noticeably abruptly, that we were hellish thirsty and that was the main reason for our late and unexpected visit. He spoke to Jacob in a condescending, sarcastic and strikingly self-assured or straight dogmatic tone of voice on the whole. Without protesting, kindly and obediently, submissively in a way, Jacob put on his dirty worn overcoat and disappeared for an hour, returning with two bottles of juniper aquavit. Our delight knew no bounds.

Jacob von Bladh's studio appeared as strange and alien a place to live in as he himself seemed as a person. I couldn't understand how anyone could live in such disorder. All along the wall under the window was a work-table covered with tubes of paint, brushes, pots, chisels, carver's tools and all kinds of rubbish, and against the opposite wall was a narrow, spartan, unmade bed heaped with a ragged blanket and horribly dirty sheets. Two strong working lamps, a standard lamp, an old armchair with ragged upholstery, some rickety wooden chairs and a table covered with yellow oil-cloth, dirty coffee cups, bread crusts, glasses and a large ashtray full of butts and pipe ash made up the rest of the furnishings. It was all very threadbare. Apart from the paintings, of course, which covered most of the available wall space.

Seppo was behaving with great self-assurance and asked me in bantering tones what I thought of 'Jacke's' paintings. I had never had the slightest chance of taking an interest in painting and naturally had no opinions. Seppo knew that. He simply wanted revenge on me for my earlier advantage.

'I don't know. I don't understand art,' I said.

'No sensible person understands Jacob's art,' said Seppo.

The paintings were mostly dark streaks on light surfaces, or geometrical figures arranged in some kind of pattern on large, almost colourless surfaces. They all appeared meaningless on the whole, although in some cases I could have said that I found the colours attractive, that I just thought they were . . . beautiful. But naturally I did not dare. I was puzzled and felt ill at ease, and the thought arose that life at the front was in some ways considerably easier and safer than visiting an artist's studio.

Jacob von Bladh rinsed four tumblers under the cold tap and we started drinking out of them. We talked about the war and our defeat. He was very patriotic and depressed. But he had been exempted from war service because of a bad heart, ulcers and a whole lot of other complaints which he rambled on about until it was impossible to go on listening. When he had a good deal of liquor inside him, he suddenly leant across to me and said slightly aggressively:

'What kind of bloody Bladh are you, then?'

I didn't know what he meant. I shrugged my shoulders and looked appealingly at Seppo and Helga.

'His father was the caretaker in Skarpskytte Street,' said Seppo.

'Caretaker? No member of the Bladh family has ever been a caretaker, as far as I know,' said Jacob von Bladh acidly.

'And I thought you were cousins or something!' said Seppo, laughing, malice in his voice.

I was suddenly angry.

'What the hell's wrong with being a caretaker?' I growled.

'By all means, I just wondered by what right you'd taken on the Bladh family name.'

'I think you should stop getting at Donald,' said Helga. 'He can't help his name, can he?'

'But it's quite interesting, nevertheless, when suddenly a completely strange young man appears in my studio maintaining his name is Bladh.'

'It's Blad without the "h", Jacke,' said Seppo.

I still didn't understand the point of this conversation and was feeling humiliated. I reckoned if he continued his bullying tactics a moment longer, I'd punch him on the jaw. He was being superior. Seppo had also become superior in his company. I couldn't stand superior people.

'My grandfather was called Blad, too,' I said uncertainly.

'My god, grandfather, too! Things get better and better. And what was your grandfather, if I may ask? Something very grand, no doubt?'

I leapt up from my chair.

'That's enough of this bloody nonsense. Your bloody family name can go to hell and you with it, fucking bloody artist!'

He sat there without moving, looking at me with a mocking smile.

'How very familiar of you. Are you a communist, Mr Blad?'

'Yes, I bloody well am.'

'Calm down, and stop it, for God's sake,' said Helga.

She knew me.

I went over to the chair where he was sitting and struck him in his watery right eye. His chair tipped over backwards and he made feeble attempts to scramble up from the floor.

That was our first meeting. I was convinced it would be the last. But I was wrong.

Seppo did his best to excuse himself after this disastrous postprandial event and our friendship did not come to an end. He admitted that, in his cups, he had brought us together deliberately, secretly hoping to make a fool of me, for he knew how sensitive Jacob von Bladh was about the family name. He admitted he had already been irritated with me for quite a time because, he maintained, I had started behaving in a demonstratively superior and domineering way. I presumed much of it was because of Helga. He had no female company and perhaps felt tormented and superfluous on occasions. I thought I would try to persuade Helga to sleep with him one night, so he could be rid of his bourgeois chastity complex. When I suggested this to her, she laughed uncertainly and behaved as if I had offended her in some way. Then Seppo's mother and brothers and sisters came back from Österbotten and I moved in with Helga permanently.

Helga's hair was black with a few grey streaks, and she had big brown eyes. She looked younger than she was, despite her considerable consumption of alcohol and tobacco and her generally irregular life. Her complexion was smooth and downy and surprisingly unlined, but when she was naked it was evident age had already begun to take hold. Her breasts, stomach and thighs were of a woman no longer young. She had a gentle expression, and in some respects it

32

was true, she was far too kind and compliant a person, the kind of woman predestined to suffer. Her first husband was an alcoholic and had committed suicide after a few years of marriage. Her second husband had maltreated her and been unfaithful, a bounder in every respect. She had separated from him at the time when I, as a fifteen-year-old, met her at the end of the 'thirties. Helga had no children of her own, and I think this was a cause of much secret grief. She never complained about the financial burden I obviously involved, but I knew her resources were limited and also that this arrangement was doomed to be of short duration.

But we got on very well together. My war experiences made us almost completely equal, despite the differences in our ages, and she was no longer a mother to me in the way she had been before the war. My life now began to run along smoother tracks. Helga was on stage two nights a week and also had a number of free-lance jobs, some of which were on the radio. She was often out in the daytime, and I drifted round the empty apartment, doing nothing. But I was thinking. The concrete result of my thoughts was that I joined the Communist Party and became an active member.

Perhaps it was the meeting with Jacob von Bladh that actually made me turn communist. Whenever I recalled in my mind his arrogance and right-wing conceit, I was always disturbed and annoyed. What right had he to get on his high horse just because he happened to have a certain name? I remembered Seppo telling me his father had been a senator or a civil servant or a general or something high up. Why should the son of a senator consider himself better than a son of a caretaker? Just like that, and as if it were perfectly obvious? Seppo had also told me that in fact Jacob was not nearly so badly placed financially as one might think from the dump he lived in, but on the contrary, he had quite a lot of inherited money from which he drew dividends. The shabby surroundings he lived in were really only silly studied artistic scenery, nothing to do with his own circumstances. Wasn't that really an insolent challenge to those who were genuinely poor, with no chance of creating a pleasant, comfortable life for themselves? He quite obviously thought he was superior to me in the way the bourgeois class all thought they were superior to the working class. In other words, some people thought they were born superior without having to raise a finger for their own superiority, while others, according to this way of looking at things, could never be superior, however hard they worked or tried. Just because they weren't *born superior*. Under no circumstances could that be considered just. Not only unjust, but illogical, a flawed concept, a false interpretation of reality, nothing to do with how people decided to live together, but how they *ought* to live together. It was an unashamed consequence of personal desire for power, selfishness and avarice. Why had a few people such power, while most had no power whatsoever? Some people had huge amounts of money, but the majority, on the contrary, had far too little. Father and Mother had struggled and toiled for a lifetime, only just managing to scrape enough together to keep us alive and to keep me, the 'scholar', in school. Things were bloody wrong all round. Somewhere there must be a basic fault that should be corrected. I went around thinking like that, reasoning my way on my own to a perhaps childish and incomplete, but probably deeply felt communist view of life. So I joined the Party. . . .

Then things started happening. Brother Emil suddenly came back from America and immediately started in business in a grandiose manner, thus becoming the direct reason why I finally found a living which would later develop into a lifetime's work on my part, if I may say so. I also made contact with my father's old father again, now eighty years old, a smallholder on a little holding called New Farm just outside Helsinki. And finally I went to see Jacob von Bladh again.

Grandfather told me something quite fantastic.

This is how it happened. We were standing out in the woodshed and Grandfather was sawing, I chopping, our breath coming out of our mouths like smoke, as it was a cold winter's day with snow in high drifts outside as dusk was falling. We talked about this and that as usual, as we had always been good friends and the war was nothing but an odd parenthesis which had not seriously been able to harm our friendship. I happened to mention I had met an unpleasant artist called von Bladh, who had started making a fuss about our family name and had behaved so arrogantly and insolently I had finally had to punch him on the jaw. Grandfather was silent for a long while, looking at me with a thoughtful expression. Then he spoke in his special hesitant way, calmly and circumspectly:

'That's Brynolf's cousin,' he said.

I let the axe sink slowly down on the chopping block and stared at him.

'You're joking, Grandfather,' I said.

He shook his head, that grey, weather-beaten, ravaged head.

'It's true as Amen in church, for that's how things went in days gone by, and still do today perhaps, how should I know?'

Said he.

We sat all evening in the kitchen, drinking coffee and talking. Grandfather told me about his mother and father and his own origins and I was told a story about which neither Brynolf nor Saimi had even whispered a single word. I had not been interested, either, had I? Origins? When have the young ever been interested in their origins?

It was really only the same old story of human strength and human weakness. And of lusts of the flesh and a lonely woman's determined struggle for her rights against an opponent which was really a whole world, or the whole apparatus of a power-conscious social system's hypocritical and accepted values and heartless hostility to intruders, and to those who were neither called nor chosen.

Grandfather's mother was called Kreetta and had walked from northern Tavastland to look for work. She was sixteen and alone in the world. Her mother had died of consumption and her father had already disappeared two years earlier while hunting for something to live off, and she knew nothing of her siblings, because they were either dead or scattered to the cold winds of a class society. That was the great year of 1863. Kreetta got a job at the Finnish Clothing Factory, which had been founded by some gentlemen, one of whom was Professor Walter von Bladh. The professor's son was called Karl-Johan and was destined to become a director in time, because the professor had put up the most capital. And Kreetta was sixteen and Karl-Johan was twenty-one and Kreetta was beautiful and Karl-Johan was randy, so he got her with child. He sowed his gentlemanly seed in her proletarian virgin womb. That was a terrible and oh, such a painful mistake. So much more so as it did not happen simply as a pastime, or an ardent impulse of the moment, or a thoughtless passing fancy, but out of pure youthful and reciprocated love.

Then the fruits of sin and shame ripened and Kreetta grew large in the belly and, in 1864, she gave birth to a healthy infant boy and that was Grandfather. He was not allowed to be called Karl von Bladh, but had to be called Kalle Hämäläinen. And Kreetta no longer had a job at the Finnish Clothing Factory, because now she was a servant and wet-nurse to another distinguished family with another distinguished name. Karl-Johan knew nothing about her or his son, because he had been hastily packed off to Manchester to study the textile industry.

But Kreetta was no fool. She was not made to wipe the floor with. They bribed her into silence with a modest gratuity. And she promised, oh so humbly and sensibly, to be loyal to poor Karl-Johan in his misfortune (because you'll understand yourself, Kreetta, that . . .). But, on the other hand, she never promised to keep to what she had promised. Need knows no laws, Kreetta thought, and anyhow justice and morality are only inventions of the rich and powerful. So there was a little bit of something like blackmail when it came down to it, i.e. Kreetta promised to keep to what she promised, as long as the von Bladh family on their side ensured she and the boy did not have to take to the beggar's bowl and so on and so forth. The von Bladh family raged and prayed to God and pleaded meekly and threatened her with whipping and the stocks. But Kreetta just stood her ground. Because that was what she was like.

And Kalle Hämäläinen went to a Swedish elementary school and learnt Swedish and to crown everything Kreetta became a little Swedish, too, and started signing herself Greta. When Kalle left school, he went to sea. When he came back a few years later, he was a grown man and very much inclined to try his hand as a farmer. Kreetta, who was Greta now, a mature, wise and experienced woman, went to the love of her youth, the doughty Karl-Johan, now indeed titled and a director and all and happily married and father of many children, and she told him straight out what the situation was, that Kalle wanted to be a farmer.

'What the . . . you don't mean New Farm is . . .'

'D'you want to see the deed of gift?'

'But thirty hectares!'

'It weren't thirty then, only five.'

'But all the same? What else was he afraid of, then? After so many years?'

'They was different times, Donald, keep that in mind. Scandal was scandal, however old and forgotten it was, for the gentry and their mania about scandals. There was a wife and children now, of course, and he couldn't come along with me saying here's your big brother . . . and . . .'

'What?'

'He hadn't ever forgotten her and she knew it. So there was a bit more in later years. . . . Mother saw to it . . . for the sake of New

Farm. As security, so to speak. And getting her own back. For it was kind of change of rôles now, and he was the one who had to go without. And when Kalle Hämäläinen had become a farmer, he took the name Blad. No one could object to that. But I've never had nothing to do with that fat family. No doubt that was best, though sometimes I've thought about it all right, especially when I saw how rotten they was to Brynolf . . . that there artist, that Jacob von Bladh, he was, Karl-Johan was, Karl-Johan, I say, dad, Karl-Johan I mean, that was his granddad, that was.'

Grandfather's astonishing revelation gave me a new perspective on my life. I had suddenly been given a concrete, genuine foundation for both my hatred and my self-esteem. In a way I took the story of my origins as an extreme confirmation of the rightness of the communist interpretation of reality, and at the same time it gave me a wonderful, dazzling sensation of being *someone*, despite everything, of having a place in a meaningful human perspective of time, despite everything, of being a link, however modest, in the historical family tradition. I did not need to found a dynasty; I already belonged to a dynasty, if only a minor branch. One was less important than the other, and even if the two experiences were irreconcilable and contradictory, they existed all the same in the same consciousness, contained within the same consciousness, my consciousness. I, Donald Blad!

This new insight, which naturally I never for one moment doubted, gave me a strong, malicious and heady desire to seek out the loathsome Jacob von Bladh and ring his doorbell and say straight to his face: 'Hi, Dad's cousin!' But he forestalled me.

One March Sunday afternoon of extreme cold and swirling snow, the telephone rang at Helga's and it was him. He was evidently slightly drunk and wanted to speak to me. He apologized for his bad behaviour the last time we had met and said he had had a guilty conscience ever since. He was not actually a snotty upper-class type, he assured me, but he hadn't really been himself at the time. He had been off the rails because of the Control Commission's arrival in Helsinki, and a number of other things of a personal nature. On the other hand, we were in some ways quits as I'd punched him on the jaw. Now he was wondering whether I would consider coming to see him. There was something he wanted to talk about and he had a bottle of brandy smuggled in from Sweden. We could sit in peace and quiet, in all simplicity, etc., etc., etc. I accepted without a moment's hesitation and set off in the raging snowstorm, not without a sense of superiority and malicious glee.

'You can imagine the bang here in 1939 when they bombed their own legation to smithereens. I hadn't a whole window left and everything was a mess. You can see the marks from splinters over there on the wall. God, I was scared, but I went down to the shelter only twice in the whole war, both times compulsorily, so to speak, on principle, for my father's sake. He never went down, either. He prayed to God and went to bed and slept as the bombs exploded and the anti-aircraft guns roared. Lived in Kronhagen; one night an incendiary bomb fell through his bedroom window, but there was something wrong with it and it didn't explode. The finger of God, Father thought. He lay there all night with an incendiary as a bedmate. Extremely odd. Plenty of curious events from this unfortunate war . . . but sit down, do, help yourself. I've bought some buns. They taste foul. I'll throw them away, no, one shouldn't waste God's gifts, even if they are extremely modest these days . . . he does his best, Father's God, oh, the way I go on . . . cheers. How're things with you? Are you studying . . .'

He was moving nervously round the room all the time, from one wall to the other, shifting things from one place to another, or arranging them in puzzling formations which he soon dismembered and replaced with others, matchboxes, coffee cups, spoons, tubes of paint, anything. He was wearing a great baggy sweater which, a long time ago, had once been white. His hands were dirty, the nails black, and he had a black beret on his head. His thick lips were wet with saliva, his fleshy nose red. From a cold? Alcohol? The cold? It was very cold in the studio. On the wall immediately opposite where I was sitting at the table, one hand resting on the yellow oil-cloth, hung a very large picture, black squares in different sizes on a yellow background, rather like an imaginative plan for a large apartment, but not so few rooms. I told him I was working voluntarily for my brother, who had just come back from America, in his firm (unusually well paid, but I did not tell him that). This did not seem to interest him much and I started feeling uncertain and embarrassed, as on the previous occasion.

'Let's wipe out the past. We might as well. Your fists are terrible, I must say. I was ill for a week afterwards, headache, black eye. I suppose it's how you were brought up. I understand, I understand, and I behaved unforgivably badly. I should have . . . but as I told you, I wasn't myself. You must forgive me. Let's forget it. Let the dead bury their dead. Oh, sorry, perhaps you've got someone in the family who . . . you never know after a war. I've a lot. My nephew was killed a year ago, my cousin, my sister's brother-in-law, lecturer at the university, twenty-seven years old. This country has only inferiors left, like me, a failed artist. What can I do for the rebuilding of the country, nothing, absolutely nothing. We must put our hopes in you, the new generation, new blood in old bottles . . . or what the hell it's called, but that wasn't why I phoned. I ought to be able to offer you something, a post, a job for the future, a loan . . . but I can't. I've no say in things. No one listens to me. A real Mister Nobody, that's what I am. They just laugh at me, glancing meaningfully at me and whispering and moving away, the black sheep, the shame of the family. It was nice of you to come. I didn't think you would, actually, after what went on, but there's still a bit of humanity left in the world. I very much value your friendship. I like you, I really do. Cheers! What about dropping the mister stuff. Jacob's my name.'

We shook hands formally and touched glasses. I had never been through that ceremony before, but nevertheless I realized it must constitute one of the high points of bourgeois life. He just went on and on talking and I hadn't the slightest idea what he was getting at. My flesh began to creep and my brain kept repeating all on its own: 'Hi, Dad's cousin, hi, Dad's cousin, hi, Dad's cousin . . .' Then suddenly it was 'Bat's cousin Bat's cousin Bat's cousin'. I'll go soon, I thought. But then he fell silent and sat looking piercingly at me, as if expecting me to say something. I didn't know what to contribute.

'You know already, don't you?' he said then.

'What?' I replied, shaking my head.

'No, of course not. But you see, I've made a little discovery which I think is interesting. That house you lived in before the war, where your father was the caretaker, did you say it was number seventy-six, Skarpskytte Street?'

'Yes.'

'Do you know who owns it?'

'No.'

'The Lehtisuon-Lehtinen family.'

'Yes, that was the manager's name, anyhow.'

'Quite right. And do you know what that family is?'

'No.'

'The Lehtisuon-Lehtinens are the Finnish branch of the von Bladh family. My cousins, in other words. Rather a remarkable coincidence, isn't it?'

My heart suddenly started thumping. Grandfather had said nothing about this. Perhaps he didn't know. And how much had Brynolf known? For some reason, I felt myself turning red, my cheeks flaring.

'So one really starts to wonder . . .'

I had it on the tip of my tongue, but couldn't get it out.

'What was your father's name?'

'Brynolf.'

He shook his head.

'I've tried researching a little into the records, but there's no one by the name Brynolf there. There's one thing that's certain though . . .'

'My grandfather says . . .'

'What does your grandfather say?'

'. . . that his father was awarded a title and was called Karl-Johan von Bladh.'

He laughed, stiffly, wearily dismissive, and then said very coldy:

'I don't understand. My grandfather was called Karl-Johan and he was awarded a title, but I've heard that . . .'

'He was an illegitimate son . . . or whatever it's called . . .'

'That's the most insolent thing I've ever heard.'

'Anyhow, that's how it is.'

'How the hell can he prove it? Is it in the parish register? No, it isn't. What's this really all about . . . a conspiracy to get at the von Bladh money, or what?'

'You were the one who started talking about it, Skarpskytte Street and the Lehtisuon-Lehtinens, weren't you? You suspected it yourself, though perhaps it wasn't your own grandfather who . . .'

'I don't believe it. Grandfather was a man of honour, not an old goat.'

I burst out laughing, suddenly feeling certain. At last he was the one sitting there stammering.

'This is no laughing matter. Anyhow, it's impossible when you think of the spirit of the time. One just didn't do that sort of thing in the 1860s. One was . . . honourable . . . loyal . . .'

I just went on laughing.

'No von Bladh has ever had illegitimate brats, I'm convinced of that. We're not the type in our family. We've never been loose-living, that's one thing you can be sure of. We're serious, ambitious, successful, often true believers, and we've always had damned high morals. You're an impostor, I sensed that from the start. Let's not talk about it any longer.'

I just laughed and laughed.

I told him all about Kreetta and Kalle Hämäläinen and randy Karl-Johan and how Kalle Hämäläinen became Kalle Blad, and about New Farm and the deed of gift which still existed for viewing by anyone interested, and so on. I told him everything, the whole story.

Jacob von Bladh sighed. He sat leaning on the table with his arms folded, staring at the oil-cloth. A broken man. All illusions shattered. I felt wonderful. Serve you right, you bloody upper-class twit, you bloody conceited upper-class twit, I thought. He gulped down his brandy. 'All right,' he said and got up, slapping his hands together with a bang and rubbing them in a military kind of way. Finally he made a smacking movement at the corner of his mouth, which meant approximately I give up, but don't you go thinking it's amusing.

'If it hadn't been for that bloody nose of yours, I'd have thrown you out,' he mumbled angrily.

'What nose?'

'Your nose, your nose,' he shouted, suddenly furious. 'You've got a typical Bladh nose, a wide strong bridge, a strongly marked tip and quite large triangular nostrils. Look, now, look! I saw it the moment you came through the door for the first time. Where the hell did he get the family nose from, I thought . . .'

As he was speaking, he came over and started eagerly poking at my face with his dirty fingers, and I jerked by head away and lightly slapped his hand. He immediately turned his back on me and walked away across the floor.

'He's got the Bladh nose and he bears the Bladh name, and in addition to that he maintains he has Bladh blood in his veins, to hell . . .'

Then he swung round violently and stared at me, saying tight-lipped:

'But you'll see. Do you want to see, yes, damn me, you *shall* see your ancestors, by Christ, your ancestors . . .'

Out of a pile of all manner of rubbish, old magazines, art books,

41

illustrations, loose sheets of paper and newspaper cuttings, he extracted a photograph album of a very old-fashioned kind, with hard, brown, finely-worked leather covers and an intricately engraved metal clasp.

He brought the album over to the table, slapping it a few times to rid it of the worst of the dust. Then he opened it and carefully began to turn the stiff, almost half-inch-thick pages, into which there were inserted, four to each page, photographs of old men in an endless sequence, clean-shaven or with large moustaches and sidewhiskers, old men in uniform and frock-coats and jackets and greatcoats, with epaulettes and high collars and starched shirt-fronts, old men in black and old men with colourful braids and stripes and queues and shining buttons and gleaming watch-chains and sparkling rings and monocles and ruffles and medals and charms, old men with long hair and short hair and with no hair and black hair and grey hair and white hair, with sharp eyes and kind eyes and large eyes and small peering eyes, with thick lips and thin lips and loose lips and tight lips, with smooth foreheads and frowning foreheads, fat and thin, harsh and amiable, stern and good-natured, pompous and modest. And old women in bonnets and hoods and large hats and wasp-waists and laces and simple costumes and linen cloth and buns and corkscrew curls and pearls and brooches and plaits and parasols, fat old women and thin old women, with kind eyes and sharp eyes, with smooth rosy cheeks and flabby wrinkled cheeks, with cherry mouths, sorrowful and smiling, stern and languishing, ugly and beautiful, with clever faces and foolish faces and intolerant faces and motherly faces . . . page after page, an endless overwhelming succession of faces.

Jacob became more and more excited, pointing and exulting as he went on:

'Look at that, you see, look there, absolutely clear, there and there and there, the Bladh nose, right the way through, the Bladh nose, strong bridge with a marked tip, triangular nostrils, the same thing everywhere, look, isn't it amazing, except the ones who married into the family, of course . . .'

I could see nothing. I saw no likeness. Naturally they were noses, but different noses, each and every one his own nose, as it is in human beings. However much I looked, it was impossible to see the nose as something in common, a distinguishing mark, a characteristic feature. It was a family myth, quite simply; later on I found out that this was only one of many. They cultivated them all, but Jacob was especially energetic . . . the Bladh nose, like the Habsburg chin, the labyrinth of family vanity, the dreamed-of emblem of bourgeois family consciousness.

Jacob just went on and on.

'You see, the Bladh nose, right through, the Bladh nose. Here, for instance, Johan Emmanuel, Director of the Mint and founder of Finnish railways, he wrote a book on the presence of God in the flow of capital, and another about the institution of money and the universe. He lived for ten years in the USA and was a very devout man with pure, high ideals. Note his eyes. I've rarely seen eyes that so clearly radiate goodness. That's Jacob Ossian Walter, the nose again, a financial genius, one of the many universal geniuses of his century, began as a priest, very strict and incorruptibly pious. Slightly later we find him as a teacher and reformer of the entire Finnish education system and founder of the Finnish Clothing Factory. He discovered a method of improving the durability of wool and homespun cloth, then later discovered a method of counteracting that same durability . . . a remarkable man, he founded several sawmills in eastern and central Finland and died at ninety-four the richest man in Finland. That's Karl-Johan, my grandfather, who carried on the work and was awarded a title, note the likeness, the nose. This one's Johan Gustaf, legal prodigy, wrote books, *On the Right to Castigate* and *On the Right to Defiance*. He pacified the wild tribes of East Karelia, a kind of Finnish Livingstone, and brought a little western culture to the primitive backwoods peasants and was killed in thanks, lynched by peasant scum when he tried to introduce compulsory vaccination against smallpox, a *cause célèbre* of the time. That one's the founder of the bourgeois branch, Peter Johan, official of the East India Company, later independent shipowner, landowner, farmer, introduced cattle breeding into the country, refused honours, founded towns and owned fifty ships and was immensely rich, wrote about freedom and equality, was taken prisoner by the Cossacks in the 1808-1809 war and made to run behind the horses with a rope round his neck, fifty miles from Kaskö to Vasa. He survived, a genuine son of the eventful days of the Age of Enlightenment, a true Gustavian. This one is his son, Karl Edward, who went into exile when Finland became Russian, travelled all round the world, wrote books on wonderfully strange places, almost became king of San Salvador and was chosen to make a Swedish colony out of Uruguay at King Karl XIV's request but did not succeed . . . as you know, later on he introduced the use of coffee into our country just as his father had introduced the use of tea. These are four Bladh brothers who all went their own ways, upright men, convinced of the existence and victory of the only rightness; pity the only rightness was so different for them. They couldn't pull together, or to put it briefly, they hated each other profoundly for most of their lives. That's the eldest there, you see, see the nose? Jacob Bladh, went Snellman's way and became Jaako Lehtinen, later ennobled to Lehtisuon-Lehtinen, thus Russian nobility, founded a dynasty, professor of history, politician, senator, financier, founder of the National Bank, farmer, Finnophile, hot-tempered and terrible, was shot in the shoulder by an activist and lost his left arm, hence the nickname "one-armed devil", opposed to Jews and persecuted gypsies, was high church. Here's the second. Johan Sigvard, quite bald, lost his hair during a sleigh trip from Åbo to Brahested in forty degrees below zero, fought off hungry wolves with a burning torch and a sheath-knife, killed twelve in one single night but lost his raccoon-skin cap, a legality man, constitutionalist, long-standing chairman of the bourgeoisie, senator, Swedish, professor of civil law, zealous supporter of legal and social protection of ethnic and linguistic minorities, reformed our penal code, died rich, owned half of Nyland archipelago, low church. The third one looked like this, Oscar Johan Emmanuel, note his long beautiful hair, even more beautiful than Topelius' hair, officer in the Imperial Life Guards, general, university chancellor, director of Rautakoski copper mine, founder of Atlas tobacco factory and father of Finnish gymnastics, wrote the epic *Hercules Conquers or the Secret of Male Strength*, an academic document *On God's Purpose with Man*, and *On God's Purpose with Woman*, built and managed four apartment houses in Helsinki, died rich. The fourth brother looked like this, his nose unusually atypical . . .'

'What was remarkable about him?'

'Nothing.'

'That's strange, isn't it?'

'Well . . . no . . . no one knows for certain . . . he was different even when young . . . rather individual . . . one suspects . . . that is, he . . . to put it briefly, he was probably a socialist. He died relatively young, presumably of syphilis, we know very little about him. He . . . he . . . but look, here's Emelie Thérése, Ossian's first wife, who died in childbirth when she was only twenty-two, buried in

44

Kexholm. Fifty years later, Ossian wanted the coffin transferred to the family tomb. The grave in Kexholm was opened up and the coffin looked as new. Ossian felt called upon by some inner voice to have the lid opened, and there she was in her beautiful silk shroud, perfectly preserved, as if alive, the dark curls round the fine oval cheeks of her face. Already an old man and a widower for the second time, Ossian gave a sob of surprise and emotion, and she opened her eyes, smiled and also tried to rise. "My darling" she whispers, then sinks back and decomposes before his very eyes. Ossian was as if transformed from that day on, having apparently received a sign from another world and evidence of the indestructibility of pure unselfish love. This is Aunt Cathrine . . .'

'Whose aunt?'

'What? Aunt Cathrine? Aunt, aunt, aunt only in general, everyone's aunt. Don't you know anything about these things, genealogy and history? There were paternal aunts and maternal aunts. They populated the world in their way, had special tasks. Do you understand . . .'

'No, not at all.'

'Oh, well, you come from such a different background, don't you? Aunt Cathrine, now, you can see the nose again, a genuine von Bladh, she was very artistic, painted, drew, played the piano, used to have the piano taken down to the rowing-boat. Some labourer or crofter took the oars and rowed slowly out on Björknäs Bay and on early July mornings she played beautifully on the still, sun-drenched water, Liszt, Chopin, Scarlatti, yes, my goodness, things were different in those days . . .'

'Who is your father?'

'My father? Have you never heard of Johan Konstantin von Bladh?'

'No, never.'

'He was my father. General in the Imperial Army, served with success in the Russo-Japanese war, was Mannerheim's right-hand man in the War of Liberation, crushed the rebellion in Poland and was called the Napoleon of Lapland, because he had the courage of a lion but was rather short of stature . . .'

Thus Jacob von Bladh continued his story and I listened, believing every word, my heart filling with envy and loathing and pride and triumph and a sense of conquest, and I made an irrevocable

45

resolution that one day I would outshine them all, my right-wing relations and ancestors, all those fantastic, glorious, invincible von Bladh ladies and gentlemen.

CHAPTER THREE *(Donald Blad's childhood)*

My first memory is of silence. The alarm-clock ticking on the chest-of-drawers. Green colour, a green bedspread, a green knitted jersey, always green, on the peg on the door, green twilight through the window from the trees out in the yard. Loneliness. Being alone at home and in some way out because all the others were out. Doing nothing and having nothing to do. Not receiving an answer to a single question and feeling the questions slowly disappearing like the dust of indifference in the silence. Having my head full of admonitions and not remembering a single one, the spirit of the admonitions present but their content absent. Perhaps that's why they are so clear in my memory. The incomprehensible trickle of prohibitions through the uneventfulness of life and the irrestistible desire to defeat it. Striking a match, then another and another. Pushing a chair up against the chest-of-drawers in a way so that the top drawer could be opened and Father's pistol taken out from underneath the towels, shirts and underclothes. Playing with it, examining it. (How did Father come to own a pistol? Since when? For what purpose? The matter was never mentioned. He did not know that I knew.) Burning my fingers by touching the stove, the heat, knowing you'd burn yourself and doing it again. Crawling underneath the sewing-machine, kneeling on the treadle and transforming it into an aeroplane in flight. Taking the scissors from the kitchen table and cutting fringes in the green bedspread. Eating sugar. Eating soap. Eating oats. Eating grease. Eating ski-wax. Strewing salt on the floor and going skiing. Strewing flour on the floor and going skiing. Being beaten.

I learnt early on that the world I had been born into was evil; a world of prohibitions. A world of injustices. A world without joy. If you wanted some fun in life, you had to ensure it yourself, for you could expect nothing much from others. Lying was a sin, but a necessity. Telling the truth was pointless, simply because no one ever believed you anyhow. You had to keep out of the way of adults, for

46

few of them could be trusted. Adults were not kind and it was wise to be afraid of them. There was wealth and poverty. Wealth was good, but for other people. Poverty was for us, dully grey, eventless, fenced round with hostility and scarcity.

How many times did I see my mother smile? How many times for my sake, at me? I have no memory of her face smiling. It was expressionless, bitter or submissive, sorrowful or threatening. But Father smiled when we were together. With his eyes. I knew he liked me. He did not smile at home. Silence reigned there. Except when Emil cursed and swore and slammed the outer door. The sounds of silence. Father's newspaper rustling as he sits reading in the rocking-chair. The fire in the stove as it blazes. Bark being ripped off a birch-log. Water boiling. The lid of the potato pan rattling as it is lifted off and put back. Oskar's heavy wheezing breathing as he sits with his elbows on the table, doing nothing. Mother's sewing-machine humming and clicking and stopping and humming again. The chink of china, coffee cups, soup plates. Steps, Father's heavy, Emil's impatient, Oskar's shuffling. Water splashing, into the washing-up bowl, into saucepans, into the bucket. That's what silence sounded like. My first and most vivid childhood memories.

Mother was small and slender, but sinewy. Her hands were hard and rough, seldom touching me. Her eyes were blue and her gaze always elsewhere. Her nose small and pointed, mouth pursed, a cranberry mouth. She scolded. You could never do what you wanted. Never take anything and look at it and examine it, not the framed photographs from the chest-of-drawers, nor the box of strange metal parts from the drawer in the sewing-machine, not the ladles and whisks from the kitchen table, nor the logs from the wood-box. Everything was prohibited, because everything made a mess and you were in the way everywhere. She pulled your hair. She boxed your ears. I had no toys, except the boat and car Father carved out of wood. And the sled standing in the porch. And my skis. She made all my clothes, shapeless clothes; no one at school had clothes like them.

We're walking across the yard, she and I. It's a dark evening. A little snow has fallen, making the contours of the trees stand out in the dim light. I am holding her hand. Am I holding her hand? It's not cold; December, wet snow. We go through the back entrance and up the murky kitchen stairs, a steep spiral staircase with high stone steps. We knock on a door, a yellow door. Someone opens it, they talk, we go into a gigantic kitchen bathed in light. The smells! Ginger-biscuit

47

smell, cake-mixture smell, sugar smell, syrup smell, marzipan smell! Heavy, hot, almost suffocating. The stove in the middle of the floor, work-tables in all directions, huge ladles, white china vessels, copper kettles, ceramic jars, pans, stone jars. We walk through long bright corridors and room after room. At last we are standing in front of her, an ordinary mistress of the house with her brown hair in curling-tonged ringlets. The room is dark and she is sitting at a table, a red lamp lighting up her face and hands. Her eyes are brown. She smiles. She says something and Mother curtseys. Her hands are white and beautiful, the table covered with bright shiny paper, a deep shimmering green, red, blue-gold and silver, which she is cutting into figures with a large pair of scissors, Christmas Santas, decorations, and there is a strong smell of Christmas, lacquer, glue, fruit, chocolate, I cannot distinguish between them. She explains something, requesting. She looks appealing, mild, very kind. The light from the red lamp falls softly on her face and hands, the rest of the room in darkness. I don't know where I am. Like in fairyland. Mother nods and says yes, yes. Far away to the right, a door opens into another room, which is brightly lit. Two children stand there in the doorway, dark silhouettes. I feel them looking at me. I look back. 'Mummy,' they say. 'Mummy!' As if in a dream. I'm given a banana sweet wrapped in red cellophane. The smell! Oh, how good it smelt. She was dressed in a black woollen dress, her throat smooth and white. 'Wait a moment. I'm just coming,' she said. Her voice so gentle. Mother curtseyed again. She curtseyed and curtseyed. And I bowed. My only childhood memory. Where had we been? In heaven? At the house of Mrs Lehtisuon-Lehtinen, wife of the manager, who had asked Mother to do the Christmas washing-up, or see to the Christmas cleaning?

Mother was small, but Father was large. His hands were big and fleshy and rough and quite dry on the inside. When you held his hand, it was as if your own hand had crawled into something large and warm, like a bird's nest. His stomach was like a large quilt which you could lean against when you sat in his arms. It felt safe; a safe place. When he sat in the rocking-chair reading the paper and you half-lay there rocking against his stomach, you sometimes fell asleep. Father's face was large and heavy. He had big cheeks, his nose large and curved, narrowing down towards the tip and big nostrils, like a triangle. His lips were full and rather loose, his chin small, his eyes dark and sorrowful, except when they were looking at me. Then they glinted in the corners. Sometimes. Mostly.

In the evenings, he took me with him to the theatre while Mother went for a fitting with one of the ladies for whom she sewed. I sat on a chair right at the back of the coat-racks in the cloakroom, watching as the women rushed back and forth between the counter and the pegs, laden with fur coats and black overcoats with fur collars and hoods and hats and bowlers and fur caps and white scarves and galoshes and overshoes, then hastily back again, holding out small worn number-plates. People crowded at the counter, waving their hands, waiting impatiently for their turn. One of the women called Kirsti soon became out of breath, red patches appearing on her cheeks and beads of sweat on her temples and round her nose. She often snapped at the most impatient people on the other side of the counter. If they snapped back, she became angry and they stood there squabbling for a while. She was always kind to me. One evening she wasn't there any longer, and Father told me she was dead. When I was older and more familiar with the theatre people, I was allowed backstage to watch all the busy preparations before a performance. Some actors were conceited and irritable, finding me in their way, and I did not become friends with them, but most of the scene-shifters were friendly and joked with me, sometimes offering me toffees or calling me nicknames I don't remember any longer. That was the way I got to know Helga, but many years later, after I had already taken part in many plays as a supernumerary, among others in *Regina Emmeritz* by Topelius. Father stood tearing tickets at the entrance into the auditorium, wearing his black uniform coat with gold braid on the collar.

Father got up at six o'clock every morning to unlock the outer door. When it snowed in winter, the alarm-clock sometimes went off before four, so that he would have time to clear the pavement and the yard of snow before the traffic started and the gentlemen in the block went to work. If it was a very bad snowstorm, Mother used to help shovel away the snow. Sometimes when Father had finished shovelling and come in between nine and ten, he was so exhausted he could only lie gasping on the bed, on top of the green bedspread, his arm across his eyes. Mother was angry with the manager then. She was afraid Father's back and lungs would give out. But when it came to me, she usually took the side of the gentlemen. And of their wives. The older I grew, the more often that happened.

Tapio was my best friend, or rather my only friend during the years before we started school. We were neighbours in that ramshackle wooden building, his father a metal-worker who rented a room and kitchen, as we did. In the spring, we made catapults out of forked twigs from the elm growing in the garden. Naturally, this was strictly forbidden. But we soon learnt not to give a damn about that. Everything was forbidden. Transgressing against prohibitions, ignoring rules and decrees, challenging the guardians of the law and defying the upholders of power were a vital necessity, a condition of life.

With our catapults, we hunted rats, the gentry's children and the odd cat. And crows and small birds. Even before we reached school-age, we had acquired considerable accuracy.

There was another place in another world, a brighter place in a better world, a borderline in time and space at which prohibitions and admonitions ceased and joy and freedom took over. With Grandfather at New Farm in the summers! All childhood summers? Some of my childhood summers? One happy summer, one single one? I don't remember. But I remember the sun, the flies, the smell of hay. The quiet, warm, sun-drenched mornings with long shadows and dew on the grass, all the animals already awake and talking as they thought of food, cows lowing, sheep bleating, hens cackling, the pig grunting and the cuckoo in the woods and all the birds of forest and garden and the swallows under the eaves and the butterflies, and the flies, the flies. Grandfather kept rabbits, and he had a dog and a cat. The dog was a black pomeranian called – well, what else could it be called but Musti, and the cat was old and called Mama, because it had always been good at bringing kittens into the world.

When I think about it, I wonder why so many obstacles were put in the way each time I was to go to New Farm. Could it have had anything to do with Grandfather's free-thinking and Mother's religiousness? Was Grandfather's home in some way an unsuitable place for the son of a true believer? Grandfather had been a widower for a decade, but he did not live alone; he had Svea, and Svea and he were not married. Grandfather was of a happy disposition, and so was Svea. He was certainly no churchgoer. As Mother was. Could that have been why? For I was always made welcome at New Farm, wasn't I? Svea was my friend, wasn't she? As Grandfather and the pig and Musti and Mama and the flies were my friends? And all the things Grandfather had been involved in, born in 1864 as he was! The inception and birth-pangs of a whole nation! How little one

50

knows about the circumstances of one's childhood, about what happens or doesn't happen, and just why what happens happens or what doesn't happen doesn't happen. A child is an oddment, shifted hither and thither to make room for what is more useful, more comfortable, more purposeful, more profitable. That's what it was like, and still is. If only I'd realized that before. Grandfather's New Farm was the animals' New Farm; meant living among animals, feeling oneself an animal among animals, with no ulterior motives, no desire to take advantage at the expense of others, or do any harm to each other. The pig and me, the sheep and their baa-baa and me, Mama and me, and the flies and me. To have been part of that once, too.

At home in town, the dirty window and the shadow from the wall, me by the window, unoccupied, wearing a knitted grey jersey, flannel shorts and long brown knitted stockings. And the cat, Mirre, grey. On the right, the grey windowless wall of number seventy-four and on the left, the narrow gravelled space between our house and the shed or store, where nettles grew. Straight ahead and up towards the clouds or the clear blue sky, the green foliage or the pattern of branches, according to the season. Then the garden, the yard and, on the other side of the yard, the high yellow wall of stone with its rows and rows of windows. Five rows of windows, with white linen curtains and blue check kitchen curtains, or blank green roller-blinds in the bedrooms. Green everywhere. And beneath the green of the trees, a few garden chairs and a table, a swing for the children and a large sand-pit. Mirre's privy, forbidden by humans to be used as such, but, according to natural rights, irrefutably designated as such by herself. For me, on the other hand, an alien world which for unfathomable reasons I was prohibited to enter, the black shadow of the worn wooden wall beneath our dirty window a mercilessly sharp boundary between two worlds, the great, bright, well-filled world of the bourgeoisie and the workers' dreary, silent little nook in creation.

But I did not think like that then. Saimi and Brynolf never complained in that way. We were poor, but our poverty was not related to anyone else's wealth; non-political poverty, so to speak. Or was it? What parents talk politics to their children? It was almost like death and sexuality: not in front of the children. If Brynolf was a socialist in secret, then Saimi certainly was not. The reason for the silence between them? And what did Brynolf's pistol mean, so well hidden beneath the shirts and underpants? Simply a legal weapon of defence in disturbed times, officially allotted by Mr Lehtisuon-

Lehtinen and approved by the authorities? Or dangerous contra-
band, a concealed token of unswerving faith in a movement and a
conviction never to be betrayed and never forgotten? What had
Brynolf done in the civil war, those blood-stained weeks of successful
counter-revolution? Even that I didn't know. Was Brynolf White or
Red? Or neither, passive in a petit bourgeois way, with wife and
children to support, frightened of losing his meagre livelihood
through political ventures, content to be allowed to keep to himself,
to be left in peace, leaving others to improve the world as best they
could and as they wished? Was that the truth about Brynolf? Was
that my father?

Mother had her Christian faith and her Bible, and there was
nothing in the Bible about socialism, rebellion and equality. Her
morality was the morality of obedience, her social concept of the
world imprinted through and through by the frequent visits she paid
to the grand ladies for whom she sewed and made clothes.
Consistently disloyal, in all conflicts she was on the side of the gentry,
and in their well-mannered gentry style she saw an ideal of
inestimable value. She worshipped Svinhufvud and admired von
Born, despite her Finnish origins; in a word, she was foolish, and we
all suffered for it. . . .

But it couldn't have been like that, and now I cannot begin to fathom
what it *was* like. Quite different. In another way. I don't know. I
don't know how to go on, or whether I shall go on at all. On the table
I find a note among the papers I'd jotted down at a time when I
hadn't really seriously been trying, but considered memories
unambiguous and reality describable and therefore possible to
organize according to a pattern which when completed could be
called an autobiography. I had written: 'Each stage of life demands
its special woman.'

By implication, of a man's life, of course. What self-absorption! For
the content is perfectly clear: woman is there for man. To satisfy
man's need for woman is the woman's task in life. What an amazing
thought! For I no longer have such simple and conventional notions.
I have had in the past, perhaps, but no longer consciously after the
severe but edifying lessons of the many long years of five marriages.
Several years ago, I once read an essay called 'On Women as Human

Beings', written in the Victorian days of the turn of the century. I don't remember the essence or content of it; presumably hatred of women. But the title! Just the very idea. On Women as Human Beings! But as far as my jotted note is concerned, the whole thing could be reversed and it could equally well be asserted that every new woman demands or presupposes a new stage in life. The question is just which comes first, love or the will to act, sexuality or social vanity, the family or society, comfort or ambitions, the need for pleasures or the sense of duty.

There is something childish about the whole argument, this division into two, this drawing-up of boundaries, this categorizing. As if the one could demonstrably be separated from the other, woman on the one side and a stage in life on the other. As if the woman or wife fundamentally had no definite part in stages of life. Foolish speculations. Women naturally belong, decide, assume stages of life and vice versa. And what do 'stages of life' stand for? Don't women have 'stages of life'? Isn't it enough that a man and a woman meet, like each other and start living together? A stage of life here seems to mean only what a man experiences alongside his erotic life, as a member of society, in the business world, 'in public service'. What a dull, superficial, truncated idea! Must have been hatched by an incurable romantic with a pressing need to mystify women and conjure with the motive of love. Am I such a person? It almost seems so. Fantastic! Because I certainly don't feel that I fit the part. It seems too trivial and arbitrary and pointless to attempt to classify and examine it all. Human beings are different. Why did I launch into this unfruitful theme?

Women are an integral part of my biography. Isn't that sufficient reason? On the other hand, I have just explained there is to be no biography. Why do I go on with it all then? Well . . . in self-defence. That's something I've spent quite a number of pages trying to explain away. But it is useless. I am writing in self-defence. People have tried accusing me of a crime. His Grace, the Master Painter von Bladh, who persecuted and harassed me for so many years, has actually gone to the trouble of composing a writ to the Attorney-General. In it I am accused of theft, gross theft. It is a lie, of course. But that is not all. Indirectly and in devious ways, I have been accused of an even worse crime. My God, it is no more than just that I should have a chance of clearing myself once and for all.

I have a copy of Jacob's idiotic writ here on my desk. Such are my connections. No measures will be taken, of course, as Jacob is insane. But it is painful enough, all the same. If Jacob thinks he is justified in writing to the highest guardians of the law in the country, then for Christ's sake I'll show him I can reply tenfold. But I'm not base, as he is. His capacity is limited to defamatory statements and other foolish rubbish. I myself am quite incapable of writing sheer libel.

I have done much wrong in my life, I must admit. At least, much that has been ill-considered. But there has always been something grandiose and supreme about it all; no one can deny that. So now that I am clearing myself, I shall illuminate the circumstances. I shall establish the merciless inner logic which decides all human actions. And it will not be a case of meaningless argument proving, for instance, that A is A and not B. But of things concerning the emotions and life and the pathos of life. The incongruous. So I must tell of the women in my life. All those women. (No, not all of them.) For without them, my self-defence would be sadly incomplete. They are the stages in life, damn it. I have acted most often for their sake. The gilt-edge in my life? No, the blood and veins of my life. So at last that has also been said.

I have been living with Vanessa R. for two years now. A mature, clarified and absorbing relationship. She is undoubtedly the first woman who has managed to bring a little order into my emotional and erotic life. I have never been able to keep myself in check before. I've been incapable of preventing myself from kicking over the traces. Woman have been my overriding interest, my passion and my hobby. I have had a fixation on women, and to be without a woman, to be celibate when circumstances have forced it upon me, has been a terrible torment. A day without sex has been a wasted day, filling me with anguish, making me lose the will to work and the ability to concentrate, painfully filling my mind with monomanic thoughts of women, naked women, women's posteriors, breasts, swelling hips, and that soft, warm, marvellously modelled miracle of skin and flesh and mucous membranes called the vagina, the female sexual organ; the cunt, in other words. Eroto-man? With such an insatiable sexual appetite?

I have been notoriously unfaithful in four marriages, without the slightest inhibitions or moral misgivings. And just as notoriously prepared and happy to be able to satisfy all the possible sexual desires of my respective wives. I have been a connoisseur of cunts. There are no two identical cunts. No cunt is quite like another, just as no human face is quite like another. But these are banal facts well known to most men. I become aroused writing about it and shall not continue.

Vanessa has such a tremendously strong personality, such tremendously powerful personal radiance. She has authority in her way of existing that demands a kind of . . . well, a kind of response I have never experienced with any other woman before. Her performance, her way of presenting herself, briefly her aura (is that what it's called?), includes a manner that is as inexpressible as it is obvious and demanding, claiming equality and personal respect as a quality and as a fundamental prerequisite for living together. It is her nature, absolutely and indisputable and impossible to reason away or evade. Least of all is it anything to joke about. Or joke away. She loves with a thoroughness that excludes every kind of surplus desire in any other direction. I have been very faithful to her over these years (almost). Quite voluntarily and with no temptations, as well. Her dominance and strength? In that case, all right with me. Or growing weakness in myself? That I'm beginning to get old? Receding abilities? No.

She is not here. She went away weeks ago. I am alone, and that doesn't suit me. That's not good for me. It makes me restless, lacking in concentration and depressed, giving me insane, compulsive ideas. She has said nothing about her return and it's a worryingly long time since her last letter. I don't understand. What is it all about? Perhaps she has found a young Greek or Spaniard whom she's making love with in the bushes of city parks? No, of course not. For Christ's sake. I am not jealous.

It must be emphatically stated that her trip has nothing whatsoever to do with our relationship or possible future conflicts between us. We love each other. Everything is stated simply enough in that way. She travels a great deal because of her profession, which I much admire and cannot imagine being jealous of. It would really never occur to me to attempt in any way to prevent her from exercising her profession.

Vanessa is a concert pianist and goes on tour for a few months every year in various parts of the world. When she left me three months ago, she was on her way to Australia in order, as she said, to try to swim through Rachmaninov for the hundred and fiftieth time without getting out of breath. She has indeed been home once or twice since then, but only on lightning visits for a night or so. She should have been in London three weeks ago. She should have been playing Saint-Saëns at Covent Garden, Piano Concerto Number Five in F-major, 'The Egyptian', which I usually call 'My-hat-it-has-three-corners Concerto', after the main theme in the first movement so reminiscent of that popular old song.

I can't really make head or tail of it all. She should have been back during the first few days of December, in good time before the sixth. As it was, I had to go to the President's reception at the palace on my own, which was painful. For a stupid reason, of course. I am proud of her. Childishly proud of Vanessa. My Vanessa. To be honest, in some strange way I find it solemn and significant to appear with her in company. It is empty without her, almost humiliating sometimes, for some silly reason. But certainly not because she is a famous person, because she is not famous here, and I am not vain in that way. She has given no concerts here in our country, as she wants to keep Finland as a kind of place of retreat, her holiday country, her refuge of rest and anonymity. I am proud of her natural authority, her regal radiance, her incredibly stylish appearance (as it says in the women's magazines). Because she's just her.

We first met in London (while I was still living with Elina) during what were for me extremely tragic and disturbing circumstances. I had gone over to find out about my eldest daughter, Rosa, about whom we had received some alarming news. But I arrived too late. She was dead. She practically died in my arms of an overdose of amphetamine. She was an addict, only twenty years old. She didn't recognize me, although I kept calling her name, one of those unhappy victims of . . . I can't talk about it now . . . later, when I tell about Miles, naturally I'll have to . . . I'm writing in self-defence, am I not . . .

Vanessa and I did not meet by chance.

During the days when the police investigation was being carried out and other bureaucratic formalities were being tidied up, I was waiting for the cremation of poor Rosa's remains and had time to roam round my beloved London and in my despair consider how pointlessly and brutally destiny sometimes strikes. One day I saw an advertisment in *The Times* which said that a pianist unknown to me by the name of Vanessa R. was performing in two consecutive concerts, playing through all of Bach's *Das wohltemperierte Klavier* in the Queen Elizabeth Hall.

For special reasons (Jacob's foolish fixation on Bach), I had always been ambivalent towards this master in the world of music, and not least towards his great piano sequence. But I had nothing else to do except wait, and other horrors, so bought a ticket for the first concert. Later, I sat there listening and I don't mind admitting my tears began as early as the first beautiful prelude, so sensitive am I at times. This wasn't because of the music, of course, but mostly because of Rosa, the memory of Rosa, my thoughts circling round her dreadful death and short sorrowful life. But I would be dishonest if I refused to admit that my emotions and sensitivity were not more involved in something as yet quite indefinite – but none the less powerfully effective. The sight of the pianist herself, Vanessa R.

There are pianists who by their actions at the piano can easily make a comical impression. All too emphatic involvement is often taken by the spectator as comical. I have seen female pianists carrying out impressive labours with their backsides, and if the backside happens to be unusually large, the comical effect is very apparent. Or male pianists who close their eyes and with a soulful expression turn their faces to the ceiling and the next moment hunch over the keys in a sophisticated *ritardando* as if looking for a needle in a haystack. Vanessa played with enormous dignity, her back straight, without any mannerisms, radiating concentration and self-discipline and a controlled intensity that had an overwhelming effect on me. Perhaps because I was so completely unprepared. Her beautiful face glowed, her glossy black hair, gathered in a knot at the nape of her neck, enhancing the pallor of her skin, the high forehead, the slightly curved nose, the narrow line of her lips – I perceived that even then – expressing intelligence, strength of will and self-confidence. I sat there paralysed, staring.

I desired her after the second prelude in C-minor, and was sure of my case after the fifth fugue in D-major, with its explanatory, almost childishly informative and safe, light, relaxed tone. As if with that she wished to send a secret message to me in particular, saying that everything was already arranged and clear between us. At the end of the concert, I knew that for the umpteenth time in my life I was in love, helplessly and definitively out for the count, or 'powerfully emotionally involved', as Torbjörn would put it.

That feeling of happy expectation fought in the most strident manner with my grief over Rosa. But as usual, it was a passing conflict. Nothing could stop me, not now, as little as ever before. And when a few days later I happened to be invited to a cocktail party at our Embassy, I persuaded the Ambassador, whom I knew from many earlier visits, to send an invitation with some suitable excuse to Vanessa R. She came. Which, to be honest, I hadn't really expected.

Later on she told me that at first she had had no intention of going. She loathed Embassy receptions, just as I had presumed. And the Finnish Embassy of all embassies! What did she know about Finland? What did Finland mean to her? Nothing. Perhaps that was why, she said. Out of pure curiosity. To have a taste of the unusual and unknown for a change. Then she added with her short ironic laugh that it had really been a kind of telepathy. A strong inner voice had urged her to go to the Finnish Embassy, for something new and exciting and pleasant was awaiting her. I don't know if she meant it seriously. Perhaps she did. In that case, she saw it as a personal weakness she was unwilling to admit to. Superstition could not possibly find a place within the framework of her rational view of life.

The cocktail party was as all similar affairs usually are: fifty or so people gathered together with no other natural connection with each other except a certain social status, a strong social vanity. Their underlying duty is to be as spiritual as hell, but most of them lack personal resources for that purpose, and the result is painful, hysterical conversation so crude or unspiritual one could burst into tears (if one had not already long become immune to all kinds of human stupidity and social hypocrisy). Vanessa R. was standing alone in a corner, refusing food and drink and all the other sophisticated and unhealthy culinary inventions that are part of those pretentious affairs.

I went across and introduced myself, telling her I had been at her concert. She showed no pleasure in my attentions, simply noting them as self-evident. One might have considered her extremely haughty, but I took it as the naturally dismissive attitude through which a simultaneously shy and self-confident person demonstrates that she is on her guard, watchful. I tried flattery. I piled it on by saying I had heard both Richter and Wanda Landowska play 'The Well-Tempered Clavier' (which was not true), but that neither interpretation had gripped me as much as hers had (which, on the other hand, was to some extent true).

'I don't believe you,' she said in icy tones.

I refused to be brushed off, indeed felt egged on to renewed efforts; the question was only whether I should make a frontal attack or encircling movements.

There are thoughts or phrases in the mind rather like sayings,

which in certain situations recur with such regularity and infallibility
that they seem to be some kind of primitive intellectual equivalent of
the physiological responses to given stimuli in Pavlov's experiments
on dogs. I myself have some recurring thoughts like that, as inevitable
as they are annoying and stupid. I think they occur in most people,
only without being especially awkward or compromising; they seem
to be so private or unnecessary and meaningless that they are never
spoken aloud. A foolish thought of this kind suddenly came to my
mind with all the supreme certainty of a computer response evoked
by Vanessa R.'s cool look and ostentatiously dismissive attitude.

'If I haven't gone to bed with you within twenty-four hours, I'll go
mad,' I thought, just as I have hundreds of times before in my life. I
think she could read in my eyes what I was thinking.

We did not sleep with each other that day. But we had dinner
together at the Villa Bianca in Hampstead after the reception. She
took me there. Naturally I didn't know the place from before, a
modest little Italian trattoria. I usually ate at the Hilton, or the
Sheraton, or the Lancaster, or wherever I happened to be staying.
Eating was part of business, and business affairs were not carried out
at the Villa Bianca. Not mine, anyhow. Apart from love affairs, of
course. One could settle those better at the Villa Bianca.

What was it that made her change her mind about me? What
made her change her attitude, exchange her earlier contempt and
spontaneous revulsion of first impressions for an incipient warmth
and sympathy and personal interest? Nothing special. She had taken
me for an ordinary conceited and successful ass, from her point of
view one of the unbearable kind of which there are thirteen to the
dozen at all embassy receptions all over what is known as the
capitalist world. She presumed I was a business man of some
heavyweight class, or a diplomat, or something else important in the
hierarchy of our country's bureaucracy. But she was utterly
indifferent to all that. She knew the type and they did not captivate
her.

What was it that despite everything persuaded her to take me in
her lovely little outmoded twenty-year-old almost antique Mayflower
and drive off to Hampstead? She had not been mistaken about me at
all. In her view I was a boor. But I had changed tactics. I had
changed my tone of voice as soon as I realized what the situation was.
I had abandoned Bach and the concert and all things well-tempered.
Changed the subject. I had started talking about Rosa, the reason for

my being in London, about my little daughter who was dead. That got her.

Her eyes, previously full of indifference, now filled with compassion. Half a victory already. I exploited not only my own grief, but also my eldest daughter's unlovely death and her previous wretchedness, in order to bed as soon as possible an almost completely unknown woman over whom I had become randy at first glance a few days before. I didn't even reflect on what I'd done. I did it because I knew it was as good a method as any. I am like that. Was that reprehensible? I shouldn't bother to argue about it, as moral niceties have never been my field. But now, unfortunately, it happens to be part of the subject of this opus, this writ of defence. So I must return to it, but later. When it comes to Miles . . .

Anyway, Vanessa came with me when I returned to Helsinki with Rosa's urn.

I can't help going on considering this business of women and stages of life. My marriages or relationships with women in fact follow such a clear geometrical or elliptical, in other words such a definitely consistent and inevitably logical, graph, that I am almost convinced it is possible to de-materialize it or transform it into an abstraction and express it in purely mathematical terms. Whatever purpose that would serve. But apart from such objections, the manifest and inexorable logic of it never ceases to fascinate me. On the other hand, one might ask oneself what kind of logic is it I think I see here? Is it philosophical logic? Or social? Or psychological? The whim of the dilettante.

I was only twenty when I married Sinikka, young but hardly inexperienced. We had two children together, a son we called Miles after some American trumpeter who wasn't Miles Davis, and a daughter we called Rosa after Rosa Luxemburg. That sounds rather childish, but in age we were more children than adults, although I had been at the front for almost two years and learnt to kill people and spew with disgust over such a foul and shamelessly false activity. I think Sinikka was slightly older than me.

We met through our mutual involvement in the Communist Party of Finland. Sinikka had been in the movement almost since the moment she was born. She had experienced the terror and persecution and underground activies of the 'twenties and 'thirties, as well as during the war. Her father was a veteran. He had been sentenced to death in 1918, but had been pardoned and then had survived starvation in the prison camp at Ekenäs. He had been flogged and tortured by lawless right-wing gangs during the Lappo years and arrested in that connection, and given a prison sentence, but had been released a few years later. Only to be arrested again in 1940 for a period of internment that did not end until peace was declared. There was practically speaking nothing in the way of illegal political activity and political persecution in which he had not been involved. Hence perhaps, paradoxically enough, the happy, secure open-mindedness characteristic of him. He had been through everything. He had faced the firing squad and literally seen the whites of death's eyes, and yet he still existed here among the living. He had nothing more to lose, but nearly everything still to gain. His name was Hannes. Hannes Kaapola, a great man. His courage was legendary, his violently hot temper similarly. But also the unselfish, almost tender care with which, without thought, he treated his fellow human beings in need, and the irrepressible belief in the future which was his driving force and sometimes appeared almost to border on blind faith. When it came to excitement and fantastic adventures, his stories about his own fate surpassed most of those I had read in my youth in comics and cheap adventure stories, or seen in films. I admired him without reservations and was proud of marrying his daughter.

Sinikka was probably the human force that brought a little social sense, a little stability and determination into my life, something that two years at the front and army discipline had far from succeeded in doing. I became a university student in 1944 without taking any special examinations. I had been given a week's leave to be able to receive the white student cap personally at my old school in Helsinki. On the morning of graduation day I got drunk and was far from sober at the actual graduation ceremony. But that was magnanimously overlooked, for in contrast to most of my fellow students, I was a real war hero. In Henriks Street (now Mannerheim Road) I refused to salute a passing colonel and responded to his harsh reprimand with a swift 'stuff it up your arse'. This should have landed me at a court martial, had not that same colonel through a strange whim of chance been a close friend of the headmaster of my school, who in his turn had long held me to be one of his favourite pupils.

61

Mercy prevailed over justice, the procedures were broken off and the matter settled with a thorough and unanimous but still rather more paternal than officer-like scolding from the gentleman's side.

I mention this side-issue as an example both of my violent and insolent temperament that has played many dangerous tricks on me over the years, and also of the fantastic, sometimes inexplicable luck that has followed me in nearly everything I have set about, good and bad, stupid and sensible. Scarcely a year later, I was lucky again in a similar situation, though of a much more serious kind. A bagatelle from the start, an act of thoughtlessness, youthful tempestuousness, after a year of forgetfulness it was suddenly turned into a terrible dark and disastrous memory. That was the lieutenant in the porchway, and the murderer, who was not revealed until he had married . . .

At the end of the Second World War, international Social Democracy was as deeply compromised as after the First. The innermost and central purpose of the workers' movement had been crudely betrayed and cowardly allied to the great capitalist imperialism in its cruel and bloody war games. For a newly awakened socialist consciousness, there was thus no choice. It was self-evident that one chose communism and joined the Communist Party of Finland, which was also enjoying a period of outstanding growth and dynamic expansion.

I was a student, which from the Party's point of view did not lack significance. I was also intelligent, eager to learn, studious, energetic, and keen to fulfil as best I could the tasks set for me by the Party and for the benefit of the common good. At first, that is. I am hardly exaggerating if I maintain that at first they had great plans as far as I was concerned. They clearly saw in me a guarantee of regrowth in the leadership. At the direct instigation of the Party executive, I started studying economics and political science a the University of Helsinki. I went to evening classes to learn the foundations of Marxism and also read Marxist literature in my free time, as the university wisely kept quiet about such dangerous knowledge. I know they were planning to send me to Moscow at a later stage for more thorough grounding. But nothing came of that.

I was received in the Party with a comradely friendliness which made a great impression on me. Never before, neither at home nor in school nor in the army, had I experienced being with people who scarcely without knowing each other could be so cordial, open and full of thoughtfulness and helpfulness. It wasn't I I and mine mine as at home and school and in real life, but we we and our our. We shared things equally and everyone joined in, and that was tremendously safe and liberating. It felt like freedom. The work and new human contacts in the Party gave my life new content and a new and more purposeful will to live, and the post-war desperation and the evil, bloody memories of the front no longer ached so badly. Gradually they dissolved and solidified into distant abstract images which more and more seldom caused me nightmares or appeared in my waking consciousness as panic and anguish.

I had come back from the war a raw, uneducated and in most respects asocial hooligan. I had found nothing edifying or instructive in life at the front. I sought trouble at the slightest provocation. I liked fighting and was bitter, frightened and filled with hatred, uninterested in the future. Generally speaking there were two occupations that took up my time and energy, sex and drinking. That was life enough for me at the time. But marriage with Sinikka not only strengthened my self-assurance, not only gave stability to my life, not only staked out a lucid, tempting and constructive aim and direction for my life, it also awakened my slumbering so-called careerist tendencies to life. I was not going to be just something, but something more. For I realized my marriage to Sinikka was the real reason why my position in the Party had been so swiftly confirmed and had given me such an amazing amount of insight, responsibility and confidence in such an amazingly short time. Hannes Kaapola supported me with a loyalty that knew no reservations. For me he was authority and master, an admired model, but with one important reservation, that one day I would go further than he had, would have achieved more than he had, would be superior to him.

Hannes Kaapola had read Marx and Engels with great care, and his Marxist explanation of the war and the causes of war naturally did not match up with what we had read in the bourgeois newspapers, or with what Churchill maintained in his speeches. And yet his explanation was the only logical and convincing one. He liked to quote Lenin and knew long stretches by heart. 'A new epoch has begun in the history of the world. The family of man is throwing off the last form of slavery: the capitalist slavery or wage slavery. In that humanity is liberating itself from slavery, for the first time it becomes real freedom.' That was how he felt. That was how he always felt. That was how he felt the world was. And as he felt that, and Sinikka felt that, so did I. For a short while, it was also my unclouded view of the world.

Then Emil came back from America.

Emil had emigrated to the USA just before the great depression began. He was eighteen then. We knew he was having a bad time, not so much from the few signs of life he gave, but because for a long time there were very long gaps between any signs of life at all. A few years later, his letters began to come more regularly and we realized he had been able to do something to enable him to survive. Exactly what he was doing, however, remained an unexplored question, as his letters were always very general and remarkably reticent when it came to concrete information about his actual activities. We didn't even know for sure whether he was married. Towards the end of the 'thirties, he addressed himself almost exclusively to Mother in more or less sentimental epistles which he might begin, for instance, with the pathetic words: 'My darling and painfully missed little Mother'. I thought it sounded revolting and the image of my previously gruff elder brother became puzzling and contradictory in my mind. I had never got on particularly well with my mother and certainly wouldn't have missed her 'painfully' had I been the one to go to America.

But now he suddenly appeared in Helsinki, a gentleman and magnate in great style. That was the winter after the armistice. He was staying at the Kämp. He wore a dark, pin-striped director's suit with a grey tie and waistcoat, a gold watch-chain across his stomach. A distinguished and tremendously amiable man in young middle age. As at that time I refused to have any contact with my family whatsoever, I would not have had the slightest idea of my brother's arrival had I not happened to meet Oskar in the street, who abruptly and disapprovingly told me Emil was in town.

Oskar was two years younger than Emil, but over ten years older than me. We had never been able to stand each other. He was a clerk in the town hall, a humourless, bitter person with a weak heart, who sat at the kitchen table at home with a gloomy expression, as kind and helpful to Mother as he was assiduously unfriendly to me. I remember hesitating before greeting him that time in the street, but I controlled my reluctance and said hullo after all, which was a good thing, considering what I was told about Emil.

I went to see Emil at the Kämp. He was genuinely pleased to see me, overwhelmingly friendly, offering me a wonderful meal of peacetime food, giving me money, and in a flash acquiring good clothes for me and fixing things so that only a few days later I could move into an apartment of my own in Töl Island, and he then generously paid the first few months' rent for me. In short, he behaved like a capitalist magician and hypnotist of note and performed Imperialist or Disney-like acts which were astonishing, quite overwhelming, in most people's eyes quite unbelievable in the ravaged ruins of Europe.

Emil no longer spoke really pure Swedish and his Finnish was even worse. He was very effusive and emotional about the family at last being reunited after so many years, about Father's tragic death and about our beloved fatherland and brave little people who had had to endure such terrible and unjust suffering. Again and again, he came back to how proud he was over his younger brother volunteering so young and filling the breach, prepared to sacrifice everything for the cause of freedom and western culture. I just thought he was talking balls and that he'd got a whole lot of things quite wrong, but oddly enough I agreed with him and felt no desire to contradict him or shatter his foolish pathetic illusions. I liked Emil at once and sensed that we would get along well together.

We were sitting in his room at the Kämp and he offered me whisky out of a large bottle he had taken out of his suitcase. Suddenly he looked at me with a troubled expression and asked if I was hungry. I looked so thin and emaciated, he said. I replied that I was nearly always rather hungry, as rations were meagre and insufficient and the black market far too expensive in general for people like me.

'Tut-tut-tut,' he said, shaking his head and smacking his tongue against the roof of his mouth. Then he lifted the receiver and spoke in English for a while to the hotel servant or porter, or whoever it was. In half an hour or so, the head-waiter, in black jacket and bow-tie, knocked on the door and we were shown to a small room where they had laid out a meal which in my wildest dreams I could never have imagined. Nothing was missing. There were hors d'oeuvres of every kind of cold meat and smoked fish and tinned crab. The main dish was roast chicken with a cream sauce and deep-fried potatoes, and for dessert we had preserved peaches and whipped cream. To cap all this grandeur, we had champagne throughout the meal and when one bottle was empty, another immediately appeared. Emil only sipped at his glass, but I swilled it down and became slightly drunk. How could this be possible? When most people in the country had nothing to eat but salt herring and frost-damaged potatoes? Emil simply smiled delightedly and secretively. I told him that never before in my life had I eaten so well, and that was no lie, for Mother's meals in the 'thirties had indeed mostly been pork sauce and cabbage rolls and black puddings with cranberries.

Emil was truly a magician and the more we talked, the more I liked him and the greater the confidence I felt in him. Many years later, I was to understand that quite a bit of his friendliness and sentimentality was nothing but the external mask a hard and successful business man puts on to confuse people whom on the one hand he doesn't know all that well and on the other hand from whom he expects some advantage. Not that he expected any advantage out of me, of course, but that attitude in him was habitual and seemed comfortable and natural. I myself was to use it to my own advantage when my time came.

I did not tell Emil I was a communist.

Emil didn't like communists. And yet within a few months of the Armistice he found himself back in Helsinki, which in practice if not also in theory was more or less occupied by the Russian Army in the form of Sjdanov's Control Commission. Largely with American capital, he had set up an import firm of his own (the same one I later took over, expanded and ran for several years) and he drove round Alexander Street or from the Bank of Finland to the Ministry of Supply in a huge Pontiac, the latest model.

'First at the mill is first to grind,' said Emil, offering me a post in his new firm. I accepted on the spot, astonished at the good fortune that had suddenly come my way. Emil was my big brother and, in less than one afternoon, had become the best friend I had ever had. Seppo gradually vanished from my horizons, and I took a melancholy but determined farewell of Helga; a new life had started.

In the daytime, I sat in an office in Mikael Street learning book-keeping and business finance and sales techniques. In the evenings, I studied Marxism and discussed methods of overthrowing capitalist society. I was released from the obligation to attend lectures at the university and studied at night for my exams. On top of that, I made love. After Helga, there was a period of semi-prostitution and temporary relationships, but gradually it became Sinikka in more and more stable forms. What more could I want? A few months before, I had been running like a maniac round the East Karelian forests, shitting in my pants with terror and utter exhaustion, my comrades falling like bloody skittles all round me, the machine-guns rattling, planes sweeping low over the tree-tops and bombs and grenades constantly exploding, and I was convinced I would never again see the sun rise over my home town. And suddenly that became nothing but a vile but unforgettable dream. Conditions of life change that fast. The transition between hopelessness and unforeseen prosperity is that swift.

A less unscrupulous person with a more conventional understanding of what was right and proper would perhaps have found the situation complicated. For me, it was an exciting challenge, rather like an introduction to a great adventure (which it was). I was a pro-Soviet communist, an active and convinced Party member, at the same time happily accepting employment - with a promise of unlimited possibilities of advancement - in an American-dominated and highly capitalistic firm. This put my hidden aptitude for acting to test, demanding that I constantly walked the tightrope between spoken half-truths and a forced artificial expression to inspire confidence, which amused me in a way and which I obscurely felt would be useful to practise. At first they were suspicious in the Party, but in the end accepted my explanations, after I'd emphasized the tactical advantages of playing the part of a fifth columnist, infiltrator and spy in enemy country. As I said before, Emil knew nothing of my political involvement.

When I think about Helga, the first woman to leave indelible marks on my life, I cannot help observing with wonder what an amazing and mysteriously symmetrical form my relationships with women have taken. Love is like music; just as the inner coherence of the notes and the interplay in harmony and disharmony seem to follow the musical conformity, so do the variations and periods of love in a secretive way seem to follow a similar conformity. The women in my life are like the voices and counter-parts, the thematic developments in a fugue, like the instrumental conversation in a *concerto grosso*, like the internal relations of the movements, the logical unity of thematic and rhythmical contrasts in a romantic symphony. My life has run a contrapuntal course, which is almost the same as saying dialectical.

The age difference with Helga, almost a whole generation backwards, corresponds to the age difference with Elina, almost a whole generation ahead. Helga was almost twenty years older, Elina almost twenty years younger. And Sinikka's everyday energy and drive, her independence, her sense of reality, strength of will and practical, illusion-free way of life, influenced by bitter experiences of childhood and youth, correspond to a kind of mysterious but inevitable inner logic of Vanessa's mature, lucid, intellectual and aesthetic view of life, her speculatively imaginative philosophy and attitude to life, in contrapuntal antithesis, with independence and energy and drive, the will to love and wilfulness as common themes. Or Helga was the prelude to which Elina was the fugue, just as Sinikka was the *allegro* in the symphony in which Vanessa is the *adagio*. Though not *sostenuto* but still – *con moto*. *Adagio con moto!*

Gunnel succeeded Sinikka as naturally as C-sharp minor succeeds C major. And Laura again was a typical subject, in relation to Gunnel a counter-subject. After long dependence, liberating independence, after stormy proximity, harmonious distance. And yet no more than a *cadenza*, interlude: Laura. I don't really know why these musical comparisons are captivating me so strongly at this moment. They are not really particularly meaningful. Music is music. (And a rose is a rose . . . is a rose) But they help me in a way to bring some order to the whole, to understand, if only in a limited, superficial, geometrical sense.

It has to be remembered that I come from what were in every respect very ordinary and poverty-stricken circumstances, although, 'on the wrong side of the blanket' as it is so condescendingly put, I happen to belong to that many-branched, famous and confident von Bladh family – Bladh – Lehtisuon-Lehtinen (and Blad – Blaadh). Everything I have learnt, attained or achieved has thus been the result of my own efforts, personal talents, my unquenchable thirst for knowledge and independent initiative. I have not had the advantage of growing up in what is called an educated home, where books and intellectual conversation are, so to speak, everyday nourishment, and where from the very atmosphere of the home the children can absorb knowledge and fruitful impulses for their imaginations and growing minds.

As a child, the only contact I had with the world of art, with education and that variant of bourgeois vanity called refinement, was the theatre, through Father, though not the theatre as a temple of festive art, but as a highly prosaic and ordinary, if also to some extent exciting and adventurous, place of work. Father was interested in the money, the niggardly wage, not in what happened on the stage. Neither he nor Mother read books. No one in our family went to the city library. Brynolf read the daily *Huvudstadsbladet* in his spare moments in the evenings before it was time to go to the theatre. Saimi read the Bible and Prayer Book in as much as she read anything at all. She was absorbed by her religion and her household chores, which gave her troubles enough to think about. When they talked to each other, if they ever did, it was mostly of trivial matters, the stairway light that didn't work, some family moving in or out, affairs of the courtyard, whether any of the grand ladies had been stuck-up or rude, or whether the manager had for the umpteenth time been abusive or complained for no apparent or valid reason. It was often about me, harping on about some mischief I was said to have been up to, 'damage to property in the yard', or bullying the refined and delicate children of the gentry, in whose games in the yard outside our window I was forbidden to take part.

Oskar was totally unintellectual, sluggish and uninterested in everything except his illness and his wretched monotonous work at the town hall, which he carried out with a strong and unimaginative sense of duty. We could not afford a radio; indeed, radio was not common in working-class homes in the 'thirties. And Emil, the most intelligent, ambitious and talented of the whole family, had left home before I even started school. The narrow circles of home had been too suffocating, the atmosphere fusty, the space too cramped. How well I understand him.

What I mean is that all this business of music, books, art, knowledge of various subjects and mastering several foreign languages – I've had to fight to acquire it. I've had nothing free. So forgive me if I seem boastful sometimes. Be indulgent when I brag about discernments and knowledge which may seem superficial and out of place in the context. I am not a cultured person in the conventional bourgeois sense. I'm an upstart and always have behaved and always will behave like one.

This business of music, I mean my love of music, is an especially sensitive area for me. When I emerged from the jungle of war in the autumn of 1944, I had never read anything other than school books and a lot of cheap magazines. My musical knowledge was limited to popular music of the time, film music and popular songs, and I knew nothing whatsoever about painting. The whole of that immense field of human activity was alien to me, unimportant, and at most awakened in me an immediate distaste, at which I tried to conceal my feelings of inferiority and humiliation with ostentatious and immediate dismissive scorn. I was wholly unintellectual, or anyhow had no conscious intellectual ambitions.

But I was clever and sensitive enough to sense which way the winds were blowing. So I realized quite quickly how inescapable politics were and the necessity and positive value of personal political views and political standpoints. Everything started from my recognizing politics, not fearfully and reluctantly as the bourgeoisie did, but actively and combatively, as a proletarian among proletarians. Without the slightest doubt, it was the study of the writings of Marx and Engels and Lenin that unlocked for me the closed door to the world of literature and art, enabling me to take my first hesitant (and frightened) steps on the road that leads to the immensely rich landscapes of human culture.

But that was just a preparatory stage, a still somewhat passive and inarticulate recognition. For it was Gunnel, with whom I have three children and to whom I was married for ten years, Gunnel, who was profoundly musical, but on the whole not literary, uninterested in books – illiterate, as the cultural snobs say – it was Gunnel, who herself could play Schubert and Sibelius on the piano, she who in some peculiar indirect way taught me to appreciate books, literature, to read, to gain knowledge through reading, reading for pleasure. It was Gunnel who gradually provoked in me a revelation that it was useful and valuable for human beings to read books, partly perhaps as a result of a complicated educational rôle she considered she had to play in our relationship. For it was not the bookish value of books, their moral or aesthetic or intellectual value she emphasized, but their value as objects of conversation and external evidence of education. To have read such and such was an educational medal. I reacted contrarily, made a mental note of what she left unnoticed, with the kind of puerile but quite natural protest of a pupil: she leads me but she leads me astray; wherever she wants me to go, I will not go with her! Neither was I wholly inexperienced in this area. We had read quite a lot together, Sinikka and I. On the other hand, I could never share that musical interest with her, with Gunnel.

It was exactly the other way round with Laura, Laura was a real bookworm. Perhaps that was the reason why I left Gunnel for Laura. Gunnel had in a quite unforeseen way given me a taste for books, and in Laura I thought I'd found a soulmate. Although it didn't quite work out like that. Laura knew literature like the back of her hand. She had a degree and had written her thesis on the feminist movement. But it was difficult to talk about books with her. She had

70

such definite opinions, such great knowledge. That inhibited me. I soon started feeling simple-minded and rather stupid. I cannot endure that feeling and have always done my best to avoid it.

Laura's interest in music was probably surface on the whole and slightly absent-mindedly snobbishly intellectual. In some mysterious way, it wasn't really the thing to like Tchaikovsky and Rachmaninov and Sibelius. You had to sit immobile and listen to the creeping bloodless flow, the descending or vanishing sound of Stockhausen and Ligeti and Luigi Nono. I yawned my jaws out of joint. In the end, naturally as a kind of protest again, I began to take to the old masters on my own. For if literature seemed to be one huge minefield in the company of the literary Laura, because of her musical indolence, music was a considerably safer art form to devote my time, attention and empathy to. During my years with Laura, my interest in music deepened and matured. That was when music became part of my life, as they say. I still remember my first conscious, if also confused, musical experience which I think in an unguarded moment of spontaneous frankness I expressed to her. It concerned Beethoven's Fifth Piano Concerto in E flat major, about which I maintained: 'The orchestra just thunders on while the soloist plays scales on the piano.' At the time, I had not yet learnt to understand the pattern of music.

But isn't this also, in a transferred and double meaning, a contrapuntal theme? The musical but unliterary Gunnel teaches me in a roundabout way to love literature. And the literary but unmusical Laura teaches me in a roundabout way to love music. Like a fugue, in which unity of counterpoints is finally attained.

A psychoanalyst would naturally have an interpretation of his own.

Sinikka was in many respects an admirable and magnificent woman. She was not exactly beautiful, but she had a wonderfully soft and fulsome body, which offered a kind of suction, an almost pneumatic counter-pressure of remarkable strength and intensity, which I still remember and which still thrills me slightly if I become engrossed in the memory. We were so young then and utterly indefatigable in our eagerness to give each other orgasms. But what was admirable about her is naturally not on that level.

What was admirable about her was her character, her sense of responsibility, her incorruptible faith in ideals and people once she had pledged herself to them. And her courage, the courage which in French was originally called *courage civil*. The memory of Sinikka

71

makes me think of Bernadette Devlin. She never hesitated to speak up, to defend her political and ethical convictions, or her friends, who for some reason or other were in difficulties. Her capacity for work was impressive, probably no less than my own. Perhaps fundamentally this was what first attracted us to each other, our common desire for and pleasure in work, soon developing into a deeply honest love and finally marriage.

When Miles was born, Sinikka at first thought we should call him Yrjö, after Yrjö Sirola. I come from a bilingual home and naturally had nothing in principle against such a choice of name. On the other hand, it was hard to accept, too ordinary, too modest. My social ambitions, my vanity, my most personal and most secret and most private dreams for the future anticipated in some way a grander, more eye-catching and distinctive name. So Sinikka suggested Karl, after Marx and Karl Liebknecht. Or King Karl XII, I protested. Also Karl seemed to banal, too used and worn-out, too unambitious and compromised, despite certain great and dutiful predecessors.

Sinikka met my objections with some impatience. A name doesn't mean all that much, does it? What is essential in a human being is not what he or she is called, but what he or she does. And it is always safer for a child to have an ordinary name rather than an unusual one, she thought. She was right in that. But I was stubborn. I had decided to have my own way. Perhaps in some obscure, subconscious way, I considered it part of a father's right to decide his son's name, while on the other hand the mother's wish was decisive when it came to daughters.

Emil brought with him an electrically driven gramophone or record-player and a heap of records from the USA. The record-player was an advanced model which we hadn't seen before in this country, and the records were no longer the old slabs. Emil gave them all to me, as I seemed to be the only member of the family who might be interested in such a gift, and naturally I was delighted. There was some 1930s jazz, some Glenn Miller and Artie Shaw, but mainly rather mediocre wartime dance music. Nevertheless, much later, Laura was to speak of them as 'real rarities'. Among them were a few records by a trumpeter called Miles something, but not Miles Davis. Not that I admired this Miles to any great extent for his musical achievements, but the name itself had a certain exotic and enticing quality. It sounded grand and dignified in some inexplicable, almost magical way. Perhaps partly because I happened to know how to

72

pronounce it properly in English. Was there one single Finnish citizen with Miles as his first name? I didn't know of any. Miles was to be the boy's name.

'We don't have to import names from the States, do we?' said Sinikka. 'Isn't it enough with tobacco, cosmetics and bad Hollywood films?'

'And dubious business men?' she added, alluding to Emil, whom she regarded with great suspicion.

I protested that this Miles someone was a black man and we were showing our respect and solidarity towards an oppressed and discriminated-against racial minority in the richest and most powerful country in the world if we named our son after him.

So I had my way, and we registered Miles as Miles at the registry office.

About two years later, Sinikka gave birth to a girl and then, with no protest whatsoever from me, she decided the girl should be called Rosa after Rosa Luxemburg.

My relations to children have always been ambivalent and ambiguous. I loved begetting them, and I never loved my wives with such tenderness, with such – I wanted to say – raging fervour as when they were pregnant. But then things became complicated. I couldn't take them in the long run. It's fun with children now and again, for a while when there is nothing better to do. But in the long run? Until they become adults? For years, night and day, day and night, without a break? I cannot endure it. Yes, I admit it quite openly, I lack the strength of mind, the endurance, the capacity to efface oneself demanded of a good parent, child-rearer and father. I have not been a good father. I have tried, but have failed. Children demand total attention for an unlimited space of time, and for a personality such as mine, a rhythm of life such as mine, my whole way of life protests most violently against such self-sacrifice and generosity. A whole evening in the company of a child who has to be fed, entertained, amused, comforted, washed, and denied this or that, makes me feel totally destroyed, depressed, useless and exhausted. I can't sleep at night afterwards. I feel aggressive and irritable, at the same time full of a rumbling sense of guilt, like a kind of gas formation after eating too much pea soup. Quite apart from the fact that children's yells drive me mad.

With her active and extrovert attitude to life, Sinikka no doubt had similar problems, but we could never bring ourselves to talk openly about them. Presumably because we both considered them weaknesses, and both of us, to the same extent, regarded weakness as shameful. We had difficulties and secret worries about the children from the very start. And the effects are horrifying.

Sinikka, as I did, wanted to be something in life. But our dreams and plans for the future did not coincide in several important respects. Her ambitions were nearly all exclusively on the political level. For me, politics were not so sacred. They were a means among other means, by which one rises, to be quite honest. I think that at the time, Sinikka dreamt of a joint place for us in the executive of the Party hierarchy, at a time that was post-revolutionary, which in practice meant in the leadership of the whole country. Rather romantic, one might think, but to what should one aim, if not the stars? She has long been a Member of Parliament.

I myself had begun as an eager and purposeful enough communist. Emil gave me something else to think about. I was a typical child of my time. It was not difficult to switch tracks from justice and equality to profitability and monetarism.

Basically, I have probably always followed the principle of profitability. Even when it came to women. My life has been staked out and its direction decided by the modern principle of monetarism, the brutal and unconditional profit motive, so ugly and repulsive and so frightening to see when it is naked, that clever people feel they have to disguise it and drape it with all manner of virtues and significances, moral and economic artificial jewelry and a little cultural trumpery. Monetarism as the foundation of the country's strength and welfare, monetarism as the presupposition for full employment and the guarantee of provision for the masses, monetarism as the support and nourishment of art and science. When did I grasp this humbug? Jacob always preached it, but I laughed at him. No one took Jacob seriously. Miles was the person to open my eyes. And that was humiliating. Of course it was. What it cost in terms of the struggle with oneself.

I left Helga when she was no longer profitable. That is so obvious it requires no explanation. Sinikka was profitable as long as she could procure or guarantee important contacts (from my business career's point of view) with the Communist Party of Finland's suddenly influential representatives in the municipal and state administration. I have always been convinced of the invaluable importance of having good contacts. I have in fact had a sixth sense when it came to good contacts in various directions. I left Sinikka for Gunnel because I no longer needed her. I could arrange my contacts in that direction on my own. Gunnel Lindermann belonged to another social and political world. And that was where I so passionately wanted to be. Now I needed close and diverse contacts with that world. So I fell totally in love with Gunnel Lindermann and loved her beyond all sense, leaving Sinikka stranded in the other world, the world of justice, equality and human solidarity. Sinikka and the children. Sinikka, Miles and Rosa.

What would have become of them if I had stayed with them? A meaningless question. I did not stay with them.

Sinikka maintains that she was the one to leave me, not I her. Because I suddenly showed myself to be a different person from the one she had believed in, not the person she had fallen in love with, not a good person, but almost a traitor, a bastard, in fact. She blamed a great deal on Emil, his poisonous American influence, his filthy capitalism. So it was Emil who really seduced and destroyed me. She was rather like a mother who blames her children's weaknesses and failures and social peculiarities on 'bad company'. Perhaps she was right in one way. Perhaps I would have stayed in the Party if I had rapidly been given a really good opportunity, and if Emil hadn't appeared. For it was Emil who gave me the thrust ahead. It was because of Emil that I cheated both Sinikka and the Party and went off. But I cheated Emil, too. That was the beauty of it.

I am really rather proud I came across this profitability business. Naturally it concerns far more than just financial profitability. Modern capitalism has infected practically all areas of life with its objectives. People also talk today about 'spiritual capital'. On the other hand, to maintain, for instance, that I married Gunnel exclusively because I reckoned it would be profitable from a social and financial point of view is clearly a simplification and falsification of reality. I loved Gunnel sincerely. I married her for love and it would be a lie to deny it. Which leads me to the thought that the course of life is not formed by one principle, but by many. Mankind has not only one lodestar in life, but many. Stages of life are not decided by one force, but by many. Life is not unequivocal, but multi-equivocal.

Starting from nothing but the profitability principle, how could it be explained, for instance, that over the course of the years I have accumulated six children to love and support? Children are not profitable. Not in our capitalist consumer society, anyway. Why then? Not one of my children has been unwanted. Some of them, such as Torbjörn, my second child with Gunnel, have arrived as amusing little surprises. But never disagreeable surprises. I have experienced a kind of spontaneous and overwhelming happiness each time I have been told that another child is on the way. Difficulties have always started after the birth, and grown at the same pace as the child. Why have I accumulated all these children? In an age of sophisticated condoms and coils and pills? Despite the fact that from very early on I was aware I was not entirely adequate as a father.

Is it because certain individuals are governed by an inexorable wish to immortalize themselves? Children are a kind of guarantee of immortality, if not very satisfactory ones from the point of view of individual consciousness, but they are a kind of substitute immortality all the same, perhaps the best available. Like books and other works of art. Writing books must be one way of trying to make oneself immortal, creating monuments to oneself. Perhaps that is the real reason why, after a successful career in business, I am now trying to establish myself as a writer of memoirs? Author? Immortality?

But founding a company, making technological discoveries, playing a central part in your country's political and social life, that's also creating monuments to yourself, leaving it to posterity to dispense with you. A great man? That is what historians call them, all those people who have done something significant, who have merited a place in the history of their country in their time. A great man? Is that what my ambitions have fundamentally been about? To be called a great man one day? To be counted as a great man among other great men in the von Bladh – Bladh – Lehtisuon-Lehtinen family? And finally my own contribution to the variations of the line of names – Blaadh, the upstart variation, the immortalized upstart? Wasn't the first von Bladh an upstart in the then aristocratic world? Just as the first Bladh was an upstart in the middle class? What the hell is an upstart anyhow? A clever man all round? Why do I keep chewing over the word?

Many children, or multifold paternity, do not make anyone a great man. The one has nothing to do with the other. On the contrary. In the section of the population in which the number of children is

76

conspicuously high, there are conspicuously few great men, are there not? In the conventional sense, that is. In the working classes and the undeveloped countries. Why have I had such a need to surround myself with so many children, to leave behind me so many human traces, so costly, so totally unprofitable.

As there is a profitability principle which decides our ambitions in life, perhaps there is also a principle of perfection? The magical driving force of the upstart. To be perfect in every field and in every respect. As a father of children and procreator of new life as well. How the hell should I know? But for anyone who wishes to measure my inadequacy, to know the measure of my failure, this business of children is clearly where he should start. Because that is where the chasm yawns between desire and ability, at its most mocking. That is where the gap in the armour of perfection is greatest, where it glows brightest, the colour of blood, soiled with throbbing warm young human blood. My children, oh God, if only you had had another father.

Sinikka was profitable. But Sinikka stopped being profitable, just as Helga and Gunnel did. The same thing happened with Emil. He stopped being profitable. Or to be more accurate, he became directly unprofitable.

At first, I didn't tell anyone I had stopped reading economics and had registered for agriculture. I had come across something really good, something truly profitable, and I realized perfectly well that the longer I could keep it all secret, the better it would be for me, the greater the chance I had of succeeding. When Sinikka found out I had changed faculty, she did indeed grow thoughtful. Or rather angry, surprised and disappointed. I tried to explain the point of it all in phrases as mild and veiled as possible, but as she was an intelligent girl, she immediately saw through it all; in other words, to put it brutally, it was really a kind of treachery, a kind of, well, swindle, the way I had thought it out. And also, if the first to be affected would be my brothers, that was bad enough, morally speaking.

It concerned Grandfather's farm.

Before he left America, Emil must have already ferreted out that Grandfather was dying. Perhaps he had corresponded with Svea. None of the rest of us knew about Grandfather's illness. He had leukaemia. Emil told me, in his most emotional and sympathetic way. That was why he had come tearing back to his 'poor shattered country'. By no means for Grandfather's sake, as he so delicately hinted. But for the sake of New Farm. I soon realized that. For even if Emil were a tough business man beneath that amiable and sometimes unbearably sentimental exterior, he found it even harder to lie and dissemble than I did, within the family anyhow. I saw through him. He was out for the farm. I was soon almost completely convinced that he had secret plans to get hold of the farm in its entirety, for himself. After he had bought me and Oskar out for a suitable sum – which meant a disgracefully small sum – in all brotherly harmony, presumably.

Emil knew things about New Farm of which we were ignorant. If Oskar was so stupid that he fell into the trap, that was his problem, I thought. But Emil was not going to cheat me. The question was whether Emil knew something else which was being kept from us. For clearly this was not just about New Farm. It concerned considerably larger issues, investments.

Did he know, for instance, what Stalin and Roosevelt had secretly agreed in Yalta concerning boundaries of spheres of power in the new peacetime Europe? He couldn't have known that, could he? But he had perhaps worked it all out for himself. In the long run, under what flag was Emil sailing anyhow? Naturally I was not perspicacious enough to ask myself these questions at the time. But I do so now. For how was it possible that Emil had succeeded in accumulating such a sizeable sum of spare American capital so soon after the Armistice, to invest in a country to all intents and purposes occupied by a great power which would certainly be the number one enemy in the Cold War that was already breaking out? Had Emil known that the communist upheavals of the kind that arose later in Czechoslovakia and Poland would never happen in Finland? That the dollar would thus be safe? For that was how the powers had thought it all out. Was Emil a CIA agent? A discreet infiltrator sent from the headquarters of capitalist imperialism to contribute to holding the balance of terror even in our northern corner of Europe? Was New Farm simply a pretext, or was New Farm land designated as the indigenous framework in some larger acquisition of capital of another kind?

How would I know? Nowadays only the brain-damaged and sclerotic reserve officers seriously believe that a communist coup was really planned in our country in 1948. No historical facts speak for such a fantastic assumption, for the simple reason that from start to finish it was nothing but a propaganda lie. On the other hand, there is a great deal of major and minor political evidence for the impossibility of such a dramatic political event to have been planned at the time. Why? Amongst other things, because the great powers had thought quite differently.

But in 1948 Emil had again shaken the dust of his country off his feet and returned to America. After completing his assignment? Because he had failed in the assignment? Anyhow, I had occupied New Farm and sat there in lone majesty on fifty hectares, almost a gentleman and landowner, enjoying to the full the first economic, political, diplomatic, not to mention military victory I had ever won in my whole life. Oskar remained at home as before with Mother, now even more bitter than before, wheezing away worse than ever.

So it was about New Farm, and about New Farm's situation in advantageous proximity to Helsinki, taking into consideration an almost certain immediate and swift rise in land values. And it was about Rapid Colonization, the compulsory state transfer of agricultural and forest lands to the tens of thousands of evacuated refugees from the areas in Karelia and Porkala handed over to the Soviet Union in compensation. We had visited New Farm together in his large black Pontiac, Emil and I. Emil had questioned Grandfather sympathetically and cautiously about the harvest and the quality of the forest and present profitability of the land and finances in general. He had arrived like a magician with expensive gifts for both Grandfather and Svea from the great country in the West. Emil had been conspicuously curious and Grandfather had replied with conspicuous reserve. None of this escaped me. I also began to be curious, but I did not show it. Grandfather had worked and expanded New Farm over a long, hard and industrious lifetime. He confided in me that he feared Rapid Colonization. But he did not trust Emil. He could not bring himself to be frank with Emil. Because of the big black car, the gifts, the worldly-wise, artless, amiable manner.

That was when I changed faculties at the university and, without telling anyone except Grandfather, decided that my career would be that of a farmer, for the time being, anyhow, and formally speaking. In name, so to speak.

Naturally no one voluntarily gives up his land to landless evacuees. But it had to come from somewhere, that was clear, no more than just. If one were a clever landowner, a big landowner, with little respect for the law, used to exploiting loopholes and contacts, one could get away with it cheaply and relatively lightly, but if one were credulous and law-abiding and not in with the authorities, the position was often bad. For the law had been drawn up by the powerful, among whom there were several large landowners. Corruption occurred. Bribes were not unusual. Especially sought-after by the Colonization Commission was tenanted land, land which was farmed by someone other than the owner. Grandfather was very old and, to most people, more and more obviously dying. He had no heirs who would immediately and logically take over the running of the farm when he passed on. He had three grandsons, of whom not one was a farmer at the time. In other words, then, New Farm in its entirety was in the immediate danger zone, a snip for colonization. But then I appeared like a spoke in the wheel of the course of events, and forestalled my clever brother Emil. I was on the spot, disguised as a farmer.

I studied the laws with thoroughness until I knew everything about land tenure, rights of inheritance and this new and complicated law called Rapid Colonization. First and foremost, I had to win Grandfather's confidence. At Emil's expense. That wasn't difficult. For while Emil went back and forth in his Pontiac, I stayed as long as I possibly could, helping here and there, not hesitating to pull my weight, even in the muckheap. I was strong, quick-thinking and a good learner, and I confided in Grandfather that the free life of a farmer was really what I had always dreamt of. Grandfather could hardly conceal his emotion when he heard this, and there was no mistaking his joy over my frequent and useful visits to the farm.

I never mentioned to Grandfather that I was a communist. On the other hand, I had a great many confidential deliberations with Party comrades in the Colonization Commission.

Finally everything was down in black and white, all that I had been after so long and so persistently. A properly witnessed, guaranteed accurately drawn-up legal document, in which I was named as Grandfather's sole heir, the only legal legitimate title-holder of the New Farm property after Grandfather's death.

It was an important document, solid gold, it could well be said. My delight and pride in its existence knew no bounds. I regarded it for a long time as my first great diplomatic success, the first really brilliant chess-move I had made in my life, even more marvellous and satisfactory in that both my brothers, Emil and Oskar, had no inkling of it.

The situation was that, had not special measures been taken in time, the steam-roller of colonization would have rolled mercilessly over New Farm after Grandfather's death, leaving behind hardly more than a few worthless crumbs for the legal heirs. Naturally Emil was just as aware of this looming danger as I was. But he undoubtedly considered he had his own reliable channels through which the ownership of New Farm could be arranged and its indivisibility finally assured. To his own advantage. He was mistaken. I, too, had channels, and at that particular time, more reliable ones than his. As was soon to be shown. Emil had not reckoned with his younger brother having a mind a few degrees sharper than his own. Emil had dollars in a bottomless pit and powerful American contacts. But I was a communist. And that actually had the edge in post-war Finland.

What Emil didn't know, or perhaps did not bother about, living as he did in the belief that I was still studying economics, was that the farmer or landowner who could produce a direct heir, with legal right to inheritance, who demonstrably was considering devoting his future to farming the ancestral soil, could live relatively securely in the knowledge that colonization would not fall on his property too heavy-handedly, and that his land and his home would in future remain more or less intact. As long as that heir actually took over the farming of the land when the time arose.

This meant I had cheated my brothers of their share of the inheritance of New Farm. As far as Oskar was concerned, although it sounds rather unsympathetic, I felt nothing but pure unadulterated malicious pleasure. I had taken my revenge, and soundly, too, for all the small slights and intolerable bullying of the past. But with Emil, I did have a slight twinge of conscience. He really had helped me when he had literally appeared like an knight errant, and he had never been anything but good to me. On the other hand, I knew for certain he had been going to cheat Oskar and me. What then was more natural, especially considering the difference between us in age and experience, than to weigh up the twinge of conscience against a sense of triumph and victory that was almost exhilarating?

Emil was no bad loser, indeed no. He could see the funny side of it all, and laugh at it all after he had recovered from the first shock. We were rather similar in disposition when all was said and done, Emil and I. It wasn't exactly a matter of life and death to him, either. Perhaps he even had a certain paternal feeling for me, which meant a kind of secret pride in the trick I had played on him, as one feels pride over a son's success. Instead of just harsh fraternal bitterness.

But Oskar took it badly. He had to live miserably off his tiny state salary, even if he was a bachelor. He saw my triumph as a terrible humiliation and was furious, even refusing to greet me in the street for a while. That didn't worry me. At the most, it simply increased my contempt for the pitiful creature. And Svea? What happened to Svea then? Grandfather's right hand for many years, his all and sharer of his bed, his faithful escort through life, or through the autumn of his years. Well, naturally, we saw to it that she was looked after. We put her in an old people's home. With a room of her own and all.

At the transfer of ownership, some time after Grandfather's death, the inventory officials could do nothing but establish that there was a legal will and such and such contents. This information fell like a bomb on the gathering. Emil's chin fell to his navel. He was dumbfounded. But he quickly pulled himself together in his experienced business man's manner, and at once instructed his own lawyer, who made a really fine job of attempting to declare Grandfather's will invalid. We then reminded him about the colonization issue, and I introduced a man from the Commission, who happened to be an old friend, a reliable and efficient Party member. This important and influential person, an invaluable connection for me, clarified the situation calmly, factually and convincingly to my astonished brothers, making no effort to conceal that he had the whole crushing weight of the power and authority of the Party behind his words. There was nothing Emil and Oskar could do but resign themselves.

I had won. I was rich. We did in fact move out to New Farm and I did a little farming for a while, alongside all the other things I was involved in, waiting for the price of land to soar. Then I sold at the same time as I bought my way into the construction firm of Rapi Ltd and became a director of it. But that is really already another story. My – I mean, what was then Emil's – newly-formed import firm served, and still does for that matter, as one of Rapi's main suppliers of a certain kind of building material.

What one gains in one direction, one loses in another. Such are the laws of life, are they not? What I gained in financial assets and prospects for the future, I lost in love and human warmth. One would have thought Sinikka would not have reacted quite so violently to what was from her ideological viewpoint such a minor matter as the hateful capitalist Emil losing an agrarian investment. But as I've said, her sense of honour was incorruptible. I had proceeded treacherously and treachery could under no circumstances be associated with her morality. The class struggle naturally could approve certain forms of treachery, in that they expressly served the cause of the class struggle in a positive direction, but this was not a question of ideology or even practical politics, but only one of personal gain. I tried to defend myself by saying that the potential capital New Farm constituted was in fact now at the disposal of the Party to a far greater extent than if Emil or Oskar had had a two-thirds share of it. She just laughed scornfully. She knew me for what I was. She had realized that for me personal advantage meant more than collective solidarity, and that for a sufficient profit I was prepared to sacrifice any ideals or principles. In other words, I had revealed my unworthiness, my falseness and worthlessness from the point of view of the communist movement. My fall was indeed great, from golden-haired boy to a near traitor and a potential risk factor.

To Sinikka's embitterment against me personally must be added her disappointment in principle that there were Party comrades, previously apparently reliable and trustworthy, who were now suddenly acting in a way that appeared close to corruption. That was because the Party had grown enormously during the postwar years, of course. The membership had increased hugely, and among those applying for membership were some who were far from ideologically unassailable or even ideologically aware. A large number of cynical fortune-seekers were concealed among the mass of decent people, hoping for a swift and easily acquired political career in a suddenly re-established fashionable socialist party. There were many suspect elements among the loyal and committed, elements who joined for opportunist reasons, thinking the Party would offer them protection and that they would be able to conceal an unfortunate or criminal past in the extensive embrace of the Party. Unexpected discoveries of this kind disturbed Sinikka, even more so when they – in the name of justice it must be admitted – partly also concerned me, her husband. And yet Sinikka was not naïve, but honest. Absolutely honest. A very unusual person.

This monetarism. Emil returned to the USA eventually, perhaps when his secret mission in Finland had been completed? He was not in a good humour towards the end. He had constant lengthy skirmishes with the Ministry of Finance, the Ministry of Supply and the Bank of Finland. The Social Democrat Minister of Finance held a different view of economics from Emil's and besides that, he cursed the fact that at every level he kept coming up against some damned

Communist who tried to put a spoke in the wheel of free enterprise, as he expressed it. 'Stupid dumb people who don't know what's best for them,' he growled. Then one day he had had enough and he left. But I was to look after the firm, already established and running surprisingly smoothly. He decided that. Those were his express orders. I became Managing Director, at not yet twenty-three. That was also how it began. But that's another story, anyhow.

When Rosa was born, my marriage with Sinikka was already crumbling at the edges. I met Gunnel and her gang. I was a director. Sinikka decided on divorce and I resigned from the Party, but ensured that certain valuable contacts remained intact. There was never any question of Sinikka not keeping the children. In any case, Gunnel did not want them dumped on her. If you want to succeed in business you can't be a member of the Party. That wasn't explained to me by Gunnel. I understood that perfectly well myself.

Talking of profitability, I should like to mention an episode I was once involved in in Stockholm. In my opinion it illustrates the profitability principle in its most naked (Christ, all attributes are given ironic hidden meaning and nuances of crude amusement in this context) and most merciless form and reveals its most brutal consequences. It concerns a stripper, the modern variant of a prostitute who usually prefers the 'respectable' professional title of strip-dancer or sex-club hostess.

I had gone to negotiate with executives of Swedish Railways over the sale of a technical discovery a young sanitary engineer had made here at home, a simplified and improved, and most of all considerably cheaper, water system to install in trains, which had eminent advantages, especially for sleeper-carriages. The hidebound railway officials met my suggestion with considerable suspicion, questioning its profitability and efficiency with all kinds of pseudo-arguments and conservative and prejudiced evasions. Their resistance presumably arose from the fact that this step forward in development happened to come from Finland, a former colony. Swedes are like that, and that is how their ancient great-power complex functioned. Their opposition was on nationalistic grounds, and had the idea come from the USA or West Germany, they would naturally have immediately started sweating and lapping the proposition out of my hand. With no petty irrelevant thoughts about profitability, which was crystal clear and indisputable.

Well, I later came to be the supplier of this new water system to the railway systems of half Europe (Belgium, Austria, Poland, Hungary, among others), large parts of Latin America, South Africa and many other countries. But my setback in Sweden truly annoyed me, and I had one of those, nowadays rare, urges to protest by striking out and living out my anger in definite forms of debauchery. In some ways, I was in a state of regression. The old, youthful, *nouveau riche*, and long since abandoned, apparently compulsory desire to spend money came to life in me. The huge enjoyment of splurging money in the secure knowledge that I couldn't go broke.

I hired a large black Chrysler and drove out to the Stallmästärgården restaurant, where I had dinner alone, as expensively as possible. That means I know both the menu and the wine list and the rules of this shameless form of vanity (it took me about three years to learn them during marriage with Gunnel) and I know the most expensive or the best is not necessarily the most expensive in the literal sense, when it comes down to price. But I had a very expensive meal, and drank accordingly. I know the vintages of both Bordeaux and Bourgogne, studying them during my morning crap to save time. My standard whisky has a black label and my brandy cordon bleu. I could boast of several more sophisticated or rustic variations if I wanted to. Although that only really applies in restaurants in London and Paris, as the cellars of Helsinki and Stockholm usually stock only the most ordinary limited choice. This is also a kind of confession, isn't it?

From Stallmästargården, I drove to one of the more fashionable sex clubs in Stockholm which I had visited once or twice some time before. I had four bottles of Cordon Vert in the back, and tried offering the girls champagne, but they refused through their boss for the night, a fantastically good-looking dark-haired girl of about twenty-five, with a hard face and almost black make-up on her eyelids. 'We don't drink on duty,' she said, with a kind of ambiguous allusion to professional morality. I didn't insist. Perhaps they preferred more discreet and sophisticated means of relaxation. 'And for the time being, we unfortunately have only a light beer licence here,' she added coldly. She treated me with a kind of stern indifference, behind which I perceived quite clearly something indefinably threatening. Her tone of voice was somehow in marked contrast to the intimate and arrogant amiability with which she had welcomed other less aggressive guests. I realized I had made a mistake. There were invisible boundaries it was wise not to attempt to cross. The staff would now keep an eye on me, suspecting me of intentions of which the rules of this abstruse and singular game did not approve. Anyway, I went in and sat down to watch the floor-show.

Heavy draped curtains, subdued lighting, stairs with soft carpets making one's footsteps soundless, secretive almost invisible doors here and there on the way into that holy of holies, the place where for what on the whole was quite a moderate sum, one could watch two real people screwing for real. The atmosphere was anything but relaxed. No women visible among the spectators. A bar counter in the background where coffee and tepid beer could be had. Loud, thumping, obstinately indefatigable pop-music. There was a kind of interval when I came in, the curtain drawn across the stage and the lighting lowered.

This was the World of Men in its grotesque, distorted, perhaps also tragic meaning. They sat there in their armchairs, their eyes rigidly turned towards the curtain, soon to be drawn back to reveal new sensations, new inflammatory or frustrating voyeuristic experiences. They tried to hide their faces in this way, by keeping their eyes rigid. Some of them stared down at the floor between their legs. Lone middle-aged men - like myself, for that matter - and one or two old men. They were ashamed. They were not at home here. Reluctantly and with beating pulse, they had been driven here by a force stronger than their inherent decency and petit bourgeois instincts. Back at home there was no one, or a woman they had long since ceased to desire or have anything in common with. She was as lonely as they, but had an even harder time. A handful of younger men, some hardly more than boys in this dull, disconsolate crowd of greying, middle-aged loners and already white-haired elders, took it more lightly, talking, exchanging foolish jokes, their beers beside them, clearly already having drunk a good deal before they had come. They were here for fun rather than out of need. They were in control of the situation, not like the older men straying shamefully from the paths of virtue.

What about me then? For fun or out of need? Well, I must admit I am in a way fascinated, or directly obsessed, by that environment. It attracts me with all the power of a magnet. I cannot resist it. In fact, I like it. I'm stimulated, revived and sometimes aroused; better a sex club than a lonely double whisky at some desolate restaurant table. And as I've already said, I am an incurable connoisseur of the parts of a woman's body her panties conceal. This evening I was to sample something new. This place was only to be regarded as the prologue, a sad little prelude.

I knew the programme more or less by heart. There weren't many possibilities for variation, and on the whole it was not that amazing. Quarter of an hour of American sex film with close-ups of the actual procedure from odd angles. Close-ups of ejaculating pricks resolutely being milked by small female hands, close-ups of red cocks between red female lips and semen dripping from the corners of her mouth, close-ups of elastic red cunts being indefatigably licked by red tongues, or palpated by hairy male hands with dirty nails. Lesbian acts and 'educational' acts, naked bodies in a confusion of every imaginable position, but always with the sex organs in focus.

After that, a fairly advanced striptease act, and then on with the sex film, occasionally supplied with the most peculiar story as a kind of hopelessly misdirected offering to what is perhaps thought to be due to the media of film. And every half an hour, the star-turn of the programme, the live show, a real sex-act on the stage, executed according to all the rules of the art by real sex-artists on soft underlays, a sophisticated custom-made red mattress. Only the orgasms fail to appear.

Let us for the moment exclude the social and economic side of it all. Let us forget the humiliation, the compulsion, the cruel exploitation of human beings in weak social positions or in distress. Let us for once look at it purely aesthetically. For even in this there is a kind of aesthetics. There is something admirable about these young people who undress in the spotlights and who with studied or even quite natural grace and complete technical proficiency, but without a suggestion of natural empathy or emotional involvement, often carry out the sexual act in front of an audience for money. It is sexual choreography at its best, sexual ballet, sexual equilibrium with given obligatory figures, a rehearsed set of movements in which nothing is left undone, everything carried out with a phenomenal control of limbs and muscles, a total exploitation of the capacity of the human body. As in *Swan Lake* at the ballet. As on trapezes, or juggling with skittles, balls and rings at the circus.

There are couples who can't do it, who do it clumsily and

reluctantly, the prick suddenly slackening and panic rising in their faces, rigid in tormented grimaces. They are painful moments and, to a sensitive person, the audience can appear as a unified mass of spontaneous sympathy and compassion. There is seldom anything importunate or aggressive about this audience. The atmosphere is tense, passively aroused, palpitatingly expectant, but benevolent. Hemingway created the philosophy of bull-fighting. I could create a philosophy on the theme of a live show. It is the same thing. Though the other way round. (Considering the life-rituals being carried out, I mean.) It's the same at the circus. Those who can, those who master the task completely, they have raised it to an art. They are artists. Bread and spectacle. Spectacle as bread. The art of killing a bull for money. The art of carrying out an act of conception for money.

I saw two sex artists in action. Then I left. The girl who had given me the brush-off, refusing the champagne, looked blankly at me and did not even reply to my ''Bye' when I'd put on my overcoat and given her a tip.

It was almost midnight. I drove to the south of the city to a place where I knew a couple of the girls from previous occasions. Not all that well, but so that they recognized me when I went downstairs into their little basement and they smiled and said: 'Well, hullo, are you in town?' and I replied, 'No, still in the country,' and we laughed and embraced each other and I felt I was welcome. I felt a kind of warmth. Although naturally I knew that was primarily to do with my being a good customer. Everything costs something in these contexts, embraces and human warmth as well. That's what I'm trying to write about. Don't forget this chapter is about the principle of profitability. But all the same. It was a kind of real warmth, all the same.

The place was called Funny Birds, considerably more modest in pretentions and décor than the place I had just come from. Cheaper, too. The atmosphere was more relaxed, less tense, the audience younger, happier (and drunker), the atmosphere not so imprinted with sophisticated ambitions, not so over-tense, almost church-like in its wordless dignity. Not so unpleasantly charged with the shameful tormented silence of unsatisfied, oppressive sexuality.

The girls I knew and who received me in the entrance were called Sonja and Siv. They did a lesbian number together, and also some recurring and carefully rehearsed solo performances. Both of them were colossally experienced, professionals worthy of respect, and bright, friendly girls you couldn't help liking. Sonja was formally the establishment's proprietor, but naturally there were male bigwigs somewhere up there, invisibly keeping their hard gangster hands on everything and picking up the profits.

'What've you got on offer tonight?' I said.

'The usual and a bit more,' said Sonja, winking cheerfully. 'We've got a girl you really must see. She's fantastic.'

'Then I'll stand you champagne afterwards,' I said, and Sonja laughed.

'There's always a bit of a party when you come,' she said.

I pushed my way through to an empty seat in the front row to have a clear view when the new fantastic girl appeared to do her number.

The films here were much like those at the previous place but of an inferior technical quality. On the whole, a miserably wretched affair. They really were an illustration of the most revolting results of the supreme rule of the capitalist principle of profitability in the world of bourgeois culture. They often involved men and women long past their youth, their bodies already having lost the vigour and firmness that make them attractive to look at. With anguished brightness or strident, grotesquely exaggerated expressions of passion and excitement, they tried to give a semblance of enjoyment and desire, as they fought a desperate and excruciatingly obvious and manifestly uneven struggle against humiliation, shame, and the merciless ghost of impotence. How much were they paid for this sophisticated and, on the principle of 'free enterprise', legalized form of sexual torture as a living and source of income? I didn't know.

How much would I demand to perform a directed sex-act in front of a camera, like a dressage number, in which the reaction on my face would be registered and portrayed with the same impertinence as every part and every crease of my loins, and the reactions or lack of reactions in my sex-organs? I'd demand millions, millions. Perhaps not even for millions. But these poor wretches, these rejected, burnt-out people, at the most earned a hundred or so. How much had I myself offered?

Yes, I once made a guest appearance even in this filthy trade, long ago. That was when my debts had begun to pile up, when I bought and furnished an enormous apartment, 'a business apartment', as a worthy framework for Gunnel's and my *nouveau riche* upper-class entertainment, when a temporary ban was put on imports into the country just as company tax was increased, when no credit could be had and building activities had practically ceased. Just once, the only time in my long successful career when I was really in a spot. Then in a kind of panic (and naturally in the greatest secrecy) I joined a peculiar consortium that was to produce and distribute illegal pornographic films.

It was not even profitable, and my debts simply increased. We were rather ahead of our time. There was no real home market, and we never managed to build up an efficient international network of contacts. The cameraman was a semi-alcoholic bungler and my other companions were also generally unskilled amateurs. It was dangerous too. The police were a perpetual risk factor and we were constantly worried about being denounced.

But I remember with tremendous clarity the evenings, nights and afternoons when the films were being made. The girls we lured out of ordinary dance places with vague promises of huge sums of money and prospects for the future. And the unemployed youths we picked up at the railway station and persuaded to perform for a hundred or so. The result was if possible even worse than the films now being shown at Funny Birds. But the atmosphere during actual filming was concentrated, to say the least. The heat from the lights, the alcohol we were always well supplied with, the semi-drunken naked actors clumsily performing what in themselves were ancient natural rôles, on the floor, on the bed and in armchairs. And the sexual excitement which gradually gripped us all, so that the whole thing usually ended in chaos, an enormous act of group sex, or to be more accurate, collective rape.

I soon backed out of it when I realized its unprofitability. And only just in time, because shortly afterwards things went as one might have expected. The firm was reported to the police by an incensed father of a nineteen-year-old girl who had misunderstood everything at the introductory stage and happened to be an undergraduate. A little bourgeois cuckoo.

The new girl, the fantastic one, the one I am supposed to be telling you about, oddly enough turned out to be an old acquaintance.

She came on wearing black panties and black bra and black stockings and black shoes. Over everything she wore a pink bed-jacket trimmed with ermine. Very sophisticated and tasteless. She moved slowly, thrusting her pelvis forward and swaying her hips, rather like a sleepwalker. So this was to be a slow-motion number, a calculated contrast to the previous girl, who had carried out her number to very quick and forceful music with an urgent rhythm.

I had actually admired her stamina, the clothes whistling off her, and then she went on doing a belly-dance and a bottom-dance and breast-rolling, bending and twisting and turning her body this way and that, all with a violent frenzy and rhythmic precision which was really impressive, and must have demanded enormous training and tiptop condition, and God knows, perhaps some professional ballet training behind it all.

But now it was the new girl's fantastic turn. She began to caress her body, using the transparent bed-jacket very skilfully, so that one moment it exposed and the next concealed fields of bare skin shimmering golden-white in the sharp light. I recognized her at once, but could not immediately recall where we had met, whether she was one of the innumerable girls I'd slept with in Stockholm over the years or someone else, a more delicate meeting, of which I had only a dim recollection. I couldn't place her in any particular memory slot. Well, anyhow, she knew her stuff.

The music to her performance was clinging, her movements were clinging, and she was performing with a sensual empathy which appeared surprisingly genuine, almost as if she herself were enjoying exposing herself.

I suspected the jacket was the important factor in the actual act, and I was right; bra and panties slid off, shoes flew to the left, then it was the stockings' turn, but her breasts and the dark triangle between her thighs remained more or less concealed by folds of nylon and white ermine. She was in no hurry. She showed her straight white legs from foot to groin, first one, then the other. The light remained the same all the time, a hard white spotlight, in contrast to what was usual for this kind of number, alternating white and red and blue and green, then back to white again for particular poses. But this girl needed no assistance from the lighting director. She stretched her legs out towards the audience, wiggled her toes and smiled. For this, she received a shy but spontaneous and appreciative little burst of applause. Good, she thought. Now she had them with her. Now she could begin. She was very attractive. I already knew what I would do when her act was over.

Suddenly she stood up, turned her back to the audience and, with her legs slightly apart, she started slowly pulling the ermine trimming up over her backside. She had a very lovely white tail, with oblong buttocks like pumpkins. Then she turned slowly round, stretching out her arms as the jacket slowly slid off and fell to the floor. She was quite naked now, the tuft of hair between her legs a golden grey. End of first act. New music, second act, and a slightly brisker tempo. Her body was amazingly lovely, slim and firm, her breasts quite small, but round and elastic, her nipples shining like small briar roses. She caressed them with her hands. She continued caressing her body. There was a fur rug on the floor, and she fell to her knees on to it, her thighs now far apart. Slowly and conscientiously, she now started massaging her cunt as she gradually leant further and further back, her legs still tucked under her. Then she separated the labia with her fingers, very carefully and thoroughly, and slid her forefinger over the clitoris, her breathing becoming heavier and heavier. Was it possible that she was doing this for her own immense enjoyment? Suddenly she skilfully, almost acrobatically, scissored with her legs, lifting them straight up, close together, her ankles as straight as a ballet dancer's, her buttocks squeezed together. Then she relaxed, opening up slowly and elegantly, like a flower, like a sea-anemone, and we sat there breathlessly staring straight into her lovely archipelago of brownish coral-red crater islands.

What she was doing was in fact a masturbation act. It took a long time, perhaps twenty minutes or more, and ended with something that looked very like a genuine orgasm. It really was fantastic; I mean, for anyone with a liking for that kind of entertainment. (Jacob would probably have thrown up with disgust and revulsion.) She received long and enthusiastic applause. When she rose, her face was quite serious, small beads of sweat glistening at her temples and on the ridge of her nose.

'Well?' said Sonja with her warm smile when, slightly stunned, I came out afterwards.

'Just as you said. Fantastic! I'd very much like to meet her right now, if she's free,' I said.

'You promised us champagne,' said Sonja.

I went out to the car, unlocked it and took a couple of bottles off the back seat. Sonja unlocked a door on the left of the hall and we went into a rather narrow passage, where the cold struck inhospitably and the light shone gloomily from two naked bulbs in the ceiling. Small closed doors on each side exuded silent expectation and tempting secrecy. We went into a room at the end of the corridor, slightly larger than the others as I remembered them, perhaps furnished with slightly more thought for amenities and comfort, a kind of parlour reserved for VIP guests, I self-confidently assumed.

There was no doubt whatsoever what this room was meant for. The musty, stifling, vaguely or ambiguously enclosed brothel-atmosphere adhered to the walls and the scant furnishings within. An ordinary bed, neither especially wide nor luxurious, with a worn, second-hand, brocade bedspread, a wash-basin with a bit of soap and a small already-used towel, a large mirror opposite the bed, a couple of hard chairs to fling clothes on to, and a little table covered with a red fringed cloth, an ashtray lying on it. A bizarre element was a bunch of red tulips, looking quite lost and out of place in this room, which was a basement room just as much as a cheap boudoir, or some kind of carelessly composed mock-boudoir.

Two lights, one in the ceiling, the other at the head of the bed, both with red shades, spread a covetous and in some way audaciously inviting half-light over the room. Stuck to the wall above the bed with tape was a photographic enlargement of an ejaculating prick and dripping semen over an open cunt, to give hesitant customers a little more strength and inspiration. The odour was importunate, sultry and stagnant, as if the memory of thousands of acts of intercourse had been stored between the walls, in far too small a space, the odour of perfume, stale tobacco smoke and human sweat with a strong spicy flavour of male and female sexual excretions.

Sonja had four beer-mugs with her. I opened one of the bottles of champagne and poured some out. We said cheers and I told her about my troubles with the Swedish railway authorities. She agreed that officials were a loathsome tribe. On the other hand, she admitted she knew some officials from a more human viewpoint than they showed in their standoffish and strictly bureaucratic rôles. Some of them slipped down here after municipal council meetings after midnight had struck.

'They need us just as much as other men do. The only difference is that they use us so damnably insolently. It'd never occur to them to defend us officially, in court or parliament. They take what they want from us, but never support us. On the contrary, they work against us as soon as it pays them in their political careers, the hypocritical bastards,' she said.

'That's life,' she added.

Siv came in with the new girl after a while. I poured bubbly into beer-mugs for them.

'This is Doni, a filthy rich director from Finland,' Sonja said to the girl.

'You were really great,' I said, kissing her on the cheek.

Her eyes flickered uncertainly. She did not want to look me in the eye. She seemed timid, or as if she had a guilty conscience about something bad she'd done, and she did not want to tell me.

'Her name's Marghita. She comes from Finland, as a matter of fact, don't you?' said Sonja.

'Yes,' said the girl, nodding.

At that moment, I knew who she was and where I'd met her before. It was the name! Marghita! Of course, it was an 'artiste's' name, like Sonja and Siv, but revealing enough to me all the same. Marghita as in Marghita Lehtisuon-Lehtinen! Her real name was Sirkka-Liisa, or Miss Järvinen, and some years ago she had been children's nurse to some of my so-called relations, Juhani and Marghita Lehtisuon-Lehtinen, he a gynaecologist and she a paediatrician. I chuckled and she smiled. For the first time, I saw her smile. With relief, it seemed.

'For Christ's sake, we know each other. We're almost related,' I said cheerfully.

She admitted she had recognized me immediately, but had been uncertain of my reactions. The atmosphere in this nest of lust suddenly became almost exhilarated.

Marghita was really delicious to look at, short black hair and small round face, straight little nose, full red lips and bright eyes. Sonja and Siv soon left us, and she started undressing.

'Let's keep things just as they are,' she said in Finnish. 'If you start fussing and asking me how I landed up here and so on, that'll be the end of it, remember that.'

She sounded very definite. Her voice was cold. Professionally cold.

'I hadn't thought of asking you any questions you wouldn't want to answer,' I said to calm her.

'And one more thing; I'm a bit more expensive than the others.'

'Why is that?'

'Because I do things they don't do.'

'Such as what?'

'Take it in the mouth and swallow it down. Some people like it like that.'

'I prefer the usual way.'

'Sonja never takes it in the mouth.'

'No, she doesn't. I remember that. She's afraid of getting throat-syphilis.'

'You can whip my bottom, too, but that's very expensive, because then I can't perform until the marks have gone. Sometimes it takes days, as I like my bottom to be quite white when I'm performing.'

'I've no desire to whip you. I prefer your bottom quite white.'

'But I'm expensive, all the same,' she repeated stubbornly.

'What are you fussing about? Do you think I won't pay?'

'You never know. I thought perhaps you were like your relatives, those quacks, dead mean, rich but dead mean.'

'Then you thought wrong. I always pay a little more than what it costs, and anything can cost a little more than usual when I'm in the mood.'

Then she smiled.

She was quite naked now. I was sitting on the bed, half-dressed. She came over to me and slowly massaged all ten fingers in my hair as she pressed her stomach against my throat and bent my head back so that she could look me in the eyes. She had green eyes.

'Then we're agreed. I'm a sort of supermarket,' she said softly.

Afterwards, I uncorked the other bottle, but she refused, explaining, again with that professional indifference, that professional dismissiveness in her voice, that she had no time for more as she soon had to be back on stage.

'Don't you like it with me?'

'For heaven's sake, it's not a matter of *liking* here,' she replied irritably.

I suggested I should ask Sonja that I should be allowed to buy her exemption from her duties for the rest of the night and she agreed to that.

'You can try,' she said blankly.

'It's fixed,' I said when I came back. 'Sonja has nothing against it. I gave her a thousand. Was that enough, do you think?'

'I should think so,' was all she said.

I myself thought that damned good pay for one girl and a few short hours, pretty good hourly payment, in fact. I was slightly offended at her lack of appreciation, and felt like getting my own back on her in some way. I thought I'd be able to break her resistance and get her to talk about herself with slightly less professional coldness. So I cooked up – I thought it not very believable – a story about not actually having anywhere to go that night, as all the hotels were full and my luggage was at the left-luggage at the Central Station. A man of my age and position could hardly spend the rest of the night on the streets of Stockholm, she must see that? Mustn't she? So the only alternative was for me to sleep at her place and perhaps the hotel situation would be better tomorrow.

She didn't believe me, that was fairly obvious. She just looked at me with a scornful smile. Contemptuously.

'I'll give you another thousand,' I said. 'For yourself. Promise.'

She hesitated for a moment. Taking men back home was not part of her working schedule. The mocking smile vanished. A small wrinkle appeared between her eyebrows (black and very finely shaped, by the way).

'OK. Let's go,' she said.

I stayed with her for three days. We acquired a liking for each other of a rather singular kind. We were very alike in certain respects, and when we realized this, a mutual trust arose, a trust which on my part at least was perhaps stronger than any I had ever felt for any other woman. Never mind that I bought her trust, even bought trust is nevertheless fundamentally real trust. Worth handling with care. I learnt that, or on the contrary, that was just what I had always known. That was the basic insight of my life. That's what I thought. That's what my life had been like. Like hers. In round figures, it cost me about ten thousand kronor altogether.

She lived alone in a rather sleazy room plus kitchen on Västmanna Street. It was a slum. The whole Vasa area seemed to be more or less a slum. Anyhow, when you got behind the façades, but even the façades were shabby, dismal and grey, a heavy, resigned world. A numbed world from which human hope and dreams of the future had long since fled. The ruined town of the old bourgeoisie.

She was not noticeably impressed by my hired Chrysler. That was also rather hurtful. I needed to show off. I needed to show what a fabulous man I was, strangely enough probably just because she was what she was, no sought-after so-called respectable and well-brought-up upper-class girl, but a woman for sale, a parasite, an excrescence, not wanted but desired, concealed almost invisibly in the foliage of the cultural tree of the bourgeoisie. Why did I feel such a strong affinity with her, stronger perhaps than with my own habitual but nevertheless fought-for world? Because I was basically an intruder? Because I basically lived on the same terms as she did, only on such a tremendously enlarged scale that it wasn't noticeable? In daylight?

She was not impressed by a big black Chrysler. She took things as they came, accepting situations in the form in which they occurred.

She had little to lose in a world in which she had already lost, subjected to the merciless pattern forced on her from above by those who ruled the world, to whom I belonged, a part however small. At one moment, I felt like saying she lived like the birds, letting each day contain sufficient of its own torments, but I can't get away with such crude explanations any longer; no one can bear such false witness these days. Had the King of Sweden or the Duke of Edinburgh come to see her, she would have treated them in exactly the same way she treated me, just as uninterestedly, disrespectfully, with arrogance, the swift and monotonously applied contempt, an indispensable and well kept weapon of defence. Practically the only weapon of defence she had available.

Sonja would have behaved differently. She would have swaggered, laid it on a bit. Sonja was more like me, had more to gain and more to lose. But I would never have gone off with Sonja like this. Perhaps just because of that. Perhaps it was a matter of human dignity? Or honesty? Daring to reach down to the point in your life where you can look yourself in the eye; these are your conditions, this is what you are. This is Sirkka.

After we had taken off our outer clothes and I had fired off the third champagne cork of the evening, I had an idea and started joking rather nastily with her.

'I have a confession to make,' I said, quite innocently, regretting it all slightly. 'That thousand I promised you. I'm afraid you can't have it, because the truth is that I haven't any cash left at all. Sonja got the last I had on me.'

She looked at me as if she couldn't quite grasp what I was talking about.

'You see, I nearly always pay with this,' I said, pulling my Eurocard out of my wallet. 'Then I don't have to carry so much cash about with me. But it's not exactly a bank book either. I'm broke. Sorry.'

She had a neat little attack of rage.

'I knew you were up to some bloody mischief, you great bastard, you,' she shrieked. 'Whenever they produce champagne and great black cars, you can always bet your bottom dollar there's trouble ahead, sooner or later, you bastard. I don't usually let myself be cheated these days, but you . . . you Finn-bastard you – with all your smarmy words and kissing me on the cheek and we're almost related and Sonja's old pal and all that . . .'

Her Swedish was almost perfect, almost totally without accent. I listened to her with amusement . . . she had even learnt 'Finnbastard', a very Swedish epithet.

'I can stay all the same, can't I? Just for one night . . . Sirkka, dear . . .' I said, trying to sound as pitiful as possible.

'Sirkka dear, Sirkka dear,' she repeated. 'Christ, what a nerve! God, what cheek! No, you bloody can't stay! Out you go, out, this moment! There's the door! Scram!'

It was no longer funny. I suddenly felt very tired.

'I'm sorry,' I said. 'That was a stupid joke. Of course I've got money. Here's some in advance, in consideration of unexpected . . .'

I couldn't finish the sentence, not knowing whether to say 'services' or 'requests', or simply 'expenses', straight out.

We were in the kitchen. I took two thousand-kronor notes out of my wallet and put them down on the table. Quite unexpectedly, she had started to cry.

'You mustn't do that. You mustn't treat me like dirt. I'm human, too. I'm not a dish-rag, am I?' she sobbed.

'I've said I'm sorry,' I whispered.

'Yes, you have,' she said. She sounded pitiful, though at the same time she slowly put her hand out towards the notes and pulled them towards her.

Then she raised her eyes and looked straight at me, her eyes glittering through the tears. We both smiled. I had an almost uncontrollable desire to ask what the price of the word 'sorry' was, but I managed to stop myself. She came over and put her arms round my neck and started playing in my ear with the tip of her tongue.

'A ten would do,' she whispered.

It was almost like a telepathic miracle. She had read my thoughts. We were suddenly that close.

She didn't set a foot inside Funny Birds for three days. We spent most of the time in bed, wandering naked round the little apartment, making coffee and heating canned food. I got dressed only to go out and buy food, go to the wine store to stock up on champagne, and to cash cheques at the bank.

She told me she had gone to school in her home town of Joensuu and that she was a trained children's nurse. There was a guy she had loved very much and had been going to marry, until everything had fallen through when he became a student and saw their joint future prospects in a depressing vision of endless years with no hope and inexorably barred means of making a living. In Helsinki she had became pregnant and Juhani Lehtisuon-Lehtinen had fixed an abortion. That was when she had been looking after his and Marghita's kids. It happened a short while after that.

What happened? Well, Marghita had given her her cards, to take immediate effect. Why? Well, you see, she was suddenly considered unsuitable to look after the children of the Lehtisuon-Lehtinen family. Just like that, for no real reason? We-ell, not exactly, but all the same, damned unexpected and unfair. She hadn't done anything special, then? Tried to seduce Jussi, for instance? We-ell, not exactly, but . . . I burst out laughing. Marghita was wildly jealous. Was that it? Yes, you could say that. That's what it probably was, absolutely wild with jealousy. But she had no reason to be, of course. Not really. There was nothing for real between Sirkka and Jussi. But it was a close thing? Or what, very close? Yes, you might say that. And now she was taking some kind of revenge on Marghita by using her name when performing a masturbation act at a third-class sex club in Stockholm? Revenge? What do you mean, revenge? That wasn't revenge. But, of course, it was rather fun when you thought about it, performing as Madame Marghita Lehtisuon-Lehtinen, a society lady from Finland. But perhaps not. Marghita was a very good name for an artiste, anyhow, wasn't it? Yes, it was. So it was no more complicated than that? No.

Then she went to Stockholm, just like thousands of other Finnish girls of her age, with great hopes of better money and work conditions. At first, she had worked in a restaurant, then as a hospital orderly, and for a while she had had a steady job in a day nursery. She could speak Finnish as well as Swedish, which was a great advantage. She was trained for the job and she could stay. But there was something in her incapable of standing the strain of a dull, ordinary and constantly repeated working day. She found it hard to be on time. The regularity in the end became quite unbearable. Is this living? she asked herself. And if this was what life really was, then it was little better than back home in Joensuu. She certainly hadn't imagined her life to be like this.

So it was only too easy to eke out her income with a little semi-prostitution occasionally. And . . . Yes? And she had suddenly realized that she actually enjoyed it, was excited by it, liked . . . in fact . . . showing herself . . . it was nice standing there in that *merciless* light, undressing, bending forwards and backwards, opening herself, masturbating . . . it was shamefully nice, knowing a whole lot of foolish gaping men, their lonely erect pricks in their trousers, were sitting somewhere out there in the dark staring at her, at one particular spot on her body . . . right into . . . it gave her a sense of power, too. She was controlling them as she subjected herself, gave of herself, humiliated herself, for it was that, too, humiliation. She owned them and they owned her, and from that peculiar combination came enjoyment . . .

'Is that perverted, Doni? Do you think it's perverted?'

'So you do really achieve an orgasm, then?'

'Sometimes, in fact, not always, but sometimes. It's easy to pretend when you've learnt how. It depends on the audience a little, too.'

'How peculiar. I simply couldn't, not even if I were twenty years younger.'

'But is it perverted? Tell me if you think it's perverted?'

'That's not all that important, is it?'

'Perhaps not, but it's my living.'

'During the war, in our unit there was a priest's son who thought it was perverted to screw from behind.'

'That's not true! You're lying?'

'No, on my honour. He had eight children with the same wife, later.'

'And all of them by screwing in the same position? Ugh, how dull.'

'What are you going to do later on?'

'What do you mean, later on?'

'In a few years' time, when you're older, when no one wants to watch you any more . . . or sleep with you. That time will come, whether you like it or not.'

'I might marry someone then.'

She said it so simply, so self-evidently, it was almost moving.

On the morning of the third day, she suddenly asked me a peculiar question. I was already on my way. The time had come for farewells, and I was to take the evening flight back to Helsinki.

'If I say I'm in love, a little in love with you, how much is that worth, Doni?'

At first I didn't understand what she meant. Then I said:

'As much as if I answered with the same words, no more, no less.'

'You don't understand what I mean,' she said.

'I understand exactly what you mean, but you can't measure

100

emotions with money, not emotions like that, or words like that. You just can't.'

'Really? Fancy you being so naïve. You maintain you've had three wives, and that you have five children, and that there's a woman waiting for you back home in Helsinki. Have you never paid her anything? Haven't any of your wives been paid? I mean, they must have largely lived off your money, mustn't they?'

'Sirkkuli, darling, you can't really compare the one with the other . . .'

'Why not? What hyprocrites men are. I'm a little person. I'm worth no more than what's between my legs. You don't care about me. No one cares about me. You amuse yourself at my expense, as long as you want to, and then you leave. You all do. Our time together is very short. I don't have time to do much for you and you don't have much time to do anything for me, but we have done something for each other these few days, haven't we? We haven't had time to say many things to each other, but we have had time to say some things, we've eaten together, and slept together and screwed together and . . . hasn't it been a kind of marriage in exactly the same way as your earlier ones, only shorter, smaller . . . that woman you were married to for ten years, for instance, how much did you spend on her, if you count it all up . . . millions, wasn't it? Millions and more millions. She didn't have to think about cash compensation for every word she spoke to you, or every service she provided, or because she let you screw her bum when you were dead drunk, and because she loved you in general, did she? She didn't need to, because she could be sure the money would be forthcoming automatically. There was always money at her disposal. Marriages are generally like that. But in my case it's different. If I don't ask for cash payment for every word and every thing, for all those things paid for automatically in an ordinary marriage, then there's no money for me at all. I'm just left there with nothing. I just starve to death, you see. It's the same thing, with the exception that I'm a little person, someone who is of no account where everything worth something is calculated, so I have to ask for everything, humiliate myself and request, formally apply for all the money that goes to other women on its own, flowing quite naturally, to your wives and all the other grand wives. That's life, or that's the system, I should say, isn't it?'

'Yes, Sirkka. You're right. That's how it is.'

She looked at me for a long time, a moist glimmer beginning to come into her lovely green eyes. She raised her hand and stroked me quickly across the cheek.

'So how much is it worth for me to say I'm in love with you, a little in love with you?'

I didn't know what to say to her. I was totally confused. One of the few times in my adult life when I felt truly powerless, at a loss, like when you lose grip completely. The situation was absurd, impossible, alien.

'I don't know . . . I . . .'

'Then I'll make you an offer, Doni. A hundred kronor.'

It was all unreal. I couldn't move from the spot, least of all move my hand to my wallet. She had already had more than two thousand a day as compensation for what she lost by not receiving clients at Funny Birds. I had never dared to ask what her own share was, anyhow.

She drew slightly apart from me.

'Give me a hundred kronor,' she said commandingly, with a hint of the familiar old professional chill in her voice.

Slowly and still in a kind of daze, I took out my wallet, extracted a note and handed it to her.

She crumpled up the note and flung it under the table. She would find it again and smooth it out after I'd left her.

Then she embraced me, pressing her body desperately hard against me and whispering: 'I love you, Doni. I love you,' repeating it over and over again with burning, anguished fervour, until I was so moved a lump came into my throat.

I was quite proud of my name when I was small. Donald! It did indeed sound much grander than Charlie, Willie or Lasse. Later, when I had hauled myself up into the middle classes, and ensured my bourgeoisness by marrying Gunnel Lindermann, to be honest, I would have preferred to have been called something else, something more traditional or more conventional from a class point of view, Henrik, or Carl-Gustaf. Even Max or Maurice or Nicholas would have been all right. Just not Donald. That inexorably revealed my origins. I soon found that out. In those particular circles. Like Clark, and Gladys, and Salome. It sounded vulgarly pretentious, upstartish, or painfully apt all round, when it came down to it. Sometimes it gave rise to discreet, superior amusement which caused me murderous thoughts. Nowadays my name doesn't make any difference, of course. I've grown into the kind of personality my human resources once anticipated and rendered possible. I am what I am and have done what I could. Satisfied with myself! Yes.

Emil and Oskar, then suddenly Donald! Perhaps I was given that grand-sounding foreign name as a kind of small, regretful compensation for the fact that I arrived unwanted many years after my brothers, at a time when Saimi at least regarded child-bearing as a chapter in her life long since closed? Children in my situation are usually called afterthoughts, and afterthoughts often have the implicit flavour of a favourite, rather than scapegoat, a positive secondary meaning. I was no favourite. Father was the only one to accept me when I was small, accepting me as a child with a child's special need for attention and tenderness. I was Daddy's boy. But why Donald? Was America also Father's dream? Was it Father who *sent Emil away* to America? I'll never find the answers to those questions.

Early, very early on, I was placed by my social circumstances in the school of bitterness, humiliation and hatred. The yard house, the wooden shack where we lived was in the shade, squeezed between the neighbouring façades, as I've already mentioned. On the sunny side of the yard, in the sun, the children of the gentry poured out of the yellow stone fortress to play, grand cockroaches arbitrarily taking over the whole yard. I knew little of what was concealed behind those five floors of yellow façade, with their great gaping windows, where one could occasionally glimpse amazing ornaments, almost unreal and other-worldy, sculptures, bowls, china dogs, curtains of airy white linen or tulle or coloured materials. Saimi went cleaning and did plain sewing there sometimes, and Father was responsible for the stairs and locks, the lights and conveniences. But they did not tolerate me. I was a pariah.

In the summer, this stone fortress was almost empty, the gentry in the country, each in his own mansion on his very own patch of native heath, by the rocky shores of the sea, or the fair shores of an inland lake, depending on . . . well, mainly depending on language and heritage, the Swedes by the sea, the Finns by the lake. Language antagonisms were severe and terrible, but nevertheless did not exclude living in the same block, as long as one belonged to the same class. Class antagonisms were much worse. They led to civil war.

Anyhow, the yard was all my own in the summer. More or less. Like the prairie Indians. And like the Indians, mercilessly thrust aside by white colonists and fortune-seekers when the time came, so was I also thrust aside by small upper-class colonists at the the play-level in the merciless reality of class hostility when autumn came. In winter, my lot was to sit in the kitchen window behind the grubby pane, listening to Mother rattling the stove-rings and pans behind my back without speaking to me, and staring at the gentry's children, the chosen, tumbling about in the snow out there. While bitterness grew, hatred slowly boiling within me.

They had quite different clothing from mine. Fur hoods, bright scarves, thick gaiters buttoned at the ankles, a few of them with elegant small fur coats. They had toboggans. They built snowmen and snow forts. They had tremendous fun together. In the evenings when it grew dark, I crept out and pushed down their snow forts, gave their snowmen knockout punches, levelled their work to the ground, tore it down, razed it. Like the Indians. Filled with the same kind of fury, the same kind of injured sense of justice.

I learnt early the difference between man and beast. Those middle-class brats had been inoculated with class-consciousness very early on. At first, my social innocence still unassailed, I wanted to play with them and tried to join in. 'Look, he's got a hole in his elbow,' they said. 'His stockings are always down.' 'You're dirty.' 'You smell.' 'Go away.' As a newcomer to the world of class-differences, I was compliant to start with and obeyed. But I came back. I was hurt. I didn't grasp what it was all about, but I presumed it was a misunderstanding. I was mistaken. 'Mummy says you mustn't play with us,' they said. 'Cos you've got nits.' 'You'll infect us.' 'Go away.' 'If you don't go at once, we'll tell Mummy.' Etc., etc.

Being called Donald was no help at all. If you were born a caretaker's kid, there was no cure. Then I realized it really was serious, life was like that, life was hard and you either submitted to it or revolted, and that you could either accept their insolent conditions, or create your own conditions and stick to them. I chose the latter. I was like that. I was not like Mother and Oskar.

'Nits!' I responded without thinking. I punched them on the jaw. They vanished, weeping, to seek shelter in the safe arms of Mummy. As they refused to be my friends, I made them my enemies. Later I used to sit with Tapio in a basement opening and shoot small stones at them with catapults. Then an endless parade of indignant mothers appeared at our front door, knocking and snarling and scolding and threatening. Then Saimi's whining litanies, her angry reprimands, her ear-boxing, her hair-pulling, her unfailing, unchanging betrayal when it came to me. 'Nits!' No, she certainly couldn't hold with that. But all the same.

I learnt that if you don't look after yourself, no one else will. If you don't defend yourself, you will defend no one. I learnt that my fist was my trump card. And that has never really left me. Violence is the only functional weapon of the underdog. I don't need it any longer, but it still happens that I strike out in anger, immediately, almost instinctively, which naturally has incurred disfavour in recent years. But what the hell, it's part of my upbringing, an ineradicable part of the upbringing a class society has given me.

Writ of defence! What kind of writ of defence? I keep on walking like a cat round a hot dish, constantly postponing it. Undertaking to write about the present, as the past seems to be impossible to retrieve and bring alive again, but paralytically staying in the past all the same, for page after page. Warding it off. Torbjörn is never out of my thoughts. I'll write about Torbjörn in this chapter, his difficult youth, our relationship, at the moment so difficult and filled with conflict. And about my long marriage with Gunnel, which was so happy and so fundamentally malconstructed. This last twenty-four hours has been a strange and disturbing time. I've had a letter from Vanessa, but what a strange letter, full of contradictions and evasions. She is still in London. She is negotiating with the Leningrad Philharmonic. Or necking with Richard Burton. I can't work out which. Something's happened to Miles, but I cannot say what it is. Not until the police investigation is over, which means under no circumstances whatsoever will there be any kind of police investigation. I can't make head or tail of anything. It is incomprehensible. And terrible. Then Helen phoned, Jacob's sister. She's an insufferable bore, long-winded, lacking both temperament and sense of humour. She was pretending to be upset about the rumours that seem to be going around about Miles and my firm's affairs, but sure as hell in the depths of her shallow soul she was bursting with malicious glee. She is a dentist, alcoholic, too, though in profound secrecy, married to her second cousin, Martti Lehtisuon-Lehtinen, dullard that he is, too, one of the innumerable academics in that branch of the family, professor of some variant of the law, civil law, I think it is. And who the hell would she be married to anyhow, if not a second cousin; that's the way they behave in this many-bladed (attempt at wit) family knife, like the inhabitants of some isolated East European mountain village or the island of Tristan da Cunha, constantly intermarrying within the family.

She went on and on in her whining voice about this incredible thing that had happened to Miles (as if Miles himself hadn't *done* anything, but the other way round, something had been *done* to Miles, a more or less defenceless *tool* . . . that's the way true bourgeois family solidarity works), and Miles, who had always been such an exemplary employee, so dutiful, so reliable, so ambitious, so singularly gifted, so kind and thoughtful, a really distinguished man, a distinguished man in the real sense of the word, a distinguished person, an epitome of virtue, a splendid boy, perfect in all respects, a bull's-eye, a veritable hundred-percenter, so handsome, so fantastic-ally handsome, so clever, so mature, so polite, so unselfish, so decent, so imaginative, so well-mannered, so restrained in his habits, so . . . so . . . and now suddenly this terrible thing, what underhand, insidious, devilish intrigues he must have been the victim of, poor boy, and despite everything he has the guts to admit his actions, to acknowledge his . . . well, one must unfortunately call it . . . crime . . .

Then she started, in treacherous and in the end absolutely clear terms, to explain what in all silence was being speculated 'in town', that in fact I was behind it all, that my *totally unexpected* resignation from the managing directorship of the firm was intimately connected with Miles' *deed*, our losses over the last two years had been astronomical, the company to say the least of it was on the brink, and because of my all too well-known habit of ruthlessly exploiting relationships and contacts and loopholes of whatever kind, I had *forced* Miles into this. . . . Now I see I will have to reveal what kind of 'deed' it is my eldest son has committed . . . in one single little fell swoop, or rather quite a big fell swoop, actually quite suddenly he has succeeded in appropriating, or straight embezzling exactly three million from the large enterprise which employed him as legal advisor and appointed him financial director a month or so ago, and the three million in actual fact were now to be found sunk in my own business! Naturally, she didn't believe a word of all this herself, I realized that perfectly well, didn't I? But she just wanted me to know, thinking it her duty to tell me what was being said and what was rumoured . . . blood is thicker than water, after all, she stressed with her studied duplicity . . .

106

I could see her in my mind's eye sitting in her elegant bedroom with its wall-to-wall carpeting and padded silk wallpaper, on the edge of her bed, her backside more than half sunk into the duvet, her back straight, in her neutral, beige-coloured morning dress, her knees pressed together and held slightly to one side as nice ladies should sit, decorously, her slack face expressionless, rather careworn, ageing and slightly puffy from drink, her grey, mauve-tinted hair sprayed and perfectly arranged, her mouth with its thin colourless lips talking and talking, the crimson receiver at her ear, the bedside table with her ear-plugs in their little box, the aspirin tablets, her nasal spray, the latest number of *Ladies World* and *Eve*, Victoria Holt translated into Swedish, Agatha Christie in English . . . and without the slightest doubt still Volter Kilpi's *Alastalon Salissa* Part One, which had lain there as long as I could remember, since the end of the 'fifties presumably, and which she liked to talk about with great enthusiasm at family gatherings and cocktail parties. . . . Yes, mmm, yes, uhuh, yes, uhuh, I replied, seeming to sense the faint odour of sherry beginning to penetrate into the room from the area round my ears as I tried to sound friendly; naturally I realized that she didn't believe a word of all that vile gossip. I was deeply grateful she had taken the time to phone me up to tell me . . . of course, of course . . . and at last there was a tiny pause in the flood of words and I could end the conversation without being directly rude.

If only I could find some concrete reason behind what he had done, but I can't. The whole thing is quite incomprehensible. He is an executive in one of the largest companies in the country and not yet thirty. He has carved out a rapid, brilliant career in the business world, with all the prerequisites for being awarded honours at fifty. His salary is princely, his private income increasing promisingly by dint of clever and forward-looking investments. He doesn't drink. He shares his father's genuine loathing of gambling. He has neither legitimate nor illegitimate children, or similar maintenance duties. He isn't even married, although for some years he has been living with a girl of whom there is nothing to be said except that she is unusually pretty and clever, and also self-supporting, as she has two degrees and has recently been appointed to a central administrative post in the Ministry of Social Affairs. In other words, there was no possible, or from any point of view comprehensible, reason for him to appropriate other people's money illegally. I thought I knew him. I thought of all my children he was the one who was closest to me,

107

because he was the most like me. I thought our earlier father-son relationship had developed into one of equality and a feeling of warm friendship, and that this feeling of friendship was mutual. I thought we had confidence in each other, and that had made me very happy for some time. What a lot one thinks and how little one knows! At the moment, the only thing I think I know is that there can't have been any rational compulsion forcing him to carry out this terrible deed, so much more inexplicable when everything Helen told me about him on the telephone is undoubtedly true, no exaggeration . . . he is in fact everything she maintained, an unusually sympathetic and successful young man, respected and appreciated by everyone, loved by many, a favourite of fortune, a truly royal child of the stars.

My marriage circumstances meant that Miles and I did not have much contact when he was growing up. Sinikka had nothing against us meeting, but Gunnel was on principle negative towards anything to do with my previous marriage, including the children. So it was not until Miles was a student that we were in closer and more regular contact, and that was when I had the opportunity to give him some useful advice, a certain guidance, and it was during those years that our friendship and mutual acquaintance began. Not a particularly long time when it comes to a father and already adult son. Hardly ten years.

There were never any problems with Miles. No growing child could have caused his parents fewer worries. His puberty came early, discreet and almost unnoticeable. His schoolwork was impeccable, and he came out with brilliant marks. He seldom had an average below ninety per cent in music and a hundred in gymnastics, and for a few years in the sixth form he was captain of football. Naturally he came out top student, with six clear distinctions. It took him exactly two years to take his first law degree. He is a lieutenant in the army reserve. Everything worked. Everything progressed quite perfectly. They were no flies in the ointment at all. And yet!

I remember a couple of events in his schooldays, a couple of times when Sinikka was at a complete loss and got in touch with me to discuss what to do about it. But do they lead to anything? Do they say anything about Miles which might in some way relate to him now embezzling three million in an up to now unexplained manner? I see no connection.

As early as when he was thirteen, in the early stages of puberty, he happened to make the classic remark of the extra-talented schoolboy. This is how it happened. That year he had a physical education

108

instructor with whom he did not get on. It was said that he sabotaged this man's lessons with a certain purposefulness, and to the teacher he was obviously a thorn in the flesh. Naturally, so long afterwards, it is hard to decide which was cause or effect, but anyway, relations were inflamed from the start, quite apart from the fact that Miles was already an excellent gymnast and athlete. One day at the end of April, after the snow had gone, they were to play stickball in the school yard. Miles was offered the captaincy of one team but he refused. 'Can't be bothered,' he had said, insolently. He had then received a short, and as I see it, well-deserved dressing-down from the teacher, who, it is worth noting, was magnanimous enough to accept his refusal. With no further discussion, the captaincy was given to the next pupil. However, Miles stubbornly continued being obstructive, apparently for no valid reason. When it was his turn to hit the ball, he didn't even try, but instead flung the bat aside. He didn't run, but walked leisurely from base to base, to cap it all, they said, laughing scornfully all the way. Thus he spoilt the whole game, which naturally annoyed his fellow-players just as much as it did the already sufficiently humiliated teacher. In the end, the game was stopped and Miles was hauled over the coals. The exchange ran roughly as follows, as far as I remember from what I heard first from Sinikka and then from Miles himself.

'What's the matter with you, Bladh. Have you gone crazy? Or, despite the fact that your father's a rich director and all that, don't you know how to behave?'

'Dad isn't made to trot round an idiotic school yard hitting a silly ball with a stick.'

'Then perhaps you learnt such insolent and unsporting behaviour in your mother's circles?'

'Take that back, sir. I refuse to listen to anyone insulting my mother just because she's a communist.'

'Listen now, Bladh. You're not only badly brought-up, but you're asocial and deserve a good thrashing. I've thought that for a long time, because otherwise things will go very badly wrong for you in life. Remember what I say.'

'Just you try, sir.'

'I warn you, Bladh, for the last time. What do you think'll become of you as an adult if you go on behaving like this, like an enemy of society and a hooligan?'

That was when it came.

109

'If I don't succeed in anything else, I could always become a physical education instructor.'

It was by no means an original remark in the context of school, but for some reason it is always equally apt. The effect was also devastating and totally unexpected this time. The teacher burst into tears and without another word vanished into the school and went straight to the headmaster. Miles was kept in for two hours on Saturdays. That was when Sinikka contacted me, as she thought the punishment disproportionately severe. I agreed with her. I telephoned the head and had a fairly heated dispute with him. I did not mince my words, in that way of offended and self-confident fathers. But he revealed a few details which later made me think. Was there something cynical in Miles' character, something callous which on this occasion had suddenly been expressed?

This teacher had family circumstances and a general background which made him a truly pitiable person in the real sense of the words. His first wife had borne him three children, then fallen ill with schizophrenia and was eventually committed to a mental hospital in Nickby as incurable. After hesitating for a long and tortuous spell, he had got a divorce and married again, this time to a woman who bore him two more children, and then one fine day she disappeared with a mediocre Italian pop-singer on a tempory engagement at a second-class dance-hall in Helsinki. So there he was, with five motherless children to support on a miserable teacher's salary. But that wasn't all. His old mother, who had moved in to look after the children, suddenly had a stroke and remained for the rest of her life on her sick bed, paralysed down the left side. To add to all these misfortunes, the poor man had never originally considered a future as a physical education teacher, but circumstances had simply decided it for him. His great all-absorbing interest had always been biology, and he had wanted to do research.

None of this was a secret. His colleagues all knew it, the pupils knew it, the whole school knew it. The physical education teacher was not the silent kind and liked to complain openly, indiscriminately and often. So Miles had also known. Eyewitnesses had said there was something in Miles' gaze during this brief exchange, not just insolence, thoughtless cheek or childish defiance, but something much more serious, something that told them it was a conscious desire to hurt, or even worse, in a horrible way a reminder of the triumphant and sadistic enjoyment some disturbed children occasionally show when they are suddenly gripped by an irresistible desire to torture animals, any animals, flies, birds, cats.

Some years later, the headmaster himself contacted me. By then we were more closely acquainted and long since reconciled, as chance and mutual acquaintances had brought us together occasionally. That was at the beginning of the 'sixties, either just before or just after the time when I was acting as Minister of Defence. For natural reasons, or perhaps one could say from birth and conditioning, Miles was one of the pioneers of the radical-left movement which quickly grew into a powerful wave during this time, and which rushed through the school and student world, disturbing and liberating, in most of the western European or capitalist countries.

I remember now that Miles was fifteen, so it must have been 1962, which shows that he was rather before his time and actively radical on the left several years before the radical left had seriously grown into a fashionable movement among the politically-minded young. But through Sinikka, he had communism in his blood, so to speak, and he developed young. In passing, the strange thing about him was that later on during his student days, when we were in closer contact, he showed no interest whatsoever in politics, least of all any sign that he held socialist opinions. All his energy and attention were devoted to his legal studies, which as far as he was concerned would be his entrée into a career in business.

Well, his headmaster telephoned me. It turned out that Miles was the leader in his class of a radical-left group, which in a variety of ways had stirred up unrest among the pupils and caused problems for the staff. The limit had now been reached, as this group had succeeded in persuading the whole class into a sit-in strike that had already lasted two weeks and was said to be a protest against the history teaching, which according to Miles and his companions was bourgeois and tendentious, or in other words false. They refused to take part in the lessons if the curriculum were not reorganized according Marxist principles. A basic demand from their side was that the curriculum should at least include an introductory course in Marxist historical views.

The headmaster explained that this particular demand was quite impossible to concede to, as there was simply no suitable teaching material. Neither was the history teacher familiar with Marxist theory, and nor did it interest him. He had his own methods and his own interpretations, so this new, to him unique, situation had

111

annoyed and irritated him, and to put it briefly, for prestige reasons as well as on principle, he was quite intractable and unwilling to negotiate. Unfortunately, at that moment it did seem that the only possible solution would be that Miles and perhaps a few more of the most active agitators should be expelled from the school immediately. This was a painful business, because Miles had always been an excellent pupil, but under the present circumstances, well . . . I understood, he supposed? Didn't I? That was the only way.

I was uncertain as to what attitude to take at first, but then I agreed with him and promised to speak to Miles. A regular tennis partner is after all worthy of greater loyalty than an adolescent son whom one seldom meets and hardly knows. I had a serious talk with Miles that same evening, our first meeting for a long time, and probably the first time we'd spoken to each other in adult terms. I gave him the headmaster's views, which naturally he was already aware of, and in neutral, friendly terms I also tried to take the part of the opposition. Miles was cautious and watchful, slightly brazen at first, but when he saw how reasonable I was, he softened markedly, and finally became quite open and talkative. But my words had no effect. He was quite firm and unbending in his stand, his reasoning very clear, impressive in a way in his all-or-nothing attitude, slightly pathetic in the almost Lutheran attitude of 'here I am and know no more', and rather admirable in his courage, considering his youth and what was at stake. For a moment I thought I would be angry and harangue him like a narrow-minded father or an overbearing uncle, but quickly noted how easily I managed to control myself. Miles was simply not the kind of youth one harangued. It would also have been quite useless, as he would have taken no notice, nor even accepted it. He would have simply considered it one of his father's many weaknesses of character.

So he refused to yield. He was going to have his Marxism on the school timetable. The result was that we took him out of school. We registered him at another school, with a history teacher of perhaps slightly more liberal views, anyhow younger and more willing to discuss things, more flexible, with a greater understanding of youthful enthusiasm as well as of the uncompromising attitudes of the young. So that was the end of that school conflict. I went on playing tennis with the headmaster as if nothing had happened.

I remember yet another incident from Miles' schooldays. Perhaps it was the most puzzling and difficult to grasp of them all. He was in his final year. This time it concerned his Swedish teacher. The whole class was demanding his dismissal. They maintained that he was a homosexual and that he had repeatedly, but particularly on one especially compromising occasion, made approaches to certain chosen male pupils, among them Miles. This story was later repeated to me by the same aforementioned headmaster and tennis partner, by then no longer Miles' headmaster, of course. On the other hand, Miles himself has never said a single word about this painful and peculiar drama.

This was the situation. The teacher, who was unmarried, was unquestionably somewhat feminine in manner. He was also known to be given to pawing, and not just the younger pupils, either, far from it, on the contrary. Anyhow, he seemed to have a highly developed love of physical contact, always grasping the boys' arms when talking to them, or putting his arm round their shoulders. Perhaps the whole thing had started from some such innocent act. On the other hand, there were two pupils who swore that when he managed to manoeuvre then into an empty classroom or some murky corner where he thought they were safe from discovery, he had made considerably more advanced approaches. Such as what, for instance? Well . . . approaches, shameful approaches.

A delegation appointed by the whole class (not Miles') had now gone to the headmaster and demanded that the matter be investigated once and for all at a kind of unofficial, improvised court, after which the teacher would be officially urged to resign. After considerable hesitation, the headmaster had agreed to this, which meant he thought he had no choice in the matter as emotions in the class were running alarmingly high. So after school they all gathered in the staff-room, observing the greatest discretion. The headmaster was in the chair. He appealed for calm, sense and objectivity, and most of all for tolerance. In other words, he was being loyal to his colleague. He was partisan. That condemned him from the start in the eyes of the pupils. The class was in uproar. The accused victim, the wretched teacher, sat to one side, wriggling, sweating and flushing, horribly upset. They hated and despised him. It was hard to achieve silence. Then Miles was to speak, acting as a kind of crown witness, as the teacher's indiscretion was considered to have concerned him more than anyone else.

Another youth, leader of the delegation and initiator of the whole business, testified first on what had happened. Together with Miles

113

and two other school-friends, he had been out one evening for a beer or two. It so happened that this teacher had been sitting having a drink a few tables away, but far from being indignant at finding his students in a pub with tankards in their hands, on the contrary, he seemed to be delighted at the chance of some company. He invited them over to his table, ordered some wine and offered it all round. This was all really rather pleasant. At closing time, he suggested they should all go back to his bachelor den. They had nothing against that. Once there, he offered them rum and Schweppes Bitter Lemon, and they were soon all fairly intoxicated, with the possible exception of Miles. That was exactly what the man had calculated, of course. Now he had them where he wanted them, a handful of defenceless, injudicious and helpless youths in the web of a cunning, evil seducer. And presumably he had made barefaced and disgusting approaches. He had embraced them in the most revolting manner. He had kissed one of the boys on the mouth, behaving like some dirty old queen.

Then it was Miles' turn to testify. Miles got up slowly from his place and stood in silence without moving, until the buzz in the staff-room had died down. Then he started speaking, very clearly and distinctly, his voice dry, detached, a trifle haughty. He said he had nothing negative to say about the teacher, to whom, on the contrary, he was extremely grateful, as it was he who had taught him to express himself easily and correctly. Then he informed the gathering that as far as he was concerned he had no intention of continuing to partake in this spectacle, which was unworthy and humiliating to all concerned. Then he went across to the now utterly confused teacher, embraced him, kissed him on the mouth and marched out, slamming the door behind him.

No one had expected that. Confusion arose among all those present, the whole 'court' came to a full stop, the meeting dissolved, and the matter was left to sink gradually into the mists of oblivion. But Miles had put a distance between himself and his friends. There was an ambivalence in his actions which no one could fathom. They no longer knew where they had him. What they began to feel for him from then on was a mixture of inexplicable fear and smouldering aversion. They no longer liked him. In some inexplicable way, he had betrayed them. Not that for one single moment would they have suspected him of being homosexual. His sexual escapades were far too well known for that. But because he had dared. Because he had dared to do something not one single one of them would ever have dared to do, or would ever dare to do in the future.

This Miles business. I have spoken to him. He appears unmoved. Cool, calm and collected. You can't get much out of him. With no evasions or explanations, he admits he has pinched three million, but he doesn't say how he did it. Vaguely, and with a faint undertone of scorn which is irritating even if you know it is self-defence, he keeps bringing in the words 'innovations plucked from the air'. Innovations from the air! What on earth is that? Miles says nothing. No one knows where the money is. 'That's my business, and will remain so,' he says. One fine day, he just walks into his boss's office and says he has embezzled three million marks. No one believed him. He had to *prove it* even to the auditors. That was how damned skilfully it had been done. I tried to talk seriously to him, but he scarcely responded.

'Making money's the easiest thing in the world, as you well know,' he said.

I felt I had to object for the sake of objecting.

'But it is much easier to allow the money to disappear, provided one has the trust of the executive, of course,' he added, quite unmoved. 'And I had that, hadn't I?'

That remark shocked me profoundly. I haven't stuck to many so-called guiding principles in my life. I've been – let's say – unconventional in my business methods many times. But there are certain guidelines, certain concepts of honour that are unconditional to me and from which I definitely refuse to deviate. One of these is never to betray a trust, least of all consciously exploit a trust for one's own ends. It was terribly hurtful and almost incomprehensible that my own son had been capable of such appalling shabbiness.

I found it impossible to carry on the conversation. I was much too upset, and I couldn't really reprimand him, either. That would have been pointless, partly because there were so many factors still not yet clarified, and partly because he would not have accepted it. He would have already diverted it with a kind of icy, superior, purposeful authority in his stance, in his gaze.

Miles, as I said, had recently been appointed financial director of a large firm, the name of which I have no right to give in this context. Its managing director has been a good friend of mine for many years, which doesn't exactly make matters any less painful. He is also a member of my firm's board of management. That was how Miles was given such a good start in business immediately after – in record time – he had completed his exams. He complemented his degree in law with a degree in economics by working overtime during his first years with the firm. It is five or six years now since I arranged the job for him. The idea was that one day he would be a top executive in the company. And now this! My good friend naturally contacted me immediately after the revelation. He was just as confused, as bewildered and disturbed as I was. The whole thing was one single gigantic mystery.

One morning Miles had simply come through the door, sat down in the visitor's chair, handed in his resignation as if it were a purely routine matter, and in almost the same breath, had explained the reason, i.e. in a few brief laconic sentences he told them what he had done. He gave himself up. The police have not been informed. I've managed to procure that. Miles has a week in which to make a complete confession, telling how and why, and it is hoped, to retrieve as much of the money as possible. But something in his attitude tells me that before then he will probably go to the police himself. Or . . . no, I haven't the energy to speculate any further on this incomprehensible . . .

The rumours Helen so kindly told me about have, of course, no foundation whatsoever. All sheer rubbish. My firm is not on the brink of collapse, although it is true we have had some setbacks this last year. But of course my departure has nothing whatsoever to do with it. I am simply tired. No, I'm not. Not in the least tired. But I've done my bit, as I stated before. I had stood at the helm for over two decades, and that's a long time. The time had come for younger people to take over, time I made room for youth, gave youth a good start, just as I myself had been given a really good start – and known how to look after my pennies as the von Bladh family say. Reino L. has my complete confidence. He does indeed belong to a different generation and is one of those young careerists in the business world, who certainly have their idiosyncracies, running five kilometres between six and seven every morning, and preferring to play squash to another hour over lunch. I cannot deny that there are certain differences between us when it comes to running the firm. But on the whole, I'm convinced no one could be better equipped to carry on my work and take the firm into a flourishing future. Successful, efficient and reverential. With that, enough said on the truth of those idiotic rumours Helen was raving on about.

I was really going to write about Torbjörn. He is living here with me at the moment, with his own room and key and so on. Why

116

doesn't he wash his hair a little more often? I can't make Vanessa's letter out. It really is bewildering. She's been away for over three months. She hints she has met someone and this meeting has released some kind of conflict, but she expresses herself in such vague, abstract terms, I can't make out what it's all about. To tell the truth, I haven't even made out whether the person concerned is male or female. Certain indications speak for the one possibility, while others indicate . . . it's very annoying. On the other hand, she clearly seems to have had lengthy and difficult negotiations with some representative of the Leningrad Philharmonic. They are obviously very keen on her making a guest appearance towards the spring, i.e. just the time she would have preferred to rest and have some peace and quiet here in Helsinki. That's actually quite sufficient explanation for her delay. He heard her play Rachmaninov in Sydney, and wants her as a soloist in the same concerto during her guest appearances in Prague and Warsaw. Now Vanessa says she objects strongly to playing Rachmaninov in Richter's native country. But Prague and Warsaw aren't Richter's native country, are they? And there is no question of Leningrad or Moscow. Then there are sections of her letter which are full of the old familiar warmth and affection, her honesty, her honesty and love, and those sections compensate a great deal for the anxiety and despair gnawing at me because of Miles' terrible behaviour.

I've thought a great deal about one item in her letter. She says she has had an almost mystical experience of a religious–musical kind during a visit to St Paul's Cathedral, and that the recollection was very strong, because the circumstances happened to be connected with our first meeting at the Finnish Embassy in London. She describes it all very vividly; the only thing is, her story doesn't in any way coincide with my own memory of it.

She first mentions her own distaste and loathing for the huge crowds of cackling tourists daily profaning or directly polluting this sanctuary, previously so beautiful and impregnated with such powerful religious nobility. Tens and hundreds in groups of various sizes, like flocks of sheep, shuffling below the monumental vaulted roof with a guide at their head loudly babbling his foolish meaningless homework in English, German, French, Italian, and, more seldom, exotic languages such as Danish and Finnish. Middle-aged American females in full warpaint, the smell of cocktails emerging like bouquets of poisonous flowers from their mouths, uttering silly little sounds purporting to be astonishment or rapture,

117

their husbands wallowing in their wash, cameras on stomachs, great fat hairy ape-like men, sleepy and bored. Young girls clutching tourist brochures rushing round staring at everything with empty student-like curiosity, and bearded long-haired German youths in worn American army jackets and rucksacks on their backs energetically trying to avoid having to pay fifty pence at the entrance of the high point of glories, the Whispering Gallery. There is a constant noise all the time of the tramping and scraping of impious feet against stone flags, now and again culminating in shrill giggles, sudden bursts of laughter, self-satisfied, unmuted, stupid, semi-drunken remarks round some tomb.

This deliberate commercial desecration of a sacrosanct place, for her linked with so many unforgettable aesthetic as well as spiritual memories from her youth, had been a distressing and suffocating experience. She had been very upset, and although she regarded herself as essentially unreligious, she had been seized with a violent, almost irresistible impulse to rush up to one of the church officials, the priests, monks, deacons, whatever they were, and ask them to sweep the place clean, push out, drive away these hordes of listless self-absorbed little people, creeping round like mice without the slightest feeling for the nobility of the cathedral, its silent claim for respect and veneration. She had wanted to ask them firmly, like Jesus driving the moneylenders out of the temple. Or in this case was it the other way round, that the priests themselves were the moneylenders?

When she had been studying music for a winter in London as a young girl in the middle of the 'fifties, she had spent a lot of her spare time in St Paul's. She had relaxed there after strenuous exercises, meditating and gathering strength and peace of mind in the quietness beneath those grey vaulted arches. St Paul's had been a place of retreat, a place of safety, a refuge where she could regain balance and perspective on herself and her work in moments of despondency and lack of self-reliance. She had come to love this cathedral, Wren's architectural masterpiece, its consummate sacred beauty, its nobility inviting reverence, its monumental and at the same time simple, rugged, almost ascetic radiance, so unlike the overloaded, boastful, power-conscious gaudiness of St Peter's, Rome. She had had an almost physically perceptible experience of the idea of eternity in the brilliant architectural planning, the constant movement of those colossal stone columns forwards and upwards towards an unattainable source of light far away in space, far beyond everything

118

conceivable, explained and unexplained, a mote of dust of materialized infinity.

She had wandered round, mostly alone, undisturbed by tourists or other visitors to the cathedral, roaming in and out of the small side-chapels, gazing at the lavish royal tombs, becoming acquainted with the historic monuments and religious frescoes and paintings, meditating on the effigies of the great men of English history, John Donne, Samuel Johnson, Wellington and Nelson. She had heard the soughing of the wings of history. She had felt the spirit of immortal poetry touching her. Certainly it was an intense and romantic experience of an inexperienced young girl. But unforgettable all the same! One cloudy wet day a week before Easter, she had suddenly heard angels singing. She had found herself right up at the high altar, the immense space of the whole cathedral facing her. She had stood as if turned to stone, then collapsed sobbing on to the stone floor in humble contrition, as if struck by a lightning blow, a violent, inexplicable, religious or pseudo-religious revelation, a strange combination of emotional tension, spiritual passion, painful yearning for infinity and crass masochistic desire for self-obliteration. She heard angels singing! Not until later, much later, did she come to her senses and realize the sound was of the sopranos and child voices practising Bach's *St Matthew Passion*, which was to be performed in the cathedral on Maundy Thursday.

Perhaps this earlier experience of imagined angelic voices had unconsciously remained central to her store of memories. Anyhow, something similar had now occurred almost twenty years later, with the one difference, which was that the sense of humble contrition had been replaced by indignation and impotent rage on behalf of this sacred and apparently defenceless building being degraded and exploited in a loathsome manner for a fundamentally sub-human purpose in the interests of cheap, avaricious profiteering from the tourist industry. Blinded by tears, she had rushed aimlessly back and forth between the columns, tripping over children playing, bumping into strangers, hearing the unreal chanting of the guides as ritual, idolatrous worship echoing in her ears, and feeling panic, hysteria approaching. She had wanted to scream. She had wanted to grab hold of one of the black-coated men and rip his clothes to shreds. That was when for the second time the angel voices had intoned the introductory chorus of the *St Matthew Passion* in St Paul's Cathedral. She heard them perfectly clearly, but she swears that now she cannot decide whether this was an aural illusion or whether they really were human voices singing. But her hysteria vanished at once, the panic draining away. Suddenly she was quite calm, feeling almost secure, childishly secure, the voices, real or imaginary, acting on her as when she used to say her prayers with her mother when very small. Her indignation and impotent rage were transformed into a feeling of indefinite, all-embracing grief, controlled resignation, utterly in keeping with Bach's *St Matthew Passion*, the complete musical manifestation of the actual concept of grief, divine resignation before man's inadequacy or human resignation before the God who is dead, killed by man himself, the fleeing omnipotence.

In this stillness, in this condition of melancholy or harmonious grief, in this unreal soughing of angels in which she felt almost removed outside time, my image had slowly appeared in her memory – how moved and happy I was when I read those lines in her letter – in exactly the same garments and form I had had at that embassy party in London so many years ago. And, she adds, it must have been *because you had then talked about the St Matthew Passion for so long, with such spontaneous, juvenile enthusiasm and with a kind of personal empathy.*

Had talked about the *St Matthew Passion*? Had I talked about the *St Matthew Passion*? This statement, more than any other in her letter, is what I don't understand. Did I even know the *St Matthew Passion* at the time? Yes, I probably did. But presumably still in a cautiously prejudiced, almost deprecatory way. Jacob was the one who kept dithering on about the *St Matthew Passion*. And that was reason enough for me to maintain an indifferent distance from this work, the greatness of which – I'm sure – Vanessa herself taught me to understand. She was the one who taught me to love the *St Matthew Passion* and listen to it without barriers or inhibitions, with enthusiasm and emotion. How then could I have been able to talk about it 'with spontaneous, juvenile enthusiasm' at our first meeting? At the embassy in London? Well, I suppose it was already a matter of passion then. But by no means St Matthew's. By no means Bach. I had been chiefly preoccupied with Rosa's death. I had talked about my daughter.

Or is it the other way round, and Vanessa is right, that my memory is completely at fault? In that case, this is a frightening symptom of age. Am I getting old? Or has Vanessa, during that disturbing moment in St Paul's, in some unconscious way confused me, the image of me, with the long-winded, but certainly enthusiastic enough expoundings she has undoubtedly heard from Jacob on various occasions? In that case, one may well ask what her relationship with Jacob really is? What is their real relationship? How stupid! What would she see in that wizened old bore? And even if that were so. Jacob is undoubtedly impotent. I'm convinced he has not been able to perform a respectable sexual act for the last twenty years. What on earth am I writing now? Airing my jealousy? In Jacob's direction! Of all directions! Madness!

On the other hand, when I come to think about it, that more or less failed artistic oddball, that peculiar and pathetic upholder of all kinds of traditions, what a part he has played in my personal life! Again and again, he has intervened on the most unexpected occasions. And what extraordinary powers of attraction he has had to so many members of my large and constantly growing family. As with Torbjörn now, for instance. Yes, Torbjörn.

When I got back home at about eleven last night after an important meeting with some bigwigs, and by that I mean very highly placed and influential men, with whom I had discussed the world situation, the energy crisis, and Chile, for certain politico-economic reasons of great significance to the particular branch of business I represent . . . well, Torbjörn was sitting at the dining-room table with his face in his hands.

In front of him on the table was a green plastic mug, the one he uses when he cleans his teeth, and a bottle of wine he had taken out of my cupboard. Naturally it was not cheap wine, but a bottle of Chateau Talbot '45 – already half-empty. There is something different about Torbjörn, outwardly, too. He is not like any of his brothers and sisters, either the half-siblings or full siblings. He has red hair and his whole face is almost perforated with freckles. His plump and rather clumsy hands are also covered with freckles. Miles is dark, and Rosa was dark, too. His sisters Anna and Carola, on the other hand, are both fair. And little Hans, or Hannu, is so fair you could almost say he is white-haired.

But Torbjörn is red-haired. Red in all respects, for that matter. Like most of his contemporaries he has let his hair grow, but he rarely washes it and it hangs in unbeautiful greasy strands over his shoulders. He is unusually unhygienic and looks generally grubby, his nails uncut and dirty, and there is usually a faint, almost numbing odour of sweat and stale alcohol around him. I find this difficult. He is repellent. He seems repulsive to me against my will, in spite of the fact I do my best to control my repugnance.

'You might have chosen a cheaper brand,' I said, unable to conceal my irritation.

'What the hell does it matter to you if I drink six or sixty marks' worth at your expense?' he mumbled.

'Chateau Talbot is far too good a wine to be knocked back like that from a plastic mug.'

'Go to hell.'

He was still mumbling vaguely, but he did look up in the end. Then I noticed he was weeping.

What does one do with almost adult sons crying at one's dining-table and drinking expensive wine out of a plastic mug? How does one console them? *Ought* they to be consoled at all? I felt helpless and confused, as well as slightly embarrassed and consequently irritable.

'Torbjörn,' I said, putting my hand on his shoulder. 'Why are you crying?'

He turned round, clung to my sleeve with both hands and pressed his face hard against my arm. Now he was crying at full volume, sobbing violently and uncontrollably, almost howling. I hadn't the slightest idea what to do. It was horribly painful. But I realized he must be very drunk and that this bottle of Talbot was perhaps the third that day, or even the fourth, as far as he was concerned.

'Allende's dead!' he wailed.

That was quite true, but the military coup in Chile had happened several months earlier. I thought this violent reaction seemed just slightly *post festum*, but I still didn't know what to say to him.

'Do you understand! Do you understand – Allende's dead!' he wailed again.

What does one say to that? Yes? Yes, I understand?

Then I saw that he already knew something that I didn't know. Something about Miles. He had simply been better informed than I was, because he was closer to Miles than I was. That same morning, he had visited Miles and Miles had said something, or hinted at something, or just behaved in a way that had made Torbjörn suspicious, and he had put two and two together, and now seemed to see the future as if it had already happened. But naturally he refused to believe those cruel omens, refused to believe the logical development of life at this late stage, this far too late stage, the logic of which was so obvious and the same time so brutal and inexplicable.

Allende is dead! If I'd known Torbjörn better, if my son had been less repulsive in his uncontrolled outburst, if I had then understood, had a chance to be clear-sighted and consequently had a possibility of putting a spoke in the wheel of fate? Stop him? What's the point of speculating? For others apart from God? For he had in fact been sitting there weeping for the evil of the world, clearly and unambiguously, because that is what he is like, that is the kind of person he is. But he was not drunk because of the evil of the world. Is that what I should have understood?

He drinks too much. Miles has always been careful with spirits, or tolerated spirits; anyhow I've never seen him the worse for drink. While Torbjörn as a rule clearly drinks with the definite aim in mind to get drunk. He is unreliable and unpredictable in his behaviour, but I cannot believe he is without talent. Miles was always best in class, but Torbjörn found school difficult. He passed his final exams at the second attempt, but now refuses to go to university. Somehow, he doesn't seem to want to be anything at all. He is trying to establish himself as a kind of free artist, writing a bit of poetry and doing some painting and so on, and he is always trotting off to Jacob with a kind of triumphant defiance directed at me personally, to gain inspiration and guidance and valuable advice from The Great Forerunner and Master. This does not inspire very great confidence and I must say I am extremely worried. He spends a large part of his time in an obscure artists' café which seems to be the 'in' place, in the company of like-minded brothers of misfortune, naïve world reformers, and more or less failed artists of a kind. I went there once. He telephoned one evening, as drunk as a lord and insolent to boot, and asked me to come and bail him out as he hadn't enough money to pay the bill. It was a dreadful place. His companions were dreadful. But what could I do but meekly pay up? And to cap it all, stand them all another round, insolently urged to do so by the whole bearded company.

'Why do you mix with those awful people?' I asked him.

'They're my only friends.'

So what can I do?

I can't make out why he came to live here with me, apart from the simple explanation, of course, that he couldn't stand it at Gunnel's. It's not a question of money; once and for all, it is not a question of money now in my family. He dislikes me and he shows it quite clearly with a kind of scornful contempt which is often unbearably wounding. Hasn't a father the right to be hurt by his child as much as children are by their father? I do my best to fit in with him and give him the freedom and independence he so clearly wants and presumably also needs. In other words, I try to give him everything which as far as I can see Gunnel denied him from a kind of distorted, prolonged, hard-won sense of maternal responsibility. But he is very difficult to please, I must admit. He has created an image of me which I don't recognize and which bears no relation whatsoever to reality. I am definitely not the uneducated bourgeois philistine, the insensitive bounder of a business man he imagines me to be. That is a misunderstanding. It is a pity he so obviously appears to like the misunderstanding. We don't know each other. We have never had occasion to become more closely acquainted. Perhaps I, too, have misunderstood him.

He was only nine when I left Gunnel and our marriage was dissolved. What can he remember of the time when we lived together? His first childhood years; did we know each other then? He grew up with a nurse. I saw to my work, travelled a great deal, and was often out to dinner or charity balls with Gunnel. To tell the truth, he can't have seen very much of his father. His main impression of me must have been based on second-hand information, on what he heard, or was indoctrinated with after the divorce, Gunnel's lying descriptions of me, her libellous accounts of our marriage, her deliberate and spiteful blackening of my character, brought up over and over again before our children. If in some respects she was a siren of the woods while we were married, she was transformed into a witch after the separation. Traces of this have spilled over on to Torbjörn. We don't get on very well, and yet he has dug himself in here with me in my home, and all the signs indicate he intends to say. Sometimes I have an unpleasant feeling that he is doing it primarily out of a kind of morbid desire to torment me.

One night a few weeks ago, he had come home at about four in the morning, and the first thing he did was to throw up on the hall rug, and then he refused to clear it up, or was so exhausted he was unable to. I had to do it, that nauseating, stinking job, while, staggering and swaying, he propped himself against the wall, half-asleep, more unconscious than conscious, and *stood there watching*, and, in spite of his wretched condition, with an unmistakably scornful smile spreading over his puffy - repellent - face. My desire to hit him was almost too much for me, but I didn't. Prevented by constricted feelings of guilt? Prevented by a hidden, almost completely denied, but nevertheless vibrantly active and indelible guilty conscience?

124

Gunnel was a dominating person. One might say she had a highly developed sense of territory, to use one of the fashionable words in the study of human and animal behaviour. The family was Gunnel's territory. The home was Gunnel's territory. And as a dog squirts its markers in all the places where it wishes to show it is master, so Gunnel managed the household to show just who was the heart of the home. She was no shrew for that. She was only a responsible and dutiful wife. The ideal wife, it is called. It could well be said that she had a strong need to hold the threads in all internal relations of the family, even those in which she was not a partner. When I played with the girls, she was usually very quickly there, wanting to play, too, and then it was often no longer any fun. Or when I talked to Torbjörn, she would come and intervene in the conversation, criticizing what I said, or explaining that I was talking nonsense and that she herself knew better. In that way, she was everywhere. She cast a long shadow in our home.

Of course, I had 'married above me' when I married her. The Lindermann family are much like the von Bladh family, wealthy, influential, bourgeois to the marrow. Nevertheless, it was not a question of a direct *mésalliance* on Gunnel's part. For if I had been an up-and-coming young man as a communist and son-in-law to Hannes Kaapola, then I was the same to an equal extent as Gunnel Lindermann's progressive, expectant, ambitious young husband. But the situation had its problems. Like most people born into the world within the secure and narrow framework of the traditionally established middle classes, Gunnel was profoundly class-conscious. She was also, as I have already mentioned, a dominating personality. The fact that she felt such a strong commitment to my bourgeois education came from this. I do not deny it could have its good and useful sides, but the fervour with which she set about instructing me unfortunately probably reduced the effect somewhat and was, to say the least, a trifle, well, psychologically unsound. She remarked on my table manners, she remarked on my language, regardless of the company we were in. In other words, she was pedantic, obsessed with unimportant details, and if generals and colonels are considered to be those who make the greatest plans, then Gunnel mostly moved in irritating and foolishly pedantic little circles of corporals and sergeants.

It would undeniably be a lie and coquetry to maintain that I was a roughneck when we married. Naturally I knew how to handle a knife and fork. Hannes Kaapola had already taught me how to mix with people, although that was perhaps not relevant to the more subtle variations of bourgeois rites. On the other hand, it is possible, I suppose, that I did tease Gunnel a little with my 'lack of breeding', partly out of genuine uncertainty, but also often just to annoy her. She took this fairly seriously, almost making it her life's work to eliminate the worst crudities, polishing my original, slightly grubby, proletarian façade shiny and bourgeois bright.

What did I learn? At this moment, I can only remember certain familiar comments, such useful witty statements as 'Hm, said the Count, in broken Portuguese, a language he mastered well'. That was quite a legitimate and indeed much appreciated conversational gambit, making fun of the peculiarities of dialect or linguistic misunderstandings of the 'peasants'. If someone in the company had returned in the autumn from his summer place in the islands and had met a 'bumpkin' who said 'professional' instead of 'provisional', that was a good story to laugh at at intimate dinner-parties all through to Christmas. But in fairness, I have to add that there was a generation gap. Bourgeois mannerisms among the younger generation were more modified, less ritualistic, more political.

Then I remember once when I committed a gaffe at a New Year's party given by one of Gunnel's relatives, and was given a good dressing-down by Gunnel on our way home in the small hours. We were newly married then, and I knew practically no one at the party. I was to be introduced, or to introduce myself. I was probably no more coarse or vulgar than most of the other men there, but it was just that I hadn't been able to devote myself to that special bourgeois talent of being coarse and vulgar with some elegance, saying foolish things so that somehow they sounded brilliant. We mixed in with all those economists and engineers and schoolmasters and medical students with (*avec*) wives and fiancées and Gunnel said 'Hullo', or 'Good evening', or 'How nice to see you', but I said 'Donald Duck' and each time I said 'Duck', I ducked. It was not a success. In fact, it was straight agony. I had still not learnt the bourgeoisie's special skill at serving up cheap remarks in studied, pretentious wrappings.

In the third or fourth year of our marriage, something went wrong with our sex life. Gunnel was suddenly less willing or somehow indifferent, and the so-called unfaithfulness I had occasionally previously indulged in, with a guilty conscience and as if with closed eyes, I now devoted myself to fairly ruthlessly and with fresh courage.

In the end, of course, Gunnel couldn't help noticing what was going on. She herself was largely indifferent, as I said before, and I don't know whether during all the time we were married she ever had a single serious erotic experience on the side. But mine were numerous. What Gunnel relinquished with regard to marital delights, she made up for in housewifely and instructional industriousness. She was wholly established as Mrs Blaadh. Any more radical changes in her life simply did not enter her mind. When Laura came into the picture and I asked for a divorce, she was consequently caught totally unawares, unprepared and deeply shocked.

The divorce transformed Gunnel in a frightening manner. Where she had previously been affectionate, controlled, cultivated, she now became aggressive, vulgar and ruthless. Her sense of territory seemed to overstep the pathological boundaries. And I was part of the territory. She could not voluntarily give me up.

She had to fight for *her right to me* to the very last drop of blood. It was a revolting and humiliating spectacle, not least because she forced me, or lured me, on her own simple or horribly distorted conditions, into taking part in these grotesque acts and this infamous and fantastic knife-throwing of blame. Her hatred of Laura was monumentally pathetic and odious, and the alternating organized slander and open uninhibited outbursts of rage she kept descending to were so painful they cannot be repeated here.

She quite quickly managed to isolate me almost completely from the children. She wanted a court order made out so that I should not even be allowed to see them, for I was a bad man, morally deficient, amoral and incompetent as a father and guardian of the young. Her bitterness was that boundless. Fortunately, the court could not approve such preposterous demands. But she managed it all quite well all the same, through her manipulations, dropping daily little drips of poison into the children's small defenceless ears, and they soon did not wish to see any more of me. They acquired a total aversion to me. Gunnel is a very strong person and her power over other people can be great if she so wishes. Who could she be compared with? Lady Macbeth? Hamlet's mother? Years went by before I was able to make contact again with the children, and then primarily only with Torbjörn.

He says he could not endure Gunnel's bourgeois prejudices any longer, her reactionary political views, her dominating authoritarian ways, her whining, her nagging, her vanity. So he has come back to his father – after all these years. The girls also seem to be moving out of their mother's sphere of influence, but in which direction I don't know. Not in mine anyhow. That's how it is in life. Nothing is constant. Everything is perpetually changing, some to the good, others to the bad. I don't know what to think about Torbjörn. I don't know what to do about him. It's a test of a kind. A new kind of experience. I want to do my best, because I do like him in many ways and he is, after all, my son. If only he had one single line staked out in his life, then it would probably be easier for us to live under the same roof. Together.

I had meant to go into Jacob's peculiar writ of accusation to the Attorney-General in detail here. But when I read through the previous pages, I grew thoughtful and felt I simply had to add some comment. Everything rang so falsely, so hypocritically, ingratiating and mendacious.

I don't have that kind of sentimental paternal feeling for Torbjörn. I'm not bursting with goodwill in my relationship with him. The truth is, he drives me mad and I wish him in hell, but I keep up appearances as best I can. I doubt very much it will work at all when Vanessa comes back. It's not a question of space, as there's plenty of that here, six rooms to be exact. That's more than enough for Vanessa and me. But Torbjörn is one too many, and it'd be a lie not to admit it. He takes up too much space, slopping about, leaving traces everywhere behind him, and he is ever-present with his melancholy, his loafing about, his dirtiness and the smell of drink. I cannot endure it in the long run. That's the truth.

Then Gunnel. How *could* I distort and misrepresent the picture of this woman, in many respects so wonderful, in that terrible way? True, her good bourgeois upbringing sloughed off remarkably rapidly once she realized I was not going to give up my request for a divorce, and she underwent a transformation which I cannot describe in any other way but as animal, just as the bourgeois middle classes collectively undergo a kind of animal process of transformation when their political power is threatened, as during our civil war in 1918, or more recently in the military coup in Chile. But, for all that, she was no witch on the heath as in *Macbeth*. Far from it. During our many happy years of marriage, she was, on the contrary, a good wife, a

128

warm woman, an unswervingly loyal companion. We enjoyed life together, most of all when there were just the two of us. At one time, perhaps our best years, we used to go to the tower at the Palace whenever we had a free evening to ourselves, and the head-waiter would say 'Welcome back, Mr Blaadh,' and we would have a meal and drink a bottle of good red wine and hold hands on the white table-cloth, talking about everything on earth as the lights from the South Harbour fractured in the black water and the Sveaborg ferry lights regularly disappeared and reappeared behind Blek Isle.

Gunnel loved me and did not want to lose me, and when I stopped loving her and wanted to marry Laura, she could not accept it. Of course I understand her bitterly violent reactions. After ten happy years. Or do I? I don't know. In actual fact, I am now faced with the same complicated, intractable tangle of problems as when I was to write about my childhood and parents. I found I didn't know anything for certain about my childhood. I couldn't write about it. It seemed foreign country to me, an alien time in which every recollection seemed illusory and inadequate, every definite statement an untruth. I had never known my parents. I knew nothing about them. I was unable to say anything definite about them. That was inhibiting and crippling. It is exactly the same now when it comes to Gunnel. I know nothing definite about her. I never knew her. I don't know anyone.

Consequently, it is impossible to write about a reality one only thinks one experienced. It doesn't work. If one doesn't accept that one is a liar. A liar in principle. And I don't want to do that, do I? I might as well cease now, then. Stop. I'm stopping. That task is unrealizable. I have failed and admit it. I have suffered a defeat. That's it. No!

I will never admit defeat! I'm going on! Lies or truth, what the hell, it makes no difference. I have been grossly slandered, accused of a crime I never committed. For Christ's sake, surely I have the right to defend myself as much as anyone else. In a free country. Jacob's writ, then. THAT isn't invented, anyhow. That's a document. Jacob! He speaks for himself! I can neither revise nor touch up him! Herewith his litany:

To the Attorney-General

Sir,

As I do not appear to be able to achieve justice ['achieve

justice'! *How wretchedly he expresses himself. Writes as badly as he paints. My italics.*] in the normal way, and as even approaches to the police have been met with shrugs and scornful smiles, I am venturing to write to you to draw your attention to a matter which from the public point of view superficially may appear to be trivial, but which for me personally and for the whole of my family is a matter of greatest importance.

The matter concerns an invaluable family record of the von Bladh, Bladh and Lehtisuon-Lehtinen families, which until about three months ago was in my possession, and which a person by the name of Donald Blaadh (or Blad) has unlawfully appropriated or directly stolen, with great insolence and the use of force, essential material from the aforementioned family archives. Every effort on my part to persuade this Blaadh (or Blad) to return these stolen goods has hitherto been rejected with the most humiliating audacity and arrogance (which by the way would come as no surprise to anyone aware of the underhand and base character of the person concerned).

In this context and for a person in your position and with your education, it should be superfluous to render further account or remind you of the eminent contributions representatives of the above-mentioned families or branches of them have made to our common Fatherland over the years. In the fields of statesmanship and politics, industry, science and belles lettres, the names of von Bladh, Bladh and Lehtisuon-Lehtinen are to be found everywhere, without exception represented by men of wisdom, energy and drive, initiative, irreproachability and justice. Of this, Sir, you are sure to be as aware as the undersigned, a more recent, possibly unworthy, but reverential descendant. Under such circumstances, it will surely be as clear to you as to me what an irretrievable catastrophe the consequences would be if private documents concerning the lives and deeds of these great men should fall into the wrong hands, to be exploited for vulgar purposes which bear no relation to tradition or historical truth.

So I am applying to you, Sir, in your capacity as the Highest Guardian of the Law in this country, with all your judicial and personal authority, to compel the aforementioned Donald Blaadh (or Blad) to return to their rightful owner the documents he has so treacherously and unjustifiably appropriated.

That this man has evil intentions is quite evident. His aim is to abuse the truth found in letters and journals and other documents of both a private and official nature, to create a scurrilous picture of historical reality, adapted and tailored by his primitive, bitter but self-righteous and vengeful mind. I myself have spent half a

130

lifetime arranging and cataloguing, putting these papers in order, so that now at last, on the threshold of my old age, I can approach the immensely responsible task of committing the history of my family to paper, giving a truthful and reverential picture of the central rôle its individual members have played in our political, economic and scientific development. It is obvious that a family history of this kind, based on unique source material and conceived with a loving fidelity to historical truth as well as to its essential subject, will be of interest far beyond the confines of the family circle and the perhaps more emotional attention paid to it.

All this valuable great work, that I have undertaken, not from self-aggrandisement or an exaggerated sense of personal literary resources, which on the contrary, I am painfully aware that I lack, but from a sense of duty, and a strong though humble wish to repay some of the good fortune and priceless advantages I have gained from being born into a family with such magnificent and binding traditions, is now threatened with destruction by the criminal action of one single base and ruthless deed. I therefore pray for justice, for, as will be seen from the above, there is far more than my personal honour and prestige at stake.

To emphasize the seriousness of this matter even further, and to illuminate the vile and painful nature of it, I respectfully beg to take up your time and attention by touching with a few more words on the said Donald Blaadh (or Blad), his background, character and intentions.

Donald Blaadh (or Blad) is a fraud. His morality is, to say the least, doubtful, his character remarkable for its spinelessness and a strong inclination to debauchery of various kinds. He is a man without scruples, without compassion or feeling for his kin, a man without honour or conscience. These may seem hard words, an exaggeratedly negative judgement, but I know what I am talking about, I know Donald Blaadh (or Blad) and have known him for almost thirty years. Our first meeting was in the autumn of 1944, when he had recently returned on leave from the war and was in a state of great wretchedness and need, financial, spiritual and, not least, moral. He visited me and begged for my support and aid on the pretext of an extremely frail, to say the least, family connection, of the truth of which he has still been unable to provide satisfactory proof.

As I have already mentioned, a fact which should be sufficiently well known to need no special emphasis, I belong to a family whose male members have always distinguished themselves by their irreproachability and unusually strict morality. However, this Donald B., whose surname was spelt simply Blad at the time,

131

then came along and maintained he was the son of a 'cousin', until that moment totally and completely unknown to me. This fantasy of his runs along the lines that his grandfather, a seaman, smallholder and later owner-occupier of his farm, called Johan or Jussi Blad (Hämäläinen, really) was supposed to be the *illegitimate son* of my grandfather, Karl-Johan von Bladh, that distinguished senator in the political and economic history of our country.

The insolence of his statement was in direct proportion to the absolute certainty with which it was stated. Obviously, under no circumstances could I have any faith in this unusually outrageous fabrication. Naturally Karl-Johan von Bladh had no illegitimate children. His character, his adherence to moral principles, his ideals, the whole of his attitude to life, was in sharp contrast to any deeds with consequences of a similar unforeseen and fraught kind. The parish registers show no evidence whatsoever of Donald Blad's statement, and to make sure, I have checked this. There is indeed a certain Kreetta Hämäläinen mentioned, a spinning-mill worker at the Finnish Clothing Factory, who gave birth on 12 April, 1864, to a boy, baptized Jussi (later changed to Johan), *with father unknown*.

In actual fact there is on the whole no legally binding document or other plausible documents worth mentioning to support or even less to verify the correctness of this fantasy of Donald Blaadh's, Blad in reality. Donald Blad is a liar. The similarity of name is pure coincidence, which in keeping with his devious disposition, he skilfully realized he could exploit. Similarly, it is pure coincidence that the father, or the son, that is Donald Blad's father and Jussi Blad's son, Brynolf Blad, happened to serve for most of his life as caretaker at No. 76, Skarpskytte Street in Helsinki, an apartment block built in 1896 by Professor Mattias Peter Bladh (later Matti Lehtisuon-Lehtinen) and still the property of the Lehtisuon-Lehtinen family.

Donald Blaadh (or Blad) is then, I repeat, a liar. Although I have always been convinced of this since our first meeting, forced on me at the time, considering his miserable situation and wretched status, I could not help giving him some modest financial aid, as well as, not least, moral support. Well, in the interests of truth and as some explanation and elucidation, I should perhaps add that I acquired a kind of paradoxical personal liking for him, as he by no means lacked a certain charm in all his ignorant awkwardness and crude insolence. He was not stupid. On the contrary, Donald Blaadh (or Blad) is an intelligent person, which his later career, or rampages I should say, have clearly shown. But this intelligence of his, combined with an unusually strong streak

132

of selfishness and lack of moral responsibility, has unfortunately seldom been used for the public good. I have only to recall the famous, or rather infamous, events connected with his deplorably notorious appointment as Minister of Defence in Vanne's interim government ten years or so ago. This appointment, soon swiftly to become a disgrace to the whole country, denotes in its way a culmination of his career as a master of intrigue and grandiose perpetuator of self-interest ['perpetuator of self-interest!' *Jacob, Jacob, what stylistic brilliance you have developed. My italics.*] with exalted political contacts and somewhat shady financial connections.

Perhaps it would be too much to say that, temporarily, there arose between us a purely friendly relationship. But there is no denying there was a certain affection on my part. Perhaps it would be more correct to describe what at the start of our acquaintance I felt for D. Blad as a kind of paternal protective zeal. He was thrown out into the world, alone and helpless, and I could not deny him the support of an adult man with experience and strength as well both financial and moral resources. How bitterly I was to regret my credulity and the trust I so generously offered him. But enough of that. I have no one but myself to blame and I am not in the habit of abandoning myself to pointless, self-centred lamentations.

Donald Blaadh (or Blad) is a parasite on society. His only true love and passion is for money and, most transitory and vain of all, the material goods this world has to offer. He has left three devastated marriages behind him without the slightest twinge of conscience. Faithfulness is an unknown concept to him. The extramarital activities to which he devotes a large part of his time with monomanic and self-righteous fervour are legion, innumerable. He has cold-bloodedly abandoned five children, at least one of whom was born out of wedlock, cowardly fleeing from his responsibilities as a father. The only qualities that can compete in intensity with his avarice for money are his intrigues and vanity. This is where we come to the very core of the whole matter. What are his true intentions in relation to his theft of the von Bladh family archives? Also, how is it that the police, in spite, as I have already mentioned, of being repeatedly and urgently informed, refuse to take up this obvious and serious crime? Just how corrupt is the police force in this country?

I am convinced that Donald Blaadh (or Blad) has in fact a double intention in this treacherous and criminal action of his. Driven by his boundless social vanity and insidious social inferiority, using all available documents and notes in the family

133

records, he is first intending to attempt in the most authentic manner possible to produce evidence of the lie being after all the truth, by which I mean that von Bladh blood does *de facto* flow in his veins and that in a legally binding sense, he will form a branch, unlike the others, if not also not directly specifically distinct, of the family tree. And he also intends to depict the destinies of our family through reflections in a jester's mirror, making fun of the noble von Bladh family and its now-Finnish middle-class branches, in order to misrepresent and ridicule them, driven by his desire for revenge and by his social bitterness, his social inferiority complex, in my opinion a superfluous burden he shares with many others who these days have worked themselves up from the lower classes. In short his intention is to violate history, to belittle elevated and important historical deeds, and, with falsified documentation, to degrade and sling mud at defenceless and in reality honourable historical personalities. This must not happen, and, I repeat, under the present circumstances, you, Sir, are the only person with the power to stop it.

To demonstrate the extraordinary seriousness inherent in my appeal regarding this loathsome and disturbing crime, I wish finally to remind you that Donald Blad, who today calls himself Blaadh, has an extremely dubious communist past. At an earlier stage in his life, he was an active and trusted member of the Communist Party of Finland, and through his first marriage to Sinikka Kaapola, a present Member of Parliament, he was intimate with leading circles of the party in question. There is no factual evidence that these intimate connections ceased with the dissolution of his marriage about twenty years ago, or when Blaadh (or Blad) left the party at approximately the same time as his divorce, clearly primarily for opportunistic reasons.

So I ask myself the question why it is that there are no powerful reasons for suspecting Donald Blaadh (or Blad) of general political unreliability as a result of this continued, concealed, communist double-act, an accusation which in respect of the Communist Party's present legality has no legal value, but notwithstanding should give rise in every right-thinking citizen of this country to considerable doubts of a social and moral kind. There is also a risk that the Bladh family archive in the hands of an orthodox and unscrupulous communist might give rise to the most morbid and nefarious misinterpretations of historical truth, in other words constitute what is called inflammable material for those most concerned.

D. Blaadh (or Blad) has important connections, exalted connections of extraordinary power and extraordinary influence in our country. You, Sir, know this as well as I do. The question is simply how it is possible in a western society that such connections involve power and authority to exercise pressure on the police to the frightening extent evident in this case, in such a flagrant and disturbing manner, a man putting himself above the law? I beg, Sir, for your intervention. Indeed, I demand, in the name of justice and western democracy, that a thorough, impartial and radical investigation be made into this case without delay.

Helsinki, 21.9.1973
Jacob von Bladh
Baron. Portrait painter.

This astonishing evidence of paranoia, in itself naturally profoundly offensive, but essentially nothing but a tragicomic farce, is equipped with an appendix, which if nothing else, quite eloquently illustrates the degree of popularity I enjoy in the family. 'Appendix 1' it says in the top left-hand corner, and then follows a mighty salvo:

'As the undersigned, members of the family concerned, have read the above document composed by Jacob von Bladh, portrait painter, we respectfully wish to inform you that in all essential respects we share Jacob von Bladh's, our kinsman's, views and impressions *vis-à-vis* the said person, Donald Blaadh (or Blad), and that on the basis of personal experience and with honour and good conscience, we can confirm the correctness of the facts as laid out in the aforementioned document. We wish, Sir, for your information to reaffirm that we wholeheartedly support our kinsman, Jacob von Bladh, in his determined demand that the most thorough possible judicial and impartial investigation be made of the above case which concerns us in the most disturbing manner, and also that we unreservedly associate ourselves with his expectations that the above-mentioned considerable and priceless part of our family archive, the von Bladh archive, reverentially administered by Jacob von Bladh, be returned without delay, through the purposeful procedure of the case in question, to its rightful owner and administrator, here synonymous with our kinsman, Jacob von Bladh, portrait painter.'

Martti Lehtisuon-Lehtinen
Professor Emeritus
Kaarlo Lehtisuon-Lehtinen
Bank Director.

135

It was after eleven o'clock at night when he phoned. That was already the second time this week. He asked me to come over, and all I could do was to go, although I was already in my dressing-gown and slippers. It takes just about twenty minutes on foot. He won't expect me before that, anyhow. He knows I leave the car in the garage, to get the exercise.

This has gone on for many years. Am I obeying orders? Or am I loyally fulfilling demands of a rather more unusual kind made by our friendship? After my resignation, a year passed before he made contact again. And yet I was constantly hovering in doubt as to the real reason for my appointment. Had he really thought I had the necessary resources for a top politician? A drastic way of showing me my place? Teaching me more? Because perhaps I was becoming far too familiar, far too domineering, far too importunate and know-all in our personal relations? Is that game possible at the level on which the destiny of a nation and a people is determined? Game? Whatever it was a question of at the time, he had given me a confidence which I . . . well, I betrayed.

And yet in the end I was restored to favour again. We have the same simple origins, the same modest starting-point. But so have a great many people. Perhaps it is his hunger for knowledge. His attitude to life itself? Social appetite. An insatiable appetite for life. 'You're the only one I can talk shit to nowadays,' he says. Perhaps that's so. But why should it be? Once, several years ago, we talked about personal weakness. 'What's your weak point?' I said. 'Have you any weak points at all?' He looked at me without answering for a long time. He gave me a stern look. Then he went out of the room and came back with a crumpled newspaper cutting which he carelessly flung down on the table in front of me. While I read it, he stood turned away, his hands behind his back. It was undated, a brief laconic report of an engineer in his thirties who had been killed in a road accident somewhere in the interior of the country. The name was unknown to me, and I don't even remember it now. 'That was my son,' he said, still turned away. I didn't really see what that had to do with personal weakness, and never have done. But it was a confidence. He gave me a personal confidence. Perhaps he was saying that confidence is weakness?

A drunk in a good overcoat and wolfskin cap was standing outside the iron gates, swaying and mumbling to himself. When he saw me and realized I was going in, he came closer and examined me with a forbidding expression.

'Who t'hell are you?' he said.

'Eckerman,' I replied.

'What bloody Eckerman . . . you the Prime Minister?'

'No,' I said, going on through the gate.

'Bloody arse-licker. Give him my regards, and tell him we'll drown him in the Kolera Pool in the name of the fatherland, for Christ's sake!'

I was suddenly furiously angry. Although I was almost halfway across the yard, I stopped and turned, then quickly retraced my steps.

'Shut up!' I said quietly.

'Oh, shit! You're no gent in this house, anyhow.'

I opened the gate again and went right out on to the street.

'Be off or I'll bash your head in,' I said, staring straight at him, my face no more than a foot from his.

'Go to hell, arse-licker. I recognize you. I've seen you somewhere,' he said thickly.

'Be off,' I said, gesturing with my right arm.

He began to lope off.

'Big Boy and his lackey, for Christ's sake,' I heard him drooling.

I regretted it as soon as it was over. My inexcusable aggressiveness. My unfortunate desire to come to grips even when it is quite unnecessary. Dregs! Rightist dregs! Bourgeois riff-raff!

I passed the guard standing immobile in his sentry-box. Ollie let me in. He was very informally dressed in dressing-gown and pyjamas, but with a white silk scarf round his neck like a desperate gesture to the conventions, to the guard, or to emphasize his dignity as butler under any circumstances.

'God, had you already gone to bed?' I said.

'I've got a temperature and bronchial trouble,' he said blankly, coughing.

'Dreadful of us to dig you out in the middle of the night then. I'm truly sorry.'

'We've all got our job to do,' he said, an undertone in his voice I could not fathom. Did he literally mean that, or was he discreetly pulling my leg?

He took my hat and overcoat and carried them as we climbed the stairs.

He was sitting in the library listening to Shostakovich's *Leningrad Symphony*. That slow heightening. That endless march. That tenacious endurance. That indomitability. He switched it off when I came in.

'I can't sleep,' he said.

'Neither can I.'

He pretended not to hear the insinuating tone in my voice.

'Shostakovich is for resolution what chess if for sharpening the mind, a kind of exercise-bicycle. But of course you don't play chess.'

'No, but I have a gramophone.'

'Today we'll start with a little quiz. Who made the following immortal remark: "The owl of Minerva rises first when dusk falls"?'

'I don't know.'

'That doesn't surprise me. The level of education in the private enterprise section of our country is admittedly low, but I'll help you a little. "When philosophy paints grey on to grey hair, a way of life has become obsolete and cannot be rejuvenated with grey on grey" – it's in the same sentence – well, I've made it easy for you now. Who wrote that?'

'No idea.'

'Hegel, of course. No marks for you and three for me. Now here's an easy one. On of the greatest connoisseurs of human nature in the world said: "Those who wish to describe a country stand on the plains to regard the mountain and climb mountains to regard the plains, just as one should be a prince to understand the people and a simple man to understand princes." Whose wise words are those? You've been given the answer almost free.'

'God knows, I don't. I'm bad at quotes. Mao, maybe?'

'Wrong again. Prince, prince, don't you see . . . that couldn't be anyone else but Machiavelli. Now I've got six points and you've still nil. Machiavelli is the author who in some respects has meant most to me. In his complete freedom from prejudice and illusion, before Marx and Lenin, he is the thinker in the history of the world who in many ways knew most about the condition of man . . . "The mob plays the main rôle in the world. The few wise people there are will not come into their own until the mob stands at a loss." That's not bad, if by the mob he means the people . . . or "what is gained with other people's aid becomes an enduring victory". What do you think of that? As early as in the sixteenth century and could have been said by Lenin . . . and was. I'll give you another chance. We'll move on to music. Do you remember the introductory bars of the "Jägar

March" by Sibelius . . . taadaadaadaa taadaadaadaa . . . ?'

'Yes.'

'Which great classic is Sibelius plagiarizing there? Direct plagiarism, I mean.'

'I should know that. Liszt? No, Tchaikovsky?'

'Wrong. It's Bach in his *St Matthew Passion*, first tenors in the second movement, the one that starts *"Geduld, Geduld, Wenn mich falsche Zungen stechen"*, the introductory accompaniment there. You really are a terrible ignoramus. Now I've beaten you with nine whole points to your nil. Infamous. One may well ask what would become of our people if you were in my position . . . when I was younger, I could stay awake all night over the *St Matthew Passion*. That was when I was uncertain about a crucial political decision. When the last note of the final chorus had sounded the decision was made and the following morning I went into action, Bach functioning as a catalyst for the political life of the country. You didn't know, did you, that I knew Bach? You can't beat me when it comes to Bach. Do I seem somewhat over-excited?'

'A trifle, perhaps.'

'Now you're being insolent, too. You've always been that. If you listen to the *St Matthew Passion* with attention, you'll notice something. I've been thinking about it all evening. Your present delightful partner once said to me about the *St Matthew Passion* that it contains everything, says everything about man and the life of man and the condition of man. I'm a well-brought-up old man. I did not wish to argue with her at the time, but . . . but that was a truly amazing idea. I wonder where she got it from . . .'

'Jacob. Quite certainly from Jacob . . .'

'Jacob? Jacob? Which Jacob? Oh, the one with the writ. Yes, that characterization of you he wrote was really excellent. Did you know I've had it duplicated, and I'll have it sent to eight ministers, fourteen industrialists and twenty-three heads of department. Harsh times ahead for the big double-dealers in a certain trade. We can't let just anything pass without the exalted concerned taking counter-measures, can we . . . where was I?'

'Vanessa . . . something to do with Vanessa.'

'That's right. Did you know I was a sworn anti-Marxist by the time I was sixty? Did you know that?'

'I've an inkling that I . . . that I knew that . . .'

'You've an inkling? Excellent. You must have an inkling about something . . . alongside all that double-dealing. Only now in my old age . . . well, when I think of the world situation, I mean all this gigantic consumer-geared orgy of over-production of goods which are from beginning to end really nothing but garbage. I mean surplus in both meanings of that word, like Marxism . . . everything is actually described in black and white in Marx . . . do you follow me?'

'Not really.'

'No, no, I really meant music. What I mean is that music in actual fact is a more lucid way of describing an historical epoch of society, the spirit of the time, human life, than words are. Bad words and good music, please note. Good words are inimitable when it comes to making a concrete event comprehensible, just as in Marx . . . or Machiavelli . . . or Manzoni. Ha ha, that was brilliant, wasn't it? Bringing Manzoni in, too. I'm utterly obsessed with the great nineteenth-century composers, the golden age of the romantics, Brahms, Tchaikovsky, Dvořák, César Franck, Sibelius and Mahler. Say what you like about my musical taste being undeveloped and surface and vulgar and inarticulated and facile, but there's something there that . . . you seem rather sleepy. Have you the energy to go on?'

'Naturally. This is enormously interesting.'

'Hypocrite! Huckster! But that she could express herself so astonishingly without nuances, your present delightful life-partner, piano virtuoso and all, that she thinks the *St Matthew Passion* contains everything, says everthing, when in actual fact it . . . do you know that no writer in history has made me into a more convinced optimist about the future than Marx himself. Cervantes . . . the comforter. Dostoievsky . . . the purifier. That was banal. Lenin . . . the liberator, no, the opener-up of rusted thought-channels. But Marx . . . the brilliantly clear illuminating gaslight in the bourgeois smog of London through the centuries . . . and then along she comes, your present delightful partner and maintains that Bach . . . in the eighteenth century, the Christian message . . .'

'Vanessa perhaps didn't mean it quite so literally.'

'Why not? But nothing can contain everything. It concerns a way of listening. Or experiencing. One should always separate, or differentiate as they say in grand language, divide the one from the other, understand what's what and what isn't . . . the *St Matthew Passion* as a total explanation of life. How can one think anything so . . . so bizarre, when the *St Matthew Passion*, on the contrary, embraces precisely only the one half of . . . of life, but so very much more completely, I'll admit that gladly. It's the defeat of man as a species it is about, the qualitative inadequacy and limitations of the human race. The suffering and death of Jesus is the mythologized, personified and simultaneously extended prophecy of the extinction of man as a race, as a family, and that is what Bach, with his overwhelming perception, his inimitable religious intuition, illustrates musically. The other half isn't there at all, the struggle, the struggle, the will to survive and survival itself, the antagonism of opposition, seen through thesis and antithesis, the perpetual uninterrupted rebirth of creation as an historical necessity and an action steered by will. The *St Matthew Passion* is seventy-eight complete variations on the theme of distilled and cultivated grief and resigned submission, submission as inevitable human destiny, but what drama, what overwhelming drama, and as drama quite unsurpassed, it puts even *King Lear* in the shade . . . as drama . . . do you understand what I mean? Do you understand anything at all?'

'I'm beginning have an inkling of what you're getting at, I think.'

'You're beginning to have an inkling. Good. An inkling is better than nothing at all. The human drama – *King Lear* is great drama, and *Faust*, but no one can deny that Bach is the greatest dramatist in history, if drama is to illustrate, and in the *St Matthew Passion* in particular, compared with the devoutly solemn *Mass in B-minor*, the B-minor seems profane, almost light-hearted, but please note . . . *essentially* it is not until the *St Matthew Passion* ends that the history of man arises, *begins.* . . .'

He sat in silence for a few moments with his eyes closed, then mused:

'It's strange, very strange indeed . . . I feel like playing Stravinsky to you. Stravinsky also had his vision of the beginning, the dawn of creation, the prehistory of man, which to him was, of course, quite different from what it was to Marx, more conventional on the whole. No, no. Stravinsky wasn't at all conventional, but like prehistory . . . to Marx, real or constructive history has not hitherto even begun. That's what inspires me and which must convey to every thinking, intelligent person inexhaustible reserves of hope and future consolation. Suffering is the prehistory of man, but *essentially* we haven't even begun, and yet it's strange that none of the great musical geniuses has wanted or been able to illustrate a vision of the Marxist future in the same way that Bach in the *St Matthew Passion* illustrates Christianity . . . they compose battle songs . . . by all means, battle songs . . . but for an old man like me . . . battle songs, at my age and in my position, one isn't inspired to action by such simple stimuli . . . it's strange that it is in fact so difficult, when in reality the future is nothing but part of the present . . . though the invisible part . . . that man is so obsessed with tragedy and destruction . . .'

'You said yourself that you were obsessed with romanticism, the great bourgeois symphonies . . .'

'Don't interrupt me. I'll come to them. I'm thinking of the human character and what a peculiarly complex apparatus it is, for what is the *St Matthew Passion* if not the theme of exhausted resignation illuminated all round and manifested musically, and yet for a long time I was able to gather indestructible strength and decisiveness from it, charge my will, the dynamic meeting between contrasts . . . Christianity and preparedness for death, Marxism and preparedness for life . . . Perhaps it is the same thing and not any old Christianity, but Bach's interpretation, for the innermost core of the *St Matthew Passion* which one must grasp, as the music says it, is that the Christian promise of immortality has only symbolic content, and individual immortality itself is a myth, that only man's own inadequacy is eternal and the only thing to remain permanent in man is his helplessness and anguish . . . there's a difference between faith and faith . . . but for the great exponents of the nature and condition of life, there is always a common basis independent of where they are in time and which principle of explanation they choose . . . the message of love in Marx . . . in Bach . . . in . . . thirty pieces of silver! What is that, if not an anticipation of the capitalist principle of profitability? The *St Matthew Passion* is an individual tragedy and a collective drama, in which the whole of human society takes part, with full orchestra, the political parties, the avarice, the limitations, the dogmatism, the bureaucracy, the complacency, ignorance and stupidity, the base envy and vengefulness, and the irresistible collective attraction of suggestive mass movements . . . what am I saying . . . Marx foresaw the world war in our century. A hundred and fifty years earlier, Bach illustrated the vanity and evil of the capitalist principle of profitability. Judas . . . Matthew, naturally . . . Why do the musicians in a symphony orchestra always wear tails? Have you ever wondered that, too?'

'Yes, as a matter of fact, I have. It looks rather magnificent, of course.'

'He thinks it looks magnificent. I think it just looks silly. And God knows, my vanity is not the least in the land. Brahms is comical and

Tchaikovsky is comical and Dvořák is comical and Grieg is comical and Sibelius is comical. The only one who isn't comical is Mahler, because he's more comical than all the others put together, of course, and the comical in him is therefore sublime, and yet I love them all as if they were my own fathers or anyhow my masters, because of that very magnificent vanity and conceit. The lofty pomp of individualism, great genius grandiosely manifesting itself, the remarkable movements and experiences and struggles and agony of the individual human soul tremendously depicted in a musical spectacle with kettle-drums and fifteen brass players and fifty violins in tails in palatial buildings constructed for that purpose alone and performed to a formally clad audience . . . no, that's altogether too much. One simply cannot think of it in that way, however sensitive, remarkable and passionate Brahms' unique artistic soul may have been, but there must be some moderation in claims made. There must be a more trustworthy explanation. It isn't the struggle of the individual soul in question, not entirely, not even primarily, but the historical epoch, the spirit of the time, the special claims of the actual form of society. The great romantic symphonies are about the great time of bourgeois respectability, the triumphant procession of the middle class, the invincible progress in the world of capitalist society. Think of Mahler's jubilant trips to the USA, simultaneously as they became almost provocative, supportively, almost agitatingly tendentious and constructive programme music. Remember Sibelius' second, the double final theme, "it's going well, this is going fine, we'll make it," says the finale. Or in Brahms' number three, the triumphant procession in the fourth movement, you can almost hear the regular troops victoriously marching across the bloodstained battlefield over colonized land in the name of Holy Capitalism, which was never to be questioned . . . no, no, that beauty, that musical heightening, that aesthetic grandeur was quite simply demanded. A dynamic, magnificent development of society demands a magnificent artistic framework and interpretation. That has to be there as a kind of moral counterweight, a peerless melodious smooth apology for all the terrible events of the time, the exploitation and oppression of working people, colonial genocide . . . the symphonies are about the middle classes, the bourgeoisie, the aesthetics of avarice, the philosophy of comfort promoted to artistic categories, that is why I love them with such an ineradicable love. One should never deny oneself, but one has to be able to see through one's own lies and prettifications . . .

143

bourgeois nineteenth-century man was naïve, saw through nothing, and his musical geniuses were naïve too. They thought it was the struggle and storms of their own lonely souls they were portraying in their symphonies, but I'm not naïve. I know what it's all about . . . political propaganda. . . .

'. . . I've shocked you now, I can see that. Behind the façade of every huckster's soul there's a little idealist, for equilibrium and progress . . . confess, confess! The huckster is afraid of nothing so much as being exposed.'

'I'm surprised, and rather sceptical, I must admit.'

'But I am deeply worried, utterly crushed sometimes, depressed, almost apathetic with despair. Which way are we going? What will happen to man? Can you say? No, you can't, but Marx could, which is why I became a Marxist in the old days. Constantly, over and over again, Marx restores my faith in human beings, the social capacity of human beings and the meaningfulness of life, and yet . . . the times we live in are a quagmire of shame, an orgy of subhuman behaviour, quite openly, too. That's what's so terrible. Nowadays there isn't even any lying to expose. People are tortured quite openly, as in Chile and Greece. People prostitute themselves quite openly, as in the pop world and the weekly magazines. In the great days of the bourgeoisie, they at least tried to create a moral counterweight of nobility in the expression of art forms. They still had a sense of the dignity of human beings. They weren't so damned insolent that they counterfeited pure rubbish as dignity. But what is art today . . . tell me? Semi-pornography and foolish serial magazines . . . the educated cultivated citizen has been transformed into a foolish chattering ape. My God, how lonely I've become in my old age. All my old friends, every single one of them, if they haven't died, sitting there carrying on indescribably long-winded and feeble discussions on who actually won, and who was reluctantly forced into, the Second World War. They all remained in the Second World War. Their greatest dream is to be able to prove that the Red Army was not brave. They're still sitting there imagining that western culture, what is called western culture, is something to be proud of, but it isn't, and in knowing that, I'm so damned alone, because . . . the sun never rises in the west. It rises in the east. The light has always come from the east. One shouldn't simplify. Nothing is simple, but on the contrary, horribly complicated and difficult to interpret. But if you want to see a glimmer of hope, then you should look in that direction. If you want

144

to retrieve something of man's lost dignity, then that is where you should go, socialism . . . it may seem severe and regimented and autocratic . . . but if you really learn as long as you're alive . . . as I do . . . you see that in severity lies dynamism, the only thing of use to the future our day has to offer . . . and regimentation is only a bourgeois term of abuse for co-operation . . . and as far as autocracy is concerned, who the hell isn't autocratic . . . you can't conquer nature by cowing it and then exploiting it, but by admitting its power and superiority, the inexorable circumstances of nature, to put it grandly . . . everyone makes mistakes, but wisdom, that was by that lonely gaslight in London a hundred and fifty years ago. . . .

'. . . Go home now, Donald. I'm immensely tired. You've totally exhausted me with your indefatigable volubility. I'll listen to a little Bach before I go to bed . . . go now, Donald. Go . . . I'm dissolving parliament tomorrow. . . .'

All I could do was to go. In a few days' time, he would phone again. On my way home, I thought about what he had said about the light from the east and the lonely gaslight in London. It wasn't always easy to understand.

As I sit writing at my walnut desk this morning, in my study, I have on my left the window and the murky greyish-blue dawn light over Ehrensvärd Park and beyond that Gräsvik Harbour, the docks and silhouettes of cranes in the powerful blue glare of the floodlights. A table lamp, switched on, also stands to the left of my typewriter. I woke at five o'clock this morning. I've been sitting here since half-past six. Torbjörn has not been back all night. I haven't seen him since breakfast yesterday. He looked terrible then, red-eyed, swollen, his breath foul. The photocopies are on the desk on my left, beneath the lamp, illuminated. Glazed, slightly sticky paper, which isn't really paper at all, but a hard mass pressed together, smoothed out, rolled out thin, and called paper from sheer habit, intended for fastening malicious, fateful or incomprehensible characters on to. I have not stolen anything. But it is true that a considerable section of what they call the family archive is at present here in my study.

Straight in front of me along the far wall is a low bookcase containing mainly books on economics and politics. When I lift my gaze from the typewriter, it falls with tiresome repetition on the same dominant work, *Estates and Major Farms of Finland*, two massive volumes, bound in leather with gold lettering on a red background. Why have I acquired this expensive and lavish work? As a sacrifice on the altar of vanity? In an uncontrolled moment of daydreaming in which New Farm's little red-painted house miraculously appears with a proudly painted yellow or pink Empire façade and pillars and verandas, a work by Engel, on page 135, beneath the von Bladh coat of arms, on thick shiny paper? Vainglorious object? Sour grapes for a frustrated lower-class fox? I have never consciously dreamt of the grandiose rôle of landowner, anyhow. And New Farm? Almost a generation has gone by since then. Vainglorious object, then.

Manor house memoirs, political memories, agricultural history, books which all too often distinguish themselves by their very superfluousness, read by few and remembered by even fewer with any lasting enjoyment. Books with no fundamental base or unified meaning, written to create memorials, in which all that is painful is eliminated and all that is excellent emphasized. Books for colleagues, the initiated, for shareholders, the privileged and capitalists. Books for me, in fact? 'He has an extremely dubious communist past'! When did my contact with this past cease? When did I re-establish it? Have I re-established it? Have I any contact with the past at all, of any kind? Now doubt is creeping in again. These terrible doubts. Doubts about myself. Torbjörn's vile breath. 'Allende's dead!' I had such a peculiar dream last night.

I was back at school, as so many other times before in dreams, and as so many times before, not at schoolboy age, but as an adult, my present age. It was spring or autumn and we were playing stickball in the Norsen school yard below Observatory Hill, where Fabian Street begins, flanked by the Guards' Riding School and the brick barracks. The lime trees rustle. It's my turn. The pitcher throws the ball. I swing the bat hard and strike, but don't hit the ball, striking the pitcher's head instead. He sinks to the ground, his skull cracked, blood pouring down his face and neck. The sand turns dark with blood. I realize at once what I must do, and like lightning evaporate from the place. I have no intention of accepting the consequences of something which is no more nor less than an awful mistake. The pitcher is taken off to hospital, where he hovers between life and death. I have gone to earth. But the physical education teacher is blamed as the responsible person and is at first charged with dereliction of duty. He is deeply unhappy, heartbroken. He seeks me

146

out and tries to persuade me, even begs me to go to the police and explain the tragic course of events, admitting, if not my guilt, then at least my part in the affair. I refuse. I am very cold, insolent and unfeeling. I see there is a good chance of saving my skin. The teacher has been charged, hasn't he? Without a single twinge of conscience, I let him take the blame. He is crushed. He weeps. He falls to his knees, humiliates himself, laments, pleads. But I'm steadfast. My heart is as of stone. The pitcher dies. The teacher is charged with manslaughter and ends up in gaol. But I go free, and on my own behalf am pleased and content at the happy outcome. At the end of the dream, the sun is shining and together with my wife, some wife or other, unclear which, I mean, I board the bus to the airport, and then the plane which is to take us south on a wonderful holiday on the shores of the Mediterranean beneath the burning African sun, or in the ancient crumbling countryside of Sicily.

Torbjörn came home later in the morning. Fairly sober, it seemed. He had stayed the night at Jacob's. They had talked for a long time, sitting up far into the small hours, 'discussing art' (he can't do that with me, of course). He had finally fallen asleep on Jacob's sofa. He maintained. And he wanted to tell me that Jacob had recently finished the portrait of old man Lindermann, Gunnel's father, my ex-father-in-law. So the threads had finally all been tied together, the circle closed. He had a peculiarly triumphant, rather malicious expression on his face which I couldn't make out as he was talking about it. Why shouldn't Jacob paint a portrait of old man Lindermann? Strange. Or rather idiotic, unnecessary. Implying that such an assignment should affect me in some special way. Torbjörn's maternal grandfather. A phantom from a long since closed and nowadys conflict-free stage of my life. I mean a stage to which I no longer have any conflict-relationship. Why must this youth constantly remind me of my failings and limitations and past mistakes? Why must he always behave as if he had a right to some kind of corrective rôle in my life? In this creeping, treacherous, false and not very direct manner?

My walnut desk is magnificent, I must say, an antique but naturally not inherited from the von Bladhs. In her drawing-room, Helen has an antique Chinese cupboard which one of the ancestors in the bourgeois branch of the family, in his time an official in the East India Company, brought back at the end of the eighteenth century. Why the hell then shouldn't I have an antique walnut desk? Helen's cupboard has inlaid mother-of-pearl dragons and leaves and all kinds of peculiar figures. My desk has carved lion-feet and drawers with secret compartments and false bottoms. Naturally the fact that a photocopy of Jacob's writ exists here at my place is in its way a confirmation of the correctness of part of what he is accusing me of, at least, in regard to this 'contacts' business. But most of all, it says something conclusive about the contents of his statement and how *de facto* they have been taken in relevant directions, i.e. as nonsense. Jacob is crazy, and that has simply been realized.

He himself implies at the end of his statement that I have an important relationship which even the Attorney-General should be aware of. That's no secret, not even an 'official secret'. As I tried to explain previously, it is a question of normal friendship which sometimes, in passing, is mentioned in the press, or is the subject of varying scandalous comments in the weekly magazines. The fact that the Attorney-General has ignored the complaint against this relationship of mine is in the circumstances no more than a gesture of perfectly ordinary courtesy and attentiveness. If the mad complaints of every madman were to be taken seriously, the whole country's system of justice would collapse within a couple of weeks. The police have also reacted according to that understanding.

I have in fact had a visit from a polite and genial police commissioner, and after many apologies and some embarrassment, he stated his errand. I explained to him what the situation was, i.e. that Jacob and I had been good friends since the 'forties, and that recently he had been somewhat off balance, and that I had possibly shown rather poor judgement by exposing him to a stupid little practical joke on a certain occasion when visiting him, and that this misunderstanding had probably arisen from that, but that he had anyhow handed the papers over to me with full mutual agreement, and that I had signed a receipt for them (he now denies this completely) and that naturally I had never had any other intention than to return all the documents to him in the normal course of events when I no longer needed them. The commissioner thanked me for the information, which he considered there was no reason to doubt, apologized for disturbing me, bowed, shook hands and left, never to appear again. The situation is that simple.

Helen telephoned at about eleven. If I turn my head to the right, my gaze sweeps first over the floor which is covered with a genuine Persian carpet, about a hundred years old. Then it meets a tall sturdy bookcase covering almost the whole of the opposite wall. That's where the literature is. The first works of literature I owned were Gorky's *My Childhood* and *My University*. They are still there, to the left of the third shelf from the top, in a Finnish translation, as they had been purchased while I was married to Sinikka, an eternity ago. But I never got to the end of *Foma Gordeev*.

Gunnel considered it part of anyone's general education to have read Topelius' *Tales of a Field Surgeon*. We bought it at an antiquarian bookshop, grandly bound. I never got further than the Catholic monk's amputated ears, or was it some imprisoned princess and Mr Larsson and someone called Bernhard? I could never get it into my head why this naïve mishmash ever came to be a best-seller for several generations. Gunnel sighed and said I was incurably uncultured and that my lack of interest in this foolish Finland–Swedish classic must be due to the fact that I lacked a natural anchorage in the national (I should like to say bourgeois) tradition in which *Tales of a Field Surgeon* was what might be called a cornerstone. But *War and Peace* by Count Tolstoy I certainly ploughed my way through, not exactly with burning ears, but with some profit. I also sometimes found the endless la-di-da works in French an almost overpowering strain. Then I was favoured with *With Fire and Sword* by the Topelius of Poland, Sienkiewitch, or however it is spelt. Historical novels have never been my line. Romanticized dreams of days gone by, about which we know very little definite and which under any circumstances were different from what those infantile authors would have us believe.

But they were part of Gunnel's 'cultural programme', her ambitious programme for me, to which I submitted myself so obligingly. Because I loved her. She also taught me in which direction one should tip the plate when one was eating soup. But preferably not tip it at all. And how to lift the spoon to my mouth in the most breakneck manner in order to get a few drops of soup inside, while at the same time it was dead essential not to slurp. And how colossally important it was when you took a sip from a wine-glass not to leave lip-marks on the rim. A perfectly orthodox liturgy of table-manners, I mean. With the mortal sins as well. Belching at table was a mortal sin, or even in public in general. I never learnt not to. I loved belching. When all is said and done, perhaps that was one of the main reasons for our divorce. She took it so terribly hard when I belched like a true peasant after a meal, although I was an upstanding director and owner of a seven-roomed apartment in Löv Island and all. Ah, me, yes, Gunnel, my dear. Those were the days, when I went to the school of etiquette to learn good manners and how to be a gentleman, so that I could be shown off in the very best circles. What singular people in those circles they were, especially the wives. But the gentlemen, too, by all means. They were all married hither and thither to each other's sisters and daughters and cousins and nieces and sisters-in-law second time round, though not always noticeably for love, but for the enormous mutual mountain of wealth. Their children were always small miracles of talent and if they weren't skating queens or district champions in horse-jumping, then they certainly went and won the Finnish championships at dinghy sailing. Children were a delight in these circles, except sometimes, oh, my God, but that was always spoken of in whispers. What else was talked about at dinner-parties and so on? The constant, apparently looming danger of communism. The constant, equally terrible wretchedness of East Germany, and that Wallenberg, would you believe it, said so last week! And then, of course, violence in the streets and general hooliganism, again coming back to communism. There they sat, these ex-skating queens and horse-jumping champions, now middle-aged, hard or puffy lines on their previously so enchanting faces, talking about their daughters, the skating queens and horse-jumping champions of today, while brains shrunk from twenty years of disuse to the size of walnuts rattled in their well-coiffed heads. The upper classes of Finland–Sweden! Finnish championships in the upper classes? Empty self-absorption. And I had once seriously and passionately wanted to join them. Good Christ. Wonders will never cease.

This time Helen revealed herself completely. She has plenty to hide. She is a false old witch. By Christ, how I dislike her. Almost two feet of Thomas Mann. Laura's books, really. She didn't want to take them when we separated. She didn't want to take anything at all. She even left a bra and a pair of pants behind her in a kind of hurt, half-amused, contemptuous protest against that young whipper-snapper Elina, who moved in when Laura moved out. Elina thought she could well use them and wouldn't let me throw them into the garbage bin, but I was allowed to in the end, as they didn't fit. Elina was much broader in the beam than Laura, and had considerably larger breasts.

While Gunnel had gone on and on about *Tales of a Field Surgeon*,

Laura tried Thomas Mann. She used to read aloud to me in the evenings, out of *Buddenbrooks*. In German. That was when we were still in love with each other. I interrupted every other sentence to have something I didn't understand explained. I'm not much good at German. Nor German sentence construction. In the end it got on her nerves so much, she gave up reading aloud and we bought a Swedish translation and each read the last chapters separately. Or rather I read them, because she knew them almost off by heart from her student days. We weren't so much in love with each other by then. '*Auf der linken Seite sind alle Nerven zu kurz,*' Laura used to quote rather condescendingly when we were talking about Jacob, an allusion to Christian Buddenbrook's understanding of his own psycho-physical predicament. She thought Jacob was an insufferable moaner. I did actually read *Death in Venice* in German. *Auf Deutsch.* Just to annoy Jacob, who loves it and has read it eighteen times. But *Doctor Faustus* really did make a deep impression on me. It took me six months to finish it. I was absolutely *enchanted* (intellectual snob's witticism). That was some years ago and the strange thing is that I can hardly remember anything at all about the book, when I think about it. There was a woman who fired a revolver in a tramcar at the end. And they looked at coloured pictures of animals and plants, butterflies and birds and so on in Brockhaus' dictionary when they were small. At home with Father, or Grandfather. Which they? I don't remember. Perhaps it was the coloured illustrations that enchanted me? Thomas Mann's magical description. A symbol of the solidly established bourgeoisie, with firm bonds with the history of mankind as a natural part of biological development. Safe growth. The calm self-evident acquisition of knowledge. The European bourgeoisie as the earthly process of the peak and fulfilment of creation. So unlike my own grey, poverty-stricken childhood. So disturbingly like what I secretly dreamt of and sought for so long and so jealously. How breathlessly attentively I read *Doctor Faustus*. Just as breathlessly attentively, though somewhat later, I listened to Bartok's string quartets. The tension in Bartok, hidden, threatening and almost physically palpable. The fifth string quartet composed in 1934. Nazism? The collapse of western ideas? Thirty years before the murder of Allende and yet only an omen and repetition. Like in Shostakovich's seventh. Starvation. Survival. Leningrad. That, too. That uninvestigatable complication. As if a whole era were speaking to me in a secret language I do not master, and yet do in a puzzling way, with a concealed, or distant, or half-forgotten, or dedicated and equally organic and natural part of myself, my personality, Doctor Faustus.

The telephone stands on my right on my magnificent great walnut desk. It is pale green and matches the green glass shade of the desk lamp. I've acquired one of those old-fashioned lampshades, the whole lamp, for that matter, as I thought it most in keeping. When Helen phones, then, I'll stretch out my right hand and pick up the receiver, but as my left ear is my telephone ear, I'll move the receiver over to my left hand so that the spiral cable is stretched and creases the paper in the typewriter. Then I'll be slightly annoyed and will have to change position, or lean forward slightly, and so will already be a little annoyed (with Helen) when Helen starts moaning and groaning. She is appalling.

My walnut desk was not bought here in Finland, by the way, and is guaranteed not inherited goods. I actually bid for it only about a year ago at an auction at Sotheby's in London. That was when I decided to launch into authorship. I thought I needed a worthy framework for this new activity of mine. It cost me only fourteen hundred pounds, including delivery. I feel enormously at home at Sotheby's. As soon as I am on the thickly carpeted stairs, I have a spontaneous, rare feeling of importance, a secret sense of being select, spiced with inexpressible bourgeois advantages, a genuine, almost euphoric, class feeling intermingled with superiority, self-sufficiency and profound traditions. It's the upstart-feeling, but what matter, because here we are all equal, regardless of whether we are called Orsini, Douglas-Home, Bernadotte, Taylor, Schneider or Blaadh. Money transgresses visible and invisible boundaries. The cheque or the banknote has neither lineage nor fatherland. Vanity and avarice are our lowest common denominators, as stable and reliable as the mathematically merciless, eternal, unfailing answer to two times two.

My God, how I love Sotheby's. That gaudy, costly, meaninglessly wealth-bound, completely illogical, profit-marred, ghost-like, shimmering, luxurious old junk shop – every time I'm in London, it draws me to it with the same passionate, irresistible magnetism, like the brothel, the whorehouse, the temples of sexual delight. I go round acting a part just as all the others do, although most of them, in contrast, are professional dealers. I myself am pure humbug, sir, poking rather absently with the toe of my shoe at an old rug, shaking my head thoughtfully and striding over to the next. Lifting chairs and staring long and concentratedly at the underneath (understanding

152

nothing). Swiftly riffling through stacks of paintings leaning against a wall, Mantegna, Cologna, Van Dyck, Van Eyck. Gliding my hand tenderly and carefully over worn surfaces of tables of oak, (and walnut), ebony and mahogany. Opening small, mysterious, oriental cupboards and inspecting their interiors minutely, ivory, sandalwood, rosewood, gold, silver, jade, porphyry, Meissen and Rosenthal. And so on. The connoisseur's lofty, enviable rôle. The assistants slip by in their dust-grey overalls. And those neat young men, insufferably well turned-out in dark suits and discreet ties, sauntering round with important expressions and holding important papers, stopping now and again to discuss correctly and knowledgeably some nonsense with some obvious American woman, her painted face already sufficiently telling.

I have always avoided all forms of gambling with utmost care. Gambling is so immensely foolish. Risking the money you have earned with the sweat of your brow with no real motive except the sensual thrill of irrational excitement. The capitalist desire for profit transformed into metaphysical expectations and a religious fulfilment of dreams. Pure madness. But I cannot resist the auctions at Sotheby's.

I once lost my head and started bidding for a small Rubens. I can't even remember now whether it was a portrait or a landscape. By bidding, I mean discreetly raising two or three fingers an inch or so off my knee, or making an almost imperceptible movement with my catalogue, as I had seen the professionals do. Everything happens as if in church there. Or a sex club. The self-confident young auctioneer sits up there at his lectern, whispering like a very hoarse or unusually shy teacher, his assistants beside him mumbling inaudibly as they register the slightest movement in the audience. Everything goes at a raging speed. A burly fat Italian dealer in a dark blue silk jacket and yellow tie was determined to have his Rubens. But not at any price, all the same. He stared at me with an expression of surprise and growing dislike as I went on bidding, unable to stop, almost as if in a dream. We had already gone above a hundred thousand pounds when I suddenly woke up and saw him hesitating. Two or three dreadful seconds went by, and I felt a cold hand gripping my heart. But then, thank goodness, he bid another five hundred, undoubtedly his last bid, and I was saved. Afterwards he came over to me and asked me who the hell I was, and I had had time to collect my wits sufficiently to be able to laugh in a superior manner (as I thought)

153

and reply 'a joker', or something like that. The expression on his monumental, chiselled, satyr-like face changed to one of distaste, and he left me without a word. But later on I scooped up the walnut desk neatly and elegantly. Though expensively. Damned expensively.

Helen has such an unpleasant voice, plaintive and tearful as if she were the eternal bearer of bad tidings and terrible forebodings. Fortunately she is not yet that. She is far too banal and dull for such a dramatic rôle. But she always has troubles. She manoeuvres and manages and telephones round. She organizes everyone in the best possible way. It may well be true that she has driven Jacob insane. She phones him at least once a day, asking how he is and if there's anything she can do for him. Sister, dear. Jacob rebuffs her so roughly sometimes, the saliva sprays the walls. That's how pleasant their relationship is. But she knows what's best for him and does not allow herself to be put down.

'Jacob's just a big baby. He's so terribly impractical. He simply wouldn't manage without someone to look after him,' she says, at the same time her expression turning so threatening and frighteningly serious, one knows her thoughts are quite elsewhere. She pronounces silent judgements right, left and centre, on 'that damned tart Sylvia' who left Jacob after only two years of marriage, almost forty years ago, and on the rest of us who do not show proper respect or feel proper esteem and reverence for Il Maestro. Himself.

She is peevish and vengeful, probably to some extent due to the fact that her own marriage to that immensely boring old bore Martti, the Professor Emeritus, is so immensely boring. It hasn't always been like that. There had been another Helen once. A long time ago. In another age. When I took Jacob's hand and allowed him to pilot me into the family labyrinths, not unlike the bull in the china shop, I might say, but on the whole as politely and well-manneredly as I could, occasionally, here and there, in subdued tones, Helen was mentioned with the expression 'the one who undresses at parties'. Actually, it was years before I began to fathom what this ambiguous statement was really about, a delicate matter, one thought, very painful, best all round, not least for Helen herself, to let bygones be bygones and forget the whole thing. But no one forgot. There was tittle-tattle and whisperings. Helen was a bright, cheerful girl in those days, no question about it. The sunny days of her youth. Her drinking was considerable, it was said, even in her schooldays, and when Martti, her little second cousin, married her, he imagined he had done so to save her from the terrible fate of alcoholism, apart, of course, from the fact that he dearly and truly loved her. He is about fifteen years older than she is and ought to be like a father to dear little Helen. But dear little Helen was bored from the very start.

In reality, she never gave up drinking. Her consumption is considerable even today and she drinks steadily, in the greatest secrecy. A closet drinker. That is the real reason why she has reduced her dental practice to an absolute minimum, a few hours a week only, largely as a hobby, for her friends and relatives and faithful old patients. I myself would never dare entrust my expensive array to the care of such a trembling hand. Martti still bravely tries to convince himself that she prefers to look after home and hearth, and that she sacrifices herself 'to her brother Jacob'. In reality, though, she has never managed to combine sherry and dental drill harmoniously.

Helen was a model member of the women's services during the war. Naturally, not one of those young tarts about whom so much lying slander was written later on in the name of history and truth. But a servicewoman of the genuine kind, from the right generation, and the right social class one could say, brave and self-sacrificing, in field kitchen as well as field hospital, with skirt and woollen knickers buttoned according to regulations and kept up on duty as well as off. That is hardly something to be ironic about. She was one of them. Most were not. I was not. She was chosen, and for a long time it was the chosen's preserve to create the myths, build the monuments, shape the memorials. Then other times came, a time for less directed truth. And Helen felt as bitter and betrayed as all the other previously selected ones. She also had her murky past to rehabilitate. Perhaps that is partly why she sometimes reacts disproportionately violently when anyone speaks light-heartedly of her elevated, illustrious war.

She is an obstinate creature. Nowadays there is nothing more important to her than the conventions. She always disagrees. She never agrees. She is monomanic at objecting, and yet she usually introduces her objections with that little phrase . . . so insufferable and indescribably petty . . . 'one usually . . .'

'One usually . . .' does this or that. '. . . One usually . . .' says this or that. '. . . One doesn't usually . . .' Blah blah blah. That's what Helen is like.

As far as her murky past is concerned, that she 'undresses at parties' – it all turned out to be a ridiculously innocent little affair. In

155

the 'thirties, at a New Year party in student circles, in the small hours, Helen once took off her jumper and revealed her left breast to a (more or less) professionally interested medical student, who had requested, in the interests of sacred science, to be allowed to study a sweet little birthmark which she had an inch or so above her nipple. As far as I can make out, there was nothing more to it than that. But enough for the von Bladh family. Helen was earmarked, birthmarked, for years and years to come. That's what happens when prudery reigns and etiquette rules. In our circles.

But things are different now, even the crudest Victorian crimes long ago proscribed. The Helen who telephones is another person, an aged Helen. She starts complaining about some old pier-glass that used to hang in her childhood home and which, God knows, has in some mysterious way disappeared and did I by any chance know . . . ?

'Why do you phone me about old von Bladh mirrors,' I say, with no attempt to hide my irritation (the telephone cable and the crumpled paper in my typewriter).

'Now, Donald, dear, don't go airing that complex of yours again. *I* have always counted you as a valid member of the family, you know that perfectly well.'

(No, really, Helen dear, on the contrary, that's news to me, valid, too, just imagine - like hell.)

'Yes, yes, but anyhow I haven't seen any old pier-glasses anywhere, I assure you, on my honour, cross my heart,' I say resignedly.

There is a significant little silence. What the hell have I said wrong now?

'It must be somewhere,' she says then, in a rather absent voice.

'Well, not here, anyhow. Perhaps Martti's pawned it and lost the pawn-ticket.'

'I don't think you can afford to make such nasty jokes, Donald, not just now, anyway.'

'What do you mean, not just now?'

'Well (silence). You know that best yourself.'

I really don't know what she means, but she sounds menacing.

'We've had an unusual amount of snow for December,' I try.

'Donald, there's something I want to talk to you about, so don't try to wriggle out of it as usual.'

'Yes?'

'Donald. Listen, to me Donald. I really mean it.'

'Yes, I'm listening. I'm listening.' (But not to the bloody celestial harp.)

'*Bien.*'

'Who's been? Has someone been and gone?'

'Donald! I *asked* you . . .'

'Sorry, sorry. I'm all ears, I promise.'

'It's Jacob. His nerves are all to pieces. He's really ill, I think, and that's largely due to . . . well, you know perfectly well what I mean . . .'

'You mean someone's broken into his treasure chest?'

'I still think you should express yourself more . . . what shall I say . . . more subduedly. . . .'

'I've not stolen anything.'

'Maybe so, maybe so. . . .'

'But, good God, we've agreed on that. We've agreed with the police, and the Attorney-General, and . . . the whole fantastic affair is just a gigantic bubble, don't you see that?'

'One usually shows consideration, Donald, a little sensitivity and tact would not have been too much to ask, when you know how incredibly vulnerable and sensitive he is.'

'I'm a boor, Helen . . .'

'No, you're not.'

'Yes, I am. A boor and clod and a pusher, but I bloody didn't grow up in a hothouse like Jacob. . . .'

'Our childhood home was not a hothou . . .'

'Yes, it was. But I went to the hard school of the back yard and learnt what sharp elbows are worth . . .'

'Donald!'

'Yes, Helen.'

'You're sitting on a gunpowder keg.'

'Good gracious me, I thought I was sitting on my chair at my desk.'

'*Donald!*'

Her voice soars into a falsetto. She will burst into tears any minute now if I don't curb my tongue and show 'a little consideration'.

'You mean the archive contains inflammable material?'

'I mean what I mean.'

'You mean that without my knowing it, some papers have slunk in – papers profoundly compromising to someone, and now you and Jacob and the whole family are keen that this someone's spotless reputation shall be preserved at any price. . . .'

157

'When I said that *you* were sitting on a gunpowder keg, I really did mean *you*.'

'Well, if I'm the one sitting there, than I am the one sitting there, even an uncultured careerist understands that.'

'I can't talk to you. You're impossible.'

'And Jacob is suffering?'

'Yes, Jacob's suffering. Because of you. And your bad habits. Why can't you . . . Jacob practically dragged you up out of the gutter. . . .'

'Thanks very much indeed.'

'You might at least talk to him. I mean in a decent way . . . like old friends talk to each other. There are things that ought to be sorted out and that can be sorted out . . . if only you'd show a little goodwill . . .'

'Well, I've nothing against that, but to be honest I didn't start all this, and to be honest, I think it's up to him to take the first step. I wasn't the one to write to the Attorney-General, and he can have the papers back as soon as I've finished with them. I've told him so a thousand times. . . .'

'To be honest . . . hmm.'

'Exactly.'

Then she suddenly comes out with her true errand and fires with no previous warning:

'And they say Miles has gone and given himself up to the police. That's what I've always said he . . .'

'You're lying!'

I shout. Taken totally by surprise. He couldn't have done anything so insane, could he? Christ Almighty! I could do nothing but slam the receiver down on her. And that was just what she had been expecting and hoping and wishing I would do. Like a dreadful magnificent confirmation that her insidious suspicions were true. Bitch!

My first impulse was to phone Miles immediately, but the next moment there was a strong counter-reaction. Under no circumstances could I phone Miles. I shied away from the very thought. I was quite simply frightened of him. What would I say to him? There was one question which was impossible to ask. One single question. But unaskable, quite unthinkable, almost. At the same time, I remembered his dismissive attitude, his cold, hostile, almost rancorous look at our last meeting. No, I couldn't think about Miles. Which means Miles was what I *had* to think about, to the greatest possible extent, inescapably, but not to talk to him. There was also a slight possibility that in spite of everything, Helen had been better informed than I had and that Miles had really done what she maintained, so was already under arrest, in gaol, although I'm convinced she was talking nonsense, consciously and calculatingly lying to me. The thought was unbearable. I had to contact a human being of some kind. I had to consult someone. Someone reliable. Why wasn't Vanessa here at this dreadful moment? She would have been able to help. I mean, I would have been able to confide in her. Vanessa! Vanessa! The only person in the world I can talk to these days. Intimately. Personally. Trust.

I felt a strong desire to put a call through to her in London, but I changed my mind almost immediately. She had her own problems, and she also might not be at her hotel at this time of day. Probably not. I couldn't endure such a miscalculation. And the cost, too. That would mean a private call of at least half an hour. Very expensive. I could afford it, of course, but all the same. No, not Vanessa. Who then? One of my ex-wives? Sinikka? Gunnel? Laura? Elina? Sinikka, Miles' own mother. Wouldn't it be no more than natural to contact her in particular? But she would be in session, of course, and couldn't be disturbed. Or at some damned committee meeting. Laura? In South Africa or Ethiopia, God knows where. Elina? Too young and selfish. Almost Miles' age-group. Wouldn't understand. Reino L.? What had he got to do with my private complications? He was a confidant of mine, that was undeniable. But on another level. He would only be painfully affected and I would embarrass him. On the other hand, he was involved to some extent, when I came to think about it properly. Although he knew nothing about it. Good heavens, Reino was the last person on earth I could talk to about this. But I had to phone someone. Who? Had I no real friend in the whole world? Gunnel?

Unthinkable. Had Gunnel ever in her life shown the slightest positive feeling, or any feeling in general for Miles and Rosa? Had she ever bothered at all with them, because they were, after all, my children, blood of my blood? I couldn't remember. At the same time, I knew it was very unjust of me to say that. I have not been so unfair to any of my wives as I have to Gunnel. Poor Gunnel. Not because she hated Miles and Rosa, but because she was frightened of them. They were a part of me to which she had no entrée. She didn't know how large that part of me was, either, how essential (competitive).

Gunnel, with her upbringing, her money, her traditions, her glowing social background, at root was scared. Scared and uncertain.

I remember how immensely sensitive her touch was when she played Schumann's *Kinderszenen*. What an extraordinary complicated combination of sensitivity and determination. Dear Gunnel, how wickedly I had treated her just because I did not realize all this in time, and if I had, in that case perhaps our marriage would have lasted . . . what on earth am I drivellng on about . . . senility creeping up on me. Sentimental. Unconcentrated. Miles!

This is about Miles. Jacob! What if I should contact Jacob after all, to 'talk like old friends' as Helen says . . . because we have, after all, known each other for thirty years, because . . . Friends? Frictions? Damn it, of course there was friction. But deep down at the bottom of it all, still some kind of . . . yes, friends. And also, blood is thicker than water, Helen says. I'll phone him. No, I can't phone him. He'd just slam the receiver down, as I did with Helen. I'll put the papers back in his old trunk and take them with me and ring his doorbell and then the whole silly business will be done with once and for all. A great deal of trouble for nothing, in other words. Cherished labour in vain? Now you're really going soft, Donald Blaadh. Pull youself together! I won't return the papers until I've finished with them. Certainly not until I've used them for the purpose I've planned. Hell and damnation! What the hell shall I say to the Attorney-General if he phones? That I worship the ground Jacob treads on? That I've threatened to burn up the whole caboodle? That I . . . I'll go to Jacob now and shake his hand in reconciliation and in all honesty ask him to forgive me. I'll do that. Because I have to talk to someone or I'll go mad. And who would that be if not Jacob, who so innumerably many times before has . . . my friend and protector and . . . foster-father since days long past . . .

I know Jacob like the back of my hand, or . . . no, of course I don't, but I know him well, very well, far too well to know who he really is, to say anything about him apart from platitudes, insults, banalities. He is too close – in contrast to my children, who are too far away. Naturally he's mad. Why shouldn't he be? Most people are mad. I am probably mad myself, too. Reino L. must be definitely be mad to take over this bankrupt firm. What do you mean bankrupt firm? On the contrary. Who took it over, then, nothing more. I'm the one who's crazy. All successful entrepreneurs are crazy. And then – sooner or later – when they stop being successful . . . there's a Bohemian hidden behind every entrepreneur and the more successful, the more insistent . . . Simon Spies and Salvador Dali, the imagination unites the entrepreneur with the artist. One has to invent, judge the effect, combine in the right way, and also discover the logic in the contradictory, binding together what is incompatible into a credible and profitable synthesis. Fundamentally, it is, of course, a matter of improvisation, an inexhaustible ability to improvise.

On the other hand, the differences are obvious. After all these months at the trade of authorship, I see them very clearly. The imagination of the entrepreneur is an abstract imagination. It is obsessed with quantities, adding quantity to quantity, building a mountain of quantities which can never be too large, or too high, or too extensive. Fantasy, quantity of. Whereas the artist's fantasy is a fantasy of events, a fantasy of reawakening, constantly prepared to revise its alignment, as jittery as a compass-needle in a magnetic field, even bringing alive and making clear the apparently incomprehensible. First and foremost, precisely that. Then common to both and a necessary condition, faithfulness to logic. Being also able to see the logic in what is ambiguous and not yet extant, uniting the trivial and obvious with the unbelievable and unlikely, *guiding the vision*, economic or human, through unprejudiced, unbiased analyses of logically tenable syntheses, maximally profitable, maximally lucid.

Most profound in both cases is knowledge of human beings, not just feeling your own strength and weakness of others, but seeing through dissimulation, judging beforehand which human reactions certain given social combinations have to offer as a result. And if that knowledge of human beings is lacking, or when it fails . . . when the vision fades . . . Has Jacob a vision? What does the conservative vision look like? Like the flow in a sewer? Like the superfluity at Sotheby's? And my own? What am I? The tightrope-walker at the circus with no safety-net above the sawdust, yet without knowing if I'm going to fall on either side and kill myself. Entrepreneur or author, visionary nonetheless, and nonetheless already condemned to death? For incompetence? Inadequacy of imagination?

I'll never give up.

Jacob's dream. What does Jacob's dream look like? What does my own dream look like? Have I a dream . . . that Miles . . . that Miles doesn't . . . no, I have no dreams. All my dreams have been fulfilled, bigwig that I am. But Jacob. Jacob's dream. 'He practically dragged you up out of the gutter.' *Me* out of the gutter! Oh, really. And what gutter? By what means? Of course, I was without means, that cannot be denied, but the gutter, for Christ's sake, when, on the contrary, he did his level best to humiliate me with his class-conscious superciliousness . . . and his money? Jacob lent me five million old marks in 1957, the year I . . . and since then he has not seen a penny of it. Then more and more money, in 1946 when I married, and in 1950 and 1953 and . . . his friendliness, his cloying friendliness, his inextinguishable friendliness, in spite of everything I . . . and that business of *Death in Venice*, for which I mocked him, and yet his unswerving loyalty, my perpetual betrayal. His dream.

Treachery? Treachery? Why treachery, when I never asked him for it, but on the contrary, he insisted, year after year, taking not the slightest notice of what I . . . 'if you find yourself in a temporary fix, you really mustn't hesitate to come and . . .' That's what it was like, or . . . but it was his friendliness, his imperturbable unbearable cloying friendship. What in the name of God is there in *Death in Venice* which could bewitch him to that extent? The dream of the artist? The dream of beauty? Ruin? Decay? The stinking dissolution of a whole culture, a culture to which he was inseparably bound, symbolized by the disintegrating city of Venice? Jacob? Who is Jacob? There is something about Jacob I've never fathomed, an enigma. Who is he? How does he think? How does he experience things? *What* does he experience? Jacob's life, what is it like?

What is a conservative person's life like? Lamenting over everything that has gone and is going and will go. Seeing threats and danger everywhere, where others see natural change. Being afraid, constantly on guard, which means feeling very brave without realizing that the oppressive, artificial courage is really camouflaged fear. What is he so afraid of, this conservative man? That everything will be taken away from him. He wants life to be unchanging, and life is not unchanging, but the opposite, a series of constant uninterrupted changes. He thinks change is dangerous, but of course it's not dangerous, or it is as dangerous as life itself is dangerous. Most people adapt to life's changes and mature as individuals in step with it. Some people see that as a personal duty, wishing to influence it and decide its direction. The conservative man finds dangers in change, concretizing change as dangers of various kinds, but the dangers are mostly unreal. They are fears in his imagination, like dreams. His life is a bad dream. The conservative man's life is a bad dream.

Is that Jacob's life? Is that Jacob's dream? That everything will be taken from him? That life is change and change is a threat to his personal existence? He never woke up after the nightmare of war. He remained in the 'thirties. Hitler, Stalin. He hated Hitler and Stalin. In some secret paralysing manner, they still cast their burdensome shadow over his life, blinding him, preventing him from waking and seeing that the world today is another world, evil the same, but the world different. He does not believe in the Friendship and Aid Pact. He doesn't believe historical facts. He doesn't believe that Lenin signed Finland's Declaration of Independence with his own hand in 1917. He doesn't trust the Russians. He thinks Russia wants to enslave the Finnish people. He thinks Soviet Russia is one gigantic workhouse. He thinks communism is slavery. He's expecting the invasion from the east. He is still waiting for the invasion from the east. He's waiting for the revolution, the bloody revolution. He trembles when he hears the word socialism. He is not alone in his fear. He has many brothers and sisters who tremble in unison with him. Jacob is a cultured man, and for a cultured man, socialism is the same as barbarity. Is that Jacob's dream? Is that Jacob's life?

His occupation alone presumes a conservative experience, a congealed dream of life. Jacob wrestling with material, with artistic tools; once it was different, he took to a hand-to-hand struggle with forms of reality, as a sculptor and painter, working like Juan Gris and Braque and Brancusi and Hans Arp, but he was too before his time for this country, fatally before his time, and it is a long time ago, a very long time ago. Jacob was laughed at, despised and mocked. He became bitter and unhappy, so immensely unhappy. He started painting portraits instead, and on the whole does a more conservative occupation exist? Killing the moment to immortalize it. Stopping the course of time, paralysing the human expression of an individual in a definite phase of his route to death, to give him eternal life in that way, preserving for the afterworld a poor, dead reflection of eternity, in uninterrupted mobility, the inscrutable composition which every individual human personality represents. Painting portraits is personifying the actual idea of conservatism itself, its impotence, its helplessness, its pointless, appalling, useless fear of obliteration through change.

But aren't I throwing stones in the very glass-house I am in myself? Writing, painting – are they not the same thing? In our case. The same impotent wish to perpetuate what allows itself to be perpetuated, the human form? Isn't that exactly what I'm doing at this moment, a self-portrait, a word-portrait, the inspiration for which is fundamentally the same fear of death and obliteration, the same anguish when faced with the unforeseeable imperative of change, the same panicky, helpless counter-measures against the fearful, inflexible, implacable threat of perishing? I don't know. How should I know? No. Yes.

Why should I be afraid of dying? I'm not afraid of dying . . . I'm not yet fifty. I'm healthy and strong. My body functions almost as faultlessly as before, apart from, apart from . . . and my brain functions better and better and better. I probably have half a generation left. More than that. A decade of healthy, active, satisfactory life. Nothing to be afraid of. Afraid? I'm not afraid, for Christ's sake, I'm not at all afraid. Life's wonderful. It *is* wonderful.

But naturally I am aware of the unforeseen, all the things that can happen suddenly, coronaries, lung cancer, stroke, leukaemia, road accidents, and plop, that's the end. I often think about that. I am constantly prepared. Aren't I? Death. No, I never think about death. This is nothing to do with death, but my honour. Now it's about my honour, my human dignity, justice. Which I have already stated a great many times. Miles! Jacob! I'll go and see Jacob this very day. Now. I'm already on my way. Because Jacob knows my son better than I do. That is what our life has been like. Circumstances, those disorderly rascals. Or that I preferred to . . . My God, the recoils of self-accusation. I need Jacob! Today I need Jacob and I shall crush his aversion to me, as I have always done before. Miles hasn't . . . Miles mustn't . . . Miles cannot have done it!

Now I'm deciding to go. Now I'm going. Now I'm putting on my hat and coat and leaving. Poor Jacob. Conservative maybe, but nice, nice, so indescribably nice, the only thing wrong with him really is that he has always had such appalling bad luck, the tragedy in his life, sheer bad luck, quite simply, and that he has always been so completely helpless when faced with it, quite incapable of safeguarding himself. As with Sylvia, the first and only woman in his life, whom he married, still so young, so inexperienced, so innocent, well . . . it's forty years ago now. She betrayed him, the false piece. The wedding bed had hardly had time to cool before she was running about, the little beauty, spicing her noble, elevated and oh, my God, so boring artistic marriage with a little ordinary, simple, sturdy, peasant eroticism here and there. How stupid and misplaced she must have felt, Sylvia, draper's daughter, in the ritual dance in which the von

Bladh cranes did their rigid upper-class turns. What was she like? Really? Like me? Just as unwelcome, but less purposeful, weaker? Or perhaps the other way round, stronger, uncompromising, so that she soon saw through the humbug and realized she would never be able to endure it? And put an end to it all in her own desperate, shameless way? God alone knows, for she has long since been buried under a high, inpenetrable mountain of slander.

Jacob's marriage lasted eleven months and then the divorce proceeded with a huge hullabaloo and a monumental mobilization of the family's collective legal, moral and sentimental expertise, so that finally not much was left of old (i.e. young) Jacob, previously so full of *joie de vivre* and hopes and plans for the future. Not to mention Sylvia, who during the course of the divorce case was almost completely transformed into some kind of vermin, a revolting spot of dirt on the previously clean and unspotted von Bladh coat of arms. This was told me (by Helen), because it happened long before I came trudging in on the sacred solidarity of the family.

But Jacob went on painting, somehow always before his time, if one considers Finnish time, that is, but naturally not before his time in the context of Europe. He painted like Mondrian with Mondrian and like Vasarely with Vasarely. He condemned Edelfelt and scorned Wäinö Aaltonen and made himself impossible in every way, painting sausages more than ten years before sausages had definitely taken over from the naked female body as the artist's favourite motif in world art. And that wasn't conservative at all, but the opposite, colossally radical and far-sighted. The disappointments, the utter lack of understanding and appreciation were what made Jacob von Bladh conservative. And now it is too late. Now he is sitting there, bitter and gloomy, daubing silly portraits of industrialists and bishops and professors. The commissions pour in, making him richer and richer, because he has the right social background, he is a professional artist people can converse sensibly with, as opposed to the more or less revolutionary and drunken creatures who otherwise seem to dominate the art world these days.

So he assuredly is and will continue to be a product of circumstances, and who the hell isn't and doesn't continue to be that?

But he is undeniably a trial, is our Jackeman (Helen – nickname from his boyhood), in his hermetic bourgeoisness, its blazing and yet somehow shamefully concealed class-consciousness, its almost blind dependence on meaningless social rituals and ideas which mostly lost all reality long ago. Correct table manners are in all circumstances more important than, for instance, showing an active interest in a starving world. For what can one individual do in that respect? Nothing, unfortunately, nothing at all. But putting your knife in your mouth at dinner, *Mon Dieu, quelle horreur*! Once some years ago, he surprised me by maintaining quite definitely and seriously that 'workmen didn't drink out of glasses'. That was when he had had considerable repairs done to his apartment, and I had urged him to offer the workmen a kind of improvised 'topping-out' ceremony. I suggested *snaps* and beer, cold meats and cognac with their coffee. He became quite confused. 'Can they manage a brandy glass?' 'And my best *snaps* glasses?' He had thought of putting the bottle on the table and offering hot-dogs. Out of pure human consideration, so to speak, so as not to embarrass the workmen!

Jacob is like that. He has a considerable stock of definitions of a 'cultured person'. A cultured person does not push ahead in the queue, but patiently waits his turn. A cultured person does not lose his self-control over a little physical pain. He does not complain loudly. His definitions of the opposite of a cultured person, the uneducated, are equally numerous. 'An uneducated man is one who smokes in the lavatory and leaves the butt in the WC without flushing it away.' Etc. etc. It is utterly laughable. He is mad. He is actually mad. And still this puzzling *Death in Venice* business. In spite of everything he knew that one day it would all collapse, and sensed destruction somewhere deep down, or more than that, was completely obsessed with this creeping inner rot that inexorably would cause the whole bourgeois world to crumble away from within, the plague, spiritual decay, the atrophied dying capacity of western man for constructive creation. . . .

I will subjugate him. His loyalty is bourgeois loyalty, limited to the family, at best just outside it, which is to my advantage; the family is sacred and to stand up and defend a member of the family and relatives in difficulties is a matter of honour to people like Jacob, whatever infamous deeds or brutalities they have committed, deeds which against all better judgement, unambiguous evidence and sworn testimonies, also have to be smoothed over, explained away, denied. That is what Jacob is like and I shall exploit it, for even if I myself have never been accepted, despite Helen's statement to the contrary, made in all her bottomless falseness, they have undoubtedly accepted Miles, anyhow Jacob and Helen, if for nothing else, then for his personal superiority. This now concerns my son, my son's honour, and myself not all that little as well. . . .

I shall fight like a lion for my son. I'll crush Jacob's resistance, his personal aversions, his envy, his foolish ideas of inferiority, as I have crushed them so often before. I shall drag him by the hair up to my level. I shall press him down to my level with my clenched fists on the top of his head, because now I need him, Jacob. I need Jacob! I'll go to Jacob! I'll ring Jacob's doorbell and push my way in and talk him under the table, force him over to my side, force him to use his influence, do something decisive which affects everything in a better direction, even if it means I'll be driven to using force. . . .

If he doesn't agree, I'll murder him. Jacob, the madman, my friend, my only support in the whole world! I need you again now, Jacob, and you'll yield just as you've always yielded. Let's forget bygone grudges. What's done is done and cannot be undone. Jacob, thirty years' friendship, think of that, thirty years – that's a long time, and as Helen so rightly says, the years mean something, they are binding. A friendship that lasts that long never rusts. I'll go to Jacob. . . .

At the moment I think he has more influence in high places than I have. . . .

He doesn't want to let me in. He tries to close the door in my face when he sees who it is. I put my foot in the door and say: 'Jacob, for God's sake, I must speak to you. It's vitally important. It's about Miles . . .' Then he interrupts me, his watery blue eyes glistening in the dim light of the doorway, like pig's eyes.

'. . . I'll speak to Miles, but not to you.'

I press my shoulder against the door to open it enough for me to slip inside, but he leans on the other side with all his huge weight, and I notice it is going to be difficult to take this first obstacle by force. We stand there for a while, pressing from both directions.

'Jacob, let me in!'

'Not bloody likely.'

'I've got the papers with me. They're in your trunk here beside me.'

'Liar!'

'Of course I'm lying. I lie all the time, and I've never done

167

anything else but lie in my life. I'm the world's greatest liar, and the whole of my life has been one long lie.'

'Oh, stop that nonsense, Donald. No one believes all that any longer.'

I go on pressing against the outside of the door, while he goes on pressing against the inside. It begins to seem rather foolish, but what else can I do?

As I'm standing there in that distinguished patrician old building on the spacious landing's patterned marble floor, feeling a whole century's bourgeoisie whispering discreetly in the cool dim light, an elderly lady suddenly comes waddling slowly up the stairs, straight towards me, puffing like a locomotive, a bulging plastic carrier-bag in each hand, and staring at me with an expression of growing surprise and distaste on her wrinkled, rather puffy pink face. She is not tall, but she is voluminous. And in mink. When she reaches the landing, she stops and glares menacingly at me. Her wheezing breath wafts towards me in a cloud of the distant odour of red wine.

'Jacob, are you there?' she says sternly.

'Yes, I'm here,' says Jacob

'What's going on? Is anything wrong? Shall I telephone the police?'

'No, no, Hillevi, dear. It's nothing. You go on home. It's only my cousin having one of his attacks.'

He sounds both ashamed and irritated.

'Are you sure you don't want any help?'

'Yes, absolutely sure.'

'Shall I fetch the caretaker?'

'No, Hillevi, dear, don't bother, just go on home,' he says, almost pleading, and the door suddenly opens so quickly and unexpectedly I nearly fall into the hall. I see him making a few dismissive gestures out on to the stairs as he energetically shakes his clumsy great head. Then the door slams behind me.

'In luck again, you damned impostor, you,' he mumbles furiously.

I take off my hat and coat and hurry into his living-room, the big drawing-room, stuffed with family furniture, some Gustavian here, some *art nouveau* there, a little Empire here and a little Biedermeier there. Heavy dark paintings in gold frames cover the walls. I sit down immediately in a huge velvet armchair. He won't say 'do sit down', anyhow. He is fairly agitated.

'I can't help you, and I don't want to, and it would never occur to me to help you even if I could.'

'What do you mean?'

'The question is more likely what do *you* mean? I could almost have you charged with breaking and entering. Go away. We have nothing to say to each other.'

'Jacob, for the sake of our friendship . . .'

'Don't you go bringing up that friendship business any more, Donald. There's absolutely no point in it.'

'But Jacob, this doesn't concern me, it concerns Miles. I must have someone to talk to, and when all's said and done, you're the only person I know I can trust. You're the only person who knows Miles well enough to . . .'

'I refuse.'

'You refuse what?'

'To become involved in Miles' and your filthy affairs.'

'I thought you were Miles' friend,' I say sorrowfully.

'Miles', yes, but not yours. Get out, now, Donald, otherwise something terrible will happen.'

'Helen says Miles has given himself up to the police. Do you know anything about it? Is it true?'

The expression on his face falters. He doesn't answer for a while. At last I've got him interested.

'How the hell would Helen know any such thing?'

'Exactly what I ask myself.'

'Why don't you ask Helen? Or Miles himself?' he says immediately.

'I can't, Jacke. That's just it. They shut up like clams. They don't confide in me . . . when I ask, they don't answer.'

It sounded pathetic. I could hear how pathetic and false it sounded. But just as I'd said it, largely with calculation, mostly as an ingratiating joke, I suddenly felt that in some strange way it was true, that the situation was just that, and I was overwhelmed with self-pity, as unexpected as it was unusual in my self-satisfied life.

'As you make your bed, so must you lie.'

'Jacob . . . I'm sorry . . . I must have someone to talk to . . . Jacob . . . I'm finished, Jacob . . . don't you see . . .'

As I am saying it, unable to stop myself and not really wanting to, and as I hear quite clearly how silly and false it sounds, with no desire to whatsoever, I sink to my knees before him and lift my hands in a gesture of supplication, which in no way am I able to stop, although it is all extremely humiliating and repugnant. I'm playing a game

169

and know that I'm playing a game, but the impulse, as usual, is irresistible, but this time, somewhere at the back of my mind, there is also a glimmer of real anguish, a genuine need, which is new, frightening and inexplicable. Jacob sees it, too, and is confused.

'For Christ's sake, don't make such a fool of yourself, Donald. Get up, get up,' he shrieks at me, apparently horribly disturbed and making impatient gestures with his fleshy red hands.

He takes me by the elbows and tries to lift me up. I won't let myself be lifted.

'What the hell's the matter with you?'

He tugs at my sleeves, his voice tense and forced.

'You must speak to Miles, Jacob, now, at once. You're the only person who can. You're my only hope. If he's given himself up to the police, then . . .'

'Then what?' he shoots at me.

'Then that's the end of me!'

'I thought as much. In the end, it was only youself, not Miles at all. You bloody rattlesnake!' he suddenly shouts, jerking back his hands and turning away.

I scramble slowly back to my feet, feeling as if I had been bewitched and the spell had at last been broken.

'What are you really on about, Jacke?' I say, trying to keep my voice light and ironic.

'I need hardly tell you that. You know damned well yourself.'

'You mean I'm the great fraud. Daddy's forced his nice little boy to pinch a million, just to get his own rotten affairs in order, is that it?'

'Exactly, precisely, that's exactly it, except that it surprises me you talk about a million so modestly now . . . I thought it was three.'

'Christ knows what it is, maybe even eight, when we come down to it.'

'And now you want to know exactly how the land lies so that you can take measures and precautions.'

I go over and grasp his lapels, looking him straight in the eye.

'Jacob! *If* Miles has gone and given himself up, he'll have to spend at least six years inside for that sum, and *no one* else will be in the slightest inconvenienced by that, in any case not me, apart from my grief and shame, of course, but if he *hasn't* given himself up, i.e. if Helen is talking balls, as we both presume, then the whole matter will be settled neatly and tidily. Miles will be transferred to Frankfurt or Zurich or Johannesburg for a few years. He'll get the money back.

He'll bow and scrape a few times and admit he did it in a state of, shall we say, momentary mental confusion, and the matter will be closed. No living person will ever know a thing about the whole affair, apart from those who have already been informed, of course. Do you see? Do you see that you *must* phone Miles. Now. Immediately. He doesn't trust me for some reason . . . at the moment. But he trusts you. He'll listen to you. He's always listened to you. Hasn't he? Jacob, you're the only person who can get him to see reason, aren't you, Jacob? I'm right, aren't I, Jacob?'

He stands there without moving, breathing heavily into my face, the piggie eyes shifting uncertainly behind pink bags of skin. His breath is bad. I try not to breathe in. Then he says tonelessly:

'Where are my papers?'

I loosen my grip of his lapels, push him in the chest with both hands and go across to the window. I stand with my hands behind my back, looking down at the cars parked in long rows along the edge of the pavement.

'And you talk about selfishness and egoism.'

'I'll telephone him if you give me my papers back.'

'Blackmailer.'

'One learns over the years . . . from so-called relationships.'

'That was a damned stupid letter you put together for the Attorney-General.'

I expect him to be quite flummoxed when he hears I've read it. But he isn't at all. On the contrary, he laughs loftily.

'Oh, that. Yes, that was a joke. I put it together just so that you'd have something to bite on,' he says, smiling scornfully.

But the scornful smile is forced, his voice shrill. Is he bluffing? Is he pulling my leg?

'Really? I thought it was the Attorney-General who was to bite on it?'

'You thought wrong.'

I can feel my neck and temples burning. So Jacob has cheated me, has he?

'Are you trying to tell me you're that clever?'

'I also have my contacts, Donald, you know. You're not the only one with contacts. Why don't you use your contacts now, by the way, now that Miles is concerned, I mean. It's so simple for you, just to get on the hot line to . . .'

'Yes, yes, of course, but I'm not keen in this kind of case, all the

171

same. You must see that.'

He just laughs a little, very self-assured, but somehow forced. Is he bluffing? Of course he's bluffing. Supposing he isn't bluffing?

'The idea was that you should read it as quickly as possible. I asked him particularly, the Attorney-General, I mean, to tell you about . . . in a way which would best satisfy your vanity, and that *worked*, I notice, as they say.'

He actually succeeded in catching me out for once, and suddenly I am absolutely convinced he has deceived me, the shit. Jacob has painted the Attorney-General's portrait. That was his contact. I am ashamed. I feel myself reddening. I become ragingly angry. I walk straight into the trap.

'As far as your mouldy old papers are concerned, you'll never get them back, you can be bloody sure of that!' I shout.

'Then I won't telephone Miles,' he says calmly.

'To hell with Miles and the whole bloody mess. Don't you go thinking you can push me too far.'

'It was only a joke, I told you. A little practical joke, the kind you're not bad at yourself, either, are you? Where's your sense of humour, Donald?'

'Shit on your morbid humour, you fat eunuch bastard. No one's managed to wipe the floor with me yet, and I'm going to make bloody sure they never do, either.'

'Watch what you're saying, Donald.'

'That's exactly what I am doing, choosing my words bloody carefully.'

'And don't swear so dreadfully. It's terribly vulgar. I thought Gunnel had weaned you of those peasant habits of yours long ago.'

'Stuff it!'

'Well, then, Donald, I suggest we do this. You sign a statement in which you pledge to return my archives within, let's say, a week, counting from today, and the moment that statement is signed, I'll go over to that telephone and dial Miles' number. Do you think that's a good suggestion? A fair and correct agreement between one man and another?'

'Like hell.'

'But the papers must come back to me anyway, even if I have to commit murder – murder by poison . . .' he adds for safety's sake, because he has fairly recently found out his physical strength is not up to much compared with mine.

172

That is the moment when I begin to wonder whether . . . whether there is anything in this whole thing that has eluded me. Whether that heap of papers, in themselves harmless, ordinary diary jottings, letters, old bills, inventories, etc. which I had swept into the trunk that dramatic evening and gone off with, whether something really delicate or fateful had slipped into that jumbled heap of documents without my knowledge. Perhaps decisive evidence proving my membership of the family, a revealingly dated and signed letter, for instance. Or something even more dramatic or something compromising, nothing to do with me at all, but with some other obscure and hitherto secret event in the von Bladh family's past history. Embezzlement? Corruption? Perversion? Insanity? Murder? One of the senators, or the generals, the professors, the industrialists? Criminals? Fantastic. And if so, wasn't that just what I . . . Helen's gunpowder keg! What kind of gunpowder had she intended, apart from her treacherous accusations of me personally being an accessory to a crime? And the Attorney-General? A joke? No, it certainly wasn't that. A serious man like Jacob von Bladh, Knight of Bourgeois Etiquette, does not send joke articles to a man in the senior position of Attorney-General, however chummy he happens to be with that gentleman. Something fishy here, somewhere in those bundles of papers, and I had not even given it a thought. Incredible? Or I had had an inkling, quite a considerable inkling, but all the same, incredible. Wonderful.

'I still don't understand what you're fussing about, Jacob. You've got a receipt with my signature on it, and you've also got my word for it that the papers'll be returned to you when the time is ripe.'

'I've never had any receipt.'

'You certainly have. You were just so drunk that evening, you've forgotten and lost the receipt.'

'I wasn't at all drunk, you know that perfectly well. But I'd been severely maltreated, humiliated, shocked, almost unconscious from your vile gangster tactics. You hit me in the face, and not for the first time either. That's one of your proletarian habits and I've got used to it over the years. . . .'

'You're exaggerating absurdly.'

'But you then put a lighted candle in the archive cupboard, locked my arms from behind, and forced me to stand watching while . . . it started smouldering in the bundles of letters . . . it was . . . it was unworthy, terrible and absolutely unforgivable all round, Donald, a kind of juvenile sadism I'd never would have dreamt an adult could be guilty of . . . but you . . .'

'Yes, it was rather childish, I must admit.'

'Childish! It was unforgivable, I repeat, unforgivable, however much you try to excuse yourself by saying you were drunk, because you were the one who was drunk, not me. . . .'

'Don't try that one on me. You know I never get drunk. You know perfectly well how colossally careful I am with liquor.'

'Definitely and totally unforgivable, in that case.'

'But, my dear friend . . .'

'Don't you start "dear friending" me, too. I'm in no way your "dear", neither dear brother nor dear cousin, least of all second cousin.'

'Is that possible?'

'What do you mean?'

'Nothing.'

'Don't you come here trying to trick me into something that has never happened. There's a limit to insolence and I won't tolerate . . .'

'What do you mean, Jacob?'

'Nothing.'

'Well, *bien*, as Helen says, no "dear" then. That was a joke, and I'll gladly admit not a particularly successful one, but a joke all the same, a little practical joke, which you yourself are not bad at arranging. Where's your sense of humour, Jacob? Can't we call it quits and let the dead bury their dead?'

'God, what an insufferable boor you are.'

He would give me a week. I would have plenty of time to take photocopies of every single letter, every single diary page, every single piece of paper I'd taken with me in his damned old trunk. Why not sign? Why not agree to his suggestion? He would telephone Miles. Everything would work out. Perhaps. *Bien* (as Helen says).

'Get paper and pen, then. One week from today. I'll sign and you'll phone Miles. OK?'

But then it is his turn to hesitate. Somehow it all sounds too casual. With his paranoid, sickly suspicious mind, he suddenly sees something is in the wind. He wriggles as he sits there, mouthing and swallowing several times, scratching his chin thoughtfully, then his neck. The fleshy, freckled hand trembles slightly.

'What are you out to get? Answer me honestly, Donald. What is it you're after?'

'First and foremost, I want to get Miles out of a damned unpleasant corner, you must see that, at least.'

'Perhaps Miles is just a joker . . . as you are at Sotheby's in London, according to what I've heard.'

'Miles has quite voluntarily admitted to embezzling three million Finnish marks, and do you think that's something to joke about?'

'No, I don't. Though I can see it has its comical sides when you come to think about it.'

'Well, don't then. It's not in the slightest comical. My eldest daughter died a drug-addict and my eldest son will be imprisoned for embezzlement. Big laugh, Jacob, actually. So funny, it almost doubles me up. . . .'

'Sorry, I forgot Rosa also . . .'

'And what would I want with the von Bladh papers? Nothing special. I've told you over and over again. It so happens that I've become slightly interested in history in my old age . . . and what does one know of Finnish history if one hasn't studied the von Bladh-Bladh-Lehtisuon-Lehtinen family?'

'You're lying.'

'Naturally. I'm always lying.'

'Don't be hurt now, Donald. I know this is an extremely sensitive matter for you, this business of origins . . . the fact is, you still haven't managed to find absolutely watertight evidence of . . .'

I burst out laughing. I laugh heartily.

'Do you really imagine I still go round in a cold sweat at the thought of my "impure" origins. What laughable fantasies.'

'Not at all, Donald. That's precisely what you do do. I know you better than you think. You've always looked for proof, and now you've suddenly realized you're not exactly young any longer, and you've got to the age when you feel very strongly you want to belong somewhere, to know where you belong, where your roots are. You're desperate, Donald, and you want to find that proof, cost what it may. Isn't that right? Aren't I right? Be honest now.'

'You can go to hell with your silly quasi-psychological speculations.'

'I can assure you for the umpteenth time that you won't find the slightest suspicion of proof among those papers you stole from me.'

'I didn't steal them and you can bloody well stop using that damned word . . .'

'Aha! Just look how sensitively you react. I was right, Donald, I

175

was right!'

'No, you weren't. I don't care a fuck for origins. I never have, and never will. But to dispense with that little misunderstanding once and for all, I will reveal to you that – like Your Lordship, for that matter – I have set about authorship, or in plain words, I've started writing my memoirs . . . in all modesty, just to have something to do . . . simply to fill the time now that . . .'

'And what the hell can the Bladh family archives have to do with your memoirs?'

'Don't be an ass, Jacob.'

He is silent for a moment, then takes a cigar out of a box on the mahogany table between us and carefully lights it. The smoke starts swirling round and filling the room with its fragrance. After a while, he says almost blankly:

'In other words, quite consciously and calculatingly, you're trying to repudiate me. Sometimes I have an unpleasantly strong feeling that the whole of your life has in some way been spent finding new ways of humiliating me, just as if you were obsessed with some irresistible morbid desire to get at me as soon as an opportunity arises, to put me down, to – as you yourself so elegantly put it – wipe the floor with me. And I don't understand it, Donald, I really don't understand it, not after all we've gone through together since the 'forties and . . . what I, in spite of everything . . . in all humility . . . have done for you over the years. So *you're* going to write the history of the von Bladh family, not me?'

'I never said that.'

'But that's what you intend to do, isn't it?'

'No.'

'Just your own little memoirs then . . . in all modesty?'

'I don't know . . . I've a feeling . . . that it's slipping through my fingers.'

We sit in silence for a while, looking straight at each other, both of us profoundly serious. He energetically blows cigar smoke out into the room and the huge chandelier in the ceiling tinkles, the ancestors in their gold frames on the walls staring at us, sternly, disapprovingly, expectant – no, with total indifference.

'You were always jealous because I was closer to Miles than you were.'

'Eh . . .'

'I remember when you came accusing me of the most terrible

176

things, just because Miles came to see me . . .'

'He was sixteen and you offered him alcohol and he was neglecting his school work.'

'On the contrary, he came to me to complement his school work, to learn something about what you don't learn in school, about art, about literature, about the history of human culture.'

'And you enjoyed it.'

'Not in the way you make out. But I was pleased. Single people can't help being pleased when young people show their appreciation . . . and affection.'

'You exploited his inexperience. It was you who put all those quasi-philosophical amoral distortions into his head, so that in the end he completely lost any sense of what was right and what was wrong.'

'And that from a father who let years go by without even giving the slightest thought to his children, taken up as he was all the time with shady deals and amorous adventures.'

'You actively tried to turn him against me. You slandered me to my own son.'

'That's a lie.'

'I've never made shady deals – I'm not that type.'

'Is that what your memoirs are going to be about? That you're not "that type"?'

'But you, on the other hand, are the innocent semi-intellectual type who sees conspiracies and shady transactions everywhere where people different from yourself carry out new ideas and succeed . . . making money is no crime.'

'Is that what your memoirs are going to be about?'

'No, my memoirs will be about how you start with empty hands, as empty as two hands can be, and twenty years later, you are so rich, so rich that . . . you can afford to relinquish most things. . . .'

'Your children first and foremost. You mean how you cheat your brothers of their heritage, and become a land speculator and eventually a director in a company which is unusually ill-regarded. That sounds interesting. Will we be given a detailed and honest description of the expansion of a great company? Most interesting. . . .'

'No.'

'And why not?'

'Because business is business. It's what one does and then it's past. Sometimes you gain and sometimes you lose, but you mostly gain. It's only a question of exploiting different, more or less already given,

177

chance combinations, dry and uninteresting, for anyone not actively involved, I mean.'

'Really?'

'You forget that there have been successful business deals in the family long before me, a great many, as early as in the eighteenth century. P.J.'s activities in the East India Company, for instance. Haven't you ever been interested in a detailed and honest description of the expansion of that great company?'

'Please don't mix my ancestors up in this, if you don't mind. My family has an absolutely honourable, unblemished past.'

'I've never doubted it.'

'And my paternal grandfather had no children out of wedlock.'

I burst out laughing.

'You'll never do it, Jacob.'

'What?'

'The family history. You have a much too respectful and reverential attitude to what you call the von Bladh heritage, the obligatory traditions. Your starting point is adoration and blind admiration, but one never finds the truth, i.e. reality, through adoration. I'm sure you'll be able to write a beautiful homage to the Bladh family, but you'll never be able to write history.'

His gaze becomes slightly absent. He is silent, his jaw muscles beginning to tense.

'And you'll never be able to get down anything except beastliness and base slander.'

'He who adores often sees the truth as slander.'

'When you take the word truth in your mouth, the whole room starts to stink.'

'And when you take the word truth in your mouth, all human kind vanishes and we are transferred to a city above the clouds where the angels sing hallelujah and all the old relatives have glowing haloes above their heads.'

'It's true then?'

'What is?'

'That you seem to be obsessed by an evil spirit, and you're determined to satisfy your vile and equally passionate desire to drag my family through the mud, to ridicule it, to distort, belittle, make it ugly, turning black into white.'

On the opposite wall, beyond a huge space, hangs a large Empire mirror, tightly framed in gold with white enamel ornamentation at the top. I can just see my face in it, my complexion strangely pinkish and my forehead unnaturally high, because my hairline has retreated upwards increasingly rapidly over the last three years, my cheeks becoming thinner and small creases forming at the jawbones. But I can't see the lines under my eyes or at my temples and round my nose. The picture is generally rather unclear, my eyes, my sight is beginning to weaken . . . perhaps I ought to start thinking about glasses. . . .

'Basically, nonetheless, Jacob, I'm a Bladh. You're always indefatigably reminding me about how desperate I am to have it clarified . . . why then should I have the kind of ambitions you accuse me of? Wouldn't it be the opposite, that I would have the same interest as you in creating a memorial . . . in so far that I, generally speaking . . . but I haven't. What do I care about traditions, in my special situation? What interests me is the continuity, the chain, the great lines, pictures of the individual human being, and how those pictures fit in with each other, how together they form a whole, a picture of something whole, a social composition, a wonderful human construction, a community, the principle of change made clear, the times, life-energy made clear, the times as a picture, the picture of human life . . . not so much as individual deeds, but as change, socially conditioned attraction and repulsion, mankind as a social event, mankind as an organic segment in the social course of events. . . .'

'And the land speculator and the joker as a philosopher.'

'By all means, if you like to express it that way.'

'Anyhow, now I understand why you suddenly stopped being in business, Donald. You grew soft. You started pondering on the mysteries of the universe. At last you realized that Uncle Jacob was right after all. Money wasn't everything in life. Age crept up on you, and sleeplessness, am I not right, and it became harder and harder to sleep at night, the heart fluttering, a little doubt gnawing in Donald Blaadh's callous but overstrained heart, and nothing more is needed for you suddenly to lose grip on the whole wonderful world . . . of business, I mean . . . you still shoot your mouth off, but admit that the ground has got a bit soggy where you've been around recently. . . .'

'Couldn't you pull yourself together sufficiently to talk to Miles, now, by and by.'

He pretends not to hear.

'What's wrong with you is that you've so little imagination.'

'What's wrong with you is that you're such a bloody dry old stick.'

'The past is a bird that flies away. What is past is a dream and the present is unreal and terrible.'

'Phone now, phone, brother Jacob.'

He doesn't hear.

'I'm a good portrait-painter.'

'No one's ever denied that. A bit dry and unimaginative, but that's what they want, isn't it?'

'You get to know a living human being sitting as a model for you for an hour a day, and you can at least imagine that you can perceive his soul as well, his personality, and you express that, in movement, in position and choice of colours. . . .'

'Yes, yes.'

'But the dead.'

'Jacob, for God's sake . . .'

'But the dead are quite another matter. You've got only diaries and other mute documents to go by, and you think you know, well, you're convinced that if every human being has a certain definite rôle in his letters and equally certainly a certain definite but quite different rôle in his private diary . . . but you don't know which rôles. You can't see through them, because you never get to know the person in question personally. . . .'

'Yes, I see that.'

'Donald, I can't do it. I've no contact with them. They slip through my fingers. All I see is nothing but a gathering of freestanding disparate events, occurrences, "deeds", characteristics, human figures with no depth or life, one-dimensional, with no internal continuity, no connection even with oneself. I don't understand them. It's like standing in an empty, sterile room and staring through a translucent pane of glass at a gathering of shadowy figures moving aimlessly or standing immobile on the other side . . . they don't speak to me with human voices. History is locked away from me, or I am locked away from history, you see. . . .'

'Yes, I see.'

'I can't do it, and you may not do it.'

'Why not?'

'I've already told you. I forbid you to. Your imagination is much too lively. You're a liar. It would be unforgivable to let a liar like you loose on the defenceless dead. . . .'

180

'You don't find the truth because you don't know where to look and you won't even let me try because you're afraid I shall do violence to it.'

'I was so sure of being able to do it. It was a task, and sometimes I imagined I'd got it from them. . . .'

'Who?'

'The dead.'

'Oh God!'

'I've lived with them practically every day these last few years . . . in the letters . . . but I haven't their confidence . . . it won't work. I thought there was an invisible umbilical cord between the past and the present, between them and me, but now I see . . . in me it has withered. . . .'

'You failed with the past because you have no confidence in the present . . . perhaps it is the same with me, but the other way round. I fail with the present because I've no confidence in the past.'

'The world of today is a simple world.'

'For me, the world of yesterday was a simple world, simple, hard and unjust.'

'And yet there was dignity. There was a pride in human beings, a striving towards a goal and a sense of nobility. . . .'

'And oppression and exploitation and need and poverty without end.'

'What goals do people strive for in the world today? Cars and sex. . . .'

'They strive for what they've always striven for, to sustain life.'

He makes a gesture out into the room, at the furniture, the pictures, the valuable ornaments.

'Here are my roots. This is my world, Donald, I've no other world, and if it's taken from me . . . and it will be taken from me if they get their way. . . .'

'Who?'

'The politicians . . . the socialists . . . you, too. . . .'

'But Jacob, that isn't socialism, it's paran . . .'

'They want to wipe out the past, and not just for me, not just my world, they want to annihilate a whole era. . . .'

I don't reply. What's the point of answering?

'And then there'll be nothing left . . . neither for me nor other honourable people, except simple chasing after . . .'

'Cars and sex?'

181

'Exactly.'

I begin to sense that my visit has been in vain, but I haven't the energy to react in any other way except with dissatisfaction. Jacob's mood has infected me. Miles aches in me like an abcess far too deep down below the skin to be able to burst without great pain. When he speaks again, his voice is low and tormented.

'I sleep badly. I have terrible nightmares almost every night these days.'

'Me, too. I can't sleep, either.'

'I knew it.'

'Yes, you knew.'

'Night after night I dream about nothing but war and death, and when I eventually do wake up, I'm horribly frightened. I've not been so frightened since I was a child. I scream with terror. It's awful.'

I don't reply. I'm thinking about my own dreams, my own anguish, my own screams.

'I dreamt such a macabre dream, that we were at war again, and I was called up, or in some kind of guerrilla band, or home guard, and I had a rifle, a great clumsy shapeless rifle from about the time of the Napoleonic wars. I've never held a proper rifle, never fired a single shot, never even been called up, but it wasn't at all uninviting, the opposite in fact, like a kind of expectant joy. It was horrible, wrong somehow, everything, because it wasn't the Russians we were fighting as usual, but the English. Can you imagine, we were fighting the English and it was the English who had invaded Finland, and I hated the English, in my dream, I mean. Utterly baroque. We were in a town which was surrounded and we had to fight our way out and that was somehow . . . good. We crept along the walls and fired from street corners, a quick rush round the corner, firing, then back to the shelter of the house again, and it wasn't unpleasant or frightening. It was fun in a revolting, exciting way. We shot at the English. We killed people and suddenly someone near me said, quite calmly, in a horrible voice, more elated than serious: "We're picking the early fruits of war," as if it were only the beginning of a long, bloody . . . and pleasant slaughter of human beings, with no end. How can one dream such things? So morally indefensible, when like me, one has no personal experience of warfare at all. What does it mean? When I woke up, I was trembling all over with uneasiness and shame.'

'Why are you telling me this? Dreams are interesting only to the

182

dreamer.'

'Because in a very special way it is menacing, or fateful, like a message, a premonition, as if I myself were on my way somewhere . . . without knowing it . . . to where I shouldn't be, or someone else, or the whole of mankind. . . .'

'But Jacob, a dream! We aren't living in the Middle Ages. There are limits to how long one can indulge in one's natural inclination to superstition.'

'I'm not superstitious. But I just had to tell you what it was like. You have nightmares. What is it . . .'

'I'd rather not talk about it.'

'Another night I dreamt I was dying. I mean, I was killed. I was in my childhood landscape, in the garden, you know, the slope down towards the bay, the sandy path and lawns and the high old pine trees, all tidy and clipped and well-kept as it was long ago, when Mother was still alive, nineteen hundred and sixteen, before the War of Liberation, when I was small . . . but in the dream I wasn't small, I was grown-up, as old as I am now. The sun shone menacingly and I was completely alone. There was an oppressive silence. I stood there under one of the pines and didn't know why or what I ought to do or how I had got there. I was afraid. It was dangerous. I didn't know why it was dangerous, and suddenly one of the pine tops started to come alive, and from between the needles, the twigs, the branches, out of the green sea of tree, thousands of grey butterflies freed themselves, materialized, pine-moths, in fact, and they dived down at me like sea-birds, like terns, or some kind of leeches equipped with wings. They attacked me . . . intending to kill me. I defended myself with terrible anguish, hideously afraid, but I could do nothing against them. Within a few moments, my whole body was covered with foul, sucking, snapping, bloodthirsty pine-moths, eating my flesh like piranha fish, my entrails, my brain, my liver. They chewed up my eyelids, penetrated into my skull through my eye-sockets. I screamed with agony and terror, but they did their work swiftly and efficiently, and in a few moments it was all over. I am dead, eaten up, devoured, I don't exist any more, and above my remains, my skull, my skeleton, the white, clean-scraped bones, there is suddenly a notice, legible to my blind, non-existent eyes: "dead because of butterflies". Donald, I think, I'm almost convinced I'm going to die . . . very soon . . . a violent death . . . or was it . . . communism. . . .'

'Good Lord, Jacob, do stop drivelling and pull yourself together and telephone Miles. That's the only really important thing, and you promised. Wake up, Jacob!'

He seems totally absent. His cigar has gone out and is clasped between the freckled fat forefinger and middle finger of his right hand resting on his knee. He is staring at the grey column of ash. I wonder if he's sick in some way. Or whether he is hiding something from me, like the rest of them. Whether he knows something which only I don't know, something terrible, fateful, so terrible and fateful that he feels it's his duty to keep quiet about it. To me. And that this duty is so heavy, he can hardly bear it. He has infected me with his neurotic forebodings. He won't telephone Miles. I'll have to do it myself after all.

But I don't. I can't. Something great and overpowering and unfathomable stops me.

When I get home, there's a faint smell of alcohol all over the apartment. I realize he's at it again. I am unpleasantly affected and, naturally, I'm also irritated. I walk round the rooms in the afternoon light, switching on the lamps. His room is apart from the others, opening out into the hall. I open the door without knocking, but it is dark inside and he is not there.

I switch on the overhead light. The bed is unmade. He has fastened a huge-scale picture of Pablo Neruda on to the bed-head. On the left wall is Lenin in natural size, in a speaking pose, a black fur cap on his head. All round the poster he has taped slogans and newspaper cuttings, but the distance from the door is too great for me to be able to read what's on them. I realize I haven't been in there since he moved in several weeks ago. It smells musty and unaired, the air grey with stale tobacco smoke. On the desk is an ashtray full of butts, in amongst a sea of books and papers in dreadful disorder. I look at the titles of some of the books. *The Socialist Man, State and Revolution, Fundamentals of Marxism-Leninism*, a bulky tome of more than seven hundred pages. A book-marker between pages 122 and 123 turns out to be an unopened packet of condoms. Some slim volumes of poetry, art magazines, political proclamations and a pornographic publication, colour pictures of intercourse. He clearly has not yet been able to decide whether he will go the way of capitalism or socialism. When he has read through seven hundred pages of the fundamentals of

184

Marxism-Leninism, both the condoms and the porn will have vanished, been made invisible.

Five empty wine bottles and two unopened ones stand at the end of the bed. The waste-paper basket, piled with empty beer cans, is in the middle of the floor. His sheets are grey with dirt, the bottom sheet soiled with ⁻e brown patches of sexual secretion. I am very much affected, a mixture of revulsion and shame. Peeping Tom. I quickly leave the room and close the door behind me. Now at least I know quite well why he couldn't stay with Gunnel. Of course, she couldn't possibly accept either his drinking habits or the direction of his political interests. Could I? Drinking habits? I suppose so. Will have to. How much easier it would have been if Torbjörn had been Sinikka's son instead of Gunnel's, and Miles Gunnel's instead of Sinikka's. Easier and somehow more natural.

I finally find him in my study. He has switched on the green desk-lamp and is leaning over my desk with a half-empty bottle of wine in his hand. He turns slowly round as I come in. Then he raises the bottle to his mouth with a movement so ostentatiously slow and uncertain that I am almost sure he is pretending, that he's acting drunker than he is in reality, just to annoy me. He succeeds, too. I am at once irritated and find it difficult to keep my temper. He takes his time. He takes two great gulps, his Adam's apple moving up and down each time he swallows, his eyes fixed on me, serious, searching. Or scared? Uncertain? Expectant? When he's completed this needless, appalling spectacle, his lips suddenly part in a broad smile, an insolent smile first and foremost, of course, I seem to think, but also with timid, anxious elements of curiosity, newly awakened interest and some kind of reluctant, shy, inarticulate sympathy. Or should I say like Raymond Chandler, whom I have recently read for the umpteenth time: 'If on the whole one can read so much into one single smile'. He slurs his words slightly as he speaks.

'What shit's this you're writing?'

'I'd be very grateful if you didn't come in here rummaging in my papers when I'm out.'

'Sorry, sorry, sorry, sorry, ever so sorry, but can't you tell me what it is? Are you trying to write your memoirs or something, or are you just putting down a pack of lies to pass the time?'

'Yes.'

'Yes, what?'

'You've no right to come poking around in here.'

I'm rather upset, embarrassed, too, in a rather childish way, or simply afraid of criticism from him.

'Is it true you were once the Minister of Defence? I don't remember that. Why didn't someone tell me?'

'Because I made a fool of myself.'

'How?'

He is still smiling broadly. Suddenly I realize he would appreciate it. At last a living person who would understand the value of what I'd achieved during the brief time I had the great responsibility of the defence of my country. A small smile appears on my face, too. Self-satisfied, conciliating.

'I inspected a guard of honour and listened to national anthems together with the Commander-in-Chief of the Swedish Army with my hands in my pockets and my hat on my head.'

He chuckles a little, not exactly enthusiastically, almost absently, as if he has not understood what a dreadful breach of etiquette, what an unforgivable diplomatic insult I had been guilty of. My smile fades as quickly as it had come. I had expected greater response from my rabid radical of a son. I am disappointed.

'Then I suggested during a financial debate that the defence budget should be reduced by twenty per cent. That didn't make me especially popular, either.'

Then he explodes. He roars with laughter. He doubles up. He slaps his knees and wine slops on to the rug out of the bottle he still has in his hand. Total success, then, which means he is behaving totally hysterically.

'Is it true, is it true?' he screeches. 'God, I didn't know I had such a funny father . . . that the right wing didn't kill you. . . .'

He goes on roaring with laughter.

'Then I made a speech on Defence Day on the fourth of June, maintaining the only way to achieve lasting peace was to abolish the armed services all over the world, or defence services as they're so fraudulently called, and you have to start somewhere, so why not here just as well as anywhere else. No one applauded and a couple of majors whistled as discreetly as their upbringing allowed.'

He hiccups with delight.

'How the hell . . . how the hell . . . did they come to make you Minister of Defence?'

'Well, you know, how does anyone become a minister? Why not me, as much as anyone else? If a professor of nuclear science can become Minister of Transport, why not a director as Minister of Defence? And I'm a veteran front-line soldier, too.'

'And you've also been a communist. I didn't know that, either. Why haven't you told me anything about yourself before?'

'I haven't had much chance to, as you well know.'

'Mother never said anything about you being a communist. Did she know?'

'I wasn't a communist when I married your mother.'

'You married into a hell of a lot of money.'

'Yes.'

'Did you marry just for money?'

'We were very much in love when we married, your mother and I.'

'But you resigned from the Party, to be able to arse around in society with a clear conscience?'

'You could put it that way.'

'You deserted.'

'You could say that, perhaps.'

'You crapped a great turd on your origins and joined the capitalist exploiters. Have you ever thought what a class-traitor bastard you are?'

'Bastard? I've worked hard all my life and tried to judge situations from a practical viewpoint as they arose.'

'Your only ideal has been money, then? Status? Maximum profit as far as you were concerned.'

'Yes, that's probably about it.'

'Egoistic bastard. Class-traitor bastard!'

'Yet think what I did as Minister of Defence, because that wasn't only nonchalance and incompetence. There was some genuine protest in that, too . . . which was class-based, possibly self-righteous and clown-like, but nevertheless a genuine reflection of something that had once been a deeply and honestly felt political ideal. . . .'

'But you didn't stick to it. You deserted, you . . .'

'I loathed the war, all those years at the front. Many of my contemporaries did not. They saw all that murder as meaningful, anyhow the officers did. They thought they had something worth fighting for, their country, which was their own bourgeois country, but what had I got to fight for? Their country wasn't mine and I knew it, although I found it hard to articulate that feeling then. I was only a labourer on their sacred estate, and out there at the front it was still my task to serve them . . . as a labourer. I never shot one single damned Russian, I swear. . . .'

'No, no, you didn't kill any Russians.'

'No, I certainly didn't. When I fired I always aimed at the treetops.'

'But supposing someone had been up in the treetops? Someone not Russian?'

'What do you mean?'

'Nothing.'

He drinks again, putting the bottle to his mouth and swallowing so violently the wine runs out of the corners of his mouth. He is smiling, too, as slackly and broadly as before, but this time with quite obvious malice. He has something to say, but I forestall him.

'You drink too much,' I say sternly.

'I drink too much.'

'Your room's like a pigsty.'

'My room's like a pigsty.'

'You live like a parasite and things will go badly for you if you don't pull yourself together.'

'I live like a parasite with my so-called Daddy and I'll never be rich like he is, because unlike him, I am no despiser of people like Donald von Duck. I don't give a crap for money or honour.'

'You're insolent, too.'

'Don't worry about me, because I'm going to do exactly what I want to do.'

'I've noticed that.'

'I'm not going to be a doctor or a business man or a lawyer or a journalist or a capitalist or a Baptist or racist or columnist or Minister of Defence. I'm going to be an artist, because that's the only honest profession left in the world.'

'Do you know anything about Miles?' I say roughly.

He laughs, stupidly shrill, but with a terrible restrained desperation below.

'Miles,' he cries. 'Miles is drawing . . . Miles is drawing and tells . . .'

'What does that mean?'

'No, he's wiping it out . . . Miles is wiping it – all of it – everything . . . *tout fini* . . . wiping out your ugly expresssss. . . .'

'For God's sake, Torbjörn, control yourself. Don't shout like that. The neighbours'll think you've gone mad . . . or me. . . .'

He takes a great gulp and the wine splashes over his face. Then he

188

switches tracks, his voice shrill, forced, horrible.

'Mother used to tell me what you were like when you married, uncultured, as she said. You said "enntrecott" instead of entrecôt and "coom" instead of come, and "skelington" instead of skeleton, and when you started making money seriously, you went crazy about servants. You had three maids. We still had them when I was small, but you weren't even content with that, you had to have a black servant and an English butler and when you really got worked up at parties and started telling stories, you slipped a little "*Oh, mein lieber Gott*" into every other sentence. Mother thought it painful. . . .'

Suddenly, up it comes again, the fist, the trump card, uncontrol-. lable and irresistible, and I hit him square in the middle of his grinning freckled face, not particularly hard, but quite hard, all the same.

He staggers back a few steps and stands there rigidly, quite immobile. Slowly, his eyes widen and are finally so large they seem to fill his whole face. His gaze is blank, but expressive in some terrible way, eloquent, almost as if equipped with an audible voice. At first there is only inordinate astonishment. Then terror. Then hatred. Then he slowly lifts the wine bottle above his head and wine starts pouring into his hair, down his temple and cheek to his chin and shoulder. Instinctively, I raise my arm to protect my face, and duck. But he doesn't throw the bottle at me. He throws it in quite a different direction, over into a corner, where it smashes and the wall and floor are dyed red from the last drops of wine.

Without a word, he leaves the room, so close to me our arms brush, then slams the door behind him. I stay there, feeling the silence and loneliness surrounding me. I've done something dreadful and unforgivable, which, terrible though it is to say it, I have secretly long wanted to do. I have struck my son.

Later, an eternity later, I begin to think it is myself I have struck, that generations are substitutes for one another, and what I have loathed in Torbjörn is a reflection of what is least acceptable in me. The repulsive image of my own lost, grubby, aimless youth, reawakened in his sloppy semi-drunken figure. The unendurable in him, Torbjörn, my own flesh and blood, the extension of my life, he is not guilty of, for fundamentally that is me, myself, a blurred image of my own past, flakes of my own helplessness, the shame and degradation of my own youth. Not his insolence, not my lack of

189

education, but the old ineradicable, irreconcilable shame, the humiliation.

How fundamentally I was deceiving myself in that as well.

Unfortunately I was to strike yet another blow that fraught evening. Later on, the doorbell rings and when I answer it, Jacob is there.

'Sorry to intrude,' he says suavely.

'By all means. Come in.'

'Am I perhaps disturbing you . . .'

'No, no, on the contrary, on the contrary. I've just been in a fight with my son and he has tried to murder me with a bottle of Cabernet, but those are mere trifles. Come in, come in, my dear cousin. You're very welcome, as always.'

'What horrors are you talking about . . . what do you mean, your son . . . which one?'

'The one who lives here, who else, your friend and protégé, the splendid and ambitious Torbjörn.'

If he had seemed preoccupied when I let him in and almost as absent-minded as when I had left him in the afternoon, he now suddenly seems deeply upset in some inexplicable way, his neck muscles strained, his head trembling.

'I shouldn't have disturbed you. I didn't really mean to, but then I thought it my duty to come personally. I've tried telephoning you unsuccessfully several times during the course of the evening, but perhaps you've got the telephone unplugged? I've come to tell you that I haven't managed to get hold of Miles. I've phoned and phoned, but he doesn't answer . . . no one answers the phone today . . . what is it? What's wrong with Torbjörn?'

'Family matters, that's all. Absolutely nothing to worry about.'

'Nothing special that has . . . cropped up?'

'No, no, not at all. A passing bit of bother, that's all.'

'There's another matter with regard to your memoirs, which I thought might be of interest to you, but it's difficult . . . I don't know how to put it. I mean . . . so that no unnecessary misunderstanding should arise. . . .'

He stands there in the hall, his arms hanging loosely, his hat in his hand, and in his delightful overcoat with its fur collar, he looks so tremendously uncertain, at a loss, touching in some way.

190

'But take your things off and come in and have a brandy. We can't very well stand discussing it out here in the hall.'

'Thanks, thanks very much, but I don't think I'll . . . you see, I've come . . .'

'All right, I promise I won't misuse any historic material. The truth shall for ever be my guideline.'

'I didn't intend to . . .'

'Let me help you off with your coat. I have an excellent Salignac.'

'No, no, you misunderstand me . . . where is Torbjörn?'

'He's sleeping it off.'

'Uhuh. He seems to have trouble holding his drink these days. Donald . . . we should come to an agreement on . . .'

'Of course we'll come to an agreement. If I've understood you rightly, you want it said that the pages of the past are always like a collection of old vessels, approximately, filled with dark secrets, remnants of what has once been human life, but illicitly poisoned by time, ambiguously deformed by the teeth of time. . . .'

'How poetic you've become.'

'Getting into trim, you see. Trying to express myself in the way real authors do, rather artificial and high-falutin' and all that.'

'There's undeniably a document among those you took which could be interpreted to . . . the person in question's disadvantage, but that wasn't what I came to . . .'

'I promise to distribute merit and weaknesses quite fairly, if on the whole anything comes of all this . . . though, as you know, your grandfather must be included in some form. . . .'

'My dear Donald . . .'

'No apotheosis, but no blackening, either.'

'In those days, people were much more colourful. They had souls, they had a sensitivity, a dimension in depth which . . . people today have turned into living cash-registers. It's not very exciting . . .'

'On the contrary, it can be very exciting.'

'On the other hand, great fortunes have clearly been made with starry eyes, I know that well enough. Perhaps you think I'm naïve. . . .'

'No, not at all. The East India Company, for instance, was certainly not created with starry eyes.'

'Are you putting him in it too?'

'P.J.?'

'Yes.'

191

'No, no, you can rest assured, not as a business man, anyhow, though he was fascinating, P.J. was. Just imagine him running fifty miles behind a Cossack horse with a rope round his neck, a prisoner of the Russians in 1809, already an old man of sixty-three, wearing a yellow Chinese kimono with a crimson dragon on the back.'

'Twenty-four!'

'What?'

'Twenty-four, not fifty. And he wasn't dressed as you say.'

'OK then, twenty-four. It doesn't make any difference. It was a long way, anyhow, and as far as what he was wearing is concerned, we don't know for certain. But considering the attack occurred early in the morning, when he was presumably not yet up . . .'

'Our ancestor, *my* ancestor, I mean, never dressed like a clown. Yellow kimono with a crimson dragon on the back indeed! It's grotesque. A respectable old Gustavian gentleman. How can you think up such lunacies? Have you no historical sense? You lack any sense of historical reality. Don't you begin to see some justification for my distrust?'

'Historical reality! How P.J. happened to be dressed on one particular morning in 1809 hasn't anything to do with historical reality, has it? It's a minor detail, but it might be of some importance from the picturesque point of view. Think about it, a stately strong old man with a rope round his neck, the mounted Cossack swinging his whip, charging over stick and stone, field and meadow, the flapping kimono glinting between birch and spruce, the crimson dragon glittering in the sun. There's a verve and colour about it all that way. You want to make your ancestors into a gathering of grizzled dullards, sanctimonious, impotent, honest old men, whereas I want to do full justice to their human individuality. . . .'

'You want to ridicule them, that's what you want.'

'No, I don't want to ridicule them, but one could say I have a strong desire to add a little extra spice to an otherwise shady and hazy historical dish, and where would a bit of extra spice not fit in if not in the story of a veteran of the East India Company, head buyer of many years' standing, on Gustavian ships, who knew Peking and Canton and Hong Kong and Singapore like the back of his hand, then suddenly in the storms of the Russian War he is taken prisoner by brutal Cossacks.'

'He was wearing country broadcloth, anyhow, not some idiotic yellow kimono. He was a man of the people, even if he was also one of

192

the most cultured and well-educated men of his time. . . .'

'Yes, yes, like old man Noah, he was an honest and true man.'

'Donald, don't let's argue about this now, I came to . . .'

'You lied to me once, by the way, about our ancestors.'

'When was that supposed to be?'

'A long time ago, the second time we met, when you showed me that photograph album and said whoever it was had killed twelve wolves during a night-time sledge ride, or the one who colonized Uruguay and was to be King of San Salvador, or whatever it was. That was all lies, and yet you come here accusing me of . . .'

'Ah, that was only a joke. I only wanted to impress you.'

'No, you were younger then. You held another view of reality. You still understood the value of picturesque exaggeration to bring alive human character.'

'You mean reducing and ridiculing all that is great and elevated in an individual.'

'Or take Aunt Cathrine.'

'Aunt Cathrine?'

'You would never have been able to describe her as a living person with your present views.'

'She was a worthy and profoundly musical woman.'

'Is that all?'

'Perhaps slightly original, as were many unmarried women at the end of the nineteenth century.'

'And?'

'What do you mean – and?'

'The piano – the rowing-boat.'

'That was incidental, a one-off event, a precipitate occurrence, an instance of her impulsive, artistically original disposition. It adds absolutely nothing to the picture of her entirely respectable character.'

'On the contrary, Jacob, absolutely the opposite, it gives you the key to her human uniqueness. Can't you see that? Can't you see her, Aunt Cathrine, her yearning, her passion and shame, her romantic dreams both stimulated and soiled by the upper-class life she led? How she tugged at the chains, how she burned, manacled, her wings clipped by the spirit of the time, the class spirit. Aunt Cathrine . . . can't you see her . . . how she loved, but loved the wrong man, and that was why she chose him as her boatman, summer after summer, constantly the same boatman, Aldur the labourer. What a lovely

193

name, by the way, Aldur. How on sun-drenched calm summer mornings, she had the farm men carry down the piano and ordered Aldur to take the oars, and how he slowly rowed out across the bay as she played Scarlatti, Rameau, a Schubert *Impromptu*, Sibelius, he rowing and rowing and she playing and playing, the notes mixing with birdsong and the cries of gulls, floating gently on the still morning air far out into the archipelago, while they gazed wordlessly at one another, welded together by the fire of love, the white-hot flame of forbidden love. Aldur and Cathrine, and how finally one August morning, the sea mirror-bright . . . he rowed further and further away, the notes becoming more and more distant, until they finally died away completely among the isles and skerries . . . then just vanished. They were never found. They never returned, but two summers later, some fisher-boys diving from a rock called Death Skerry found a sunken rowing-boat and a wrecked piano nine feet below, and the year was 1896. . . .'

'But that's pure lies. Aunt Cathrine died of scarlet fever at the Deaconesses' Institute in 1924.'

'But her soul, her yearning, everything that gave her life meaning and content and joy, that died that mild August day at Death Skerry in 1896.'

'You must be mad!'

'No. That is what I mean by real and true and meaningful biography.'

'I emphatically forbid you once and for all, never in any public context whatsoever, ever in any way to have anything to do with my family history. Is that clear, Donald?'

'Man proposes, God disposes.'

'Exactly. That was what my paternal grandmother used to say and it's damned right, though it sounds like blasphemy coming from you.'

'Show a little tolerance, Jacob, towards a clever, many-sided, though perhaps a trifle crude man of the people, who in contrast to you has had to travel the hard road.'

'You're so damned self-righteous, and cocky, too.'

'And you're so incredibly unimaginative and narrow-minded to be an artist.'

'Gunnel thought quite differently.'

'Gunnel, yes. You two were the same in spirit in many ways.'

'That's quite true.'

His voice suddenly speaks volumes and is so ambiguous, I am

immediately on my guard.

'The same pride of birth, the same vanity, the same narrow perspective.'

'Exactly, so much in common.'

A small smile slowly spreads from the corners of his mouth, no friendly smile, but a triumphant smile, which reminds me of . . .

'What do you mean by that?'

His smile broadens, mocking, openly insolent, very familiar.

'Gunnel and I had a relationship for many many years.'

'Wha'?' is all I can get out. 'Wha'? Wha'?'

'From shortly after the birth of your elder daughter, Anna.'

Then the whole situation suddenly falls into place for me, striking my mind like burning lightning, as he just goes on smiling his triumphant, mocking, victorious and so unbearably familiar smile.

What can I do apart from hit him? I hit him straight on that broad grinning jaw. He lets out a small cry, bending forward and covering his mouth with his hands, groaning. Blood starts trickling through his fingers.

'Bastard!' leaps out of my mouth.

I want to hit him again, but at the same time I want just as much to lean forward, take him by the shoulders and comfort him and ask forgiveness. That is when Torbjörn comes out of his room, attracted by the noise and Jacob's cry. I don't see him, but I hear his voice.

'Can't you do anything but hit people, you idiot,' he says reproachfully, a serious, disturbed adult, more adult than myself.

'It looks like it, damn it.'

He goes over to Jacob, takes his hands and carefully pulls them away from his mouth.

'How is it? Are you badly hurt? He hit me a little while ago, too,' he says, and there is anxiety, friendship, comradeship and tenderness in his voice.

'Ah, it's twenty years ago, but he still has to act the hooligan, the bastard caretaker's brat,' snaps Jacob.

Torbjörn turns slowly round and looks straight at me. His eyes are blank and bloodshot and he is not at all sober. With collected calm, as one finds in moments of catastrophe, he says quietly, almost whispering:

'Remember, remember, remember Donald's Day!'

If only he *had* had an insolent smile on his lips, or a smile of any kind, instead of that timidity. If only he had used the word 'relationship', but he hadn't. I invented all that, first only to myself at the moment, as an excuse, and later when I wrote it down, a kind of apology. 'Hooligan,' he said. I'm certainly a hooligan.

In reality he said nothing but '. . . had acquired a warm liking for each other', and nothing more was needed for me to lose my head. Naturally, because that was enough for me to realize what in actual fact I had already realized long before in the black recesses of the mind where poisonous suspicions fasten, but I had obstinately refused consciously to admit out of male vanity and prestige. How it had happened, this Torbjörn business. Why it had been as it had, and is as it is. He is Jacob's son. What shall I do now? Deny him? Ask him to move to his real father? Take steps and measures? Avenge the shame? No, nothing. I'll do nothing. Everything will be as before. Life is difficult enough anyhow.

What's the point of trying to elucidate your memories when your memories suddenly turn out to be quite different from what they originally appeared to be? When individual memories you thought were safe and final are quite suddenly wiped out, declared invalid by themselves, and the reality you once thought was real and definitive simply dissolves like mist in the morning wind and reappears in quite a new and alien form? What is the fundamental difference, I mean in authenticity and veracity, between one's own quite personal memories and those written down by the people who no longer exist, one's predecessors, the dead? They all have the same uncertain basis, the same swampy marsh-bed, the same thick black shadows over the truth and essentials. My knowledge of myself is as limited, as superficial and modest as my knowledge of my father and his father. So stop now, stop finally!

Bury yourself in memories! At my age! As an excuse for a failure I don't even admit, I don't even mention. Pretexts and excuses! Writ of defence! When you lie, anyhow, to be able to swear yourself free! The book of lies! Memories, memories, what do memories of the past mean when the present keeps producing new memories, increasingly more and more violent, more and more bitter. What is the past worth when the present is so mercilessly present, claiming such potential strength and attention, everything, everything that can be summoned up by way of strength and attention?

I can't talk about it. I have to talk about it. And when I talk about

196

it, I seem no longer me, but someone else, a substitute, because I myself am burnt out. This is about the following day. The morning. The day after Donald's Day.

Miles was dead. Miles had taken his own life.

Rosa dead. Two of my children have died violent deaths. A third is suddenly not mine. Sinikka has lost both of her children. Our children. Why . . . no, I won't ask why. Faced with death, why is an utterly meaningless word.

It was eleven o'clock. It was twelve minutes past eleven. Torbjörn had not put in an appearance. He was sleeping it off. I was in a rather disturbed mood because of the previous day, for one reason or another confused and humiliated. The telephone rings. It is Hannele, Miles' girlfriend, with whom he lives, I mean lived, and she just says: 'Donald, can you come at once? Miles has committed suicide.'

I react almost wholly instinctively, feeling nothing except cold, by which I mean an absence of any feeling. Perhaps because in my subconscious I have been expecting this conversation, and am somehow prepared. For a moment, Vanessa's face with her warmest smile appears in my mind, then disappears. I go in to Torbjörn and wake him up. He is unwilling to be woken. When I finally manage to get him fully awake, I explain what has happened in as gentle terms I can find. He seems neither exceptionally surprised nor amazed. But he bursts into tears. I stroke his head, but can find nothing to say. I have no consolation. His hair is tangled and greasy, unpleasant on the palm of my hand. I tell him Hannele is alone over there and I must go at once. He says he will come with me and asks me to wait while he gets dressed, and I reply I can't wait, but he can follow when he has got some clothes on.

Miles has, I mean had, a three-roomed apartment in Hagalund. I was there within ten minutes. I used to drive a Mercedes, but have changed to a Saab as I get a discount on the models manufactured here in Finland. Hannele opens the door. She is as white as a sheet, but otherwise calm and collected. I take off my outdoor clothes. It is hideously quiet in the apartment. Neither of us has anything to say. I feel shivers running down my spine, from tension, a kind of animalistic resistance to what I must do within the next few minutes. See. Experience.

'He's in the bathroom,' she says blankly.

She takes me there. The door is closed. She opens it. She doesn't have to switch on the lights as they are already on. He is lying in the

197

bath, naked, lifeless, strangely reduced, shrunken, his skin white or almost grey, yellowish-grey, his lips grey, his mouth half-open in – one might think – a ghost of a smile, but joyless, quite joyless. His eyes wide open, empty as shells, with no sight. He is lying crookedly, or half-lying with his head resting against the edge of the bath where the taps are. He has gaping glistening slashes on his wrists and the left side of his throat, the side facing outwards. He also has a deep wound high up on the inside of his left thigh. He has cut the main arteries in at least four places. There are spots of blood on the floor, along the edge of the bath, and traces of blood on his body, but not much. He has been neat and tidy and considerate right into death. He has let the water from the tap flush away the flow of blood from the opened artery in his neck, and has also taken the hand-shower across from the bidet into the bath and turned it full on to rinse between his thighs, where his hands now rest. There is no more water running now. Hannele has turned off the taps. There is no blood from the wounds. He is empty, rinsed out. His knees are slightly bent and as wide apart as the dimensions of the bath allow. Between his knees on the white enamel lies a scalpel, a surgeon's knife, presumably purchased for this purpose alone. His sexual organs are half-hidden by the thin, now almost transparent and faintly hairy lower arms.

I retch, putting both hands to my face and turning away. It is still quiet – quiet as a tomb. Then I feel Hannele's hand on my arm. She leads me out.

We are in the living-room. A little time goes by. I stand in the middle of the floor, staring at a picture without seeing it, an etching by a Latin American artist whose name I don't remember. The picture is of the rage of the people. She has moved a few steps away from me and is standing quite still, looking down at the floor. She is waiting for me to do something, to take the initiative, for me to take over with my strong decisive paternal hands, but she is full of patience and consideration, giving me time to get over the shock. The minutes hum in the room like wind in a leafless tree. The seconds tick by beneath my living temples.

'Have you phoned Sinikka?' I say in the end.

'I couldn't get hold of her. She was on her way to parliament.'

'We can phone there in a minute.'

'Yes.'

'Have you phoned anyone else? I mean . . . a doctor?'

'No.'

198

'I'll call an ambulance.'

'No!' she cries out, gesturing roughly with her hand to stop me.
'Why not?'

'Leave him alone . . . leave him in peace for a little while
longer . . . he . . . give him time to disappear. . . .'

I don't know what she means.

'You have to tell the police, too, don't you, in cases like this?' I say
hesitantly.

'Not yet, Doni dear, not just yet,' she says in a low appealing voice.

She comes and stands close to me, so close I can smell her hair, and
she puts her hands on my shoulders. She squeezes my shoulders hard.
Physical touch has always come naturally to her, like part of her
language. Then she says 'Doni', to denote our equality despite the
age difference. That moves me.

'He's had such a hard time . . . grant him time to die completely. . . .'
she says slowly.

I agree to wait half an hour, realizing at the same time that passive
waiting will be a terrible trial. The awareness of that corpse in the
bathroom will not leave me, but apart from conventional and formal
reasons, what else can I do but what she wants?

'Hannele, there's so much I don't understand. Can you help me?
Why . . . no, no, I don't mean this . . . but the other, the money?'

'I can't tell you.'

'But you know?'

'We had no secrets from each other, none at all. There's nothing
Miles did . . . or didn't do . . . that I wouldn't know about.'

'He's been avoiding me the last few weeks, but I never understood
why. I had a strong feeling he . . . that he had acquired some kind of
hatred for me. Why had he, Hannele? I've never done him any
harm.'

Not consciously, perhaps.

'I think we've had a good relationship these last few years. He
might have confided in me . . . it seems so unfair.'

'Yes, I understand. Come on, we mustn't leave him alone for the
few moments he has left.'

She takes me by the hand and leads me back to the bathroom.

I shudder with aversion and uneasiness, wondering whether she is
considerably more shocked than she seems. Nevertheless, I follow her
obediently, or because of that.

We stand there in the cramped bathroom, staring down at the

lifeless naked body as if in prayer or adoration. Something has happened to it during the few minutes we've been away, but I can't really make out what. It seems to have been growing smaller, he has grown smaller. Miles is lying there and is dead.

His beautiful face, how ugly death has made it.

'Doesn't one usually . . .' I say uncertainly, bending down and closing his eyelids. I fumble. It is the first time in my life I have carried out this ritual, sealing death. It takes much more time and skill than it seems to when done by old women in films or read about books. My hand trembles. Touching the cooling, plastic-like skin makes me retch and I let out a sob I am unable to keep back.

'He couldn't endure the double class-loyalty, the double class-treachery . . . and I loved him . . . that's why I let him do it . . . there's a letter on the dressing-table in the bedroom, but it's not for you, it's for Torbjörn.'

Suddenly I remember . . . the same death but another kind of lifelessness, the same muteness, another kind of silence . . . in London, three years earlier . . . the darkness, the panic, Rosa . . . so unlike this premeditated obliteration. . . .

'She wrote a letter to Sinikka which was very confused . . . but between the lines there was a terrible anguish . . . we didn't know where she was . . . it was franked in London . . . I flew there at the first opportunity. . . .'

'Who?'

'Rosa.'

'To think that neither of them had the will to live, no will to live at all.'

'She was affectionate as a little girl, so incredibly affectionate, so loving . . . then . . . things didn't work out for her at school at all . . . a strangely passive child . . . she was afraid, or . . . as if something were missing in her. Some determining quality of life.'

'Miles didn't want to live, either. He said he ought to have lived a hundred years ago. He said he would like to be us, but he had only learnt how to be him . . . he said that a hundred years ago it was still morally defensible to be him . . . but now . . .'

'Then she just vanished. Months went by without us knowing anything.'

'He was awfully cerebral . . . there was always a theory behind what he did . . . even the simplest, most ordinary action . . .'

'Gaywood Street.'

'What's that?'

'Where I found her. She died there, in a hovel in a street called Gaywood Street. I searched for her like a maniac for two days, all over London . . . government offices, authorities, drug pads . . . God, the things I saw during those days . . .'

'To think that brother and sister could be so unlike and yet . . .'

'She was lying there in a dreadful mess of mattresses and old blankets and tins of food and bottles and bottle-tops and all kinds of rubbish. The stench was terrible. I think they'd relieved themselves there in the same room. There were several of them, all more or less stoned. I couldn't find her. I had to ask which of them was her. They just pointed apathetically at a corner, and there she was, lying on an indescribably dirty mattress, and she was so thin, so terribly weak and thin, her face quite blue. I didn't recognize her at first. I could see no sign of breathing. I just picked her up and carried her away. She weighed almost nothing. I called her name over and over again, but she didn't answer, didn't react at all. Perhaps she was already dead. I was in dreadful anguish, wandering along the street for several hundred yards, maybe miles. I wanted to find a police car or a taxi, and kept on calling her name, but none came. It was quite quiet there at that time of night, late at night, the slum area round the Elephant and Castle, a dismal dreary area of hard-working people, largely demolished now, replaced by tall office blocks and factories and complicated road schemes. God, what decay, and finally I came across a hospital quite by chance. All Saints' Hospital, it was called. They wouldn't take her in at first, because of a whole lot of silly formalities . . . I shouted and cursed at them, all the fucking saints, and then they let me put her on a stretcher and took her away. It didn't feel as if I'd been carrying anything, only like part of my own body . . . as if they'd wheeled away my lungs, or my liver, or my heart on that stretcher. Then nothing happened. It was quiet and empty and there was no one else in the whole world but me . . . and my love and Rosa who didn't exist any more and everything was too late and an eternity later a doctor came, friendly when he saw I was a foreigner, telling me he was sorry but unfortunately she was dead . . . unfortunately she was dead! I thought I would never have to go through that again . . . Hannele, what kind of terrible curse is it on me as one after another my children . . .'

'No one has said it's your fault.'

'But it is my fault, because it's always the parents' fault.'

201

'If it'd been your fault, or any human being's fault at all, he would never have done it. Miles wasn't like that . . .'

'But why then, Hannele, why? If he had managed to retrieve even some of the money, it would never have got into court, and he knew that. We'd expressly assured him of that. You would have gone to Frankfurt or Zurich for a few years. No more than a handful of people would ever have known about it. He would have had a spotless reputation, and we truly did our best to convince him of that and yet . . .'

'I've told you that the one has nothing to do with the other. Miles com . . . committed suicide because he couldn't go on living in a world corresponding so little to his . . . personal vision of a humane world.'

Her voice is almost gruesome in its calm matter-of-factness.

'We all have our ideals, of course we have, but to put an end to your life just because . . . no, I can't understand that. I simply don't believe it.'

'You don't believe it, Doni. You don't understand it. No one understands it . . . except me.'

There is a self-assurance and a lack of either agitation or grief in her voice which I definitely dislike. A horrible thought comes to me.

'You knew he was going to do it?'

'Yes, I knew.'

'You knew. He had told you about it and you could have prevented him, but you didn't. How . . . how on earth . . .'

'I loved him. I love him.'

'You love him and you let him die!'

'Yes. His life was not my life, was it? My happiness was not his happiness. Doni, there is one thing I want you to know before all the awful things start happening here. It is no explanation, only a kind of significant fact. You're going to be a grandfather. I'm pregnant.'

I feel faint and have to prop myself against the wall. I feel a hundred years old, senile and feeble, with failing mind. For the second time that evening, she takes me gently by the arm and leads me out of the bathroom.

And all that time he has lain there beside us, with no movement and no life, as if he were listening without hearing, and answering in the affirmative without showing it.

Then the apartment is suddenly full of people getting in each other's way and trying to look as if they were doing something important and necessary. Sinikka is there, and Torbjörn and Jacob and Helen. Two policemen go round asking questions. The ambulance men are busy in the bathroom. The whole scene seems unreal.

I gathered my wits and made a whole lot of telephone calls, active and efficient for a while, and once that's over I feel totally exhausted.

Torbjörn is crying. He is the only one crying, the tears pouring down his cheeks. He stands over in the corner with his half-brother's or quarter-brother's or non-brother's unopened letter in his hand, looking like Jacob and heart-rendingly lonely and desperate. I see him as if in a picture, distant and unattainable, in another world.

Jacob is trotting restlessly back and forth across the floor, mumbling to himself and wiping his face with a large white linen handkershief. Tears or perspiration?

'Can't you sit down, Jacob?' I say.

He stops and stares at me, his lips trembling. He looks so old and tired, I suddenly realize he is an old man.

'Why didn't he come to me? I could've helped him. We could've sorted it all out as we'd done so often before . . . why didn't he let me help . . . ?'

'I tried to get you to do it, but you weren't easy to persuade.'

'You, yes. You, too . . . But Miles didn't come . . .'

'You help everyone and no one, Jacob.'

Hannele hurries up.

'You mustn't start quarrelling here.'

She takes me by the hand and pulls me across to Miles' study.

'Come in here . . . I want to show you something.'

It is a picture of people, an immense crowd of people, people with no faces of their own, with no individuality, with no distinctiveness, but all of them on their way to a goal unknown to the spectator, seen from above in the picture, a God-like perspective, so to speak, or from the perspective of social consciousness, man as a herd-animal, depicted in greyish browns, all alike, a greyish brown flock of people, but not like a herd of buffaloes, not like bees in a beehive, not like a pack of wolves, not like in the antheap, working together, individual but working together, but pushing, shoving, trampling, elbowing their way ahead to get there first. Where? Yes, where? No real goal, then. An unpleasant picture. An unpleasantly perspicacious picture.

'Do you see now? That was what he no longer wanted to be part of.

He often said it hung there as a reminder of the utter meaninglessness of capitalist competitiveness . . . the crowd, the aggressive crowd . . . he couldn't cope with the foolishness of it . . . I'd rather be a buffalo, he said, or a wolf . . . or a sheep . . .'

'Buffalo . . . rather be a buffalo than a financial director?'

'He was admirable, magnificent in his single-mindedness, his uncompromising attitude, his . . . humanity. I was wrong when I said he had no will to live. On the contrary, he had a terribly strong will to live. That was what killed him.'

I feel a hand on my arm and turn round. It is Sinikka, her face expressionless, her eyes quite dry as she looks questioningly at me.

'Now I've no more children,' she says slowly, her voice breaking so that the word 'children' becomes nothing but a little falsetto squeak.

Then she controls herself, making a great effort. I don't know what to say to her.

'Was it my fault, Donald? Did I neglect my children? Did I deny them the security they . . .'

'You mustn't think like that, Sinikka. We've both made mistakes, but we did what we could, and it might have happened whatever we'd . . . look at that picture. It's not communism that eats its children. It's capitalism that eats communism's children.'

'Then we won't blame each other, will we?'

'No, we won't blame each other,' I whisper.

Then I put my arms round her and she presses her face against my neck, and I can feel her back trembling. Her flesh is a little flabby there. Her hair is quite grey. She has been transformed into an ageing woman. How on earth has that happened? Is it really that long ago? And what do I look like? Grey? A little, perhaps.

Suddenly, as I stand there with my arms round her and she soaking my neck and collar with her tears, Sinikka, my first wife, mother of my eldest children, mother of my dead children, like a revived past or an ancient abused memory, a materialized memory, while I'm standing there holding on to her, an idea intrudes uninvited on my mind and I think, I'll give up, at last I'll give up, I'm not young and strong and best and most beautiful any longer, I'm neither supreme nor invincible nor infallible, but I'm old. Old and worn out and mediocre and very very tired and very very sad.

'Donald, dear, do something, try to get the police out of here. There's no sensible reason why they should go poking about here all day long,' Helen calls in a high plaintive voice.

204

'They're only doing their job. They'll go when they've finished,' I say over my shoulder.

Then I bend over Sinikka, burying my face in her grey hair and holding on to her hard as I say:

'You'll have a grandchild instead. You're going to be a grandmother. Hannele is pregnant.'

She just goes on shaking. We're both shaking now. There is a rattle in the chains of life, the chain of generations. A link is making itself known.

Torbjörn wouldn't let me read Miles' letter.

'I don't think it'd be good for you to read it,' he said.

There was an air of self-assurance and slightly superior protectiveness about him which was new and bewildering. I tried to convince him that it would be right and that I was also entitled to read the letter, although it wasn't addressed to me, as I was, after all, Miles' father. But in vain. He stood firm, maintaining that that would complicate matters even further.

Finally, after the funeral, that weighty and trying spectacle, when life had begun to settle back into its normal groove, the situation was so embarrassing and, from a paternal point of view, so humiliating, I decided to act quite arbitrarily. One dark, gloomy, January morning, after he had gone out telling me he would not be back until dinnertime, I went into his room to search for the letter, wherever he had hidden it. Vanessa was practising Rachmaninov, the *adagio* movement, on her Bechstein in the living-room. I had telephoned her in London the evening Miles died, and she had flown home the next day. Then we had spent Christmas *à trois* here, with Torbjörn. He had refused to go home to his mother for Christmas, despite the pressure Gunnel had brought to bear on him, or perhaps because of that.

His room had changed almost unrecognizably. The empty bottles had gone, his bed was made, his desk tidy and dusted. I searched through the drawers with no special shame or guilt. Without finding anything, either, for that matter. I combed the room systematically, feeling under the mattress, behind the books, on the shelves, among the clothes in the wardrobe. Nothing. In the end, I found Miles' letter. It was inserted in a book. I had thought of that, but the question was which book? He had five hundred or so. But I presumed, quite rightly, that the hiding-place would have some kind of symbolic motivation. Neruda's poems? No. *Steppenwolf*? No. Guevara? Of course not, that was a romantic wave they shy away from nowadays. *Das Kapital*? Not there, either. Did Miles have any genuine socialist connections? More likely to be aesthetic connections, literary ones. Dostoevsky? But no letter in *The Brothers Karamazov*, or in *The Idiot*, either. Not in Thomas Wolfe's *Look Homeward, Angel*, nor in Vonnegut or Salinger's affectionate, grubby *Catcher in the Rye*. It was inside Gramsci's *A Collective Individual*. I've never managed to get through that book, as it's so terribly theoretical. But Torbjörn! And Miles?

That was the first surprise. But not the last. The letter was twenty pages long. I went into my study and sat down at the desk to read it. Vanessa was practising away at her Rachmaninov. When I'd finished the letter, for a long time I wished I had followed Torbjörn's advice and left it unread. It changed my life.

MILES' LETTER

I do not intend this to be a sentimental farewell letter. You don't need that and I don't feel it that way. But there are some things I want you to take to heart, partly because I feel a certain responsibility for you, both as a brother and a fellow human being, and partly so that no unnecessary misunderstandings shall arise. From the fellow human being point of view, this letter could be addressed to anyone, but as you are my brother, and as in my opinion we have had a good and open-hearted relationship these last few years, I am regarding you as my confidant.

First of all, I want you to know that I am not in any kind of mood of desperation. I am not doing this for the banal reason that I cannot see any other way out, but on the contrary, I am fully aware there have nearly always been a great many ways out. I don't regard suicide as a good or even acceptable solution to any problem in the social situation we both find ourselves in. I am not taking my life because I think it is right and true. This has nothing to do with right and wrong. I am not taking my life because I feel it to be necessary or inevitable. This has nothing to do with necessity or inevitability, either. One might possibly say it is a kind of protest against a situation which has been shaped more by circumstances than by my own will. But that would also be superficial and over-dramatic. My suicide is to be seen as an action among other actions, indeed the last I carry out, but anyhow fully comparable and worthy as previous ones, neither more nor less well motivated, as meaningful or meaningless, neither heroic nor contemptible, simply an action. That is how I see it, and that is also how I want you to see it. Hanne knows about it and approves of my decision. We are agreed in that respect, for we are to such a great extent children of the same spirit in all but one thing: her will to live is so much stronger than mine. I want you also to approve of what I am to do when this night is over, not as an aimless or sentimental concession in the presence of 'my last wish', but consciously and premeditatedly, when you have finished reading and thought about what I now have to say.

Please don't make the mistake of thinking that my suicide might have a direct causal connection with the fact that I have in a (rather elegant) financial operation managed to liberate three million marks of the firm's capital for other and better purposes. The one does not provide motivation for the other in any way whatsoever, although I cannot deny there is an inner logical connection. Don't believe, either, that I took over that three million to satisfy any personal material need, or any such trivial capitalist desires, which in so many tragic cases form the overwhelming driving force, when cashiers and bank officials and their equivalent give way to the temptation to embezzle. I have also embezzled or misappropriated, that is true, but the money is *in toto* safely deposited in an account in a bank in Zurich, where it will stay until the hour is struck. In a safe-deposit at the head office of the Worker's Bank of Finland is a sealed envelope with detailed information about how this money will be available and how it is to be used. But more of that later, as well as concrete directives in another sealed envelope enclosed with this letter.

I first want to tell you something about myself to explain my situation, to make my actions more comprehensible to you, for I am perfectly aware that to those nearest, suicide is always a disturbing and horrifying occurrence, although I am fairly sure most people at some stage in their lives have been afflicted with more or less powerful impulses to do away with themselves.

For a long time, I was under the impression that we had different mothers and a common father. Then, as I became adult, or almost adult, when Father had married for the third time, to Laura, and I came to mix more with your family, and the friendship your mother, Gunnel, and I felt for each other had developed into a deeper intimacy, she once told me that you were really Jacob's son. I mention this because I know it will not come as news to you. The similarity between you and Jacob is striking, although one doesn't think about it as long as the connection is not made. But I think I have even greater reason to call you my brother, and to feel for you as for a brother. The purely biological connection is in that case of quite secondary importance. Oedipus did not know his wife was also his mother and felt for her only as for a wife. I felt for you as for a brother because I thought you were that, despite the fact that biologically you were not. It is the actual experience which is the main issue, not whether the assumptions are true or false, illusory or real.

So much in our lives is paradoxical and incongruous. The fact that you feel so unhappy in the same milieu as I have felt so at home. If you wish to analyse that, you are free now to say I was still looking for a mother at an age when most people have normally already long since freed themselves from the apron strings, because Sinikka, owing to lack of time and natural aptitude, had never really corresponded to my expectation of a true mother, of a mother's care and love. On the other hand it is quite easy to see I was also seeking a father-figure, that in a slightly treacherous manner I have followed in Donald's tracks, like a small shadow or a growing shadow. My essential contact with your family was established for the first time when he left you. When Father moved out, I moved in, but only as a kind of big brother or pseudo-son of the house, as I was not yet old enough to be able to dare replace him in his own way. That Gunnel never became my lover (as they say) was really only chance, or rather, again as a result of Donald's manoeuvres. For when things came to an end between him and Laura, when he grew tired of Laura, or Laura grew tired of him, I was of age. When she returned from South Africa after that short and unsuccessful incident with that engineer, we started a relationship that lasted right up until I met Hannele. That is why I knew so much about Father which he himself is not aware of. I met Vanessa in Zurich last autumn and went with her to Paris where she was giving a concert. We took a warm liking to each other and I was perhaps rather more open-hearted to her than I should have been, telling her things she perhaps need not have known. Isn't it strange that I go and fall slightly in love with nearly all Father's women?

(You are free to try analysing again if you feel like it.)

Sometimes I have a strong sense of having been born without feeling, or that the circumstances of my life have been such that a normal emotional life has provided no breeding-ground for me. Hannele is the only person in the world whom I can say I love, have loved. And yet it is not love of the life-giving or intoxicating kind which would stop me from doing what I have decided to do, to kill myself. I cannot be angry. I have no aggressions, on a personal level, I mean. You know I am well known for my courtesy and kindness. That is not a natural love of people, or friendliness towards people, but neither is it a mask. It is *instead* of ordinary simple human emotions. I could have been a perfect diplomat (and was also once intended to be).

As a child, I was afraid occasionally. Not of ghosts or the dark or that kind of thing, as horrors of that sort didn't exist in Sinikka's world. My childhood was happily free of all irrational reasons for fear. But I was sometimes afraid because I felt an apparent gap, a threatening discrepancy between my own childish imperfection and adult people's imagined or stated or somehow obviously presumed perfection. In my twelfth year, I realized my mistake, or that I had also been deceived on this point by adults. From the age of twelve onwards until now I cannot remember a single time when I have felt fear, terror. Fear neither of physical nor mental pain, nor of external dangers or inner humiliations or personal misfortunes. This is what happened:

It was November. I was twelve, and there was quite a high wind, and a man had fallen into the water off one of the quays down in the harbour. He had already sunk below the surface of the water and had been out of sight for a while. Twenty or so people, men and women, were looking on, standing there at a loss, unable to dare to collect their wits and do something for the drowning man, but just chattering in dismay. I took off my coat and shoes and asked where among the waves he might be found and then I dived in and found him under the water and got him back up on to the quay. The adults were enormously impressed, but still just as confused and at a loss. So I started artificial respiration and asked them to get an ambulance. *They obeyed me.* When the ambulance and the police finally came, almost simultaneously, I just left. No one bothered about that, and I didn't feel I'd done anything special. It didn't seem to me to be any kind of 'heroic deed'. Just an action. I didn't even tell Sinikka what had happened. But after that, I was never again afraid of anything. And I was twelve then. I am not proud of myself. I have never been proud of myself. Nor felt self-contempt, either. Not even dissatisfaction. Nothing.

You mustn't think any blame of my parents lies hidden in what I am telling you now. I don't blame them for the divorce. I don't blame them for my sister Rosa's death. And I don't blame them for not having much time left for me. Materially and financially, they have both always been very generous to me. From my earliest childhood days, they have always treated me as an equal, i.e. as a human being. They have seldom or never questioned my personal judgement, or tried to put obstacles in the way of my personal wishes. For all this I am honestly grateful, and I would be doing them a great injustice if I felt anything but profound respect and esteem for both of them. I admire Sinikka for her magnificent political achievement as a long-standing party worker and Member of Parliament, and I admire Donald for his toughness and the stubbornness with which he has worked his way up from nothing to the position he is in now. What is paradoxical and incongruous in me perhaps has its roots in the fact that I was born to the wrong marriage of the wrong parents, the wrong combination.

This autumn has been difficult and painful. The autumn of Chile. The autumn of bourgeois reactionaries or bourgeois barbarity. I have tried to instil that into you many a time over the last few weeks, and I do so again now for the last time: Torbjörn, never forget the murder of Allende. Never forget him! Remember him not as a hero or an individual, but as a symbol of the oppressed, who in the course of history again and again make the same mistake of trying to fight with clean weapons, only to be assassinated and torn to pieces by the bourgeois ruling class, which takes to any loathsome physical means to defend and maintain their power and supremacy, their freedom to own and rule over what they call democracy. Always keep alive in your memory the picture of the murdered Allende, his bloodstained, bullet-riddled, ageing body, a helmet on his head and a machine-gun in his hand. That picture will help you remember what this is fundamentally all about: a struggle which quite unequivocably is only about the right to live a life worthy of human beings. A struggle which embraces the whole world and stretches far back into history. A struggle the irreconcilability of which continually increases at the same pace as the stronger, the power-owning side, becomes

210

brutalized, barbaric, stupefied, at the same time as the ruled, the weaker side, persists with indestructible obstinacy in its belief in the dignity of man and a future without hunger and oppression. A struggle in which the weaker are constantly defeated, mown down, perish or are mortally wounded, not necessarily because of their weakness, their material and physical inferiority, but because of their incomprehensible credulity, their ineradicable reliance on abstractions made marketable and at the same time scorned and dragged in the mud by the ruling class, the abstract myths of justice, goodness and humanity, and on following the rules of the game. In the class war.

A member of the bourgeoisie is never just when he feels his position sufficiently threatened.

He breaks all the rules of the game when he feels his position sufficiently threatened.

He is humane and good only to his own class.

He will commit without a twinge of conscience any inhumanity and cruelty when he feels his position sufficiently threatened.

He does not keep his word when he feels his position sufficiently threatened.

His word of honour is worthless.

The whole of the bourgeois welfare state is principally based on theft, on consistent fraud and icy calculation.

Never trust the bourgeoisie!

Never believe his sweet sugary words.

Always start from the fact that he is lying, because his only aim in life and only interest is to satisfy his personal greed for profit and enjoyment.

Not until the working classes realize that the bourgeoisie will use dirty weapons without hesitating and that dirty weapons can be effectively defeated only with dirty weapons, not until then is there any hope for or possibility of progress and victory in the fight being fought between the classes, uninterruptedly, irreconcilably and with no mercy. When the working classes are under arms and their leaders have grown out of their credulity, their blue-eyed innocence (did you know Allende had blue eyes!?), then, and only then will there be any hope of victory.

Be active! Be well-informed! Be courageous! Be faithful but not credulous! Torbjörn, this is what I am leaving to you in my will: an unshakeable belief in the cause and final victory of communism. It is not a great deal, but more than a great deal, and I have nothing else of value to offer you. It is essentially only a sense of reality, a true knowledge of human beings, a real ability to co-operate, and a feeling for the innermost logic of human history. It is essentially only what we all might be thought to be born with. But that is unfortunately not so. Communism corresponds to the world everyone has always dreamt of, in which solidarity is master, where love decides and oppression and need do not exist. Where human values, food, and a roof over your head and meaningful work are respected as a right for all, not just for the privileged few. But in this world, in which the majority of people fumble blindly around, one single sighted person must necessarily be regarded as a madman, a monster, a deadly threat. Like Marx, once. For in that world, blindness is natural and the rule, and seeing an exception. And even if it were so that the exception proves the rule, there is nothing about the exception to show or even less to prove that the rule is right and worth following. The exception does not confirm the rule, just as the rule says nothing essential about the exception.

If only I could say I am tired, tired and disillusioned. But I cannot. I am not tired. I am full of strength and life. It is just that I have done what I can do and can do no more. Am not *able* to do more. What is the value of a human life? Isn't three million a good price for one human life? In South America, human lives cost nothing.

There is an insurmountable contradiction in my life, which I have been unable to solve. If I had ever been a soldier by disposition, then I would have been able to go on living. But I'm no soldier. I have done what I am able to and am retiring from the game. My contribution was three million. Admit that there is something incongruous, almost ironic about this: born of originally communist parents, my mother faithful to the communist cause all her life, and I spent all my childhood and youth under the same roof with her. But I have matured as middle-class. I have lived and thought and acted as middle-class and a capitalist – until I eventually realized the filthy insanity of it and was transformed into the snake in the bosom of the bourgeoisie. Or better expressed, did as the magpie did, just so much damage, and stole a silver spoon. Torbjörn, take over the rôle of snake, stir up others secretly to do the same, become an army of snakes, go forth with lies and cunning and treachery, with broken promises and betrayal, for in that way alone can the enemy be defeated. In open battle they always have superior numbers.

212

Infiltrate the army, that is the most important. Infiltrate industry and the world of finance. Don't go forth with banners and shouts and slogans. Remember the tiger is silent. And the clown disguises himself. Be a tiger and a clown. Only paper-tigers rustle.

Presumably Sinikka took it for granted I would somehow automatically follow in her footsteps, becoming one of them for the simple reason that she already was one. But she forgot that communism, and in our capitalist society first and foremost just communism, also demands active learning to be understood and accepted as an aim and way of life. I was like one of Pavlov's dogs, reacting positively to the most pleasing impulses, created according to the most clearly produced variations of encouragement. That was true of my school marks, among other things. My school marks were always good, often brilliant. I wasn't weak in a single subject, not even music or physical education. Sinikka never failed to praise me for my successes at school. When I showed her my marks, she praised me, and for a long time that was the only active expression of appreciation on her part I ever heard. In that way, I gradually became convinced school was most important, as success at school brought the greatest and most spontaneous amount of encouragement and appreciation. But I did not learn communist virtues at school. I was born and made into a collective socialist, but grew up into a capitalist individualist. That is perhaps the main reason why I now feel I have to retreat. Sinikka's passivity, her thoughtless omission when it came to my communist education, combined with the influence of school and later on that of Jacob and Gunnel, the whole of that environment, made me into something I was not intended to be from the start, into a competitive individualistic member of the bourgeoisie, instead of a solidarity-minded communist, an 'Indian', by which I mean indifferent to personal property and selfish profitability.

It is not too late on earth. It is not too late for mankind. It is early for mankind. I believe in a better future, another kind of future. I believe in the victory of communism, I believe in a future earthly life free of hunger and suffering for the millions and millions of people who are now oppressed and martyred to the borders of death. But this development will never be a social-democratic dance of bourgeois roses. The road to a better world is paved with violence and runs through a sea of human blood. For that is what the ruling class has decided. That is what the barbaric bourgeoisie has determined. They

213

will never share voluntarily. And I cannot partake in that. For I'm no soldier. I have grown up middle-class, but I'll never be a bourgeois soldier. I'd rather take my own life.

You have grown up in a bourgeois world yourself. You live your life as a bourgeois citizen. Everywhere, you have met the kindness and 'tolerance' of the bourgeois citizen. Don't be deceived; he is kind and tolerant only as long as he doesn't feel threatened. When he feels threatened, he becomes a wild animal, or rather, not even a wild animal, not at all animal, but cruel and terrible, non-animal, *subhuman*. The whole of this capitalist affluent society in which you will continue to live is becoming a dump for subhuman garbage, avaricious, cruel, insensitive and intellectually atrophied. You'll be constantly exposed to capitalist destruction which Sinikka in her idealism and haste forgot that her children were also exposed to.

Chile today is a country ruled by subhuman garbage. Torture is subhuman. To imprison, murder and allow people to starve to death for power and money, is subhuman. But sexual exploitation of social need for commercial aims is also subhuman. Copenhagen and Stockholm, and soon Helsinki, too, are being turned into huge subhuman brothels, where what is subhuman is legalized in the name of the sacred mixed economy. Sex as a commodity is indeed nothing new in the history of the world. But sex in this officially legalized, multi-capitalistic, richly and vilely varied form is new, a typical bourgeois concept, an expression of subhuman bourgeoisie. In those curious memoirs you told me about, Donald boasts of his contacts with prostitutes, how much money he has spent on them, how deeply they 'loved' him – for a suitable sum, how aesthetically attractive and interesting he found public performances of sex acts on the stage, carried out by people who have nothing but their sexual organs left to sell to make a living in this bourgeois world of usury. I do not want to criticize my father, as he has never actively done me any harm, but I must confess I do not understand him.

Don't make the mistake of believing Chile to be any kind of exception. Or Latin America in general. Or Uganda. Or Indonesia. Don't believe it is a matter of race or 'national character'. Bourgeois man becomes a barbarian wherever he feels threatened. Don't forget Germany. Or Finland in 1918. In Santiago, the Brazilian police teach the techniques of torture to the Chilean 'order authorities'. But who taught the Brazilians? The Pentagon. For every two murders carried out by the Red Guards in 1918, two hundred were carried out

214

in revenge by the White gangs of murderers in the mopping-up operations and prison camps after the German occupation forces in May had fixed the victory for Mannerheim. Blood-lust and a desire for murder are pronounced bourgeois qualities regardless of language, race or geographical situation. In the prison camps in Hennala in the summer of 1918, a small food parcel, sent by loyal relatives from the outside world, had on one rare occasion got through to a starving woman prisoner. Such parcels were usually confiscated on the orders of camp commandants. Naturally you know how many people died of starvation and malnutrition in those foul establishments of revenge by our glorious White country, don't you? More than twelve thousand people died there of starvation within a few months. Well . . . that parcel contained a piece of sausage, which this prisoner immediately started to eat greedily. But her longstanding state of malnutrition meant that she couldn't hold down the food, her digestive system was no longer functioning and she vomited whole undigested pieces of sausage as she stood there on the gravel of the camp site. And seeing this, her fellow prisoners, half-dead with hunger, threw themselves at her feet and fought over her vomit, like animals, yes, just like animals. For this was not subhuman, this was nothing more nor less than an extreme and terrible expression of excessive human hunger and a memorable picture of human degradation the bourgeois barbarians exposed their fellow human beings to in order to satisfy their primitive desire for revenge. Never forget that picture. And remember hunger in itself can never be subhuman, nor actions carried out in the name of self-preservation or the will to live. But to *allow* people to starve, that is subhuman. Coldly watching the starving without intervening, that is subhuman.

Perhaps when all is said and done, even suicide is subhuman in a world in which so many people have to die when they really wish for nothing better than to live?

When it comes to facts about the cruelty of the ruling classes, fiction can never really surpass reality. The left-wing, which represents the oppressed and is behind the grim revelations, is always right. The right-wing is always wrong, as it speaks in self-defence and can only operate with lies and excuses. The ruling classes throughout the course of history have become consistently more cruel at the same rate as the value of their possessions, the capital to be preserved, has increased. Bourgeois cruelty is thus greater than aristocratic cruelty was greater than feudal cruelty and so on and so on. What are called 'primitive' people, the persecuted, the humiliated, the scorned and now almost eradicated South American Indians, weren't at all cruel. Their lives included ritual violence and death which could be regarded as cruel if one were ignorant of their ritual background, but they were never cruel for the sake of cruelty alone, or for personal gain. As the bourgeoisie is. The noble art of scalping they learnt, by the way, from the Spaniards.

Economic progress is not social progress. Technical development is not human development. The human being by the freezer is different from the human being by the tripod over the fire mainly in that his cruelty and indifference is so much more profitable and the value of the possessions he is defending so much greater. If you can't see this, that is simply because the perspective has been widened so enormously during our century and the context has become so enormously more comprehensive and more immense. When North American genocide or wars of extermination against the Indians was going on at the end of the nineteenth century, an Indian said: 'The white man can make any articles under the sun, but he has no idea how to apportion them.'

We live in the days of degenerate bourgeoisie and I'm sick and tired of being bourgeois. I can no longer endure being a bourgeois intellectual, an intellectual humanist. A few weeks ago, I was walking along Salomon Street in Helsinki. It was dusk, and there were a lot of people about, the temperature about freezing, slush on the streets, a biting cold wind. I was walking past the petrol station, and a man was lying by the wall, sleeping or unconscious, sick or dead drunk, dressed in rags, his bare red-frozen hands and his head in a small puddle. He was quite still, in fact perhaps already dead. A whole lot of us walked past him at the same time, but no one reacted. This is not unusual in Helsinki, the rejected or defeated lying in the street and dying while the middle classes pass by wanting nothing to do with them. Naturally that wasn't the first time for me, either. But I remember this particular time for a special reason. I was vividly aware that I ought to do something, take some measures, call the police or an ambulance. But I didn't. I just walked past like the rest. And I noted that I just walked past like the rest. And I noted that it was wrong, that it was unforgivable neglect and actually an expression of the same bourgeois indifference I accuse other people of. But even then I didn't turn round. Not even then did I feel any agitation, any compassion, any urge to do something. Only indifference. My conscience was equally still, petrified, exactly like the semi- or wholly-frozen body of the man lying there in the street. So much for the theory and practice of humanism, of poisonous bourgeois solidarity.

There isn't much to add. From what I have already said, it should be clear why I regard taking my own life as a logical inevitability. As I said, the money is in Zurich, and you will find further information about how it will be available and for what it is to be used when you open the smaller sealed envelope enclosed with this letter. In that, I have also broadly outlined how I went about it. Of course, I could not carry out the operation entirely alone, apart from the strength of unlimited confidence I could reckon on from the firm, which in a fit of pride and also as a safety measure I mentioned to Father. Naturally the theft would soon have been discovered, probably at the following month's audit. I took the safe way out and gave myself up, less for the sake of honesty than for single-mindedness and simplicity. To some extent, the whole affair occurred in some kind of atmosphere of faintly puerile radical protest, but mainly for other and more serious reasons, which you probably understand without my having to go over them all over again. As far as the use of the money is concerned, I want you to know now that the whole sum is reserved for a particular resistance movement in a particular country and is expressly intended for the purchase of arms and ammunition, as a contribution to arming and equipping a people's army. But more of that in the smaller envelope.

There is one more thing that worries me because I do not know with any certainty whether I ought to talk to you about it or not. This is about my physical father and your pseudo-father, the inimitable and indefatigable Donald Blaadh. It is not a question of what you can 'stand', but entirely one of confidence: can I trust you never to tell him what I am going to tell you now? With that, the matter is decided. I know I can trust you. So . . . we both know that he is a conceited braggart who hasn't succeeded in everything quite so marvellously as he himself imagines, but who on the other hand has succeeded in certain things better than he could ever have dreamt of doing. This may sound puzzling but the riddles will soon be solved. This partly applies to Jacob, partly to Laura and partly to myself.

As far as Jacob is concerned, it is nearly all at a psychological level. Isn't it tragicomical, almost grotesque, and how can it have come about at all that Donald has never understood what kind of relationship exists between the two of them, indissoluble and mutual, a highly mutual interdependence between them? Donald is eternally grateful to Jacob and he defends himself against that as violently as it makes him feel guilty. Thus the constant rows, the puerile collisions, are actually nothing but distorted expressions of secret love, love-hate. Jacob is Donald's father in a much more real sense than he is yours. He 'made' Donald, giving him self-esteem and self-confidence at exactly the most favourable moment. For Donald, Jacob is the god of the most favourable moment – and that is what he has been unable to forgive him. We have all been more or less dependent on Jacob, and you, the youngest, perhaps still are so. Jacob has constituted a kind of axle round which our adult lives have revolved. First Donald, then Miles and finally Torbjörn. This in its turn is because Jacob possesses an ambivalence in his emotional life which makes him especially sensitive to and especially observant of a particular kind of human need in a particular kind of person at a particular age, or a particular ambivalent stage of human development. Jacob is fixated on the age of youth, on youth. It sounds clumsy and unfair to say straight out that Jacob is bisexual, but that is what he is, and you know that as well as I do, although in your capacity as his natural son, perhaps you can be presumed to be the least well qualified to do so. We have both been aware of this, and I dare say we have both taken that into consideration. We have gratefully accepted his generosity, at the same time sensitively keeping a suitable distance. Isn't that so? Doesn't that apply to you, too? Although I am perfectly aware your situation in this case has been infinitely more complicated than mine. Jacob must have found the relationship with you much more difficult, more painful and more full of conflict than his relationship with me. Only Donald has been blind and consequently plunged on, exploiting with ruthlessness and humiliating impertinence which must often have been an almost unbearable strain on Jacob. If you can bear to swallow yet another bit of psychology, then I would say you are in fact the fruit of Jacob's unhappy love for Donald. His relationship with Gunnel was nothing but a surrogate for another relationship which he knew could never be realized. And so you were conceived. There is nothing remarkable about that, simply history repeating itself, though in a different disguise, a new disguise, so hard to identify. Just think about what Donald has spent such a large part of his life researching into and deciding on – the truth of his origins!

One of the most honest and honourable of my father's characteristics is his genuine pacifism, his hatred of war and the emphasis he puts on that. He was terrified, and he admits it openly. But there are some ironical paradoxes here, too, of which because of his conceit, his self-absorption, his curious variation of 'blind clear-sightedness', he has fortunately remained unaware. First of all that in his boundless vanity he even considered taking on the post of Minister of Defence, although he must have been aware he would make a fool of himself. Then that he managed to persuade himself the appointment was a result of his own efforts, of skilful political intrigue on his part and the result of the extremely important contacts he has undeniably managed to make over the years. Naturally he is only one small fish in a very much larger (party) political sea, and naturally he was meant to fail. True, it was an interim government and Donald non-political, but political opponents are also to be found in interim governments as party politics inevitably function there, too. He fell with a crash, but as always, despite everything, landed feet first, because no one had reckoned on his total lack of conventional ambitions and what is meant by a sense of timing. When he realized he was not up to the task, he didn't do what others would have done, retreat into the wings with bureaucratic solemnity and wounded dignity, an offended victim of underhand political intrigues. Instead he chose to do a turnabout and made the most astonishing and bewildering move, for the game was anyhow lost. He chose to play the clown. In that way, he fooled all his political opponents, spread confusion among the leaders and achieved a semi-victory. Admit that there was something magnificent about that way of doing things. He has enthusiasm. He is in his way a dreamer and visionary, but he's no dullard.

We both know he boasts about 'never having killed a single damned Russian' during the war. So it was much more ironic that after the ceasefire, he did in fact murder a Finnish officer. We know that shortly after he came back on leave, he beat up a lieutenant in a porchway somewhere in Jägare Street, after first being insolent and breaking army regulations. What Donald doesn't know is that the lieutenant died of his injuries. And how do I know that? Laura told me. The lieutenant happened to be Laura's elder brother. The world is that small, some women are that sensitive, and love can gloss over that much. But you can imagine the shock when she finally realized who it was who so long ago had committed that meaningless and sadistic murder of her favourite brother. Fundamentally it was

219

probably that revelation, unplanned and chance as it was, which meant the end of their marriage. Laura couldn't cope with being married to her brother's murderer. On my part, I regret telling Vanessa this during a confidential moment in Paris a few weeks ago. She took it rather badly. She said it changed her whole image of Donald. And I have no reason to harm him.

Donald believes or hopes or dreams that I stole three million in order to put them at a suitable moment into his own firm, thus filling up the worst gaps that have arisen from longstanding mismanagement on his part. You can gladly disillusion him on this point, so that there is at least one element of uncertainty fewer in his life. How he has thought this might be done in practice I can't imagine; all I know is that he has been feverishly active recently, keeping the police at bay for as long as possible, seriously thinking I could muster that much filial loyalty. Incredible! On the other hand, what will forever remain a puzzle to me is why he hasn't been able to manage his own affairs for the last two years. He really is a very good business man. I've always admired his manner at the negotiating table, able to switch like lightning from the jovial whisky-swilling raconteur to the flinty uncompromising bidder, operating with the most ruthless lies, the most amazing fantasies. He is a gambler by disposition. Perhaps only genuine gamblers succeed in business. Whatever has happened to him now, the fact is that he has been none too secure recently, despite his satisfactory share majority and that in the end he received a generous handshake from the board, by which I mean an honourable retreat. But he can never admit that to himself.

I have written at length and am rather tired. In a few hours' time, I will no longer exist. I wish I could at least say that is a strange thought. But I can't. Dying is only reverting. So simple and undramatic. Do you believe in God? These last weeks I have begun to believe in the Indians' God. It's a Marxist God, who says that the world is common to us all and that the land and the products of the land do not belong to anyone special, but to us all, and that that is the way it is, and must be if human beings are to continue to be human beings in a world of human beings. The white man's burden is his own blindness, from which has come his avarice and terror. Torbjörn, my brother, be sighted among the blind! Act like a seeing man. It is not too late for man on man's earth.

It is only the prehistory of mankind.

I sleep. I wake. I have had a nightmare every night for weeks now, and I am as terrified as I have been every night for weeks. I try to lift my hand to turn on the reading lamp above my pillow, but note that my hand will not obey my will. I cannot move my hand. I cannot move at all. I am paralysed. I have had a stroke in my sleep. I lie on my right side, facing the window, my back to the room. I am seized with terrible anguish and call out to Vanessa, who is sleeping in the next room. Even my speech organs are paralysed and I cannot call, only achieve a little squeak. She doesn't hear, of course. But someone else hears me. There is someone in the room, in the darkness behind my back, someone who wishes me ill, now soundlessly moving closer in order to murder me. For some reason, I think it is a long butcher's knife coming towards me. I make a great effort to turn over, but don't succeed. I cry out as loudly as I can, but my vocal cords simply whistle. Just as the unknown enemy reaches the edge of the bed, my paralysis breaks and at last I get my arm up and switch on the light. Thank God, it was only a dream. But what a horrible dream, I think as I regard the quiet order, the familiar old furniture and objects in my familiar old bedroom.

Then it suddenly happens again! You were dreaming, I say to myself, but now you're awake and now you're afflicted with paralysis. It's true, I'm lying there and cannot move, knowing I'm awake, because I can see all the familiar objects in the room and with all my strength I try to cry out but cannot get out more than a squeak. The door slowly opens, the secretive enemy comes in with his horrible long knife, and my head is turned and fixed so that I cannot follow him with my gaze on his way across the room. I know he is approaching. He is already close to me, so close the knifepoint brushes my left shoulder. Then at last I regain my voice and scream with all my strength and Vanessa is there on the edge of my bed holding my shoulders, and I wake for the second time, this time for real.

I feel wretched. I ask her to get in under the covers beside me, but she refuses. She says it is the middle of the night and we should both sleep. I don't want her to leave me, and start telling her about my dream. She listens for a while, polite but uninterested, then interrupts me.

'You should make an appointment with a psychiatrist,' she says calmly.

She is changed. All her old warmth and consideration have gone.

She behaves as if we had been married for fifteen years, indifferently, her manner towards me that friendly formal indifference in someone you have lived with for a long time but stopped loving. It makes me despair. I ignore it. I go on talking.

'I have such terrible dreams these days. Do you know what I dreamt the other night. I was in Stockholm, outside the Sheraton Hotel and a young, rather drunken Finnish emigrant met an elderly lady with a little . . .'

'You must try to go to sleep now, Donald. It is very late, and I have a lot do do tomorrow . . .'

'No, no, I can't sleep. Let me tell you about my dream. A pissed Finn meets one of those upper-class Swedish females with a little dog on a lead, and he asks her in abysmal Swedish what the time is, or something, and she at once starts insulting him in that disgustingly superior way only silly upper-class Swedes can descend to, the superciliousness of the average silly upper-class Swede . . .'

'Donald . . .'

'Yes, yes, and then I grew angry listening to her insults and hurried over to my poor drunken defenceless countryman's aid. To hell with the old bitch, I grabbed the dog instead, the sweet little poppet, by the back and pressed downwards so that one leg came off and the poppet yelped. The old girl was very upset and tried to go for me with her umbrella, but I shoved her away, brusquely, then I gave the dog a karate blow, snapping its spine with the side of my hand, simply killing the old lady's little dog, and then I woke up in terrible anguish . . .'

'You mustn't get over-excited, Donald. Do try to sleep. . . .'

'I can't sleep, Vanessa. Play something for me. Play for a while and then we'll go to bed.'

'Not now in the middle of the night?'

'Yes, now, in the middle of the night. Please, I beg you.'

'What will the neighbours say?'

'To hell with them. I own this apartment and anyhow I'm richer than all of them put together.'

'Are you?'

'OK, OK, what if I'm not, to hell with that. Come on, now.'

I scramble out of bed, take her by the hand and drag her with me into the living-room. She is wearing nothing but an almost transparent nightdress and I glimpse the lines and shadows of her lovely body underneath. I am wearing my striped pyjamas.

I get the piano ready for her, feeling a strange over-tense fervour, as if I were somehow outside myself.

'Play Rachmaninov, the swan-song of bourgeois Russia. Play now, play. I'll do the orchestral parts.'

Reluctantly, she sits down and stikes the introductory chords of the piano concerto she is to perform in two months' time in Warsaw with the Leningrad Philharmonic Orchestra, while I, at exactly the right moment, intone the violins, or a travesty of the violins, with my voice, gradually increasing the volume of my voice to full strength, or orchestral strength, feeling colossal joy, excitement over my voice carrying, the voice I thought in my dream a few minutes ago was lost for ever, and that I think I'm mastering the assignment and can follow her, compensating for both Okku Kamu and the Leningrad Philharmonic with my vocal cords and my incredible musicality.

'To heeelll with empathy and immediacy, Vaneeessaaa, plaaaaay like Brecht does theatre, play with distance as Richter taught you. No one can take bitter old depressive bourgeois nostalgia seriously, then he becomes comical . . . like Soltzhenitzyn. . . .' I sing.

She laughs, not all that appreciatively.

'Can't you heeeeaaar how he laaaaments his loooost privileges,
and old velvet curtaaaaaaiiiins,
he is so gloomy because the revolution has taken
everything great and beeaooootiful
and now there's nought but boring equality leeeeeeft. . . .'

She goes on laughing, more and more uncontrollably, finally striking some hard pom-pom-pom chords and falling doubled-up over the keys, her hair in disorder over both bass and treble.

'I can't co-operate with such an undisciplined orchestra.'

'But I'm right, aren't I? Isn't that what he's trying to say? He has a very understandable tonal language, I think. I understand him completely, but I don't share his views. They are Jacob's views. Rachmaninov is a crony of Jacob's.'

'One can't interpret music properly like that.'

'But I can. Play something else, then. Schubert. I'll keep quiet. I understand nothing but music these days. Words are hard to understand, living and dying and all that, living your life with dignity. I can't make head or tail of anything. No, don't play anything. Let's put on something magnificent, Brahms, no Mahler. Brahms was the perfect bourgeois. He believed in the victory and greatness and constancy of the bourgeoisie, Brahms did.'

'Who? Miles?'

'No, Brahms, for Christ's sake. Can't you listen to what I say? Sorry, Vanessa. Don't you think there must somewhere be a species of creatures who make themselves understood and communicate entirely through music? A scrapes away on a violin, and B replies with a piano sonata, and they go on like that, conversing until C comes along with a symphony and they establish, yes, that's right, that's how it must be . . . a string quartet is just like a conversation between . . .'

'What are you going to put on?'

'Mahler's seventh.'

I put Mahler's seventh on to the turntable, turn the volume up full blast and the speakers begin to rasp and roar. She shuts the lid of the piano and goes and sits on the sofa. I feel feverish. We sit listening for a while, then I cry out.

'Listen, listen to this. Can you hear how he scorns Brahms! Can't you hear, the first movement of Brahms' third, he's just taken Brahms' main theme and now he's kneading it and deepening it and having fun at his great master's and predecessor's expense. . . .'

'Uhuh, yes, he is,' is all she says.

'Just listen! Listen, here he's exposing the naïve bourgeois idealism of the great Brahms, his devout one-dimensional experience of beauty. How frightfully sarcastic Mahler is, smashing a whole concept of life, a whole image of the world, showing how endlessly much more complicated and contradictory life is than they thought in the great days of the bourgeoisie. This is truly the swan-song of the bourgeoisie in another way. . . .'

'If you're trying to read political messages into Mahler's symphonies, then you're definitely on the wrong track, I assure you. Mahler believed in absolute beauty. Few people have been more bourgeois than Mahler in particular . . . with his social background.'

'No, no, I don't mean that. The great composers describe the spirit of their age or argue with it. They illustrate the spirit of the time much better than words do, bad words, I mean, without really being aware of it. That is exactly their greatness. Why do you think our generation is the first to appreciate Mahler according to his deserts, to understand him? Naturally, because he was long before his time . . . without knowing it, of course . . . he predicts the dissolution of the secure bourgeois image. He directs his corrosive bitter satire at

224

all that is triumphant and consummate . . . in Brahms and Mendelssohn and César Franck . . . while he is always an organic part of the same age and spirit of the time . . . think of Bach! A hundred years before Marx! I mean, that says everything . . . if only we could explain it . . . the *St Matthew Passion*. . . .'

'Donald, calm down a bit, now.'

'Everything, everything is in the *St Matthew Passion*. Or how was it . . . half of everything, exactly half of everything, neither more nor less, you said once . . . but everything isn't . . . nowhere. . . .'

I sob. She gets up from the sofa, comes over and takes my hand.

'Donald, let's go to bed now. It's not good for you to sit up late like this.'

'But can't you hear how he scorns Brahms!' I cry.

'Yes, I can hear, Donald dear. I hear . . .'

At that moment Torbjörn appears in the doorway, also in pyjamas, his feet bare.

'What the hell are you up to, you two . . . in the middle of the night,' he says sleepily.

'We're playing music and solving the problems of the world,' I say.

'Must you do it so loudly one can't sleep?'

'They're important things of concern to everyone,' I say.

'OK, and what have you arrived at then?' he says, sitting down in an armchair.

Vanessa switches off the music with a determined hand movement.

'We'll all go to bed now,' she says.

'No, we won't. Torbjörn shall have a drink now. He'll like that,' I say, going across to the bar cupboard.

'Not for me, thanks,' he says.

'No? Won't my liquor do any longer, either?'

'Donald, be sensible now,' says Vanessa.

'Dad. . . .'

I turn slowly round and look at him. It hadn't just slipped out of him. He had said it for a special purpose. To calm me down? Like Vanessa? Or to imply a loyalty he knew I doubted, a cautious attempt to establish new contact . . . ? I feel I can't cope with it. We can't look each other in the eye.

'Let's have Sibelius then. I'll teach you two to listen to Sibelius in quite a new way. Sibelius was in reality a truly sexual composer. All his symphonies are actually screwing in one way or another . . .'

'Donald . . .' says Vanessa, now clearly irritated.

225

'The number two is the perfect great potency-symphony, pompom pompom pompom, one long scraping in-out in-out, with thunderous spurting orgasms on every other page. It's great when you realize it. Then we have the delightful innocent little third, pure idyllic marriage, when he walks hand in hand beneath the cherry trees with his young wife. But then comes the fourth, when everything's suddenly gone wrong as a result of all too great a consumption of alcohol, who knows. It is the great supreme impotence-symphony in the history of European music. You really hear how he's trying and trying, but it just won't work, all is lost, there it is hanging slack and refusing to rise, pure misery, what a dreadful fate and shame, but then the fifth comes along and then up it goes again, inhibitions overcome, only a temporary little hitch. Now things are going for him again and oh, how triumphantly happy he is, one can really hear how he snorts with delighted surprise, 'By heavens, look, I can after all, in-out in-out, wonder of wonders, go on, go on,' and everything ends in a wonderful orgasm in a long sighing spurting taadaataadaataadaa-taadaataadaa, can you hear it . . . what a bloody great fucker Sibelius was . . . that's why the second and fourth and fifth are played most of all. The theme is so near to people's hearts.'

'The Bellman of the symphonies?'

'Yes, exactly. The Bellman or Gyllenbom of the symphonies.'

'You've read the letter, haven't you?'

Now I have no other contribution to make in any sustained battle.

'Yes, I'm sorry. I shouldn't have done so, but I didn't know what was in it . . .'

'It doesn't matter. It was to mankind; he says so himself at the beginning . . . I was just thinking for your own sake . . .'

'How do you know I've read it, for that matter?'

'It shows.'

'Thanks very much indeed.'

'And, to be sure, I sealed Gramsci with a hair.'

'Pure James Bond, in other words,' says Vanessa.

'Why just Gramsci, Torbjörn?'

'Because Gramsci is constructive. He is writing in prison, and yet he has more than one foot in the future. He has been put out of action by Mussolini, but knows more about politics than fifty little Mussolinis all put together. He differentiates between "be" and "ought to be" in politics. "Be" is the average mediocre politician's starting point. "Ought to be" is the realistic alternative. There is no static "be". Everything is constant movement, so is . . . the vision, the visionary will. "Ought to be" is the only realistic foundation for progressive politics . . . if you see what I mean.'

'I've never understood Gramsci.'

'If that's the case, it's only because you're so obsessed with the permanent.'

'That "small envelope" . . . I didn't find it . . . fortunately.'

He shrugged his shoulders.

'Neither did I . . . unfortunately.'

'What? But he says perfectly clearly that . . .'

'He must have collapsed in some way before he had time to finish it all . . . there were only a few almost illegible notes.'

'You're lying.'

'If you want an absolutely honest reply, then I prefer to say nothing.'

'That's what I thought.'

'The safe-deposit is empty.'

'Empty! But the money? Where's the money?'

'Gone. Gone with the wind.'

'Oh, my God.'

'He simply couldn't manage to complete it.'

'I'll go mad. The money must be somewhere!'

'Somewhere in Switzerland, yes, but where we'll obviously never know.'

'And I'd have given such a lot to know at least how he set about it.'

'I know.'

'What?'

'How he set about it.'

'Indeed, so you know how he set about it. But you do not reveal such secrets to your poor old Da . . .'

'Poor Donald.'

'Poor Donald, poor Donald, don't go showing off with that poor Donald stuff. You hate me. You've been as icy as the Snow Queen herself ever since you came back from London, and I know why all right. Because of what happened in Paris and if he wasn't dead I'd . . . I know why you despise me. I know exactly what it's all about. You're going to leave me, one day, you'll be off because it revolts you to live with a murderer . . .'

'I admit it was a shock.'

'There you are, you see . . . you're going to leave me. Everything

227

goes to hell for people like me. . . .'

'Donald. You know the period for prosecution has long since passed and that very old . . . offences long ago are . . . forgotten or . . . forgiven . . . come here, Donald.'

'No, I'm not coming. I'm fine where I am.'

'Come,' she whispers.

But I'm brazen and stubborn, remaining by the bar counter and pouring out a whisky for myself.

Torbjörn is sitting, or rather half-lying, in his armchair, his long legs nonchalantly outspread, his bare heels resting on the carpet. I note that his feet are clean. The fly of his pyjama trousers is not quite closed and half his member and a wealth of red growth of hair are just visible. He knows, but ignores it. He sits there staring at Vanessa through half-closed eyelids! No young scamp, I notice, but a young man.

She feels his gaze and realizes she has practically nothing on and he is sitting a few feet away from her, gazing at her nipples. She laughs.

'Must I put my peignoir on?'

'By all means, just show yourself naked. All my wives seem to have done that to all my sons, so that's truly nothing to get hung up about. We could have a little group sex, too, to pass the time.'

'Another time, eh?' says Torbjörn.

'You slept with him in Paris, didn't you? Admit it. He insisted on sleeping with all my wives, one after another.'

'Don't be silly, Donald. What if I did sleep with him. In Paris. What does that matter? At our age?'

'No, by all means, it doesn't matter at all, not in the slightest, at our age. I just wondered . . . you're a free and independent woman . . .'

'Without a doubt.'

I gulp back my whisky. Things calm down a little and no one says anything for a while. Torbjörn is the one to break the silence.

'He mucked up reality, my brother Miles, changing its course, like when they dam up a riverbed and give the water a wholly new direction . . . and that requires a rare constructive imagination, that does. . . .'

'You might well say so. Three million gone up in smoke. Highly imaginative.'

'I think one of his intentions was to show how little money is worth, or how abstract and theoretical the whole money-value philosophy is, when it comes to a sufficiently large sum of money . . . money is really only worth anything to small salary-earners. . . .'

'A catastrophe is what it is, utterly catastrophic. You've no idea of the laws of the financial world. . . .'

'No one's said anything yet about a catastrophe.'

'You don't understand. Such a tremendous loss is practically impossible to cover up. It'll be years before . . .'

'On the contrary, I think it's like that bank robbery in Norrmalm Square in Stockholm. "No loss to us," said the director of the Swedish State Bank. "We just print new banknotes . . ." and that's what it's about here, too, not gold ingots. . . .'

'How did he do it, Torbjörn? Can't you tell me how he did it?'

'It was a loan granted to a subsidiary company somewhere in South America, or a transfer of capital, I don't really know . . . and some forged cheques . . .'

'You're bluffing. You don't know anything about it, do you?'

'Maybe not.'

'You don't know anything at all.'

'Maybe so. Nothing, apart from what Miles meant by a particular resistance movement in a particular country.'

'And that was?'

'Finland.'

Suddenly I feel it again, vertigo. Things go black before my eyes and I have to lean against the wall.

'My God, then he really must have been crazy . . .' I hear Vanessa say far away in the distance. Then violently, frightened:

'Donald! What's the matter?'

They leap up and come across to me, taking me by the arm and leading me to the sofa. My legs will hardly bear me. Did I fall? Did they lift me up? They're talking over my head, as if I weren't conscious.

'He's had a few attacks like this before. It's his heart. He's pretty well worn out . . .' Vanessa is saying.

'So that's why he gave up the firm. He wasn't chucked out after all, as Miles maintained. . . .'

'Ssh. Don't talk about it. He . . . take that quilt over there and put it under his head, his feet on the arm . . . that's it. Donald, dear, how are you feeling?'

'Fine,' I mumble.

'Armed revolution in Finland! But Torbjörn, you must admit that was . . . if not pure madness, at least quite dreadfully starry-eyed,' I hear her say.

'Yes,' I hear him answer.

I feel her hand behind my head and something cold on my lips. 'Drink this,' she says.

It's something in a small glass. I swallow it down. It tastes unpleasant and I start coughing, then gradually start to feel better. I want to talk. I sound hoarse and distant.

'I had such great ambitions. I was going to expose it all, show up the merciless inner logic of all human development . . . and what happened to that – belly-flop – nothing but one great belly-flop. I knew nothing . . . a conceited braggart, oh, yes . . . a conceited braggart, dying too, for Christ's sake. . . .'

'You're not dying. All you need is rest . . . and everyone has his own view. Perhaps you're no brilliant judge of character, Donald, but somewhere . . . somewhere you have a warm heart. . . .'

'And you're going to leave me. Just leave me. I'm not worth your love. A warm heart. Oh, indeed, I have a warm heart, have I? Done in. . . .'

'I'm not going to leave you.'

'Good, good. She's not going to leave me. She's sacrificing herself for me, she . . .'

'When I'd read Miles' letter, when I'd got over the shock and grief, all that horrible . . . I realized . . . something happened to me. . . .'

'Miles knew a hundred times more about women than him,' she whispers.

'In some way I'd lost my grip on the firm . . .'

'I was given a kind of internal jab, almost like an earthquake inside me, or as if the flow of perception had been dammed up and given an entirely new direction . . . I'd been so terribly dependent on Miles and suddenly wasn't any more. . . .'

'It'd be very much easier for me if you bothered about me as a person, too, as the person I am, not just . . .'

'Yes, yes, but the truth was actually that international competition had become terribly fierce, very much fiercer than long ago when Emil and I started . . . the worst thing was that I didn't recognize them any more . . . suddenly they were twenty years younger, all business men were twenty years younger than me and I didn't understand them. I didn't know what they thought, or how they reasoned. I just sat there staring at their poker faces without the

230

slightest idea what was behind them . . . a new generation . . . so damned . . . didn't even take a brandy with their coffee. . . .'

'You ask nothing of a woman except that she'll be Daddy to you . . . and a mattress . . . don't you see how difficult it is . . . I love music. The first time I . . .'

'It was like a great leap forward. I seemed to be raised a little bit above reality and saw where he was right and where he was wrong. . . .'

'The first time I heard music was one summer when I was small. I was alone in the yard and I heard a piano playing from an open window where the light curtains were flapping in the wind. I listened. I remember listening. I stood still for a long time, and if I could have found the words, I would have said to myself it was beautiful . . . it came from the gentry side – one of those damned gentry wives playing up there alone and the strange thing is I still remember . . . almost remember the notes, and later on I was able to identify what it was, one of Beethoven's sonatas.'

'He was bound to a schedule that was far too severe, far too lacking in the various possibilities, and he knew it, and wanted to escape, but he couldn't, except . . . in a destructive way, because he was a political bastard, just as you've always been a political bastard, and I myself . . . we're all political bastards because of our starting points, our origins . . . it's a moral duty, a theoretical necessity . . .'

'I don't understand what you're talking about.'

'That "sea of human blood" he writes about, Torbjörn. Do you all really think like that? Does it really have to happen like that?'

'No, no, it doesn't have to, not *have* to. But it's one of the possibilities, one of the probabilities, and for Miles, in his view, the only one. . . .'

'I'm tired. I want to sleep.'

'We'll go to bed.'

'There's a destructive pessimism in the world today I want to fight. There's a terror, a self-effacement in mankind which is perilous, more dangerous than anything else . . . bourgeois society as a constructive social alternative has actually already ceased to exist . . . it's a corpse spreading like poison . . . the question is only how to bury it. . . .'

'I read through Jacob's damned papers and do you know what I found? Heavens . . . I found love and friendship and solicitude for fellow human beings and anxiety and alarm and joy and harmony, and infidelity, financial fiddles, adultery, treachery, lies, misery, even

231

murder . . . just like today, everything just like today . . . the world doesn't change. . . .'

'The world is changing all the time and if it doesn't, I'm going to make it. . . .'

'Not tonight, I hope.'

'Do you notice that we're passive, allowing ourselves to be prepared for violence that is meaningless and poverty that is unnecessary . . . this appalling sense of doom . . . I want to stop it. I'm going to stop it . . . with every means. . . .'

'Every means? Miles' "secret" means? My means?'

'Yes, anything, everything . . . your patience, too, my paternal heritage.'

'Well, goodnight then. Sweet Prince.'

'Goodnight. But remember, we start tomorrow, early in the morning.'

'It's too late.'

'No, it's early. I know it's early.'